PRAISE FOR TERRY

"Soul Forge is an exhilarating
Even if you haven't read the other novels in this series,
characters will draw you in."
- Antonio del Drago, author of *The Mythic Guide to Characters*

"Reading *Soul Forge*, I have discovered the new Michael Moorcock, Terry W. Ervin II. Fantastic work. Thoroughly enjoyable. Seriously recommended."
- C. Dean Andersson, author of the *Bloodsong Saga*

"Blood Sword is a tremendous installment in one of the most inventive and compelling fantasy sagas I have read in years!"
-Stephen Zimmer, author of the Fires in Eden Series and The Rising Dawn Saga.

"Blood Sword continues the adventures started in Flank Hawk, in which Ervin created a unique and detailed post-apocalyptic world where magic works but ancient technologies from the First Civilization--our world--still exist. You'll cheer as they face off against griffins, fallen angels, gargoyles, and worse, in a fun, engaging adventure filled with wall to wall action."
-David Forbes, author of the Osserian Saga

"A worthy successor to the original novel, packed with action and entertainment."
-Jim Bernheimer, author of the Dead Eye series and Confessions of a D-List Supervillain

"A classic epic fantasy with plenty of original twists. You won't want to put it down, even when you've reached the end."
-David Debord, author of The Silver Serpent and Keeper of the Mists

"Grab hold! Ervin's got the magic!"
-C. Dean Andersson, author of the Bloodsong Trilogy

"A curious blend of epic fantasy, modern techno-thriller and non-stop action-adventure."
-Erica Hayes, author of the Shadowfae Chronicles

"Buy it or chalk it up on that long list of things you regret not doing!"
-Stephen Hines, author of Hocus Focus

Books by Terry W. Ervin II

First Civilization's Legacy
Flank Hawk
Blood Sword
Soul Forge

Crax War Chronicles
Relic Tech
Relic Rescue (Forthcoming)

Short-Story Collection
Genre Shotgun

SOUL FORGE

A FIRST CIVILIZATION'S LEGACY NOVEL

James,
I hope you enjoy
Krish's 3rd tale.
Terry W. Ervin

TERRY W. ERVIN II

Gryphonwood

Gryphonwood Press

Published by Gryphonwood Press
www.gryphonwoodpress.com

Cover art by Christine Griffin

ISBN: 978-1-940095-18-9

Printed in the United States of America

DEDICATION

This novel is dedicated to David Stace. What I miss about him most is his persistent optimism.

ACKNOWLEDGEMENTS

First, I would like to thank the members of Elysian Fields, especially Bill, Rick, Lynn and Anita. Your input helped keep Krish's story on track.

I would also like to thank my wife, co-workers, family, friends, and the members of *Flankers*, all of whom encouraged, questioned, and prodded me along to finish ***Soul Forge***.

As for Barkey, know that Chuck Braden devised the character's name. He was selected from the many who signed up for the chance to name a character in the third installment of the *First Civilization's Legacy Series*. It was a pleasure to work with him on that creative endeavor. It should be noted that I incorporated the Svartálfar thrall's 'private' name, Braden Coaliron, because it just seemed to fit.

Finally, I'd like to thank the folks at Gryphonwood Press, especially Mike Dunne for editing ***Soul Forge*** and David Wood for believing enough in my first novel to publish it, and for believing enough in Krish's second and third adventures to publish them as well.

That leaves you, the reader. You're the reason I wrote ***Soul Forge***. Thank you for choosing my fantasy novel from the tens of thousands available. I truly hope you enjoy the story. Don't hesitate to send an email or post a review to let me know your thoughts.

CHAPTER 1

I'd seen men asleep, and I'd witnessed my share of soldiers, unconscious and dying. For some reason I recognized the young enchantress lying before me hung somewhere in between.

After a moment I stepped back from Enchantress Thereese, neatly tucked under emerald green blankets with her head and long brown braids resting on a silken, tasseled pillow. The immaculately kept bedroom, holding a polished oak desk and bookshelves filled with leather-bound tomes, stood at odds with the two tattered dolls wearing blue and red aprons, and resting upon a rustic shelf to the right of the bedroom's single window. The mid-morning sun's rays, granted entrance by the window's fine glass, highlighted the foot of the quiet bed.

The floorboards creaked, disturbing the silence.

"Upon reaching ten summers my Thereese discovered the enchantment that maintains that sound," Enchantress Thulease said, standing in the doorway behind me. "It alerted both myself and the servants if she was up and about when she should have been asleep. I believe she began climbing along the bookshelves when she desired not to be discovered."

I turned to face the enchantress who wore a high-collared green dress that matched her daughter's blankets. Her face held no expression, even her green eyes hid the sorrow echoing in her words. I recalled her daughter, who bore what had to be a perfect youthful image of her mother, was even taller than her mother, who herself stood a head taller than me. I also recalled the young enchantress being less capable of masking her emotions.

"I long to hear the creak of those boards," the supreme enchantress said with a sigh. She gazed beyond me toward her daughter. "But it shall not happen without my intervention. And in that endeavor, Mercenary Flank Hawk, I desire your company."

CHAPTER 2

The young servant refilled my cup with warm cider before offering more white grape juice to Supreme Enchantress Thulease and her husband, Master Alchemist Butlir. I sat in a deep-cushioned chair across from the couple. To my right, ashy gray coals from a small fireplace offered warmth.

The master alchemist, a stocky man wearing brown cotton trousers, shirt and four-button vest, nodded and held up his glass for the young girl to refill. His gray hair, thin mustache and calloused, scarred hands and face made him look much older than his wife. Enchantress Thulease, in her high-collared dress, shook her head and set her glass on a small table next to her chair. She'd been doing most of the talking and continued.

"Grand Wizard Seelain released you from service three months ago, before returning to her family's southern estate. It is my understanding that the king's daughter, Princess Julee Ann, requested your services as a personal guard. You declined?"

After the revelation that Enchantress Thulease wanted me to somehow assist her daughter's recovery, I expected the conversation to focus on that. She was getting to it, but in a roundabout way.

"I did."

After leaving Wizard Seelain's service, I guarded Lesser Seer B'down, who'd served as Prince Reveron's advisor. He was part of a team that tracked remnants of Long Tooth insurgent cells within the King's City. There'd been a few close scrapes, including one with a necromancer and handful of zombies, and a ghoul, but the king ended the effort after trails went dry. Every enemy not killed or captured had fled the city.

The enchantress nodded and waited until the servant stepped out and closed the door. "You do not strike me as one inclined to play the part of a show piece."

"Princess Julee Ann remains within the palace most of the time," I said. "Although it's a vital duty, I have little desire to be a palace guard."

"Of course. I overheard Seelain remark to the princess that you would not be lured by any amount of gold." After a pause, she continued. "The grand wizard blames herself for her fiancé's death. In that, she is wrong."

I nodded and took a long sip of cider. The enchantress must have guessed my thoughts.

"In as much as she is wrong to blame herself, Seelain is correct in not holding you responsible for Prince Reveron's death." She held up a hand to forestall my objection. "It was the Goddess Fendra Jolain who struck the mortal blow. It was she who tossed the beloved prince into the hyrdra's jaws, to be torn and devoured."

She leaned forward and locked gazes with me. "Yes, Mercenary, you slew the ogre a fraction of a second too late. Even as the brute hurled its sword, wounding the prince from behind. Enabling the goddess to strike that mortal blow. Yet, you did all that was humanly possible." Her gaze intensified. "I was there. You took up the fallen Blood Sword and finished what the prince had begun."

She leaned back. "With the assistance of Sergeant Drux. And," she said, her voice falling to a whisper, "with my spell moving the Blood Sword away from the healing goddess's hand. Drawing magical energy from my daughter, through the Shard Staff. Because I, like Wizard Seelain, had already expended all my strength. I summoned what was necessary. More than my daughter could afford."

The enchantress sat back in her chair with eyes closed.

"Few have avoided sacrifice," I said. "Many have suffered—died—to defeat the Necromancer King. To defeat Fendra Jolain." Images of my cousin's death hovered foremost in my mind, but there were so many behind him. Some with names. Roos, Shaws, Jonas, Zunnert, Pops Weasel and Short Two Blades, and Prince Reveron. Thousands with names, but unknown to me. And those were only the ones I'd witnessed.

"They are defeated," Enchantress Thulease said between clenched teeth. "But not ended. When the Crusaders overran his keep, the Ancient Dictator escaped beneath the waves in a steel leviathan."

"An ancient submarine," her husband quietly interjected. "Yet it is believed that he may not venture far."

She shot him a sideways glance. "Our king still wars."

The alchemist set his drink aside. "He and our allies advance on the Long Tooths, and what allies yet remain to them."

It appeared an argument between them, however civil-sounding, had been rekindled.

She countered, "Fendra Jolain yet lives within the Blood Sword's steel."

"After a fashion," he replied.

"And because of me, our daughter lays upstairs, dead, after a fashion."

"You did what was necessary," I interjected before the enchantress's husband could. That caught them both by surprise. "*I* was there."

I set my half-empty cup of cider aside. "Your daughter sacrificed like so many. A sacrifice that might be undone?"

Enchantress Thulease said, "That is my objective."

"How?" I asked. "And why do you need me?"

"I intend to venture to the Southern Continent," she said, rising from her chair. "It is there that Imperial Seer Lochelle suggested I seek the Sleeping Sage."

CHAPTER 3

Since it would've been a long walk from Enchantress Thulease's grand tower back to the boarding house where I stayed, I accepted the offer of her carriage. Riding alone inside didn't feel right so I sat next to the driver, talking to him. He had to stop at the Arms Practice Yard to pick up the captain of Enchantress Thulease's guard. And, since the boarding house was nearby, it'd offer me the chance to watch Rin train. I'd paid good coin for the young stablehand to get some basic weapons training. Plus, he'd enjoy the brief carriage ride, *if* Guard Captain Flayzin didn't object.

Being related to me, even as an adopted brother, brought danger from the king's enemies. Rin lost his family, murdered by Long Tooth insurgents. The potential threat was also why I chose a boarding house over staying with my family. My mother thought it was to avoid Raina's visits—or not to discourage my sister from visiting.

I didn't argue. My father understood.

"The enchantress listens to Captain Flayzin," the carriage driver said, slowing the horse team as we came up behind an oxen-drawn cart filled with coal. "I hope he recommends me to journey with the enchantress."

Miggs, the carriage driver, was about my age and at least ten summers younger than Flayzin. Maybe a few more. I'd weapons sparred with Miggs, and with Flayzin. The driver was competent with the long-handled mace resting at his side, but I didn't think he knew much about deadly combat, or travel beyond the walls of the King's City. Guard Captain Flayzin, on the other hand, was skilled with the sword. Very skilled. I'd crossed practice blades with him once a long time back. He'd easily proven my skills lacking, and they hadn't improved much since. I didn't care for the arrogant captain of the enchantress's guard. His vocal and sometimes bullying confidence in his sword arm didn't garner friends, but being popular wasn't why he served in an important position. For his efforts he probably earned more coin than a major in King Tobias's army, an army that I had no interest in joining.

Taking a deep breath, I decided that Rin and I would walk rather than impose upon the guard captain.

Miggs pulled the carriage alongside the six-foot stone wall, allowing him to view the practice yard while perched upon his seat atop the black wooden carriage.

I climbed down and waved to Miggs. "I'm going to check on my brother, Rin, and then I'll walk the rest of the way."

"Okay," Miggs said, some disappointment hanging in his voice. I think he enjoyed being seen next to me. I wasn't recognized by the average citizen, but nobles and most city guards knew my face and that I'd been honored with two golden medals by King Tobias for my war contributions.

Preston, the stocky and capable guardsman, opened the gate for me without question. We exchanged a few words before I stepped into the practice area. The sunny afternoon took away some of the October chill. I wasn't wearing my breast and backplate, but my leather armor kept me warm enough.

The hard-packed dirt was damp, but its gravel mixture ensured the ground didn't become slick. The practice area was roughly fifty yards wide and twenty-five deep with two barn-like buildings opposite the entry gate. Their sliding doors facing into the yard stood open. Scattered to the left of the smaller arms building's doorway were several pairs of men and two women engaged in combat practice with wooden swords. The yard seemed empty, the war having claimed so many.

One of the practicing men was a fellow mercenary named Sledge Fist. We'd never fought side-by-side but had fought on the same battlefield more than once. He was being schooled by Guard Captain Flayzin. Off to the right, a retired infiltration soldier was giving lessons on balance and footwork to four youths. One of them was Rin. Hard work in the wyvern stables had made my adopted brother wiry and strong, but his freckles and unruly blond hair reminded me that he'd seen only twelve summers. Soon to be, but not yet a man.

Rin was so focused on his instructor's demonstration that he didn't notice me standing fifteen yards away. That told me of my brother's focus.

After a few minutes, Sledge Fist came to stand on my right. I looked up to him and his crooked grin. He had three broken teeth. Maybe one more than the last time we'd met. "Flank Hawk."

"Sledge Fist," I said, returning his grin. "Where've you been?"

"Throwin' drunks outta the Busted Barrel."

With his size, broad shoulders, and biceps that matched my thighs, I thought about asking how far, but instead greeted Flayzin who marched over and stopped to my left with hands on his hips. His thin red mustache and narrow beard were neatly trimmed, which was no surprise.

"Flayzin," I said.

"You expect that I should deign to speak with you, coward?"

I turned to face the captain of the enchantress's guard. Sledge Fist's questioning grunt indicated his surprise too.

"Say again?" I asked.

He turned to square off and I knew where this was going, but had no idea why.

"You heard correctly, Mercenary," Flayzin stated, his cold brown eyes meeting mine. "However, I am unsure whether it was more your incompetence rather than your cowardice that betrayed the brave and beloved Prince Reveron, and left him dead."

One of the first rules Major Jadd taught me was that a mercenary never allowed an insult to pass. Ever. And Flayzin had been around long enough to know this rule and the result of his words. It appeared he was counting on it, based on his sneering grin. He or I would soon lay bleeding or dead, but who or what drove Flayzin?

He'd chosen the proper ground. Duels were permitted within the confines of the Arms Practice Yard. I was a mercenary, and he was a guard, not constrained by the king's Military Code of Conduct. Even if I had my spear, his sword would still best me. Wondering who paid, or what drove him to pick this fight, could wait.

Survival came first.

He wore a chainmail shirt and leather greaves. That left a portion of his thighs relatively unprotected. My leather armor protected my torso, arms and legs. His leather gauntlets were sturdier than mine. His long sword gave him better reach than my broad-bladed short sword. I did have my dirk, coated in fireweed resin—a carryover from my service as a wyvern scout. After facing zombies within the city, I'd kept the habit of carrying a pouch filled with finely ground salt. I loosened the pouch's drawstrings as I stared back. Certainly he saw my action, but didn't understand its purpose.

I didn't have my helmet and he'd left his sitting next to the wooden practice sword. The older man's look of confidence—over confidence—gave me hope.

Only a second or two had passed, but the entire practice yard stood silent. Even Rin and his teacher turned our direction. Debating my actions related to the prince's death would serve no purpose. Flayzin had insulted me, named me a coward.

Sledge Fist stepped wide. "Flayzin, you sure—"

The guard captain said, "This is between this coward and me, Sledge." He offered me a false smile. "If you feel inadequately armed, you can run and fetch a spear from the armory."

I squared off to face Flayzin. "You're proposing a duel?"

My foe stood straight, with hands formally held at his side. "Mercenary Flank Hawk, I challenge—"

That was all I needed to hear. Before Flayzin uttered another word, I grabbed a handful of finely ground salt and flung half of it into his face. Maybe some it found its way into his eyes, but the goal was to keep him busy while I drew my boot dirk and flipped it to a throwing position.

Flayzin had his hand protecting his face even as he drew his sword and cursed. "Cheating coward!"

I flung some of the salt remaining in my right hand at his face again as he backed away, holding his sword in a defensive position. I flung the rest of the salt, emptying my right hand and causing him to retreat a step further. He closed his eyes again, for a fraction of a second—enough to snap my left hand forward, releasing my resin-covered dirk. Its blade found flesh in his left thigh.

Flayzin grunted and yanked my dirk free. Without a word he inexpertly hurled it back at me as I brushed my gauntlet against my leg to free it of salt and drew my sword. I ducked under the spinning dirk and smiled as the pain fireweed resin inflicts flared within Flayzin's wounded leg.

"Poison?" he shouted and tried to rush me. Hampered by his injured leg I parried his attack and sidestepped around to his right. The guard captain's leg nearly buckled as he shuffled to face me. "A cheating coward with no honor," he said between clenched teeth.

"A challenged mercenary is free to use whatever weapons are at hand," I said, and attacked with a forehand cut, followed by a stab to his shoulder, which he blocked and parried. I pressed my attack, causing him to stumble. I managed to strike a hammering blow to his left shoulder—missing his head by inches, and retreated beyond the reach of his counter strike.

I rushed him again. He stood his ground, parried and tried to catch my sword arm in a lock. He almost had me until I head butted him in the nose and followed by driving the heel of my palm into the same spot, knocking him to the ground. I kicked, driving my boot into his good leg as he tried to rise. I had to finish this before the initial shock and pain of the resin began to fade.

Suddenly Miggs stood between me and my foe. Rather than his mace, he held a white crystal in his hands, as if to show me. "Stop," he pleaded. "Enchantress Thul—"

He didn't get the chance to finish as Sledge Fist grabbed hold of the carriage driver and threw him to the ground, away from the fight.

I stepped forward with sword raised even as Flayzin rose, face bloody but sword held ready. The crystal flared white between us as a ghostly image of Enchantress Thulease appeared. She turned and raised her hands, pointing and then signaling for each of us to stop.

I stepped around the ghostly image. Whatever her purpose, this was life and death for me. I'd never again have the upper hand on Flayzin.

The enchantress's captain held his sword in a defensive stance. "The supreme enchantress bids this to end."

"She is not my master," I said, closing. "You should have weighed her desires before challenging me."

Sledge Fist and Preston held Miggs back even as he yelled for us to stop.

Then words sliced into my mind, speaking to me as a thought. A voice that had been there before—Imperial Seer Lochelle's. She demanded, "*Cease, Flank Hawk.*"

I stepped back and shouted, "Why?" with an adrenaline-filled voice.

"*Any hope for young Thereese requires the service of both you and the captain of Thulease's guard.*"

I backed away and faced the image of Supreme Enchantress Thulease. A memory of her daughter smiling and walking at my side in the King's Palace flashed in my thoughts. It shifted to the recent image of her lying silent, caught between life and death.

"Do you take back your words?" I asked, turning to Flayzin.

He wiped the blood that flowed from his broken nose away from his lips and chin. "Nay, I do not."

I nodded then said to the image of Enchantress Thulease, "You may have my sword and service." I then pointed my sword at Flayzin, who still held his weapon ready. "Or that of your guard captain. Not both."

Then I turned back to Flayzin. "When the enchantress's daughter is returned to health, we'll finish this."

"That we shall do," he said and sheathed his sword.

I sheathed mine, turned, and strode away. Before I reached the gate Rin was at my side. "Here's your dirk," he said.

It was clean of blood but still retained a bit of fireweed resin. "Thank you," I said and slid the weapon into its boot sheath.

We walked in silence for a few minutes as we made our way past porters and merchants with their ware-laden carts that filled the narrow cobbled streets.

"Who were ya talkin' ta, Flank Hawk?"

Rin was the only one in my family who called me by my mercenary name. "The enchantress and those witnessing the duel," I said.

"No, there was somebody else. When you looked up and shouted, 'Why?'"

I considered whether to tell Rin or not. "I believe it was Imperial Seer Lochelle."

Just about everyone in the King's City knew that Imperial Seer Lochelle was King Tobias's prime advisor. She was one of the most mysterious and powerful spellcasters in the land.

"Huhh..." was all Rin said as we made our way toward my boarding house or maybe my family's apartment several streets beyond. A few minutes later he asked, "That Captain Flayzin. He called you a coward and that's why you fought him. Reputation and honor. You told me about that once." He rubbed his chin and then scratched his head, just behind his ear. "He said you cheated. Did ya?"

I thought a moment, trying to look at it from Rin's perspective. "You know Guard Captain Flayzin's a better swordsman than me?"

"Yeah. Even my arms instructor said there's few that can best him."

"Well, when it comes to life and death, I'm not sure there's such a thing as cheating."

Rin thought on that a moment. "Kinda like if I had ta run a race with someone who was always faster than me. Better trip'em at the start so I can win, rather than lose for certain."

I nodded. "If it meant life or death."

"You got another plan ta get the edge on him when you finish for what he called ya?"

"I'll think of something," I said to Rin, not sure that I would.

"Don't matter what he says about cheatin' and honor anyway," Rin said. "Everybody who's got sense knows you ain't a coward. That makes him a liar ta begin with."

I sat in my second-story room in Snyder's Boarding House, mending my armor. Although I had several unlit candles, the oil lamp on the table provided enough light.

Flayzin had managed to wound me, and could've crippled me with a draw cut, probably when I'd head butted and knocked him down. Luckily my scabbard had been between my leg and his blade. Mostly.

I'd bled a little and hadn't noticed the shallow wound until Rin pointed it out just before running off to catch up with my mother and little sister Katchia on their way to the well house. I'd thought about helping with the buckets, but Rin's assistance would be enough for the job. I didn't want to explain the challenge to my mother with Katchia about. Rin promised not to say anything until my father returned home from working at the royal stables.

I could afford a far larger room with the coin I'd earned serving Grand Wizard Seelain and the king, but my father would better use the money. He planned to rebuild the family farm in the Doran Confederacy once spring arrived.

Someone strode down the hall and stopped in front of my door. The proprietor, Mr. Snyder, knocked quietly and asked, "Flank Hawk, there is a man downstairs who would like to speak with you."

I set my armor aside and buckled on my belt, which held my short sword in its scabbard. It wasn't very late; the sun had set less than an hour ago. When I opened the door, Snyder stood quietly in the narrow hallway with a questioning look on his face. He was a tall, middle-aged man with short hair and a quiet sense of humor.

"Who is it?" I asked. If it'd been anyone in my family, Lilly, Sergeant Drux or Major Jadd he'd have let them up to my room.

"He announced himself as Master Alchemist Butlir." When I didn't immediately say anything, he said, "I could send him away, if you like. I've heard you had a hard day."

"No," I said. "I'll see him."

"Here, or in the common room?"

"Here," I said, shrugging. Word always traveled fast. "I've had worse days."

"I know you have," Snyder said with a tight smile. "Surely the master alchemist knows it too. I'll have Heidi Lynn escort him up."

I barely had time to light a candle on the dresser, fold my armor and set it next to the head of my bed, near my boar spear leaning against the wall, and pull the square table away from the narrow window before I heard footsteps climbing the stairs just down the hall.

I slid the room's single wooden chair next to the table, opposite the bed where I'd sit. There wasn't much space in the room for more furniture beyond the locking chest at the foot of my bed and the narrow, three-drawer dresser near the door. Other than my clothing and equipment, the only personal thing I had was a painting of my family hanging on the wall above the dresser. My aunt, an accomplished artist, had painted the portrait. It was one of the few unnecessary things my family took before fleeing south, ahead of the Necromancer King's army.

In the painting I was about Rin's age. It seemed a lifetime ago.

Heidi Lynn knocked lightly on the half-open door. "Mr. Flank Hawk," the young maid said and peeked her head in, showing her wide eyes and a smile that did little to hide her uneasiness. "Master Alchemist Butlir, like Mr. Snyder announced."

"Thank you, Heidi Lynn," I said. "Please, let him in."

I figured the enchantress's husband was either going to apologize for the captain of the guard's actions and request I reconsider accompanying his wife along with the captain of her guard, or to let me know that my services wouldn't be needed.

Alchemist Butlir handed his cloak to the young servant before entering my room.

"Mercenary Flank Hawk," he said, extending his hand. "Thank you for seeing me."

I shook his hand. "Master Alchemist Butlir, please, have a seat." I gestured toward the wooden chair.

Heidi Lynn quietly said to me before closing the door, "Mr. Snyder is preparing wine and cheese for you and your visitor. We'll bring it up shortly."

I hadn't even thought of food or drink. I nodded to her. "That will be fine. Thank you."

The alchemist, still dressed in brown, waited for me before he sat down. "Do you entertain guests often?"

I shook my head and looked around the room from my seat on the bed.

"Like most mercenaries, you require little more than a place to lay your head when not in the field."

I nodded once and said, "My father taught me to never squander coin when it can be avoided. Mr. Snyder runs a good house. Decent food. It's quiet, clean and free of vermin."

"And near to your family," he said.

Alchemist Butlir apparently knew a lot about me. At least more than I expected. He added to that belief when he continued. "I have been told that you hold much untapped talent as a healer, if you would choose that path rather than continue your mercenary trade."

It was true. I had the ability to be a healer, like my older sister. But just as an air wizard's ability is weakened while at the bottom of a coal mine, my life as a mercenary stunted any development in ability as a healer.

"The mercenary life and healing are like oil and water," I said.

He leaned back in the chair and glanced out the window. "Yes, one cannot easily drink of both, despite residing within the same cup."

When I didn't reply, he leaned forward and rested his folded hands on the table. "Events of this afternoon were reported to me." He leaned back again. "There are so many elements contributing to the state of affairs, now and in the future—so much I desire to convey, I remain unsure where to begin. Although I have, it would seem. You see, when it comes to my wife and my daughter, their safety and wellbeing…precise and orderly logic escape me."

A knock at the door sounded before Alchemist Butlir could say more, or I could reply. I went to the door and allowed Mr. Snyder to enter. He carried a bottle of wine and two goblets. Behind him followed Heidi Lynn carrying a plate of cut cheese and a wooden chair that matched the one upon which my guest sat.

The room was crowded with so many bodies. But, before I knew it, the red wine had been poured, the additional chair had been placed, and Snyder and Heidi Lynn were gone with the door closed behind them.

The way he stiffly sat, watched and moved, it struck me that the alchemist didn't feel comfortable around people. I'd met a few craftsmen and artisans like that—like him.

The interruption gave me a chance to consider what Alchemist Butlir had said and why he, instead of his wife, was meeting with me. "Is Enchantress Thulease still interested in my assistance seeking out the Sleeping Sage?"

"That she most definitely is," the alchemist replied after tasting the wine. He nodded as if in approval.

"For my ability as a healer?"

"Primarily, no," he said. "And not necessarily for your arms skills."

"That's Guard Captain Flayzin's value."

"His and several additional members of the house guard."

While my skills were less than Flayzin's, I could hold my own, and had done so through more skirmishes and battles than I cared to remember.

The alchemist must've seen the perceived insult in my face and actions. I relaxed my hands and picked up a small wedge of the yellow and orange mottled cheese.

"You would like to know why my wife believes you are vital to achieving her goal, the restoration of our Thereese?"

"I would," I said. "And why both you and she expect me to journey with the captain of your guard? He who names me an incompetent coward and prefers me dead rather than part of the mission."

"As I said previously, there are many elements. First, my wife has closely consulted Imperial Seer Lochelle, whom you have met and worked with. As it has been relayed to me, the imperial seer can neither see certain success, nor a specific path toward it. This means that in addition to variables unaccounted for, individuals and possibly beings of power and influence are involved in the resolution. Yet, your participation is believed by the imperial seer as vital.

"Even if need of your company was not clear, nevertheless I believe Thulease would have you at her side. Not only have you proven yourself capable of completing daunting tasks, you also impressed her, as your mercenary name befits."

He took another sip of wine. "When Thulease worked spells to undo the magics holding closed the gates to Fendra Jolain's temple, despite the magical backlash that nearly slew her, you were there. Where others shied away, you imperiled your life. Assisted her to her feet, remained with her. At her side. That confidence, at that moment, meant more to her than you must realize."

"Her safety was my assigned duty," I said. "Until relieved. None with us that day shirked their duty."

At that moment I decided to accompany the supreme enchantress. What her husband said struck deep. But even more, their daughter, Thereese, risked as much as anyone who assaulted Fendra Jolain's temple. If there was a chance of the young enchantress's recovery, how could I deny her? Without her sacrifice, Fendra Jolain would've triumphed. I and all who survived would be imprisoned, or dead. The Kingdom of Keesee would by now be toppled.

Also, if I declined, Flayzin would have that victory.

I'd be going back on my claim that either he or I would accompany the enchantress. Not both. But abandoning Enchantress Thulease would damage my reputation. Even worse, if she failed, where I might have made a difference…

"Of course, Mercenary Flank Hawk. I have no intention of debating you on that count or any other of that day. Your steadfastness is why my wife believes you necessary for her success. Not only the instance I just reminded you of, but also from what Grand Wizard Seelain has remarked of you."

"Put yourself in my position," I said, not yet prepared to tell the alchemist of my decision. It was selfish, but the point had to be made. "In a desperate situation, will Flayzin have my back?" I set the wedge of cheese down, untasted. "Trust should be part of any team Enchantress Thulease puts together."

The alchemist placed his goblet on the table. "To be honest, I have never been in violent confrontations such as you. I have performed experiments where my life and wellbeing have been at risk, but, to be sure, such circumstances are not…congruent."

He picked up his goblet again and swirled the wine that remained in it. "However, I must have complete faith in my assistants, in their competence and, in that, there must be a parallel.

"Flank Hawk, do you know why Captain Flayzin challenged you?"

I reached for my goblet and tasted the wine. Sweet and good quality. "I take him at his word."

"Indeed, he is an honest man. But there is more to it."

That caught my attention. "Oh?" I said, setting my goblet back on the table. My mind again raced. I didn't ask but my thoughts settled on someone putting him up to it, even paying him.

"While serving as Grand Wizard Seelain's personal guard, you might have witnessed Captain Flayzin accompanying my wife inside the palace, serving as her personal guard?"

"I did."

"Unlike most personal guards, he accompanied her into the White Wing, where the royal suites are located?"

I nodded. It was unusual, but I'd never thought anything of it. Upon invitation, I'd accompanied Grand Wizard Seelain once and shared a meal there.

"Captain Flayzin is Grand Wizard Seelain's cousin. In addition, although they had limited contact as adults, the captain and Prince Reveron were, for several years, childhood friends."

"I begin to see," I said.

"I believe Captain Flayzin not only blames you for the death of the prince but, for whether right or wrong, he holds *you* responsible for the grief and sadness his cousin has endured. Not only her personal loss, but her elevation to royalty. A blow to all in Grand Wizard Seelain's family. There is more to that, but not for me to share."

I stood. "Master Alchemist Butlir, I will accompany your wife, Supreme Enchantress Thulease, wherever she must go and whoever she travels with in order to revive your daughter."

I offered him my hand. He stood, clasped my hand and we shook.

"I will do my best to keep your wife safe," I said. "And all that I can to ensure her success."

"Thank you," he said. "You cannot comprehend how that eases my concern. However, you should sit. A moment more of your time, if I might have it?"

I did as he bid. "Yes?"

"My wife. Normally she would be here to discuss this matter. Instead,

I came in her place. You might have wondered at this?"

"Not until you mentioned it," I said. "Your daughter's health is of equal concern to you and your wife."

"That it is. But she and I, and Imperial Seer Lochelle have a concern as well, with respect to you, which I have come to relay. Thulease is at the Royal Palace, in council with Prince Halgadin before he returns to the field. And the Imperial Seer, well, she does not venture out often and is even this night serving King Tobias. So it is left to me."

He stared at the candle on my dresser, before meeting my eyes. There was a sadness in both his eyes and his voice as he spoke. "Imperial Seer Lochelle has divined through her spellcraft that, should you come to face Captain Flayzin in combat, he will slay you."

CHAPTER 4

I decided to wear my breast and backplate but left my spear in my room. I had my sword and dirk. I wasn't looking forward to seeing Guard Captain Flayzin. I didn't think we'd fight. But if we did, what weapons I carried wouldn't matter. The chances of Imperial Seer Lochelle being wrong were small. Too small to hope. I wondered if Flayzin knew of the imperial seer's prediction.

I'd thought hard on what Alchemist Butlir said. Maybe that was why he hinted for me to take up as a healer. The practice of healing magic weakened a healer's ability to hurt others, even in self-defense. That's why any healer worth anything had a personal guard. By common practice, if Flayzin followed through with his challenge, he'd have to defeat my personal guard. If I took up practice as a healer. And could hire a swordsman better than him...

I was almost to Supreme Enchantress Thulease's tower. The red granite structure overshadowed the nearby squat, two-story brick building. From the shorter building a trio of pipes, braced together with metal and rising higher than the neighboring tower, drew my attention. They went up at nearestleast a hundred feet with several support beams running from the tower to the three-pipe structure, probably to keep them stable in strong winds. The pipes must've been related to the alchemist's work. Behind his workshop stood a small wooden horse stable, and servant quarters. An eight-foot stone wall lined with sharp metal spikes surrounded the buildings. Each spike was over a foot long, angling down toward the street to deter anyone from attempting to climb over.

Blue District was the wealthiest part of the King's City, and the safest, except for the White District around King Tobias's palace. Still, those who had something of value were wise to protect it. Even more so since the war left few soldiers for patrols, and many of those were old men or injured veterans unfit for regular duty.

A few carriages passed me as I neared the gate. I felt the need to look around. Something wasn't right, somebody was watching me. Then I spotted her, next to a blue-painted lamp post.

Lilly came bounding across the wide street toward me. "Took you long enough to notice me," Lilly said before opening her arms for a quick hug. "Been following you for almost five minutes."

Lilly should've been at her job in the palace's North Garden. Instead of her assistant gardener uniform, she wore the green shirt I'd given her over a year ago, covered by a deerskin jacket, and pants. From her belt hung

Lesser Enchanter Jonas's rapier and her old broad-bladed dagger.

After a quick embrace I stepped close to the wall, a few strides from the gate. "I have a lot on my mind."

"When don't you?" she replied, moving next to me. Her short brown hair looked a little damp and her wide-set brown eyes sparkled with her smile.

"Lilly, what are you doing here?"

"Same as you," she said. "Last night Enchantress Thulease came by my room in the palace. I was studying. She said you might be going on a mission with her and wanted to know if I'd go too."

Lilly grabbed a hold of my hands. "If you're going, of course I am. I'm your scout, after all."

"What about your studies?" I asked. "And your duties in the garden?"

Lilly rolled her eyes. "The enchantress said she'd take care of everything like that. Even Chief Gardener Orich won't argue with Supreme Enchantress Thulease. Even I wouldn't."

I smiled at her last statement, knowing it wasn't true.

My friend shook her head and grinned. "Plus, she's an advisor to the king and prince."

We turned and walked toward the gate. "Heck," Lilly said. "I'd drop it all in a second for you, Flank Hawk. You know that." Then she leaned close. "And the enchantress said you'd probably want someone along you could fully trust."

A servant girl wearing a blue dress and gray apron led Lilly and me past the staircase that spiraled up several floors. The previous day I'd taken it up to where Enchantress Thereese lay.

The house servant then opened a narrow door that led to an equally narrow hallway, dark except for the light shining in near the far end where a pair of oak double doors stood open on the left. The servant stopped at the double doors, turned, and gestured for us to enter the square room dominated by a circular table and nine high-back chairs.

Most of the light came from two narrow windows opposite the doorway. The internal shutters constructed of both wood and iron had been pulled back. An ornate silver chandelier depicting eight geese with wings outspread and necks curving upward hung centered above the table. Three of the eight white candles held by the geese's open beaks were lit, adding their light to the room.

Shelves lined with books filled the left and right walls. Various glass bottles and jars with stoppers and lids sat on the top board of each shelf. In addition to the varied colors of glass, including browns, greens and blues, the containers held various powders and liquids, themselves varied in color, I noted, based on how they affected the portion of the hue-tinted containers they filled. Between the two windows hung a painting of a man and woman, both in green. Supreme Enchantress Thulease resembled the tall woman in the picture in much the same way Thereese resembled her mother.

Lilly's time spent in the palace and having been schooled in etiquette by Tutor Roeth, and accompanying Grand Wizard Seelain during the mission to recover the Blood Sword, showed in her manner. She didn't look wide-eyed or nervous in the massive tower. She'd changed a lot since we crossed paths along a wooded riverside in the war-torn Faxtinian Coalition.

Even so, she remained at heart a small village girl with an untamed spirit. Some of that spirit arose from her werebeast nature. Something that would never allow her to fully fit in, especially among nobles and royal circles.

It appeared we were the first of those invited to arrive as the meeting room sat empty. The servant girl ushered us to our seats. Mine was to the left of the seat with the tallest back, nearest the windows. Lilly was directed to sit to my left.

I guessed Flayzin would be sitting to the right of the tallest chair where Enchantress Thulease would certainly sit.

As soon as the servant departed, Lilly asked, "We that early?"

I shook my head and observed the large tan envelope resting in front of me. 'Mercenary Flank Hawk' was scrawled upon it in black ink. The writing was so fancy that I found it initially difficult to read. Lilly was looking at the envelope in front of her.

She frowned. "It says, Scout Lilly, I think. I don't read cursive well, and can't read a lick of Mainland. I do sort of okay with the Crusader—Reunited Kingdom's language."

"You probably read it better than I read Mainland," I said.

She smiled, and then leaned close. "I don't like the king much, but he did get me a good tutor to teach me to read Roos's book of scripture."

That was her gift for helping me thwart the Necromancer King's invasion of Keesee. What Lilly asked of him when he offered her a boon.

Lilly gazed at the shelves. "You think they've read all these books, Flank Hawk?"

"Probably. There's a lot more. I saw this many in Enchantress Thereese's room."

"You saw her?" Lilly's voice fell to a whisper again.

I nodded. "It's as if she's asleep, but more." I didn't know how to explain it. "You just know she's not going to wake up."

Lilly scrunched up her nose. "Don't know what's in those jars but, even closed and stoppered, I can smell it." She looked around. "At least a few of them. What're they for?"

I couldn't smell anything except the oil polish on the table and the flame-melted candle wax above. "Enchantress Thulease's husband is a master alchemist."

"Oh," she said while adjusting her rapier and scabbard. "Know where we're going?"

I shook my head. "No."

"Me neither." She started to say more but stopped. The narrow hallway's distant door opened and a half moment later the blue-clad servant girl escorted two more individuals into the room.

Lilly and I stood as they entered.

The first was a dark-skinned woman with short tight-curled hair. The grips of two long sticks or clubs showed above her shoulders. In addition to her armament, including a sling attached to her thick belt, she wore sturdy leather armor with reinforced shoulders and thigh-high boots that had seen a lot of wear.

Even as I assessed her, the woman examined Lilly and me. Her eyes met mine as she recognized me as a fellow mercenary. Looking closer I could see her hands bore several scars, along with a healed burn wound the size of my thumb just below her left ear.

We acknowledged each other with a slight nod.

The mercenary and Lilly's eyes must've met too, but I couldn't see how Lilly responded. Only that the mercenary stepped aside with a neutral expression. From behind her a youth who couldn't be more than fifteen summers stepped into the room. His skin was swarthy, but not as dark as the mercenary's, and his short wavy hair stood on end, probably due to the orange and brown knit hat clutched in his hands. He wore a gray wool jacket over a faded brown shirt, its dark buttons matching his brown boots and pants. He carried no weapons and greeted me and Lilly with a crooked, unsure smile.

The servant girl directed the youth to his seat to the right of where I figured Flayzin would sit. He pulled a tan handkerchief from a pants pocket and wiped his thick nose that reminded me a little of a wyvern's beak. The mercenary swiftly pulled her wooden fighting sticks and leaned them against the bookcase behind her seat to the youth's right, across the table from me. The two-inch thick sticks were a little over two feet long. What stood out was the silver cord, wrapped and imbedded around the top six inches of each fighting stick. She made a point to rest her hand on the pommel of the sheathed curved dagger hanging on her belt opposite the sling.

As soon as the servant departed, I said, "I'm Flank Hawk." Since the table was too large to reach across and shake hands, I gestured to my friend. "And this is Lilly."

The mercenary said without expression. "I know." The two words revealed an accent I'd come across before. She was a mercenary from the Southern Continent. Probably not a Malgerian mercenary as she wasn't dressed as they do. However, the silver wrapped fighting sticks were something a Southern Continent mercenary might use.

Neither she nor the youth said anything else before pulling out their chairs and sitting down.

Lilly and I did the same.

"And you are?" Lilly asked, staring across the table at the mercenary.

The young man looked from the mercenary to Lilly, and back.

Lilly leaned forward. "It's written on the envelope in front of you—if you've forgot."

The man gave us his crooked smile while the mercenary frowned. I thought about saying something, but decided not to. I hadn't brought Lilly onboard and better to let things play out ahead of time—before we were on the road or in the wilderness. I'd back her, whatever happened.

Another half moment passed and I began to wonder if the mercenary was friends with Flayzin.

I placed my hand on Lilly's leg just before she began to speak. "You know us," I said. "Should either of us know you?" I shifted my gaze from the mercenary to the youth sitting to her left. "Either of you?"

The youth leaned close to the mercenary and whispered into her ear.

She responded, looking from Lilly to me, "No, not both."

The youth said to her, "Then why antagonize them?" His Mainland carried a slight accent too, one I didn't recognize in his nasally voice.

She shot the youth an angry glance. He ignored her and said, "I am Ammond, son of Rabumb." He pointed to the mercenary. "She goes by Storm Claw. She's my protector."

With lightning reflexes, the mercenary snatched Ammond's hand and pinned it to the table. He grimaced and said, "She takes her responsibility for me seriously, like everything else."

Lilly said, "Flank Hawk's been a personal guard too."

"Who failed," said Storm Claw.

At the same time I said, "So I've recently been told," Lilly stood and said, "He did not!" Her words weren't quite shouted, but close.

I placed a hand on Lilly's arm. "If Guard Captain Flayzin is your source of information," I said to the stern-faced mercenary, "you might consider asking around." I shrugged. "Maybe you'll get confirmation. Maybe you'll hear something else."

"I've heard about you," Ammond said. "Even in my land. From the stories, I sort of expected you to be…older, larger…look meaner."

"He's fought beasts that'd leave you shaking in fear," Lilly said to the youth. "Maybe you too," she said to the mercenary.

"What about you?" Storm Claw asked Lilly.

"Can't say for sure." Lilly sat down. "I never faced a bone golem."

A skeptical eyebrow rose on Storm Claw's face. "Could you take the captain of this tower's guard?"

I replied, "Ask him how things turned out yesterday."

She nodded once.

Lilly asked me, "What happened yesterday?"

"Later," I said to Lilly.

My friend glared at me a second and huffed. "I will."

"Are you a healer?" I asked Ammond.

He asked, "How did you know?"

"You didn't name yourself as a noble, you have a personal guard—a protector, and it makes sense for Enchantress Thulease to invite one to accompany her."

"You gonna tell him, Flank Hawk?" Lilly asked. "Ain't any reason to keep it a secret. You saw to that more than just about anyone."

"What?" asked the young healer.

When I didn't say anything, to him or to Lilly, my friend said, "Flank Hawk's a healer too."

"But you're a mercenary," Ammond said. "How can that be?"

I smiled. "I'm not much of a healer, really." I stared at Storm Claw. "Of course, some might say I'm not much of a mercenary, either."

Lilly looked toward the hallway and stood. "Other people are coming."

I stood, followed by Ammond and Storm Claw when we heard the distant door open.

The servant girl stepped into the room and then off to the right of the double-doorway, allowing Guard Captain Flayzin to enter. He was in his chainmail with his sword at his side. He must have found and employed a healer since he walked without a limp and his nose was straight and not swollen. Behind him came Miggs, and Sledge Fist. The carriage driver had his long-handled mace. Sledge Fist had a sword. Miggs wore a thick cotton shirt and pants, while the mercenary wore a vest of wolf fur over his gray shirt and breeches.

Flayzin ignored everyone as he made his way to the seat I expected him to take, between Ammond and the empty seat to my right. Miggs moved to the seat next to Lilly with Sledge Fist stopping at the seat on the carriage driver's left, one of the two closest to the doorway. That one was still empty.

Miggs made quick eye-contact with me before we all sat, then he stared down at the table.

"Flank Hawk," Sledge Fist said, showing his broken-toothed smile.

"Sledge Fist," I replied with a nod. I was preparing to introduce Lilly to him when I saw the servant girl turn to face down the narrow hallway and bow her head. Enchantress Thulease's voice came down the hall in quiet tones. Someone with a deep male voice replied, but I couldn't make out any words of their conversation. Lilly probably could.

Walking in with Enchantress Thulease was a stocky man, shorter than me but taller than Lilly. His hair and eyes were brown and his skin had a brown cast to it. His bare feet was the final clue that told me he was an earth wizard. Probably not a very powerful one.

With wizards, the more powerful one became the more they tended to resemble their element. I'd once seen a supreme water wizard. Her skin had become a glassy ocean blue, and her eyes were a matching blue with no whites. Her hair and fingernails were green, but it looked more like she'd colored them.

In public, especially when they might perform spells, enchanters wore masks that covered their faces just below the eyes to hide their identity. The more powerful they became, the more susceptible they became to other magics worked against them. Seers, they lost their eyesight. And healers, like me, the ability to physically harm others.

Everyone stood as the earth wizard took the remaining seat near the doorway, between Sledge Fist and Storm Claw. The enchantress strode around the table to her seat. When she turned to face all of us and nodded, we followed her example and sat.

"I trust each here knows the purpose of this meeting," began Supreme Enchantress Thulease. "Namely to seek the Sleeping Sage so that I might obtain the knowledge to revive my daughter." She paused to individually meet the eyes of everyone attending. "But each of you may not know every individual invited here to my table. Thus, I shall briefly introduce all attending this meeting, beginning with the captain of my guard.

"Captain Flayzin," she said, gesturing to him. "To his right sit Healer Ammond and his mercenary protector, Storm Claw."

She paused and continued, staring at each person named. "Journeyman Earth Wizard Stok, Mercenary Sledge Fist, Ostler Miggs, Scout Lilly, and Mercenary Flank Hawk."

The enchantress gestured with sweep of her hand. "The envelope in front of each invited here contains a contract drawn up by my husband. With some, I have informally discussed payment for participation and assistance in this venture. Others, I and my husband have researched through contacting previous employers and referencing prevailing wages, and have offered within the contract, appropriate compensation. Please refrain from examining the contents for the moment."

She paused and rested her ring-adorned hands on the table. "Until after you have learned some of the details of what will be expected. Then you may back out, or negotiate with my husband, Master Alchemist Butlir. Understand, I have contacted other parties that have expressed interest, should any or all here change their mind, or are unable to come to a negotiated agreement with my husband."

The enchantress stood, but signaled for us to remain seated. "No magics in Keesee, including the most powerful healers combined with my own spellcraft, appear to be able to alter the condition of my daughter, Thereese. After long weeks and months of research, delving deep into the archives of Keesee's Imperial Library, no solution, magical or alchemical, was to be found. Even as we speak and prepare, Thereese's condition worsens. A slow march toward death."

Enchantress Thulease began pacing around the table as she spoke. It reminded me how King Tobias had once addressed his War Council.

"Consultation with Imperial Seer Lochelle resulted in a vision, a possibility, a probability where the knowledge I seek may be obtained. The abode of the Sleeping Sage." She held up a finger. "Yet it is not a sure path to an answer. The imperial seer's vision lacked clarity. That may owe to the fact that some factions of the indigenous peoples inhabiting the Southern Continent have a faith which, similar to the Crusaders of the Reunited Kingdom, renders them both immune and hostile to magic. Seers have forever been unable to divine clear paths when the Crusaders play an integral part. It may be so with these inhabitants.

"Keesee's contact and dealings with the Southern Continent beyond its northern coastal cities are few, and this may be another factor."

She had circled the table twice and stopped behind her seat. "When powerful individuals or beings are involved, a seer's vision is clouded. The more powerful the seer, the more powerful the individual must be to cloud a vision, which legend and research indicates the Sleeping Sage may be."

This last statement worried me. By the mixture of frowns and widening eyes around the table, it did others as well.

"That, however, is not a direct concern for you. It is I who must deal with him. Obtain the knowledge from him. And that is the final potential limiting factor inhibiting Imperial Seer Lochelle's vision, and thus, her guidance. What the Sleeping Sage desires, I may not possess to barter."

She pulled out her seat and slowly sat down. "We will travel by ship to the Southern Continent. From there, we will travel south, nearly one thousand, five hundred miles, through vast expanses of desert, which none around this table have experienced, to a large, shallow lake in the heart of the continent. There, along those shores, is where the Sleeping Sage dwells.

"I have sent ahead several men to secure a guide, mounts, beasts of burden, and men to accompany us as they see fit."

She nodded toward each of us around the table, explaining our part. "Captain Flayzin will lead security. His sword along with Mercenary Sledge Fist's and those of the three of the tower guards sent ahead will both deter aggression and protect us during our travels. Healer Ammond's purpose is evident, as is that of his protector, Mercenary Storm Claw. Earth Wizard Stok will combine his magic with mine to secure water during our travels." The earth wizard nodded back with a faint grunt.

"Ostler Miggs will care for the mounts and beasts of burden, as his skill and training provide. Scout Lilly will assist our hired guide, help to warn, if not maneuver us clear of danger. And Mercenary Flank Hawk will serve as my personal guard, and be at my side when I confront the Sleeping

Sage."

The word 'confront' caught my attention. Lilly sat up straight and glanced at me, so it must have caught hers, too.

Even as the enchantress finished, the sound of servants moving down the narrow hallway could be heard. They carried in bowls filled with hardboiled eggs and plums, and plates filled with sliced ham and loaves of warm bread, including small cakes of cornbread. They deftly placed fancy white plates bearing black-lined images of the King's Palace, along with silver forks, knives, and white napkins embroidered to match the plates.

As the smell of salty, steaming hot pork and dark breads filled the room, servants filled narrow glasses with white grape juice, except for mine, which was filled with weak cider. Next to Lilly's glass a servant in blue placed a dish filled with honey.

I heard Sledge Fist chuckle. "Pickles," he remarked, and asked a brunette servant girl, "How'dja know I liked pickles fer morning food?"

At that statement, Enchantress Thulease stood. No plate had been set before her.

She signaled for us to remain seated. "I must excuse myself to attend matters. Read the contracts and, if agreeable, sign and wax-seal them and deliver them to Captain Flayzin. If not, contact my husband through Captain Flayzin. Your decision must be made before nightfall. We will depart sunrise two days hence, aboard the *Hunchback Maiden.* Please, enjoy your meal."

"And the company," added Guard Captain Flayzin. "May this be the first of many meals shared together." He raised his cup of juice.

The enchantress stopped at the door and took a glass from one of the servant's trays, allowing her to fill it with cider. "I can most certainly spare a moment to drink to that."

We all did, but after that the camaraderie and meal became mired in silence.

Ammond appeared to be observing Sledge Fist eat.

"Gotta nother tooth broke off inna fight," the big mercenary said, before swallowing the hardboiled egg he'd been chewing. "The barber plastered it closed, but it takes a while till I don't feel nothin."

"After breakfast," Ammond said, "I could examine it. Although I am not able to repair most organs, tendons and ligaments in the body, I am proficient with bones, of which teeth are an offshoot. I do not believe I can initiate regrowth of the lost parts. Still, I should be able to strengthen them and deaden the sensitivity so that all three cease to cause discomfort."

Sledge Fist pointed to the envelope beyond his plate. "I never had no contract, so I can't say there's enough coin in it."

"I could read your contract to you," interjected Flayzin. "After we finish here."

The big mercenary hesitated shoveling in his bite of ham, stared at his plate a second, then looked up and smiled his broken-toothed smile. "Naww, Flayzin. And thanks, Healer, but I been through it before."

The healer started to say something but Flayzin spoke over him, to Sledge Fist. "Address me as Captain Flayzin, unless you intend to turn down your contract with Enchantress Thulease."

I didn't know why Flayzin was spoiling for a fight with Sledge Fist. He'd dug at the mercenary twice.

"You mean *Guard* Captain," I said to Flayzin. "Unless you've recently been elevated to service in the king's military?"

Lilly leaned in to look past Miggs to get Sledge Fist's attention. "Flank Hawk can help you if there's a couple words in there you can't figure."

Flayzin said, "Certainly he'll read all the words in yours, Scout."

She glared back at Flayzin and snapped something back in the Crusader tongue, which I didn't understand. Neither did Flayzin.

I couldn't understand why the enchantress had left. It was like she wanted to encourage anger and distrust among us. How that could benefit her mission I had no idea. Then, I recalled that she'd said the guard captain was necessary for any hope of success. As was I. Maybe somehow the others were too.

Storm Claw looked like a wildcat ready to pounce as her protectee slowly stood and raised his hands to calm the situation.

"Scout Lilly," Healer Ammond said. "As the supreme enchantress has obviously researched each of us closely before inviting us on this mission, it could be that your contract is written in the language of the Reunited Kingdom.

"Guard Captain Flayzin," he said, looking at the man seated to his left. "By seating you to her right this morning, and through her directives for us to go through you before she departed to attend other tasks, the enchantress clearly placed you second to her in the overall chain of command." He gazed around the table. "Although we each have been given our primary tasks, which may lessen the degree of authority Guard Captain Flayzin might wield with respect responsibility in that area."

He then sat and said to Sledge Fist, "As we are to be colleagues in this mission to seek a means to revive the young Enchantress Thereese, I believe it only proper that I attend to your damaged teeth without expectation of monetary compensation."

As the healer spoke, he seemed to gain confidence. Confidence and insight beyond his years. Maybe he was older than he looked?

"Finally," he said, "I am fluent in four languages and offer my humble service to assist each in interpreting the contracts before you. Knowledge of contracts, both formulating and interpreting, was a part of my formal education, in addition to training in the healing arts."

Sledge Fist grinned wide and shoved a slice of apple in his mouth, beyond his broken teeth. "I'll take ya up on that. The teeth and the contract. But I can't let ya do somethin' for nothin'. What say you, if it's good with your bodyguard, let me take ya to the One-Eyed Pelican?"

The young healer obviously had never been to, or heard of, the rundown tavern as he suggested we all venture there for an evening meal.

After everyone nodded in agreement, I leaned close to Lilly and whispered, "Having to eat there is reason enough not to sign on."

She spit her bite of cornbread half way across the table in laughter.

CHAPTER 5

"Come on," Lilly said to me, laughing. "Everyone had a good time last night at the One-Eyed Pelican. Even you."

Lilly and I made our way through the mid-morning crowd. I'd just had my sword and boar spear spelled by a greater enchanter to better resist salt and corrosion. I'd also picked up a dozen superior quality quarrels for my crossbow, three of them silver-tipped.

"The company, yes," I said. "The food, no. Not even close."

Lilly scrunched up her nose. "Maybe you should've tried something besides that fish soup you always get."

"What, like that dried-out, overcooked slab of lamb you, Miggs and Sledge Fist shared?"

"It's not about the food, Flank Hawk. It's the place and the company."

"I counted six rats in the rafters."

"That's two fewer than the last time Road Toad and Drux went with us." She signaled with her head to step onto the porch of a garment merchant's shop. "Probably was more fun last night since that Flayzin didn't show up. Besides, you're supposed to tell me something about you and him, remember?"

"You already got your backpack," I said, tugging the soft leather pack holding a pair of new boots and a dozen arrows. Being a lycanthrope, she didn't get any silver-tipped ones. I held the door open for her. "What do you want here?"

"A hat with a brim," she said. "Bet it's gonna be sunny. And don't change the subject."

Lilly had a point about the sun. Plus, our contract said the enchantress would pay half the coin of any services and supplies purchased in preparation for the journey.

Lilly ended up haggling for a sturdy leather hat with a broad brim all the way around and a cord that could be cinched up under her chin. I picked up a light cotton hat with a forward-facing brim. It could be folded and wouldn't take up much space. Except for being brown instead of mottled green, it also reminded me of the hats the Colonel of the West's soldiers wore while on work detail.

"So," Lilly said, adjusting her new hat while waiting for a donkey cart to pass before we stepped off the porch. "What about Flayzin?"

"It makes sense he'd have duties at the enchantress's tower and couldn't make it."

"I don't know," Lilly said. "Miggs didn't sound too convincing. But that's not what I was talking about, and you know it."

"Miggs hadn't ever been to the One-Eyed Pelican. He was pretty wide-eyed even after Sledge Fist said he'd watch out for him." I had to agree with Miggs that half of the One-Eyed Pelican's customers looked more like thieves and cutthroats than anything else.

Lilly stopped in the middle of the street, forcing a woman and daughter with water jugs balanced on their heads to step around. I signaled Lilly to follow me into Gerlach's Café. I wasn't really hungry, but their tea was good and I didn't want to discuss what happened between me and Flayzin while walking down the street.

After I finished telling Lilly about what had happened in the practice yard, she leaned back in the wicker chair and sipped her cup of lemon mint tea. "Think you can take him with your spear?"

I shrugged. "Maybe." I wasn't going to tell her what Imperial Seer Lochelle had predicted.

"I hear he's *really* good with a sword." Although the café was empty except for us, and the serving girl was humming a happy tune while sweeping behind the floral-painted counter, Lilly had dropped her voice to just above a whisper. "You better think hard on something like fireweed resin, but different. I'll think on it, too."

"Thanks, Lilly. It may not come to it."

"Yeah, he might get killed on the mission."

"No. That's not what I was thinking," I said, finishing my tea and placing four copper on the cherry-wood table. "Remember how Prince Halgadin banished Major Jadd from all of Keesee, and threatened to cross swords with him, if he ever saw Jadd again?"

Lilly nodded. "Yeah, but good as he is, Flayzin's nowhere near good as the prince."

"Remember, it was a time of war so they didn't fight right away when Jadd returned to serve Prince Reveron? And he and Prince Halgadin both had to serve on the king's mission to slay Fendra Jolain with the Blood Sword?"

"Yeah, I remember," Lilly said. "The prince shook hands with Road Toad and told him he was forgiven—but you did nothing wrong, Flank Hawk." She pushed her empty teacup away. "Flayzin's wrong," she said, no longer whispering. "What he said about you, Flank Hawk."

"What I'm getting at is, like the prince and Major Jadd, Flayzin and I will be serving Enchantress Thulease together. He might change his mind, too."

"No, he won't," Lilly said, shaking her head. "He's got too big an ego."

"And Prince Halgadin doesn't?"

I didn't really believe my argument, and neither did Lilly.

But, for the moment, it was all I had.

CHAPTER 6

Rin shifted my boar spear from his right hand to his left, lightly thumping its butt against the weather-worn planks we stood upon. "That's a pretty big ship," he said.

The *Hunchback Maiden* was a three-masted merchant ship. Not the largest in the main harbor of the King's City, but far from the smallest.

"That she is," I said. "And the crew looks busy." Like a colony of ants, the shadowy figures worked in the rigging and manhandled the last of the crates below deck.

"And they're armed," commented my mother, pulling her green wool shawl tighter around her shoulders. It was obvious from the light of the lanterns lining the pier, especially when it glinted off the metal blades that hung at their sides.

Rin and the rest of my family had come down to the docks to see me off. My father, standing behind my mother, put his calloused hands on her shoulders.

I wanted to tell her the cutlasses a few of the sailors wore were for show. Once at sea, they'd be stowed and not seen again…unless trouble arose. Explaining that wouldn't lessen my mother's worries.

She wiped a tear as it ran down her round cheek. "You should take up like your father. Buy farm land. Or healing like your sister, Raina."

Dad stepped up between my mother and younger sister, Katchia, and put a hand on each of their shoulders. My little sister watched everyone and everything, but remained quiet. She'd grown a lot in the past two years, but hadn't yet seen eleven summers. Her brown hair hung down over her shoulders in two braids. It made her appear even younger as she turned and smiled up at me.

"It'll be okay, Mom," I said. "This is what I do. I'm good at it."

I looked over at Raina who stood several paces away from us—from me—clutching a heavy canvas sack holding something large and round. Behind her stood one of the king's guards, a stern, battle-scarred veteran. Raina was a healer and needed protection. King Tobias provided it, since she was now serving him, serving the citizens of Keesee.

I was surprised my older sister even came to see me off. She'd avoided me since Major Jadd had carried her back with us after the battle in Fendra Jolain's temple. Carried her when we fled the closing army scaling the mountain. We'd escaped upon dragons, wyverns, and in one of the Colonel of the West's troop helicopters, a relic preserved and maintained from the time of First Civilization's fall.

Nearby, Lilly talked to a woman dressed in a golden-brown sweater and matching pleated skirt. She wore wire-framed glasses and smiled as she listened to Lilly. I finally placed her face when the woman handed Lilly a book. She was Lilly's tutor.

Lilly didn't have any family. Her mother and father had been killed by townsfolk in the Faxtinian Coalition after being discovered as lycanthropes. She had an older brother but hadn't seen or heard from him in years. She figured he was dead too. It was good that someone had come to see Lilly off, and that brought a smile to my face.

In the predawn darkness, I spotted Supreme Enchantress Thulease's black carriage approaching, so I turned to my mother and gave her a hug. She hugged me back, adding a kiss on my cheek and a whisper in my ear. "Keep safe."

"I will, Mom," I said, and lifted Katchia up from the dock. She pretended to struggle and not be happy about it. "I won't be able to do this much longer," I told her.

She hugged me tight. "You're gonna be gone a long time, Krish?" It really wasn't a question.

I put Katchia down. No sense lying to her. "I don't know, but probably." I gripped Rin's shoulder. "Rin, here, will watch out for you. But there's no reason you shouldn't make sure he keeps out of trouble."

"Right," he said, balling his fist before socking me in the shoulder. "It'll be me keeping her outta trouble." To which she stuck her tongue out at him.

"Watch yourself in the roost," I said to Rin. "Don't feed any of your fingers to those wyvern hatchlings."

"That's whatcha gave me these for," he said, pointing to the pair of chainmail gloves tucked in his belt.

The echoing of horse hooves told me the carriage was getting closer. I shook hands with my dad, then we hugged. He patted me on my backplate. "Remember what your mother said. Keep safe, Son."

"I will, Dad." I stepped back and nodded to Raina. "Thank you for seeing me off, Sister."

She took a step toward me, hesitated, then strode up to me. Her brown hair continued to grow long and she remained heavier than the day the followers of Fendra Jolain stole her from us—took her because she was discovered to have healing ability. But Raina didn't look like eight summers had passed since that day.

Extending her arms she handed me the sack. "Hope this helps you do your…your…job," she said, and turned away.

"Thank you," I said, hefting the sack over my shoulder. "I'm confident it will."

Lilly ran up to me. "Here comes the enchantress. Give me your gear."

I unslung my crossbow and handed it to her along with the sack. Rin handed me my boar spear.

"Good-bye," I said to my family and donned my helmet while trying to ignore my mother's sniffles. The night before I'd told my parents about the confrontation with Guard Captain Flayzin. I knew that was a good part of my mother's concern.

Without turning back I marched toward the carriage that had just come to a stop. Next to it was Guard Captain Flayzin. He cantered forward on his white stallion and looked down at me before dismounting. "Move quickly," he said. "The enchantress doesn't want anything to delay departure."

I stood on the quarterdeck next to Supreme Enchantress Thulease, together watching the sun rise over the King's City as its walls and towers fell away in the distance.

"Although you are a reserved man, Flank Hawk," the enchantress said, "you appear uncharacteristically sullen."

I thought a moment about what she said. "Missions in the past, Enchantress. It's always been a secret departure. In the dark of night. I'd have preferred that again."

The enchantress sighed, which was uncharacteristic of her. "I would have preferred that as well, my mercenary friend."

CHAPTER 7

Lilly sat in the shade of the *Hunchback Maiden*'s billowed sails, carefully studying a small leather-bound book. We were in the third of what was expected to be a six day voyage, and she'd spent time studying the book each afternoon.

I sat down next to her, tired from weapons training Flayzin had offered to Miggs, Sledge Fist and me. I set the round shield to my right and leaned left, trying to see what Lilly was reading. The lettering of the printed words was clear, but the words they formed were unfamiliar. They reminded me of Roos's book of scriptures that Lilly sometimes carried with her.

"It's a gift from Tutor Roeth," Lilly said. "It's called *A Christmas Carol*, and it dates back from before First Civilization's fall. Before the Colonel of the West was born. It's got ghosts that are like seers haunting a cruel man." Lilly was silent for a moment before adding, "She said I needed to keep practicing my reading whenever I could."

"It's in the Crusader tongue, then?"

Lilly placed a flower-painted marker between two pages and closed the book. "I'll tell you about it sometime, once I get it figured out. I know the words, but not about things where it takes place…" Lilly trailed off in thought for a moment. "It's kind of like in the Reunited Kingdom, with steam tractors and all, but not exactly 'cause I haven't read about a tractor yet. Maybe since it's winter in the story."

She glanced over at my round shield I'd been practicing with. It was the gift from my sister just before I boarded. It was a few inches over two feet in diameter, wooden with a sturdy iron rim around it. It'd been painted gray with two green hawks, back to back with wings outspread and talons outstretched, as if ready to grasp.

"Think she painted it?" Lilly asked.

I shrugged. "Maybe. I'm not very good using it with my boar spear. But Flayzin's showing me how to use it with my sword. He showed me how and when to strike with a shield instead of just using it to block and deflect attacks."

"Why do you think he's teaching you to fight with it, if he's planning on killing you after we're done with the mission?"

I shrugged again. "What he's teaching me probably won't help much against him, but might make a difference if there's combat between now and then. Besides, I figure finding the Sleeping Sage is only the first leg of the mission." I didn't add that it allowed him to observe my skill and any techniques I might try against him.

"Oh," Lilly said. She fiddled with her book a moment. "I'll stick with you, Flank Hawk, through any mission. I'll even fight Captain Flayzin for ya."

I smiled at Lilly. "You're getting handy with Jonas's rapier, but you're not that good. Plus, rapiers aren't good against armor."

"I remember Road Toad saying once that battlefield fighting's a lot different than practice fighting. Some men don't take too well to it. Me and you do."

"I think Flayzin does too, Lilly."

"Yeah," she conceded. "Maybe. But who said I'd fight'im when he's ready for it?"

"Ship off the starboard bow!" shouted the watchman in the crow's nest. "Can just see the tops of 'er sails."

That got everyone's attention. The ship's captain, an aging lanky man with a long wispy beard and mustache, strode down from the quarterdeck to the main deck and stared up at the watchman. The rest of the sailors on the ship moved about their business, stowing ropes and securing gear, checking the sails. Three stood, awaiting orders to go below deck for weapons.

"She's two-masted," called down the watchman from the crow's nest. A few minutes later he added, "A brigantine with square sails. She's flyin' no flag."

Lilly had her spyglass out and peered through it with her right eye. "Can't see anything, yet."

"Go alert our lady," I told Lilly. That was the title we were to use for the enchantress while aboard ship.

Lilly handed me her spyglass and ran to reach the enchantress's cabin below where she spent much of her time, talking with Wizard Stok and Healer Ammond.

Flayzin signaled me to join him on the quarterdeck. After I did, he held out his hand for Lilly's spyglass. "May I?"

While Captain Skerlain barked orders to adjust the sails and for the steersman to change the ship's course, I handed Lilly's spyglass to Flayzin. "Even up here, it'll still be out of sight, except for maybe the tops of her sails."

"So, Flank Hawk, you know about curvature beyond the horizon," he said and looked anyway. "Brigantines are fast ships—far faster than ours." He paused. "Ah, there she is, or her sails. No colors present."

I looked to the flag fluttering atop the stern mast above us. Half purple and half gold, the colors of Keesee.

Enchantress Thulease emerged from below deck, followed by Lilly. She signaled to both Flayzin and me. "Attend," was all she said to us while striding toward Captain Skerlain.

Even though the ship's captain was tall, he still had to look up to the enchantress. And he appeared annoyed by her demand for attention. What surprised me was the straight-bladed saber hanging in a scabbard on the enchantress's hip. It appeared at odds with the white cotton blouse lined with frilly lace and emerald green breeches. Only her sturdy knee-high boots appeared to match.

"Can she fight with that blade?" I asked Flayzin. She hadn't carried a saber when we assaulted Fendra Jolian's temple.

"Competent," Flayzin said, "but doubtful she could take you without employing magic."

I wasn't sure if it was an insult or compliment—toward me or Enchantress Thulease. "Good to know," I said.

When we made it to the enchantress's side, she was carrying on a discussion with the captain while the *Hunchback Maiden*'s crew urgently went about their tasks, shouting directions and encouragement to each other.

"She's hoisted a black flag," the watchman shouted down. "But I canna see her design."

"Aye," Captain Skerlain said to Enchantress Thulease. "She's a pirate and we cannot outrun her." He lifted his spyglass to his eye. "And she'll have fifty or more armed men to our thirty."

Flayzin handed Enchantress Thulease Lilly's spyglass. "Don't discount those that travel with me, she said to the ship's captain. "How powerful of an air wizard is your first mate?"

"He can summon a breeze for the sails and fend off a weak elemental."

"A lesser wizard?"

"Aye," said the captain, pointing fore and aft. "But I've some special treats to deliver by ballista."

Enchantress Thulease turned and handed Lilly her spyglass before closing her eyes in concentration. "If the pirate vessel harbors no spellcasters of significant ability, it shall never come within range of your ballistae."

The enchantress stepped onto the quarterdeck and leaned back against the mast. The captain waved away sailors as she closed her eyes and began to chant. I moved to stand between the enchantress and the pirate ship, still a distance off the starboard side. Lilly stepped next to me. Standing between my ward and the enemy ship wouldn't protect the enchantress from most spellcraft, but I hoped it made her feel more secure.

Five long minutes passed as the pirate ship closed. I could see men climbing the rigging, others lining the deck, holding javelins, axes and cutlasses in anticipation. Even their shouts and jeers made it to our ship, causing the *Hunchback Maiden*'s crew to scurry about their tasks with even more urgency. Each now bore a club or cutlass. Sledge Fist came up beside me, handing me my helmet and crossbow, but held onto my boar spear.

Miggs handed Lilly her short bow and her quiver of arrows. All the while, Enchantress Thulease chanted.

Miggs fingered his long-handled flanged mace with a worried look and sweat forming on his brow. The healer's staying below," he said. "So's Storm Claw, and the other passengers for that matter."

The other two passengers that kept to the cabin across from the one Sledge Fist, Miggs, the Healer and Storm Claw shared wouldn't be much help in a fight. One was a chesty blonde-haired merchant. Maybe she was a noble. The other passenger was her middle-aged manservant. He appeared capable and intelligent, even though he grunted far more than he spoke.

Enchantress Thulease exhaled sharply. I turned to see Flayzin holding her steady. A wicked smile crept across her face as she met Captain Skerlain's gaze near the aft ballista.

"She's dropping her sails," shouted the first mate. A rousing cheer from the *Hunchback Maiden*'s crew arose, along with shaking fists held high.

The ship's captain made his way to the enchantress. "How did you accomplish that?"

"I withdrew bolts securing the grudgeon to the sternpost. Unfortunately, they discovered my sabotage before the rudder tore away."

"Aye, that'll slow them," the captain said. "How did you accomplish what you did at such a distance?"

"Precise knowledge of ship construction," she said. "My apprenticeship involved warding Keesee's warships to prevent such an attack."

Whether what the enchantress said was fully true or not, I wasn't sure. But disabling a rudder would stop their pursuit.

"I shall assume that, like most pirates, these are crafty and resourceful," said Enchantress Thulease. "So repairs can be expected to swiftly follow."

Lilly stood, peering through her spyglass. "I see a white skull with a cutlass crossing a leg bone underneath on their flag." She looked to Captain Skerlain.

The ship's captain ran his left thumb and forefinger along his wispy mustache and beard. "That would make it the *Garroted Kinsman* out there, captained by Klammer Cisco. Most seafaring folk name him the Blood Shark."

Suddenly our sails went slack, the breeze having left them.

"Spellcraft," Captain Skerlain remarked, eyeing the flat sails as he made his way to the main deck. "Weldy," he called to his first mate. "Can you undo it?"

The wiry first mate stood rigid. Some of the white that speckled his graying hair and mustache probably owed to his air wizard ability, but he was a lesser wizard, where, from the strain on his face, I guessed the pirate ship's wizard was stronger. For some reason I thought of Grand Wizard

Seelain, who would've said, "More accomplished."

Enchantress Thulease asked Captain Skerlain, "How urgent is it that this wind-deadening spell be undone?"

"We have no oars. The longer we remain dead in the water, the more time Blood Shark's crew has to repair his rudder and close in for the kill."

Enchantress Thulease glanced around at the *Hunchback Maiden*'s worried crew, and then to the distant *Garroted Kinsman*. "I see," she said and moved to stand behind First Mate Weldy. She whispered something into the older sailor's ear and then placed her index fingers and thumbs against his skull, just above the ears, and both began chanting. The first mate's chanting became louder. Although their words differed, the cadence became the same. Their voices rang urgent as they sped up and intensified.

The pair continued for a half minute, until a stiff breeze snapped the sails full and the *Hunchback Maiden* jolted forward and picked up speed.

Lilly and I rushed up to support Enchantress Thulease, ahead of Flayzin. Lilly caught the first mate with her left hand before he collapsed unconscious to the deck.

Enchantress Thulease leaned on my shoulder as she spoke to the captain without inflection. "Your first mate will recover some of his strength by nightfall. The pirate's wizard is quite accomplished. Yet he should not be able to hamper your progress until nightfall as well. Put as much distance between us as you can before then."

She then turned to me. "Assist me to my room, Flank Hawk. I must rest as well."

The cabin Enchantress Thulease, Lilly, Flayzin and I shared was cramped. Not only did the enchantress have to hunch over to avoid the ceiling, but she had to curl up on the small cot-like lower bunk that served as her bed. While she may have tossed and turned previous nights, she fell into a deep sleep less than a moment after resting her head on the tattered cotton pillow. I sat on the lower bunk where I slept and watched over my ward, in case something—I didn't know what—might happen.

The oil lamp's dim, flickering light wasn't enough to create shadows, but enough that I could see the enchantress's pale face. The noise of sailors, although muffled by the planks above our head, kept me from hearing my ward's breathing.

Healer Ammond had said there was nothing he could do to help her recover from such fatigue. I understood how spellcasting could drain a person, little though I could cast. But I'd never heard tell of an enchanter lending spell energy to another caster, except through the Shard Staff, and that was only from enchanter to enchanter. Not enchanter to wizard. I wondered if Supreme Enchantress Thulease and Imperial Seer Lochelle combined their powers to do King Tobias's bidding.

Faint but rapid knocking on the cabin's door interrupted my thoughts. I leaned over from my bunk with hand on my sword's hilt and whispered, "Who?"

"Lilly. The ship's captain needs you on deck."

I unlatched the old pine-plank door and opened it several inches. "What for?"

"Bring your crossbow. There's a hawk needs shot."

I bent over and quietly pulled the crossbow from underneath my cot while Lilly crept into the room. "I'll watch over her," she said, still whispering. "Flayzin's got my bow, but don't show your crossbow right off when you get on deck."

I wanted to ask, but then Ammond stuck his head in the door and signaled us toward him.

"I and Miggs shall watch over the enchantress, if you desire," he said, not bothering to whisper. "Captain Skerlain desires as many arrows and sling stones together in the air as can be had." He pointed to Lilly's sling.

I was uncomfortable leaving the enchantress unwatched by either me or Lilly, but the healer and the animal handler were trustworthy enough—especially if there was a new danger above to face.

Lilly took and held my crossbow and quiver of quarrels before I stepped out on the deck. The ship's captain signaled me over. "I've been told that you have shot a spying bird from the sky once before," he said.

I casually glanced upward to see a hawk circling high above the *Hunchback Maiden*. I agreed; it had to be a spying bird, a familiar of a witch, beastmaster, or some other spellcaster. Hawks wouldn't be found this far out to sea, and not circling a ship.

"I did," I said, "but had the assistance of an air wizard's spell. It provided extended range and accuracy."

The captain rubbed the back of his neck. "That's what yer scout said. We roused Weldy, and even if he had spell strength, he doesn't know the spell."

"What's the plan?" I asked, estimating that the hawk was above one hundred and fifty yards.

"Normally we'd chase off such troubles with one of Weldy's little whirlwinds." Then he gestured with a nod up to the quarterdeck. His black hawk, tethered and perched as usual near the wheel deck stared skyward with feathers ruffled. "I sent up my hawk to chase it off, but the bird up there's more fierce. Now my bird won't go up again," he finished, spitting on the deck.

"I'm a good shot," I said. "But it's really out of my range."

"I know," he said. "I've got eight bowmen, along with your Captain Flayzin with yer scout's bow, and the slinging of your scout and that woman mercenary, Storm Claw. Plus, I've got three slingers in my crew."

"It'll be lucky if any of us comes close. And we'll only get one shot."

"Aye, it'll just fly a little higher. It may be just taunting us now. But if we cannot kill or drive it off, Blood Shark will be back close on our wake by morning."

Several sailors had spread short bows with arrows along the starboard side. Lilly now stood casually next to my cocked crossbow lying on the deck. She held a smooth sling stone and stared up at the hawk. Storm Claw and two sailors with slings stood under the sails, ready to rush forward near the bow.

A few moments later, when the captain felt all was ready, he leaned an arm on one of the tarp-covered dinghies. At that signal we stepped to our bows, aimed and shot as quickly as possible. I think Flayzin came closest, missing by several feet wide left. Storm Claw's stone missed by a few feet to the right. Everyone else, including me missed by more or fell short.

The hawk circled higher. Flayzin and most of the sailors cursed. Lilly came up next to me. "Hard to sling nearly straight up," she said. "Probably even harder to shoot a crossbow almost straight up."

I shrugged and turned to go back below deck.

"Keep her on course until nightfall," the ship's captain ordered the steersman. "Get us close as you can to our destination." He stared up at the circling hawk once again, then toward me and Captain Flayzin. "Make'em think that's our goal. Come nightfall, we'll swing south. I know of a safe port of harbor we might reach before we're caught."

CHAPTER 8

The rising sun's light didn't bring good news, nor did it offer promise of safe harbor. I stood with Enchantress Thulease, along with Guard Captain Flayzin, as she consulted with the ship's captain and the first mate.

"No," explained the enchantress. "I cannot perform magics such as yesterday. A witch has erected wardings, not so much as to protect the enemy vessel, but to point back directly to me should I attempt a spell."

"How strong of a witch might she be?" asked First Mate Weldy, caressing the pike end of the boarding axe he'd looped to his broad leather belt.

"If she were wise, she studied the residue of my magic upon the keel before it faded and has some measure of my strength. I can sense her probing to locate me, with that knowledge aiding her. But until the *Garroted Kinsman* approaches within one hundred yards, my masking spell will foil her.

Captain Skerlain spat, the breeze carrying his spit over the gunwales of the foredeck and into the sea. "You can do nothing for us?" he asked.

"I shall be pressed to defend myself," Enchantress Thulease said.

"Enchanters are open to magical attacks, especially from witches and sorcerers," the first mate explained.

"Aye, I know," the ship's captain said. "At least you'll keep that one from causing us mischief."

"Can you send a whirlwind to entangle her hawk familiar?" I asked the first mate. "Whisk it to the ocean and drown it? That would distress and weaken the witch."

He rubbed his mustache in thought. "Their air wizard will likely foil my spell. Maybe in the heat of battle…"

Captain Skerlain gazed at his crew, armed for combat while working the rigging and sails, but splitting what attention they could spare between our quiet conference and the closing pirate ship. "We've no more than twenty minutes before they're upon us." He looked prepared to dismiss us to rejoin the rest of our team on the main deck when the blonde noblewoman dressed all in black except for a gray wool shawl stepped between Sledge Fist and Miggs. Showing no expression she approached the captain with confident strides.

"I am Tina Elaine, a Sister of the Black Oak Coven," she announced in a smooth, assured voice. She carried a staff, knobby and gray like driftwood. Her manservant followed her, one stride behind and to her left. "May I approach, Captain Skerlain?"

Lilly took a step forward to join us. I signaled her off, which drew a frown.

The ship's captain ran his fingers over his wispy mustache as he eyed the young woman. "So, yer a witch and not a merchant's daughter?"

Tina Elaine nodded once and then shook her head once. "I am both," she said and gazed up at Enchantress Thulease. "I can sense another of my ilk's magic. A seeking spell."

"We are aware," Enchantress Thulease said. "The witch that approaches surpasses your years and knowledge by much, young one. If you have felt her probe, you must know she will quickly undo you."

It was then that I noticed a snake—a striped viper—emerge from beneath the young witch's shawl, its forked tongue flicking in and out. Flayzin noticed it too, and we both stepped closer to our ward.

The blonde witch nodded once and removed a pearl earring from her left ear. A shimmer ran over her face like warmed air rising above a blacksmith's forge, causing years to melt away from her appearance. She looked to be no more than sixteen summers.

"That is most certainly true," she said, her voice sounding more youthful but still assured. But together we might resist. She looked over her shoulder, toward the approaching enemy. "What other choice is there for me, or for you?"

Even as Enchantress Thulease nodded in agreement, the watchman in the crow's nest shouted, "War galley off the port bow!"

"What flag does she fly?" shouted the first mate.

"Two-masted but her sails are down," the watchman said. "Three tiers of oarsmen. She's flying a red flag, with the head of a…cat. She's a Long-Tooth raider!"

"Swing us about to starboard, until we're running south east," Captain Skerlain ordered without hesitation. While the steersman complied, the ship's captain said to his first mate, "Now we're between a tiger and a shark."

The crew jumped into action, adjusting the rigging and sails as we came about, our speed dropping as we angled more into the easterly wind. That put the closing *Garroted Kinsman* on our starboard side.

Enchantress Thulease and Flayzin knew as well as I did that the Long-Tooth raiders would slay, or take for slaves, all aboard any ship flying the Keeseean flag.

"Maybe," suggested Flayzin, "a 'let you and him fight' strategy?"

At that, the captain laughed. "Oh, it'll be quite a scrap, and me and my crew will take our share down with us."

I looked at the grim-faced crew. They knew as well as me, probably better, what was ahead.

"I thought your seer predicted a successful voyage?" the first mate asked his captain.

"Maybe I should've been more specific about whose voyage," the captain replied. Then he began shouting orders and encouragement to the crew.

"Might want to get in your metal armor," the first mate suggested to me and Flayzin, stepping between us on his way to assist the crew. "You'll have to survive long enough to drown."

Flayzin decided the best chance of survival was to resist the initial boarding. I quickly agreed. With that, Enchantress Thulease, Tina Elaine and Ammond went below deck. Miggs with his long-handled mace, Wizard Stok with an engraved scimitar, and the young witch's manservant armed with a belaying pin, warded them.

On the main deck I stood with my crossbow cocked and ready. I'd slung my shield over my back and covered the tip of my spear and sword's blade with fireweed resin. Lilly crouched behind a stack of folded tarps to my right, with her sling ready and Storm Claw stood just beyond, holding her sling taught with tightly clenched fists. Having borrowed Lilly's short bow, Flayzin stood to my left, grim-faced like the crew, but otherwise relaxed. Sledge Fist hovered behind us, holding two javelins he'd coated with some of my fireweed resin and muttering about the barrel of pickles the ship's captain owed him, if we got through this.

My mind drifted between thinking about my mother's tears the morning I departed and focusing on my duty to safeguard Enchantress Thulease's life, and reminding myself to account for the swelling waves rocking both ships, as well as the salty cross breeze when aiming my crossbow. I'd already picked my target. A burly sailor, red-faced and bald, bare-chested, holding ready a boarding plank.

The dozen *Hunchback Maiden* crewmen with bows and the three slingers appeared to have selected targets as well. The first mate was at the stern ballista, preparing some sort of cylindrical ceramic containers with a tar fitting and oiled wick.

On the *Garroted Kinsman* a squat, scar-faced man dressed in black with a red belt sash drew his cutlass. He then stuck a white cloth to the end of it while striding to the ship's prow. I guessed him to be Captain Klammer Cisco, the Blood Shark.

He looked mean enough and could probably swing his blade with plenty of force. Still, I expected someone named Blood Shark to be larger, and leaner. I knew Lilly did too, after she whispered to me, "That's the Blood Shark?"

Captain Skerlain moved to the *Hunchback Maiden*'s prow as the pirate ship maneuvered parallel to us, leaving about thirty yards of ocean between the two ships.

"His crew looks tough enough," I whispered back to Lilly. "Plenty of them, too."

A sneer crossed Lilly's face. "We've faced worse."

I looked at the *Maiden*'s crew, most of which kept looking over their shoulders at the closing raider. We were moving at an angle away from it, but not nearly fast enough.

"Captain Skerlain!" shouted the pirate captain in a jovial tone. "Send over the gold yer carrin' in yer hold and we can both be away using air wizard craft before the oarin' Long-Tooths ken board ya."

I wondered how the pirate knew our captain's name. Skerlain was experienced, but I didn't think he'd be known by pirate captains and crews.

Captain Skerlain replied, "You're mistaken of my cargo. I carry no gold."

Blood Shark loosed a gutful laugh. "The king of Keesee sendin' coin to the mercenary tribes. Is it worth yer crew dyin?" He lowered his cutlass a few inches. "Drop the strongbox in one of them dinghies ya have."

"My crew knows what's in the hold," Captain Skerlain shouted. "We've bolts of silk and barrels of wine, but no gold. You're misinformed."

The pirate captain lowered his cutlass another few inches.

"If you know of me," Captain Skerlain said, "you know me and my crew are willing to die, if it'll mean bringing you and yer crew down with us."

The pirate captain laughed again. "That Long-Tooth galley's called the *Bone Yard.* More than slaves man the oars. When they die, their captain gets them rowin' again, bein' a necromancer." He paused to let that sink into the *Hunchback Maiden*'s crew. "The first mate, he's a walkin' dead too, but with thinkin' thoughts and harborin' a soul."

My hand went to the pouch of salt tied to my belt. It was the only thing that caused zombies pain. I wondered about sea water being salty, but refocused on the immediate danger.

Blood Shark looked past our ship. "The *Bone Yard*'ll soon be upon you, too close fer runnin' with the weak air wizard ya got. So send over yer gold, and we'll letcha go about yer way, and we'll be about ours."

Our captain shook his head. "There's no gold in—"

Those were Captain Skerlain's last words. He managed to side-step one arrow. A second missed. But the third arrow took him in the thigh while a fourth pierced deep into his throat.

The pirate captain yelled something, probably for us to lay down our arms, but he'd misjudged the *Hunchback Maiden*'s crew. Shouts of anger and defiance rose as our arrows and sling stones flew. Even as the *Garroted Kinsman* angled toward us, their arrows flew and grappling hooks arced across the closing span of sea that separated us.

My plank-holding target stumbled back with my quarrel biting deep into his stomach.

Lilly grunted as she pulled an arrow from her left shoulder. "Not deep," she said, preparing another sling stone.

I set my foot in the stirrup to re-cock my crossbow, an arrow clinking off my breastplate. Drowning? I doubted it'd come to that, I thought, lifting my crossbow and setting the quarrel.

Half of our crew was down or wounded. An equal number of the pirates were injured, with fewer down on the deck. They were better bowmen, and probably better with their blades as well. Even so, one of Weldy's ceramic pots had shattered against the base of the pirate ship's main mast. At first what had to be lamp oil burst into orange flame, but seconds later, searing white flames sprouted. Even buckets of water couldn't douse them. A second pot shattered and began the same process further up the mast, catching the sail which their air wizard struggled to extinguish.

Our steersman, an arrow shaft protruding from his right forearm and thigh turned away from the *Kinsman*, but it was too late. Grappling hooks already had us, and any sailor that rushed forward from cover to release the *Maiden* from them sprouted arrow shafts like needles on a pine branch.

I loosed my crossbow's quarrel at the frantically gesturing air wizard and set my missile weapon aside in favor of my boar spear. Although our ship's deck rode higher above the waves than the *Kinsman*'s, the boarding planks bore hooks, and slats for climbing. Adding to those pirates scrambling up the planks and ropes attached to the grappling hooks, a half dozen attempted to swing by ropes from their rigging across into the *Maiden*'s rigging, or onto her deck.

Captain Skerlain must've underestimated the number of pirates aboard the *Kinsman* as they scrambled up onto the *Maiden*'s deck like cutlass and axe-wielding locusts. The ferocity of their snarling battle cry put the *Maiden*'s sailors on their heels, leaving only us from Enchantress Thulease's team charging forward to meet the enemy as they attempted to board.

Spear held ready, I closed with the enemy, realizing how much we needed Enchantress Thulease's spellcraft. But she and the witch were certainly in a struggle for their own lives even as I drove into a wild-eyed pirate, knocking him back onto his ship with a bloody shoulder wound—one filled with fireweed resin.

We tried to hold, but their overwhelming numbers drove us back. Three pirates fell upon me at once. I knocked aside the far left pirate's cutlass and thrust my spear tip at his face. He ducked aside, but not fast enough and my spear tip sliced across his throat just below the ear. I didn't have time to see how deep my spear bit because I pivoted and shoved my spear shaft to the side, catching the middle pirate's cutlass in a backhand slash. Busy parrying, I didn't see the third pirate's strike coming. It rang across my steel helmet, knocking my head to the side, stumbling me to one knee.

My peripheral vision caught Flayzin's sword cutting the middle pirate down. He drove the third pirate back with a flurry of thrusts and cuts. On instinct I shoved my spear forward along the deck, tripping a pirate preparing to take Flayzin from behind.

Having dispatched the third pirate by slicing his forearm wide open and then gutting him, Flayzin turned and clove into the tripped pirate's skull before the downed man could get back to his feet. Without emotion Flayzin said, "Behind you," then turned in time to block another foe's attack with his kite shield.

Seeing that, I wondered how I'd ever gotten the upper hand on Flayzin.

Bodies and blood covered the deck, causing me to slip as I tried to stand. I ducked and drove forward, catching a charging pirate in the midsection with my shoulder. Sledge Fist must've carved into the pirate's back because my foe fell with a grunt and I saw the mercenary grin before turning away from me to engage another snarling foe.

Of remaining pirates, there were plenty. Lilly fought back to back with Storm Claw, the dark-skinned mercenary's fighting sticks whirling and thudding against pirate bodies, sometimes giving off a sparking flash and stunning her foe.

Lilly was in trouble, having only her dagger and two pirates closing. I hurled my boar spear the twenty feet across the deck, taking one in the lower back, before I ducked a slashing cutlass. I spun while drawing my sword, just in time to see the snarling pirate make a second attack with his off-hand weapon, driving the pike end of his boarding axe into my chest.

The blow knocked me back a step and pierced my breastplate, but it didn't penetrate the leather armor underneath. When the burly pirate tried to yank his axe free, I drove my sword tip deep into his armpit. Then I stepped close to avoid his cutlass swing and head-butted my helmet into the wounded pirate's face. Even as he fell to the deck, taking his axe with him, I unslung my shield and looked about before drawing my sword across the stunned pirate's throat.

A shrill whistle sounded, one short burst followed by two longer ones.

It must've been a signal from the pirate captain as his men backed away. None of the *Maiden*'s crew pressed an attack. I looked about. Flayzin took a step closer to me. Lilly and Storm Claw were leaning against the portside railing. Weldy and two other sailors were still standing, on the quarterdeck and separated from us.

At that moment, Wizard Stok swung the door open and emerged from below deck. Miggs stepped out after him, followed by the young witch. Each bore a stuffed satchel. They stood ready as Enchantress Thulease and Ammond emerged behind them. They were closer to Weldy than to Lilly, or to me on the far end of the main deck. Between Enchantress Thulease and us—her mercenaries—stood a gang of at least twenty pirates, including the captain, their shoulder-wounded white-haired air wizard, and a stooped woman dressed in black robes holding an even blacker staff. She had to be the witch. No sign of her hawk.

Near Weldy, seven armed pirates stood poised to reengage the first mate and his two surviving crewmates. All around the *Hunchback Maiden* lay the dead and dying, many of them groaning, including Sledge Fist. He was on his back to my left, pale and in shock, trying to shove a handful of his bloody intestines back into the wide gash across his stomach.

Lilly was bleeding from her shoulder and also from her scalp. The blood ran across her brow and down her cheek, dripping onto the deck. Both she and Storm Claw's chests heaved in and out for air. I realized I was doing the same.

The smell of smoke signaled danger more than the blood and foul odor of split bowels. The *Garroted Kinsman* was on fire. Her main mast was a column of flame, which was spreading through the sails, to the yard, gaff and boom.

Even worse was the sight of the closing *Bone Yard.* Locked together and steering unattended, the *Maiden* and *Kinsman* must have altered course. The pirate ship's port side was now closest to the closing Long-Tooth raider, now mere minutes away.

The pirate captain shouted out to First Mate Weldy, "I'm claiming yer ship! You and the survivors of yer crew're welcome to join us."

Even as he spoke, I met Enchantress Thulease's gaze. Its hardness told me she wasn't accepting what the pirate captain said. We wouldn't throw in with them.

I glanced at the dinghy near Lilly and then back to the enchantress. When our eyes met I knew that was her goal—our goal. A hope of escape.

The pirate captain wiped splattered blood, that of the *Maiden*'s fallen crewmen, from his face with his sleeve. "When we get to a port," he said, "any that don't care to stay can go ashore, with a fair cut of the gold."

The pirates were mostly watching what Weldy was going to say. About a third faced Flayzin and me, and a couple kept an eye on Lilly and Storm Claw. The witch and air wizard paid attention to Enchantress Thulease, and glanced suspiciously from her to Flayzin, ignoring me.

"We have little time," the pirate captain said. "Join us now, or we'll slay ya." Even as he said it, three pirates were cutting the grappling hook ropes, releasing us from the burning *Garroted Kinsman.* Fortunately the wind, probably through the enemy air wizard's spellcraft, kept the smoke and embers away from our ship.

Lilly must've been watching me and understood, because when I glanced from her to the fifteen-foot boat, she winked. After she did, I loosened the pouch filled with salt tied to my belt. This resulted in movement of my sword, which caught the attention of a couple pirates, but they quickly refocused on the *Maiden*'s first mate.

Weldy stood up straight, and glanced at the nearing *Bone Yard.* The sound of drums setting the oarsmen's rhythm came within range of hearing. The pace quickened as the war galley circled wide around to reach the *Maiden*. Her prow bore an iron ram which she certainly intended to use. Unless the pirate air wizard was powerful, and the *Bone Yard* didn't have any spellcasters to counter him, the *Maiden* was doomed. At least a hundred javelin throwers, most with shields and swords, lined the war galley's deck, waiting to get within range.

Without saying a word, one crewman next to Weldy handed the first mate a javelin from the deck. Weldy didn't hesitate hurling it at the arrogant pirate captain.

The instant Weldy released the javelin a wave of magic passed through me. It had to be from Enchantress Thulease. She whipped out a long cord and threw it at the enemy witch. Thulease's magic release and action must've distracted the air wizard pirate because he didn't see Weldy's javelin coming. Nor did he notice Blood Shark duck aside to avoid it. The javelin missed the pirate by inches and took the air wizard in the gut.

Holding up some sort of smoking herbal charm, the young witch, Tina Elaine, stepped between Enchantress Thulease and the black-garbed pirate witch as the enchantress's cord landed and snaked its way around the hunched crone's neck.

There wasn't time to see what else happened because Flayzin and I charged into the distracted pirate mass. As I ran past Sledge Fist, I dropped my salt pouch on his chest. Any mercenary who'd fought necromancers and zombies had to know what it was for. One of the first lessons a drill sergeant training me for Pine Ridge's militia was that salting a death wound stopped a necromancer from animating the corpse. It was the best I could do for my fellow mercenary before clashing with the enemy, slamming my shield into one pirate and hacking open the stomach of another, a mortal wound mirroring Sledge Fist's.

Earlier the pirates fought with coordinated ferocity. Now, with every breath bringing the *Bone Yard* one oar-stroke closer, a frantic wildness filled their attacks. Flayzin and I took advantage of this, wounding and maiming our way into the midst of the main pirate mass. His goal had to be the same as mine. Draw the bulk of the enemy onto us, allowing Enchantress Thulease a chance to escape.

Their weight of numbers was great, but their heart wasn't in fighting us. I heard the pirate captain shout, "Smeldin, take the wheel! Squint Eye, Roggin, Boxer, to the sails. We can still catch the full eye of the wind!"

The pirates broke contact from us and scattered. Maybe they did because of the captain's order, or maybe it was because everyone but us was wounded, dead or captured.

Flayzin grabbed me by the shoulder. "Come on, Flank Hawk. Over the side," he said at the same time the pirate captain shouted, "Dyin' or no, put wind in them sails or you'll be rowin' while ya rot to pieces—we all will."

I looked over my shoulder while following Flayzin. The *Bone Yard* came on, surging ahead to ram. The *Hunchback Maiden* caught the full breeze, and then some, maybe from the wizard.

I slowed a step while looking back again. Weren't we going to the wrong side? But the starboard dinghy was still there, with the raider closing. The pirates ignored us. I leapt over Sledge Fist. He was dead, dissolving salt crystals covering his bloody right hand and stomach wound. I slipped and stumbled on the blood-slick deck. I got back to my feet and sheathed my sword and slung my shield. Flayzin was already taking a rope over the side.

Javelins and axes rained down on the *Hunchback Maiden*'s deck and the surviving pirates now crewing her. A few pirates shot arrows back.

I climbed over the railing too, but already the dinghy floated twenty feet astern of the *Maiden.* I spotted Thulease and Storm Claw in it. Stok and Ammond, too. Not Lilly that I could see. I looked across the deck for Lilly, but my eyes fell upon the *Bone Yard* only thirty yards away, angling to ram. Flayzin was already half way down the rope. He, like me, wore metal armor. It looked like we both would die unless we could get our armor off. My gut twisted. I'd join Lilly in death—but not the same death. She didn't have salt in her death wound, like Sledge Fist.

A hurled javelin flew by a foot over my helmet and another stuck in the railing two feet to my left, so I went over the side and began sliding down the rope, my gauntlets protecting my hands. Flayzin pushed off the hull the last few feet before I caught up to him. He grabbed a floating disk someone from the dinghy had thrown his way.

"Jump, Flank Hawk!" Thulease shouted. "Lilly is in the water."

With that I pushed off with my feet and let go of the rope just as the *Bone Yard*'s iron prow crashed into the *Maiden*'s hull. I heard the cracking and breaking of timbers above the many shouts of triumph and the few cries of terror before I hit the water and went under.

Immediately I put my arms out to stop my descent and began kicking to reach the surface. With great effort I managed to get my head above the water only a few feet from the Maiden's hull. The release of trapped air bubbles and weight of metal pulled me back under.

I began reaching for the buckles securing my back and breastplate when something brown bumped up against me. I grabbed hold, remembering that Lilly was in the water. Even if I drowned, knowing she was still alive brought a deep sense of relief. My awkward grip forced me to let go and reach around, over the human-sized muskrat's shoulders and lock my hands in a tight grip so that I could be towed along. It reminded me of a previous escape, where Lilly in her beast form had towed me beneath a fouled stream's surface to escape under the palisade wall surrounding the Necromancer King's industrial city. That seemed a lifetime ago.

Lilly struggled to support me and my weapons and armor even as we broke the surface. I exhaled and took a deep breath, just in case we went back under.

We were nearly to the wooden dinghy when it shimmered and disappeared from sight. At first I thought it was from sea water splashing in my face, but then I recalled the spell Enchantress Thulease had used to hide our dragon-mounted assault from a battling army as we approached the Goddess Fendra Jolain's temple in her capital city.

When we reached the lifeboat's location it came back into view. I grabbed onto the side and Storm Claw helped me climb in. Next to her, Wizard Stok pulled on a rope, drawing Flayzin holding onto the floating disk toward our small boat. Storm Claw let me catch my breath, my hand gripping an oar along the side while she helped Stok and the young witch's manservant haul Flayzin aboard.

Near the bow of our small boat, Enchantress Thulease sat erect, chanting. I knew better than to disturb her as I sat up and looked around. I was soaked, as were all the others in the boat with me. Enchantress Thulease, Storm Claw, Ammond, Stok, Flayzin, the young witch's manservant, and one of the *Hunchback Maiden*'s crew.

I looked in the water, around the boat and then toward the ships only a short distance away. A few lifeless bodies and one pirate trailing blood as he swam toward a wrecked board from the *Maiden* floating nearby. Nobody else that I could see, none of our people, except Lilly in her beast form swimming nearby, preparing to climb in.

Aft of us floated the burning pirate ship, most of her deck now in flame. Off our boat's port bow was the *Maiden* with the *Bone Yard*'s prow still buried in her portside. There didn't look to be any fighting going on. Although I couldn't see onto the decks very well, I spotted three pirates being escorted back toward the Long-Tooth raider, and at least thirty bodies of fallen pirates and sailors being hauled over the shoulders of raiders, back onto their ship.

I smiled with grim satisfaction. One of the hauled dead bore a red sash; the Blood Shark would soon be rowing. Then I frowned. Did any man deserve that?

We all sat quiet and still, even Lilly after being helped to scramble onboard. The *Maiden*'s sailor, the manservant and Ammond nervously glanced at Lilly's in her were-muskrat form, deep brown fur, a little lighter along her underside, with a black scaly tail.

A few raiders inexpertly took pot shots with arrows at the wounded pirate trying to paddle away from them. But with the waves he spent more time holding on so he wouldn't be washed off the plank.

Apparently no one saw us. Not the raiders, nor the floating pirate.

Eventually, the *Bone Yard*'s crew returned to their ship, carrying crates and sacks filled with the *Maiden*'s treasures, whatever they might be. After releasing their grappling hooks, and powerful backstrokes from three tiers of oars, the *Bone Yard* pulled away from the *Maiden*. Within five minutes, the merchant ship disappeared below the waves, and the raider, with square sails raised to assist the oars, returned in the direction from which she came.

The entire time I watched Enchantress Thulease out of the corner of my eye. Watched her sweat and strain, and begin shaking as she quietly chanted, maintaining the spell that hid us from the raiders, and certain death—or worse.

Several minutes later, with the *Bone Yard* disappearing in the distance, Enchantress Thulease ceased her spell. Almost immediately the wounded pirate spotted us, raised his head and tentatively waved.

"Let us oar over to him," Enchantress Thulease said in an exhausted voice. "Captain Flayzin, you know what to do."

The pirate had sun-weathered skin and had seen at least thirty summers. He realized he'd seen his last, as his smile of relief turned grim upon meeting the guard captain's gaze. He sat up on his floating plank. "Make it clean, and quick," he said, lifting his head to expose his neck. "A better end than me crewmates."

I gripped and held Flayzin's belt as he hefted his sword. I wasn't sure how clean of a blow the guard captain intended as he said, "A wise man would have selected a more honorable seafaring profession."

"Yer right," the pirate said as Flayzin swung. "I know," were the pirate's last words.

I think only Ammond looked away as the pirate's head splashed into the south Mediterranean Sea, followed by his body.

CHAPTER 9

As soon as the *Bone Yard* disappeared beyond the horizon we took stock of our situation and then began rowing toward the Southern Continent. The dinghy had a five gallon cask of fresh water and two sealed ceramic jugs. One contained sliced dried apples and the other held chips of dried beef. Beneath two oiled tarps Lilly found a box with two coils of thin cord. Tied to each were barbed hooks attached to copper and wooden plugs decorated with feathers to mimic a fish of some sort. That was all that Captain Skerlain had stocked his emergency boat with.

Lilly had managed to toss down a coil of rope, two cutlasses and a boarding axe after lowering the boat. Before joining the battle, Wizard Stok and Enchantress Thulease had quickly stuffed small sacks with clothing and food and given one to everybody below deck. But whatever Miggs and the young witch carried didn't make it to the boat. Just like they didn't.

Delmit, the witch's manservant, wasn't much of a fighter, but he did risk his life carrying his master's body when they ran for the boat and dropped her into the ocean. Nobody had been able to do the same for Miggs. I hoped his body was so mutilated that he couldn't function as a zombie and would be left alone, unspelled.

Nobody said much about how they died, but I could guess. The young witch was no match for the pirate witch, but she was apparently powerful enough to give Enchantress Thulease time to slay the crone. Wizard Stok said Miggs fell to cutlass blades. I thought back on how many I'd met over the past two years who'd found similar deaths.

There were four oars in the crowded boat. Lilly rowed in front of me. Stok was to my left and the *Maiden*'s sailor, Swigopp, in front of him—across from Lilly who was questioning the olive-skinned sailor, digging into how he'd survived nearly unscathed.

Lilly's wounds had mostly healed through her lycanthrope shifting. I'd been very lucky. Lucky not only to have avoided major injury, but to have survived. I had Flayzin to thank for much of it. Ammond had healed the guard captain's wounded hand and calf and Storm Claw's cracked ribs. That was why she wasn't in the initial rowing team and would rotate in later. I'd helped a little with Delmit, stopping most of the bleeding from his shoulder before the real healer among us closed the wound up. My effort saved Ammond enough spell strength to repair a shallow puncture wound in the enchantress's thigh.

"You got up pretty quick," Lilly said to Swigopp after pulling an oar stroke. "Off the deck, when I started lowering the boat."

After two strokes, the young sailor responded, "I got hit in the head." He turned to show her the knot on his forehead. Sweat now plastered his long black hair over the injury. But I'd seen the welt. "Takes two to lower it," the sailor said, between strokes.

Even though I saw only the back of her head, I knew Lilly was frowning. "Left Storm Claw alone to watch my back."

Everyone paid attention to their conversation, except Enchantress Thulease, who was exhausted from slaying the witch and making us invisible to the raiders. She was fast asleep, curled up in the boat's bow, using a tarp for a cushion. As tall as the enchantress was, balled up on her side, she looked much smaller.

The only sound besides breathing was the oars slapping the water, swelling waves washing against the boat, and Guard Captain Flayzin working to repair my breastplate using the boarding axe Lilly had tossed in the boat. He was tapping flat the spurs where the pike end of a pirate's boarding axe had punched through. Seated next to him, behind us, was Delmit, holding the cord he'd tied to his belaying pin, waiting for a fish to strike the trailing feathered lure.

"We made it," Swigopp said a few strokes later.

"Little thanks to you," Lilly said.

"You all saw the pirate blood on my cutlass."

Lilly huffed. "Could've come from lying on the deck." After another stroke, she finished her statement. "Like you."

"You think I'm a coward?"

Without hesitation, Lilly said, "Yup."

Wizard Stok let go of his oar the same instant I let go of mine. He latched onto the young sailor's shoulders, holding him in place on the bench. I grabbed Lilly's arm and collar. Storm Claw and Ammond watched but didn't move from their seat on the other folded tarp.

From behind us, Flayzin ordered, "Cease now!" He didn't yell, but it was sharp enough to cause the enchantress to stir in her sleep. The authority in his voice had less effect on Lilly than on the sailor, who wasn't really looking for a fight. Lilly sat poised, still ready to defend herself.

The oars began knocking about as our boat lost momentum.

"Save your strength for rowing," Flayzin said. "Waking the enchantress will hinder recovery of her spell strength. To remove the salt from the water we'll soon need, and who knows for what other purpose." After a breath he added, "Or danger."

We all grabbed hold of our oars and returned to our rhythm.

Storm Claw sneered before shifting her seat to lean against the side, and closed her eyes. Nobody said a thing. Flayzin continued tapping, Delmit fishing, and Ammond watching the waters ahead for danger.

Around midnight, Swigopp and I were the only ones awake on the boat. The breeze appeared to be taking us southeast, in the general direction of the Southern Continent. But with thick clouds completely hiding the stars and moon, it was a guess based on earlier in the evening.

I paid attention to the moon more than I used to for several reasons, but mostly because it affected Lilly. Under a full moon, she had no choice but to allow her beast to emerge.

Swigopp proved to be the best fisherman on our boat, catching two gray-scaled fish almost as long as my arm. Nobody else except Lilly got even a bite on their line. Later, the sailor had found a single hook wedged in the box holding the lures. He'd used some of the cord and tied it to an empty sack he'd twisted tight. He attached some of the fish guts he'd saved to the hook and was now trying to supplement our food supply.

"Never eaten fish seared on the blade of a magically heated cutlass," Swigopp whispered, holding the sack with both hands, one on either side of the knotted cord. "Only a little raw."

"The effort wiped Wizard Stok out," I whispered back.

"Yeah," Swigopp said. "I didn't think earth wizards could even summon spellcraft while at sea."

We were sitting back to back, leaning against each other. The sailor suggested it. Said it would make it easier to sit longer. I felt his back tense, like he thought he might be getting a nibble on the line. After a minute he relaxed.

"It's like trying to start a fire with damp wood," I said. "Possible, but takes a lot more to get it done." After a moment, I asked, "Was there gold in the *Hunchback Maiden*'s hold?"

"Nah," the young sailor said. "Somebody would've noticed when it was loaded, or being moved around. That kind of secret wouldn't keep on a ship. Unless maybe it was in the captain's cabin."

I thought about it. Had someone told the pirates we were carrying gold? Who and why? Maybe someday I could ask Imperial Seer Lochelle. That wasn't likely to happen. Only once had I seen the king's prime advisor outside her dark chambers below the palace. Further, I no longer had access to the palace. Even if I did, I doubted she'd be willing to expend such an effort for me, even if I had the coin to pay her. She might for Enchantress Thulease, though. They worked together often and, from the small bit I knew about them, they appeared to be friends. So, the question about the king's gold might be answered—if we made it back to the King's City.

"I fought hard as anybody," Swigopp whispered with tense emotion, disturbing my thoughts. "You got to know that, Flank Hawk."

I shrugged. "I don't know one way or the other. What matters to me is what you do from now on."

"It's not that way with your scout."

"No, maybe not," I agreed. "She's not in charge. Supreme Enchantress

Thulease is."

"Ain't got fire or silver anyhow."

The sailor was truly worried about Lilly, enough to ponder the most effective weapons against a lycanthrope. I sat and stared out into the darkness and listened to the others breathe and, in the case of Ammond, occasionally mumble in his sleep.

"I've heard tell of you, and your scout," the sailor said. "Is it true?"

"Depends on what you heard."

"About you striking a blow against the Necromancer King with a weapon from the Colonel of the West. And then you both was there when the prince fell fighting the healing goddess. And you took up the Blood Sword and finished the job."

"Yes, I helped finish the job. Plenty of others there that did their part. Including Lilly."

Swigopp fiddled with the fishing line a moment. Then he asked, "So then, why do you take orders from Captain Flayzin?"

"I'm a mercenary," I said. "The enchantress hired me. She's in charge and decided that her guard captain should be second in command."

"Oh," he said. "I don't think your scout likes him much either."

He was right, but I didn't comment.

"It's kinda hard," he said. "I only been on the *Maiden* a year, but I lost a lotta mates."

"I know," I said. "It's always hard."

"You've lost a lot of mates, in the wars and on the king's missions?"

"I have."

After a few minutes he asked, "How do you handle seeing their faces when you close your eyes?"

I sighed, at first not wanting to answer. "I worry I'll forget their faces," I said, starting to see some of them while staring out into the dark night. From now on, whenever I ate a pickle, I'd think of Sledge Fist.

CHAPTER 10

It rained shortly after sunrise. Not violent but steady, and anyone under the oiled tarps managed to remain relatively dry. I wasn't one of them. My turn to man the oars extended through the three hours of rain. Lilly, who rowed in front of me, kept her head and face dry by wearing her broad-brimmed hat.

Storm Claw didn't seem to mind the rain. After refilling the five-gallon cask, she used my helmet to bail out rainwater from the bottom of our boat.

The day remained cloudy and I managed to get some sleep throughout the afternoon, crowded between Lilly and Storm Claw in the bow of our little boat. Sergeant Drux, Major Jadd's aft-guard on their serpent, would've offered a few jestful lewd remarks about sleeping with two women. All things considered, I'd rather have been flying on a dragon or wyvern, especially in their company, as opposed to the cramped boat, unsure of our exact location on the open sea.

My dream, involving Drux, Jadd, Lilly, and oddly enough, Supreme Enchantress Thulease, eating and laughing at the One-Eyed Pelican, was interrupted by Healer Ammond shouting, "Smoke! Is that smoke I see rising?"

It turned out Ammond did spot smoke, a thick column in the distance to the south, a little further east of the direction we were heading.

Everyone in the boat gazed a moment, even those rowing.

"Too much to be a ship burning," assessed Enchantress Thulease.

"Aye," Swigopp said. "A ship at sea burning that much would've gone under right away."

Whether or not he knew how much smoke rose from a burning ship, the sailor spoke with an authoritative tone. Besides the *Garroted Kinsman*, I'd seen warships burning in battle and in harbor, and he was probably right. The thickness of the smoke and how long it rose and curved with the breeze spoke of a bigger fire.

"Land," Flayzin said. "Still hours away."

Supreme Enchantress Thulease nodded in agreement.

I spoke up. "It's a marker pointing toward land, but I don't think we want to approach someplace burning. Not without knowing the cause."

"Not in this little boat," Lilly added.

"I agree," Flayzin said. Then he asked Enchantress Thulease, "Should we oar further eastward before angling again toward land?"

"What if the smoke is the result of the coastal raider?" Enchantress

Thulease asked. "I am open to speculation, if my suggested cause is accurate, as to what direction of travel would be most likely to avoid the raiders?"

"If it is indeed the Long-Tooth raiders," Ammond said, "setting fire to the coastal town or village would in all likelihood indicate their departure."

"Was their running into us and those pirates just bad luck?" Lilly asked. "Might make a difference which way they go. I don't know how, but...I don't know. If it *is* them."

Enchantress Thulease appeared to ponder Lilly's question. "Captain, your recommendation?"

"Enchantress, Flank Hawk is right. Approaching straight on toward the smoke is an unnecessary risk. If it is due to the raiders, who can know their necromancer captain's mind?"

She nodded once. "Flank Hawk, your opinion?"

"Without knowledge of the situation, there's no reason to work against our eventual goal and travel eastward. Float with the breeze, mainly eastward, or oar eastward and then south towards land. Those hold equal merit."

I paused a moment in thought. The enchantress waited for me to finish.

"It may benefit us, however, to scout and approach the town," I said. "Even ones put to the torch will have homesteads beyond the range raiders might travel on foot. Food, shelter, even horses or beasts of burden may be obtained. Or those loosed, having dead masters, might be claimed by us."

Storm Claw cleared her throat and was acknowledged by the enchantress. "Flank Hawk is right," the woman mercenary said. "But look at us. Not only are we outsiders, but we look like outsiders. Not likely anyone'd welcome us with open arms."

"Aye," said Swigopp. "Might make'm even more hostile."

"Offered payment in gold, of which I have a small sum, often allays fears," the enchantress replied after gazing down at the young sailor. "But your points are well taken. We will rest several hours. Save our strength and then work to land east of the village. We need bearings, if nothing else. Scout Lilly, Storm Claw and Swigopp will approach the town, if town it is, after nightfall to gather information so that we might make an informed next move."

Lilly didn't look happy about the selection of scouts, probably the sailor, but she didn't object. So that's what we did. Rested, then oared south so that we struck landfall just after sundown.

I stood watch along the rock outcropping's edge where we'd pulled the dinghy ashore. Without clouds, I observed the near-full moon climb high into the night sky. It gave a gray cast to the waves rolling onto the shore.

The scrub plants and scattered rocks appeared darker shades of gray, casting black shadows.

Flayzin crept up through the rocks behind me. "Anything from the west?" he whispered.

I shook my head. "No."

He gripped my shoulder. "Nothing spotted by Wizard Stok or that witch's servant, either."

I looked over my shoulder as he crept away. "The polished steel in your shield reflects the moonlight."

He stopped and removed it from its slung position across his back. "Good observation, Flank Hawk. I see now why you don't polish your breastplate."

I maintained my armor well, and it retained some flecks of black paint from a previous mission. But if stealth might be needed, I'd weigh the added protection against increased detection. Lilly'd once taught me the value of silence and speed.

"Just the rivets," I said, observing how the olive green paint covering most of Flayzin's shield blended well enough with the night. "But might be enough for someone with sharp eyes."

"The way our luck has started," Flayzin said, glancing up at the night sky, "no reason to offer more reasons for it to remain sour."

I continued to watch for another two hours, with Flayzin checking every twenty minutes. The sounds of the sea made it difficult to listen for danger, but it also masked any noise we might make.

Just as Flayzin was checking again, I pointed out across the water. "You see something out there?"

After a moment observing, he replied, "I believe so."

He waited until we identified it as a single-masted boat with a single sail that wasn't quite triangular. Probably some fisherman's vessel, but out at night without lights? That made me wonder.

The boat appeared to be making its way toward shore. Flayzin went to warn the others as I watched it drop sail and anchor about fifty yards off shore. Someone leapt overboard and began swimming toward our rock outcropping.

It turned out to be Lilly. She stood in the surf and waved her arms before approaching, just to be safe. She was wet and cold, wearing only a shirt. I signaled Delmit to stand watch before joining Lilly. She spoke to Enchantress Thulease, who was wrapping a wool shawl around her.

"The whole town's burned out," Lilly said. "You were right. Raiders, and most everyone was killed or ran off. Some fella from the militia…"

Lilly was shivering. Although it was dark, I thought she smiled at me. "Storm Claw spoke with him because she speaks his language. Said we could have his father's boat, if we took him with us. He got shot by an arrow in his leg and has some burns on his arm and face and most of his hair's singed off."

Lilly was talking fast. The enchantress let her scout continue without asking any questions.

"I'm not sure it's really his father's boat," Lilly said. "But he knows some about sailing. Swigopp can do a lot of it himself, and me and Flank Hawk know some sailing too, so Storm Claw and I figured it was better to sail in the fishing boat than row the rest of the way. The militia fella, Nidthaam Ebol, says the city we're looking for is about a half day east of here, if we use the fishing boat. It smells like fish. And burnt wood too, because it was on fire, but it didn't spread and went out after burning up the sail. There was a spare one so we used it."

I'd never even attempted to heal burn wounds, and saw that it took Ammond a lot of effort. As he said, he was better with bones and cuts. Still, Nidthaam Ebol was grateful for the repair to his leg and the partial healing of his arm and face.

We rowed out to the fishing boat before sunrise, tied our dinghy to the back, and sailed unmenaced to the harbor of the ancient city of Tripoli.

CHAPTER 11

The ancient city of Tripoli was an open city, ruled by someone titled the High Sheikh. It belonged to no tribe or kingdom, functioning as a trade city. I knew the Kingdom of Keesee was attempting to reestablish trade even though we remained at war with the Vinchie Empire. After Fendra Jolain's death upon the Blood Sword's blade, it became more of a war of skirmishes and reprisals, mainly with elements of the Vinchie Army backed by the resurgent Long-Tooth Tiger Brotherhood. Few battles occurred on the seas, but rather across the devastated lands of the Faxtinian Coalition and the Doran Confederacy.

The open city's huge main harbor held a host of ships, from three-masted merchants to oar and sail-driven war galleys. There were very few small boats like ours. Even so, a patrol skiff directed us to a pier just outside the main harbor. The salty air smelled different than the air along the shores of Keesee, or the main harbor in the King's City. Tripoli's reminded me of air rising from a cooling brick oven.

A dark-skinned official with long black hair and beard, wearing white flowing pants and robes, strode toward our fishing boat as we pulled up along the pier. Two broad-shouldered men armed with scimitars and small round shields accompanied him.

The trio ignored Lilly and Delmit, who climbed onto the dock and tied our boat to the pier. Swigopp stopped taking in the rope to pull our trailing dinghy close to tie alongside until Flayzin gave him a stern look.

I assisted the enchantress onto the deck and stood next to her as Ammond stepped forward to act as translator. The harbor official appeared surprised when our healer translated the enchantress's answer to his first question, that we carried no cargo. Enchantress Thulease offered to allow the official to inspect our boats. He declined, but counted each of us and noted the two boats before requesting from Enchantress Thulease a tax of six gold coins for our admittance to the city.

The enchantress managed to negotiate the admittance tax down by two gold and four silver coins. She was then informed of the docking fee, which, for our two boats, would be six silver coins a day, payable each morning, one hour after sunrise.

Enchantress Thulease acknowledged that we were expected to provide security to ensure our boats weren't damaged or stolen. After that, the harbor official began scribbling something into a small book.

Enchantress Thulease ordered Swigopp and Delmit to remain with the boats while the rest of us went into the city. Nidthaam Ebol, who looked like a cross between the thin official and the broad-shouldered guards, asked the official a question.

Ammond told the enchantress that the militiaman asked who he might report a raid on his town to.

The militiaman appeared satisfied with the official's answer, and told Enchantress Thulease that he'd return to the boats after reporting the deadly raid.

Lilly whispered in my ear, loud enough for Enchantress Thulease to hear, "Think the boats will still be here by morning?"

I gazed back at the two men remaining with the boats, and then over to the militiaman, who'd decided to arm himself with one of the spare cutlasses. "If the enchantress believes so," I said, "then so do I."

In truth, I wasn't so sure, but I also wasn't sure the enchantress truly wanted the boats, or the men. I realized this as we hefted small our sacks, which constituted just about all we had of value. It wasn't much.

Lilly slid on her wide-brimmed hat and hurried along the pier's graying planks to get ahead of Nidthaam Ebol. He appeared eager to report the destruction of his family and home. I fell in line just behind and to the right of Enchantress Thulease while Healer Ammond walked beside her. Storm Claw came up next to me, behind her ward, eyes alert for danger. Earth Wizard Stok and Guard Captain Flayzin walked behind us.

Despite it being October, the afternoon lacked a chilling bite as the sun shined down on the city that sprawled well beyond the surrounding wall. I figured it felt warmer ashore since we weren't caught in the near constant sea breeze while being sprayed with sea water.

Most of the buildings were squat mud and brick dwellings with reed shutters and doors. A few were immense stone and brick structures, adorned with both wood and glass. There were even spires that rivaled the towers in the King's City of Keesee. The most common trees had tall branchless trunks and broad fern-like leaves sprouting from the top. Many of the green leaves were tipped with browning edges. I wondered if that was normal.

Tripoli was much cleaner and didn't have the feel of sulking desperation like the dark city of Sint Malo, the only other free city I'd visited. Maybe the High Sheikh wasn't evil like Corradin the Conjurer.

We made our way through several markets with peddlers selling twine, rope, nets and hooks, before reaching the eight-foot high main wall built of dusty bricks. Its purpose didn't appear to be repulsion of attacks, or even to stop someone determined to scale it and sneak into the city. But Tripoli was an open city, so maybe invasion was less likely, and it held a different culture. Based on the tax official and his two burly guards, I suspected the penalty for anyone caught going over the wall into the city was harsh.

The men and women about us looked like those encountered in the King's City but with darker skin and lighter colors in their loose-fitting clothes. I didn't know their language, yet their faces appeared friendly enough. And I did catch brief phrases in Sea Spittle, which I spoke.

Lilly turned toward the main harbor's gate that enabled foot and cargo traffic to enter the city. Starting from the main harbor's gate, she knew the way to the inn where Enchantress Thulease's men were supposed to be waiting for us. We'd all rehearsed the route while onboard the *Hunchback Maiden*, before her sinking.

Lilly led the way deftly through the crowded streets and markets. Maybe it was something owing to her inner beast, but the donkeys and goats pulling carts shied away, often allowing us unhindered passage. We didn't stand out too much as there were others like us, foreigners, but Enchantress Thulease's unusual height drew attention.

Some of the foods cooking in the marketplace made my mouth water, especially the grilled goat shanks and coal-blackened fish. Others, pan-fried grubs the size of my thumb and lizards skewered on a stick and broiled before being devoured whole, chased away my appetite. The way Lilly scrunched up her nose said she felt the same as me.

Around the markets, dust and grime-covered workmen and women pushing wheelbarrows stopped and shoveled animal waste. Others of apparent low stature, crippled or blinded, sat along alleys. Many gripped clay cups, begging for coins. Several times my threatening mercenary gaze and hand movement toward my sword gave hesitation to those who looked to be cut purses. Their alert gaze and eye contact between partners gave them away. Storm Claw's actions said she'd identified them as well.

What I didn't see was an abundance of patrolling city guards as we wove from the main streets to narrower ones along our route into the heart of the city. The layers of newer construction upon weather-worn stone foundations confirmed the city's age. It made me wonder if there were tunnels beneath our feet, like there were below the streets and buildings of New London.

The dusty city smelled of hard clay, and sweat, mine being added to the mixture as we made our way to the large inn. Near as I could tell it was called *Ub-deeubdo Delab-vuab*. Ammond translated it as White Doors. It only made sense that the inn's main double-doors were painted white, as were the wooden shutters and window frames. So were the doors of the horse and camel stables next to the inn.

As soon as we got there, Nidthaam Ebol left us to report the burning of his town. The three men Enchantress Thulease sent ahead to secure mounts, beasts of burden, and a guide, were at the White Doors Inn.

The inn appeared to be the type that housed merchants, not the wealthiest, but equal to the boarding house I stayed in. I heard Enchantress Thulease explain to Healer Ammond along the way that she'd sought a reputable establishment in which to prepare for our journey's overland portion, and one where her advance men wouldn't draw unwanted attention.

I followed Enchantress Thulease onto the White Door's porch and then said to her, "Captain Flayzin or I should go in first."

She hesitated and then nodded to me.

It was difficult to see in through the windows. They were clean, but it was darker inside than it was outside. The front doors had brass handles shaped like feathered wings. They appeared old, yet recently polished. I closed my eyes for several seconds to help adjust them for the darker interior before opening the left-hand door and stepping in.

A short entry hall opened into a large room with a hardwood floor holding four tall tables with stools, eight padded chairs, and an elevated desk made of oak. Although polished, the desk bore marks indicating decades of service. The gray-bearded man matched the desk behind which he stood. He was finely dressed but bore thin scars down his cheek and across the bridge of his nose. He wore a drab brown, flowing shirt and pants, and a white hat that reminded me of an upturned flower pot.

A hard-edged man stood along the end of the desk, playing chess with the old man. I recognized him immediately when he turned and nodded to me.

"Flint," I said, seeing he and this chess opponent were the only ones in the room.

"Flank Hawk," he replied sharply and stepped away from the desk.

Flint worked on and off for the enchantress as a guard while also freelancing as muscle when merchants went to collect debts. His name not only fit his angular features, but his brittle personality as well. In the Arms Practice Yard he was a no-nonsense man and easily took offense. Best I could tell, he didn't have many friends, but I didn't have anything against him. He was better with a cudgel than he was with a sword.

He and Storm Claw might get along, I thought, stepping aside and allowing Enchantress Thulease to enter.

The old man appeared to count us and then said something to Enchantress Thulease after she stopped in front of the desk. Healer Ammond translated, "He says, 'You must be who Master Flint and his two companions have been waiting for.'"

Enchantress Thulease nodded her head once. "We are," Ammond translated.

The innkeeper clapped his hands three times and a boy and a girl hurried in through a doorway filled with a curtain made of long strings of white reeds and beads. If I had to guess, I'd have said the boy and girl were the old innkeeper's grandchildren. The boy was dressed like the innkeeper, including the hat, while the girl wore a long brown dress and a white scarf that held back her wavy black hair.

"We were getting worried," Flint said. "We got rooms like you said to. Thack and Robbins are in the stables, checking on the mules and camels.

One of us can go and fetch the guide and his son anytime."

"Unexpected difficulties caused a delay," Enchantress Thulease said to Flint. Then she asked the innkeeper, "May we see our rooms?"

Ammond translated her request for the innkeeper, who nodded and introduced himself to us as A'waan, and his son, Timin, and daughter, Sa'ida. He then instructed his children to show us to our rooms, men on the second floor, women on the third.

I began to object, but Enchantress Thulease looked to Ammond. "Keeping with the customs, might it be acceptable with you that we exchange personal guards during our stay in this establishment?"

Storm Claw frowned when Ammond said, "Absolutely."

The female mercenary and I shifted positions behind our new wards. I didn't feel as bad as Storm Claw probably did, knowing Lilly would be near the enchantress. Still, I returned her hard glare, delivering the same unvoiced notice: I'd hold her responsible for anything that happened to my primary ward.

Enchantress Thulease said to Flint, "Please have Robbins arrange for a common room at a nearby establishment where we might all meet over an evening meal, including our guide."

She looked to Ammond. "Would you ask Innkeeper A'Waan to have a bath set up? Sea water is fine, if that is less expensive."

Made sense, I thought. She could remove the salt. Me, I'd settle for a bucket of fresh water and a clean rag—if I got the chance.

We dined on lamb and fish in a small banquet room. The tavern, whose name roughly translated as High Tide, wasn't within sight of, let alone near the sea. Lilly thought maybe it was named after a flood of some sort.

It appeared to be a tavern that served common artisans and less affluent merchants, with the small banquet room used for minor celebrations. The wooden tables and chairs were worn but stout. The thick door promised a measure of privacy. Compared to the One-Eyed Pelican, it was like dining in the King's Palace. Still, it could've used more than two overhead lamps to supplement the single candle on each of the three tables.

Although Storm Claw and I initially stood guard next to the closed door leading into the High Tide's common area, Enchantress Thulease directed Flint and Thack to do so. Their trip had been easier and they'd had over a week to rest and prepare. Flint wasn't too happy about standing guard while we ate, but Thack, a heavyset older guard didn't seem to mind. He might've wanted to be a bard or minstrel in his younger years because he loved to tell stories to anybody who'd listen. Normally Thack found listeners since he was pretty good at spinning interesting tales.

Taking a bite of the roasted lamb, I did my best to enjoy the peppery flavor, knowing we might not have a good meal for quite some time.

We sat at three tables set in a U shape to make room for the fourteen of us, including Ghaiz our guide, and his son, Dastgir. Both the guide and his son spoke Mainland. Only Ammond, Robbins, Thack and Storm Claw spoke the language dominant in this part of the Southern Continent. Besides Ammond, Robbins was also supposed to be able to converse in a dialect found in the central portion of the continent where we were preparing to march—or ride. Even so, I'd learned that Sea Spittle was more widespread than use just among sailors. It was a trade language spoken in the lands across the Western, or Atlantic, Ocean. I knew Flayzin, Thack and Storm Claw spoke Sea Spittle as well.

Even though we ate in near silence, I think everyone who'd survived the voyage aboard the *Hunchback Maiden* appreciated the hearty meal that included grilled onions, boiled carrots and fresh bread.

I was sitting to Enchantress Thulease's left, and noticed she'd pushed her empty plate away. She surveyed the group before gripping her mug of beer. It looked like she was preparing to propose a toast with the bitter, but welcome, brew set before each of us. Flayzin, on her right, whispered something into her ear. He then got up and left the room for several minutes, returning with a plate of thin pickles. He offered one to each of us at the tables and those guarding the door.

Enchantress Thulease stood, raised her mug and said, "In memory of Miggs, a loyal guard, the witch, Tina Elaine, and the crew of the *Hunchback Maiden*, especially her captain and first mate. Without whose bravery and sacrifice we'd not be here tonight."

We all responded with raised mugs. "To Miggs, Tina Elaine and the *Hunchback Maiden*'s crew!"

After everyone drank deeply, Captain Flayzin lifted the pickle lying on his plate. With a wry smile, he said, "To Mercenary Sledge Fist, for his courage and sacrifice. He will be missed."

All in the room responded, "To Sledge Fist," and took a bite of their pickle.

I had to smile, knowing Sledge Fist would've laughed at our salute to him. A few around the table did laugh, but grew somber as we returned to our seats. Those we toasted, they were gone. I guessed that like me, the others around the room were pondering if they'd survive the journey, and what might be said about them if they didn't. Maybe they wondered how many of those we toasted were now aboard the *Bone Yard*, below deck, mindlessly rowing.

Lilly stared hard at Swigopp who sat at another table across from her. Enchantress Thulease had offered him, Delmit and Nidthaam Ebol, the option to join her mission. The sailor and witch's manservant accepted. The militiaman declined, even after Enchantress Thulease had sold the fishing boat and dinghy. The Enchantress did, however, give Nidthaam Ebol one quarter of the gold from the boat's sale, as he had nothing. I don't think she believed he was truly the original boat owner's son, especially when he didn't complain about his share.

Sailor Swigopp stared back at Lilly, then sought out a knife to slice himself another piece of bread.

"We depart the day after tomorrow," Enchantress Thulease said, getting everyone's attention. "We shall re-equip tomorrow morning and then rest, for it appears our journey is destined to remain arduous."

"Lucky you found that boar spear," Lilly said to me as we wove our way through the market crowd. "Maybe they don't have zombies much on this continent."

I thought about what Lilly said. The wings behind the blade kept prey, like boars, from running up the shaft once stuck. Foes like zombies, too. They helped keep a spear from piercing too deep and getting stuck when braced against a charging horse, or ogre.

"Walking dead can be found here," Storm Claw said. "Not in large numbers."

"The raider ship," I reminded Lilly. "But they don't have the Necromancer King, either."

Two months ago in the King's City I heard that the Crusaders had finally laid siege to the Necromancer King's fortress, but the Ancient Dictator escaped before they managed to breach the defenses. Jadd said he'd heard the Necromancer King disappeared beneath the waves in an underwater ship preserved from before First Civilization's fall, like the Colonel of the West had preserved flying machines such as his *Osprey* and *Hercules*.

The Necromancer King's fall from power would reduce the number of undead on the Mainland Continent. Maybe boar spears would become harder to find there as well.

I led Lilly and Storm Claw around a corner onto a broader street, away from the markets and shops and among dusty brick apartments. "Lilly, with the Necromancer King defeated, boar spears might become scarce in the King's City."

Besides getting a spear, I had the hole in my breastplate patched over, and purchased some oil and a small pair of pliers to use in repairing and maintaining my armor and equipment. And a pouch of finely ground salt as well as white oak bark—something that I truly felt lucky finding at an herbalist's shop. The last thing I got was a new crossbow. This one had a wooden prod and functioned well enough.

Everything had cost me over half my gold and silver coins, but what good would the coin do me if I was dead?

Lilly didn't have much to purchase, except a short bow, a few more arrows and a new backpack. She even got me a light gray cotton hat with a brim in front and a cloth that hung down over my neck in back. I wore it as we walked since I'd left my helmet back at the White Doors.

"Ha, Flank Hawk," she said. "Finding no boar spears in Keesee? You're funny."

"Lilly, I don't think he was joking," Storm Claw said.

She came along mainly as our interpreter, although the blacksmith that patched my armor spoke Sea Spittle. Flint and Thack remained behind as guards for Enchantress Thulease and Healer Ammond back at the inn where they were finalizing plans with the guide and his son. Everyone else had broken into groups like Lilly, Storm Claw and me to reprovision ourselves.

"Maybe I should've gotten that wooden canteen," I said, still wondering if Robbins had gotten enough waterskins for the desert journey.

"Maybe we should've taken a different street," Lilly said, just as I noticed mothers calling their children inside, and shutters closing at the street level. In those windows above, women and some old men peered out with expectant gazes.

Ahead of us, five men in flowing black shirts and pants, wearing leather vests studded with metal plates advanced in a line across the street, blocking our path. Three rested a hand on the pommel of a sheathed scimitar. Two carried flanged maces.

"You're right," Storm Claw said. "Three more unfriendly men are twenty paces behind us."

After another few strides I stopped, rested the butt of my spear on the dusty road and said quietly, "We need to avoid getting wounded, or arrested."

"Or killed," Lilly replied. "I'll watch them that's behind us, Flank Hawk."

The men ahead of us had dark beards and wore grim expressions. I figured the men behind us did as well. The ones ahead stopped, except for the center man, who continued for another two strides, leaving him about ten paces away. He said something in the local language I didn't understand.

Storm Claw said, "He says this is his street and wants to know who gave us permission to use it."

I replied in Sea Spittle to the foremost man, tallest among them, "We are visitors to the city. We'll return the way we came and use a different street."

The man smiled and it wasn't a pleasant one. In Sea Spittle, he said, "You and your women are already halfway down my street. To return means you'd still walk its length."

"What'd he say?" asked Storm Claw. I told her, keeping my eye on the group ahead.

Lilly said, "This is why I hate cities."

"Three on eight," I said. "I don't think they expect much out of you two, so we have a chance."

Storm Claw placed a hand on my shoulder. "Let me handle this, Flank Hawk." Before I could object, she added, "If anybody gets killed, we won't be the first."

From what I could see, the leader was getting ready to give the order to close on us. Storm Claw was an experienced mercenary, so if it was going to come to a fight, better they start dying first. "Okay," I told her.

As Storm Claw stepped forward, Lilly said to me in a low, even voice, "I got these guys here. Just tell me when."

I appreciated Lilly's confidence. Maybe the men behind didn't look as dangerous as the ones I was looking at.

Storm Claw spoke to the leader in a strong voice that carried up and down the street. Whatever she said, she wanted everyone watching to hear. The man smiled, apparently amused. I didn't imagine Storm Claw was smiling.

They exchanged words for a moment and he laughed again, and then nodded his head, saying something to his men. They relaxed and chuckled among themselves.

I took a step toward Storm Claw and said in her ear, "They going to allow us to pass?"

"We'll see," she said, pulling her clubs from their sheathes along her back.

"What'd you tell him?"

"We agreed, if he can wrest these clubs from me, without him striking or kicking me, he can have me. If he's forced to let go first, without me striking or kicking him, we go past unharmed." She frowned. "He wants to know if you agree."

"I won't let them take you," I whispered, in case one of them spoke Mainland. I knew Lilly's ears would catch what I said.

Storm Claw half turned to me and whispered back, "Either we win or lose, but any way it goes, they don't win." She shook her head. "Not in full."

Sounded like a result I'd arrange, if I could've figured a way. "Okay," I said in Sea Spittle to the leader. To Storm Claw I said, "Good luck."

"Luck will have little to do with it," she said, stepping forward, gently waving her fighting sticks back and forth several times before stopping with them extended, silver laced end toward the leader.

I recalled seeing what happened to several pirates Storm Claw clubbed and wondered if she had something like that planned. If she did, even if the deal fell through, it'd be better odds. Seven on three.

The leader swaggered up but, when he was within gripping range of Storm Claw's fighting sticks, he spread his feet for balance and became serious. Storm Claw spread her feet as well, preparing to keep hold of her end of the sticks.

Just as he was about to grip them, a small spark flashed from each stick, striking his hands. He jumped away, shouting, "Aahhh!" Then he yelled at Storm Claw. It was impossible for me to tell what he said, but he was furious.

She yelled back in the leader's tongue. One of the leader's men began walking forward. Storm Claw shouted louder, pointing one of her fighting sticks at the leader, then at the closing man. The follower stopped when the leader signaled with a hand and said something to Storm Claw.

She pressed the silver end of her clubs to her cheeks, said something sharply, and then extended them again.

The leader steadied himself before shaking his hands and flexing his fingers.

Storm Claw said something to him. It had to be a taunt.

He grunted and snarled back at her, then reached for the ends of the fighting sticks.

Just as he grabbed hold, Storm Claw shouted, "Ha!" causing him to flinch, leaving him with a weak grip on each stick, and leaning back, a little off balance. Immediately Storm Claw spun to face my direction, keeping hold of her sticks over her head while yanking forward.

Trying to keep his footing, the leader staggered toward her but lost his grip before she could throw him over her shoulder.

The leader reached for his scimitar. I stepped forward, spear held ready, pointed at him, shouting in Sea Spittle, "You let go first! *You* lost!"

Storm Claw spun on him and shouted in his tongue, looking not only at him, but to his men and the people watching from the windows and balconies. What she said made the leader hesitate drawing his scimitar, maybe more than my spear did.

A false smile spread across the leader's bearded face as he stepped aside and stiffly gestured for us to continue on our way. He barked something to the four men blocking our way and they stepped aside as well.

"Let's go," Storm Claw said. "But not too fast."

Storm Claw fell in line beside me. I said over my shoulder to Lilly, "Not a word."

She mumbled, "Not like they'd understand what I said anyway."

The leader hissed something at me, or maybe at Storm Claw—maybe both or all three of us as we strode past. Whatever he said, it sounded a lot like a threat.

I sat on a cushioned chair next to Enchantress Thulease as Storm Claw told her how she'd gotten us out of the bad situation on our way back to the White Doors. Lilly, Ammond and Flayzin each sat in one of the inn's cushioned chairs, listening too.

"The street boss laughed at me when I said he could include any air wizardry skills he might have during the challenge, because I intended to."

"You have air wizard skills?" Enchantress Thulease asked Storm Claw. "I have occasionally observed latent spell energy stored in your weapons."

Storm Claw shook her head. "No. And I obviously don't have any of the traits indicating I might."

She pulled the fighting sticks from their sheaths. "These were made by a weapons master who also was an air wizard," she said. "Through movement, flash energy like small lighting builds up. I don't know how or why it works, but it does."

"How did you obtain them?" Healer Ammond asked.

"A gift, from the weapons master for saving his wife," Storm Claw said, before resheathing her sticks and refocusing on her tale. "The street boss had to make a choice. Allow us to pass and suffer embarrassment, or break his word in front of everyone on the street he runs."

Enchantress Thulease pressed her hands together and rested her chin on them.

"He said he'd kill me, my man and his other woman, if he ever sees us again," Storm Claw said without a trace of concern.

Enchantress Thulease turned in her seat and said to Ammond, "Inform Innkeeper A'Waan of what happened and ask if it might result in trouble for him, his family, or his inn."

Ammond got up and spoke with the innkeeper. A'Waan smiled and shook his head, then said something to the enchantress, which our healer translated. "He says it will lead to no trouble for him or his family. Unless we venture to the markets around the street boss's territory, it is unlikely we will encounter him or his men. Unless he had you followed, he will not find you. Certainly not before you depart in the morning."

"Nobody followed us," Lilly said after Ammond returned to his seat.

Enchantress Thulease leaned back in her chair. "I suspect it was more than keeping his word that motivated this petty street thug. I do not know him, but I have encountered his kind, working with Imperial Seer Lochelle to track such as him down."

She smiled and rested her hands on the arms of her chair. "I imagine he swiftly came to realize that he had selected poorly as to his choice of victims. Deep down, Mercenary Storm Claw, he was relieved you offered him a route that did not threaten his survival."

I sat back too, with my hands resting on my chair's arms, wondering. It would've been bloody for both sides, and I couldn't imagine Storm Claw, me, or Lilly emerging without at least one of us maimed or killed. Then I thought back to Enchantress Thulease consulting Imperial Seer Lochelle. How, or for whatever reason, Storm Claw came to take part in the mission aimed at reviving Enchantress Thereese, it was a wise choice.

CHAPTER 12

After riding an hour south out of Tripoli I decided to give my mount, a gray spotted mule, a different name. I couldn't pronounce his given name anyway. Our guide, Ghaiz, said it translated as Eater of Reeds. That didn't sound like a good name. He was a patchy gray, like thunder clouds, I figured he'd respond to Thunder as good any other name. As mules go, he was sturdy and responded to firm stirrup kicks and stern tugs on his reins. If Thunder stopped responding, I'd make use my pliers and fit something sharp into the stirrups to encourage cooperation.

Travel was warm, but easy on the sand-covered road, wide enough for four mules abreast. We numbered fourteen travelers, counting our guides, Ghaiz and his son. They rode tawny-colored camels that appeared even more ill-tempered than the worst of our pack mules—even the one Delmit re-named Turd. The mule's coat certainly resembled the name.

We rode upon twelve mules. We also had six pack mules led on strings of three each by Delmit and Swigopp, and one spare horse, a stout bay, should speedy travel be needed. Thack led the bay, which carried four large waterskins.

We weren't nearly the largest group or caravan on the road, at least measured against those few travelling north, past us toward Tripoli. One caravan numbered over seventy riders, not counting their beasts of burden. Most wore the loose-fitting desert clothing and, like all groups, they had a large proportion of members armed for combat. I thought the sand and rock-filled desert would be sparsely populated, with only scattered nomadic tribes to worry about. Whatever might be found of value out there had to be fiercely guarded.

Despite my effort to securely tie them down, my helmet and breastplate eventually began to clank and rattle as Thunder plodded forward. The only people seeming to enjoy themselves were Lilly, riding next to Ghaiz on his camel, and Stok, bringing up the rear and riding alongside young Dastgir on his camel.

During our rest alongside a large rock outcropping to wait out the intense afternoon sun, Lilly told me some of the desert lore our guide had shared with her. Prior to departure Enchantress Thulease had informed our guide that Lilly was a lycanthrope. The revelation didn't appear to astonish or cause fear in Ghaiz or his son, Dastgir. Rather, they were curious as to why a water-loving beast would choose to travel the desert.

Earth Wizard Stok simply seemed to enjoy solid, dry ground under his feet after so much time surrounded by the sea. Even if that ground consisted of dry caked earth and sand.

Along the hard-packed road there wasn't much plant life to speak of. In the distance, I sometimes spotted bits of brownish green. Rain in any large amount had to be rare; it would've eroded large swaths of the trade road we traveled. The only birds I spotted were the occasional high-flying buzzard and a single desert hawk.

The evening's camp held the day's only excitement. When the full moon rose, Lilly's beast emerged. She didn't remain in our fireless camp when she changed from human to werebeast. It would frighten our mounts and pack animals. But, having learned from our experience in Iceland, she promised not to venture far.

The other interesting event was Enchantress Thulease and Wizard Stok combining their magics to obtain water. After selecting a low spot on the desert ground near a large boulder, Wizard Stok pressed his hands against the earth and began chanting. Within moments a three-inch diameter shaft formed. As he worked his magic, extending the shaft down into the ground, Flayzin uncoiled a long tube made of well-oiled leather and fed it down the hole. The coordination between Stok and Flayzin told me they'd practiced this.

The slow process appeared to be tiring the earth wizard. After about fifteen minutes and almost fifty feet of leather tube pressed down into the shaft, the wizard sat back and mopped sweat from his brow.

Enchantress Thulease patted Stok on the shoulder and said, "My turn, my friend."

She knelt in Wizard's Stok's place and gripped the leather tube where it emerged from the ground. After a moment of silence she began chanting. Flayzin signaled to Flint, who hurried over with the empty waterskins.

Five minutes later, after a tense nod from Enchantress Thulease, Flint inserted a wooden funnel into the mouth of an empty waterskin while Flayzin held the end of the leather tube above the funnel. A minute later a small but steady stream of water poured from the tube into the funnel, slowly filling the first waterskin.

I guessed the water poured about one quarter the rate beer drained from a keg. I thought she could do better, being a supreme enchantress, one of the most powerful in the Kingdom of Keesee. Then I reminded myself, it was water from desert soil. It might've been a decade since rain last fell where we camped.

Over the next hour and a half the rate fluctuated, but she managed to fill our six empty waterskins and provided each of our mounts and pack mules a half bucket of water.

While the enchantress worked, Storm Claw and Thack stood watch. Ammond, Dastgir, and I set up our four small A-frame tents. The canvas of the tents had been dyed a mottled brown to help them blend into the desert landscape. From a distance, it might prove effective.

Before Enchantress Thulease retired to her tent and I stood the second watch, she signaled Flayzin, Flint and me over to her.

"Tonight was a test," she said, "to see how well our combined magic works in an actual desert. It made sense to test tonight since the full moon forced Lilly to release her beast. For those reasons we strayed off the main road to avoid contact with other travelers."

She frowned and looked over her shoulder into the tent she was preparing to share with Wizard Stok. He'd begun snoring. "It appears," she continued, "I can draw enough water to enable survival without my spell strength being overly taxed. If we travel hard, drawing sufficient water for all of our mounts will be an uncertain prospect."

"It will enable us to cross great expanses, even if slowly," Flayzin said.

I warned, "It'll take more than water to maintain the strength of our mounts and pack animals."

"True, Flank Hawk," the enchantress said. "Tomorrow evening, Guide Ghaiz will lead us to an inn frequented by travelers. There is a well there, and stables where we might feed our mounts without resorting to what grain we carry."

I felt a lot better about not paying coin for the wooden canteen I'd seen in one of the Tripoli marketplaces.

"We should avail ourselves of all such stops possible," Flayzin said. "If they're safe."

"Everyone but Delmit is handy with a weapon," I said. "If we let that be known in subtle ways, and appear alert against trouble..."

I didn't need to finish my thought as both Enchantress Thulease and Flayzin nodded in agreement.

"We have two of the tubes," Flayzin said. "Since having at least one will be vital to our survival, let's pack them on separate mounts."

"I'll keep one with me," Enchantress Thulease said. "Let Robbins carry the other on his mount."

"I'll see to it," Flayzin said. "Flank Hawk and I will see to everything, Enchantress. If you have the strength in the morning, it might be good if you could draw more water for the mounts."

Wizard Stok's snoring increased in intensity. I caught Flayzin's white teeth gleaming in the moonlight. "I'll cover the shaft," he said. "If Stok was able to drill it the way he practiced, this one shouldn't collapse and we can use it again in the morning."

"It *might* be possible," Enchantress Thulease said. "If any moisture seeps back into the soil surrounding the cavity. I drew it forth from quite a distance."

She looked over her shoulder into the tent. The full moon revealed her frown.

"Don't let him sleep on his back," I suggested to the enchantress. Flayzin and I stood as she prepared to crawl into her tent. "Get him to sleep on his side. It always stopped my cousin Guzzy's snoring."

We rose well before sunrise to cover as many miles as possible before the intense afternoon heat. Enchantress Thulease had managed to draw only a quarter a bucket of water for each mule. We gave them some of our carried water too since we planned on stopping and an inn called the Vulture's Foot Crossing, or that's how Ghaiz translated the name. They were supposed to have a reliable well.

Storm Claw was next to me as we walked alongside our mounts in the late afternoon. I asked her, "How hot does it get here in the summer?"

She shrugged. "I'm not from this region, but I heard talk in Tripoli that it's hotter than usual for this time of year."

"Where are you from?" I asked.

Enchantress Thulease and Ammond were a short distance ahead of us, far enough that I could hear them talk but not what they said. More importantly, far enough that we weren't eating dust their mounts, and the mounts ahead of them, kicked up. Same with Robbins and Thack. They followed about fifteen yards behind us. Flat and empty as the land was, I couldn't imagine anybody sneaking up on us.

She hesitated for a moment. "Far west of here. Malgeria." She shot me a cold smile. "Yes, I fought for the Healing Goddess before her fall."

I shrugged. She was a mercenary, just like me. We fought for whoever paid us. "What do you think of the Long-Tooths?"

It was her turn to shrug. "Cruel. Effective fighters. When the goddess fell, they came to dominate. I took my final coin and left, like most from my tribe."

"How'd you come to be Healer Ammond's personal guard?"

"Luck," she said. "We crossed paths when he was in need."

The silence that followed indicated she wasn't going to say more. After several minutes she said, "I heard Captain Flayzin blames you for Prince Reveron's death. Believes cowardice played a part." She adjusted her grip on her mount's reins. "I've also heard tell of the deeds you performed on Keesee's behalf. The two don't fit."

I looked at the dry road and snorted out some of the dust from my nose. I didn't much like to think about that day. "An ogre threw its sword and struck Prince Reveron from behind. I didn't slay the brute quick enough. Because of that, the prince fell."

"There's no quick way to slay an ogre," Storm Claw said.

"There is if you're good enough. Maybe fearless enough."

"You're a mercenary," she said. "*And* a healer. That's unheard of. Means you'll always fight like a weight's tied to your sword arm."

"I took it in the throat with my spear," I said of the ogre.

"Then you picked up the prince's sword and finished what he'd begun." She looked over at me. "I was there—not in the temple when it happened," she said. "My company was fighting the Crusaders. I watched the dragons and bladed flying machine leave."

"I don't remember that."

"I've heard tell the goddess didn't die. I've heard King Tobias holds her hostage in the Blood Sword's blade."

I shrugged. "I don't know," I said, thinking it might be true. The Colonel of the West might have hoped for it to happen when he returned the Blood Sword to King Tobias's hand. "The evil in the Blood Sword was trying to kill her. She fought back. Prince Reveron was dead, thrown to the hydra's venomous jaws, and Grand Wizard Seelain was helping me to my feet. Shouting, blood, smoke and the smell of charred flesh. That's all I remember."

I folded up the memory, or what I had of it, and tucked it away in my head.

She must've read the sorrow and regret on my face. "Sorry," she said. "Shouldn't've asked."

"Now, you know more than most," I said, forcing a smile across my face. "About as much as I do."

"I saw how you fought those pirates. How you were ready to fight those street thieves. I think the captain is wrong about you. About what happened."

"Everyone sees the world from a different vantage," I said. "That's what my dad told me."

Ahead of us, Enchantress Thulease signaled us to mount our mules.

"The wisdom of fathers," Storm Claw said, then cursed as she fought to get her mount to cooperate.

"Give your mount a better name than Shummessah Mesheya," I said to Storm Claw, laughing while sitting atop Thunder. "Worked for me."

The Vulture's Foot Crossing wasn't really an inn. More like a sprawling shack built of brick-like clay and gray, weather-beaten planks. And the well house, it looked more like a fortress. Circular and stone, with an iron door, always guarded by at least two alert, burly men armed with wickedly curved falchions and bucklers painted blue and brown, Tripoli's colors.

The inn's name came from three roads that converged into one that continued north, toward Tripoli. Our guide said the High Sheik's men guarded the well, and collected the water tax. It made sense, as it aided traders from the desert traveling to his city. And the taxes were minimal, probably not even enough to pay the guards and workers that maintained the well house. The inn? I wasn't sure anyone maintained it. Everyone in our group chose to sleep in our tents, under the cooling night sky. Two other caravan groups camped like us, a short distance from the well house.

They apparently weren't impressed with the Vulture's Foot either. The only difference was our camp was fireless, whereas theirs had small smoldering fires. I thought it was fueled by dried animal dung. Lilly's nose confirmed it.

Storm Claw kicked my foot, waking me for my turn at watch. "Five minutes," she whispered. Lilly, sleeping next to me stirred awake, so the female mercenary moved on to awaken Delmit.

Lilly helped me buckle on my breast and backplate after taking a drink from her waterskin. "Don't know why anyone would wanna live out here," she whispered so she wouldn't wake anyone. "Always hot. Always thirsty."

I whispered back, buckling on my sword. "Weather's cooling some, I think. Plus, they're probably used to it."

Lilly handed me my spear. "Probably don't know any better."

Captain Flayzin came up to Lilly and me and signaled Delmit over before leading us to where we'd hobbled our mules. "Storm Claw saw two men from the inn out for a night stroll. Might've been looking over our animals."

"Seeing if we're easy marks?" I asked.

"That'd be my guess. Continued on their way when they spotted her watching them. Just wanted you to be aware."

"They won't get the jump on us," Lilly said.

"I'm going to stay up an extra hour," Flayzin said. "Then rouse Stok to finish being the fourth man. We'll have the healer stand fourth man on the third watch. Can't fight, but his eyes and ears are good as anyone's."

I asked Flayzin, "Did you clear that with Storm Claw?"

"She's not in charge," he said. "If she's uncomfortable about it, she can stand with him or take his place."

"What about our guides?" Lilly asked.

"Not unless we have to. We count on their being alert during the day's travel."

Lilly frowned at that, but didn't say anything.

Storm Claw wasn't happy, but couldn't argue that Ammond was any less safe in his tent than watching from his post near the tents. The rest of the night went quietly and, as the sun's light was just climbing into view, most of us were lined up with our animals, preparing to water them. A group of carpet and garment traders, mostly wool and goatskin, waited ahead of us.

Enchantress Thulease, Flayzin, and Robbins had gone over to the inn to negotiate for what food might be had to supplement what we'd eaten and for a weed-ridden bale of hay to feed our animals.

"There they are," Storm Claw said to me, pointing at two men leading two sturdy horses out of the rickety stable attached to the inn. Like the men, the bay roans appeared healthy and well-fed.

They got in line behind us, ahead of a group of traders that looked like they'd banded together and hired a half dozen mercenaries for protection. Their camels carried sacks filled with copper and bronze dishes, at least from what I'd seen and heard when they broke camp earlier in the morning.

I watched the guards collect the tax and hand buckets to the lean carpet and garment traders ahead of us, and allowed them in the stone well house. Soon the traders were moving among their camels and mules with water-filled buckets.

"Hopefully it'll be a cooler day," I said to Storm Claw.

She grunted agreement.

Lilly stepped out of our line as our guide stomped past her, and continued past me and Storm Claw. "What's he so mad about?" Lilly asked.

He grabbed his son by the arm and yanked him away from the two men who'd been near our camp last night, cursing at his son by the sound of it.

"Watch Shummessah Mesheya," Storm Claw said, handing me the reins. I handed the reins to my mule and Storm Claw's to Lilly and followed the female mercenary over to our guide. He hadn't let go of his son's arm as they began walking toward us.

The two horsemen laughed.

Dastgir's camel began to wander out of the line. "I'll take care of that, and watch them," Storm Claw said.

"Okay," I replied, knowing she spoke their tongue and I didn't. "Lilly, see if there's a problem with Dastgir."

A few minutes later, Lilly marched back. "No problems, Flank Hawk," she said into my ear. "Ghaiz doesn't like the looks of those men and didn't trust his son talking to them."

I didn't like the looks of the horsemen either, especially since they might've been scouting our camp. "Okay," I replied quietly. I didn't want the two horsemen pretending they weren't watching us to hear me. "Captain Flayzin knows about those two men from last night. Make sure our guide reports what his son said to Flayzin and the enchantress."

"Yep, will do, Flank Hawk."

Two days later Storm Claw kicked my foot, waking me for my night watch. Lilly was already crawling out of our tent. "Five minutes," Storm Claw said and walked over to Delmit's tent.

Lilly yawned and said, "Yup."

I checked my boots for scorpions and put them on before crawling out, dragging my breast and backplate with me.

"Want help with that?"

I took a drink from my waterskin and held it out for Lilly. "Sure."

It was a clear night. Stars glittered and the waning moon added its light, giving the reddish tan rocks and desert sand a silvery gray cast. A breeze caught the tips of my matted hair.

She took a drink, capped the skin and set it back inside our tent. "About three miles before the road ran out, you think there really was a spider the size of a prize bull waitin' to ambush us?"

"You don't believe our guide?" I held my breastplate in place. "He named it…a trapdoor spider?"

Lilly sighed and held my backplate against my back, lined up the shoulder buckles with the breastplate, and began with my left shoulder buckle. "Uh- huh," she said.

"The mules' ears were perked. Something had them spooked."

"I didn't sense anything, Flank Hawk." Lilly began working on my right shoulder while I worked on buckling the sides. "Didn't see what he was talking about when he led us off the road and wide around. Besides, nothing that big could live out here."

I knelt to retrieve my sword belt and shield from the tent. "Why not?"

"What's there to eat? Scorpions? Little lizards, bugs, like they eat in that Tripoli city?"

"Maybe that's why it set up along the road, Lilly." I slung the shield over my shoulder and began buckling my belt. "Catch lone travelers."

Lilly stepped past me and signaled silence. She stood on her toes, sniffing. Listening. "Robbins?" she whispered, looking sharply toward our tethered mounts. "Alarm! We're under attack!"

I grabbed my spear and remained crouched while debating for half a second about getting my helmet from inside the tent. Would it be worth the time? Having it might save me from harm, but with our camp being attacked at night, a wide field of vision and clear hearing were more important. I heard Thulease and Stok moving about within their tent five feet to the left of ours.

As I stood, Lilly pointed to a pair of shadows rising from the ground forty feet beyond our tent. I thought the one on the left had a bow. Shouts in the form of undulating whoops and piercing yodel-like howls rose from all around our camp. It was meant to confuse and intimidate. It worked on the mules, but not on Lilly and me. We'd stood to much worse.

Rather than waiting for the enemy to close, I said, "Lilly, with me." Our action would draw the enemy to us and away from the enchantress's tent—better than making a stand there, defending them.

Running between the tents, I hurled my spear at the shadow bowman as he drew back an arrow. He fell back, clutching at my spear buried in his gut.

Three more shadows stood to make four facing Lilly and me. Two were bowmen.

Lilly said, "Sounds like at least forty of them." She held her rapier and dagger ready as we closed. I slowed a stride while readying my shield and drawing my broad-bladed short sword.

I heard the *twang* as the enemy ahead of us loosed their arrows. On instinct, I raised my shield, catching one with a *thunk*. Lilly grunted but didn't have time to do anything about the black shaft protruding from her left shoulder before we clashed with the two falchion-wielding men.

Orange light from somewhere behind us lit up the camp. It was bright as a bonfire, magical and above the camp based on the angle of my shadow.

I ducked a two-handed slash and slammed the rim of my shield into my foe's chin. His head snapped back. That gave me time to take Lilly's foe in the back with a quick sword thrust as he tried to parry her attack. It wasn't a killing strike but enough to give Lilly the upper hand.

My foe remained between me and the bowmen who were stepping right to get a shot at me. Before the falchion-wielder recovered I drove into him with my shield, snapping off the arrow buried in its wooden face. He fell backwards so I charged among the two bowmen. Another *thunk* on my shield and a *twack* against my breastplate told me both men had loosed their arrows. They swung their bows at me. One broke on my shield. The other caught me across the sword arm but my armor absorbed most of the blow. I hacked one bowman down while the other turned and ran.

Lilly shouted, "Behind you!"

I ducked and spun, bringing my shield up. I was rewarded with a hammering two-handed strike which I deflected, leaving one of my two new foes off balance. I caught him in the stomach with my blade and drove it upward, into his lungs. His eyes went wide and he feebly reached for my blade as I side stepped, keeping him between me and a scimitar-wielding man. The fiery light danced off his flowing black shirt and pants. His long beard had some gray. His smile carried confidence. Beyond his shoulder I saw chaos in our camp. Flayzin and Storm Claw were surrounded by a dozen men, and there was another skirmish around the mules. I heard Lilly cursing above the enemy battle cries somewhere off to my right. I didn't see the enchantress's tall form and didn't have time to search more.

Sometimes you can just tell when you're facing a sword master, in this case, a scimitar master. It showed in his face, stance and the lightning speed of his attack. I wasn't a sword master, but I was a veteran mercenary. His blade slid off my parry, slicing down into my right thigh. He moved away, fluid steps putting distance between us.

My counter wasn't fancy. Once out of sword range he spun to face me again. I threw my sword, letting it go, spinning end-over-end at him. The aerial bonfire was in his eyes, hampering his vision. He didn't bring his buckler over fast enough. My sword's tip bit into his chest, just to the right of his sternum. My leg was cut, but I couldn't yet feel the wound. I knelt even as my sword fell away and my scimitar-wielding foe recovered from the shock of his shallow chest wound. It might've been different if the sea water hadn't washed the fireweed resin from my blades, and the *Hunchback Maiden* hadn't taken my tin of resin down with her.

He smiled again with confidence. I tugged my boar spear from the dying raider's stomach. I wasn't any good spear fighting one-handed, so I dropped my shield. While I did, I felt blood from my leg wound trickle down my thigh and onto my knee. Although I'd injured him, my wound would slow my movements more. But with my spear, I could keep him off me for a time—time enough for his fellow raiders gang up on me.

We were outnumbered, and I was bleeding, so fighting defensive played to his advantage.

He circled left, trying to force me to maneuver on my bad leg. I stood my ground and prepared to attack when a horn sounded from the east, not too far off. Three short soundings, followed by a fourth, a long one.

The scimitar master took notice and backed away from me before turning and disappearing into the darkness. There was no way I could catch him. I thought about throwing my spear but decided to turn about to where Lilly had been fighting. She wrestled on the ground with a burly raider. Both had daggers drawn, but she was on top.

Other raiders retreated from our camp, giving me wide berth before disappearing into the darkness.

"Hold him, Lilly," I said while closing with her. The raider became frantic in his struggle to throw Lilly off. Lilly was stronger than she looked. I found an opening and thrust my spear through his ribs, up to the crossbar.

Lilly finished him with a slash to his throat before pushing herself away and getting to her feet.

"You're bleeding," Lilly said to me as I surveyed the camp and searched the perimeter for bowmen.

"I know."

"Heal yourself before you lose more blood!" She pulled off her belt and tightened it above my thigh. "I see the enchantress is up and about."

That news was a relief. And Lilly was right. Still, I said, "You're bleeding too." She was, from her shoulder where that arrow had gotten her. Dampness in her hair said she had a scalp wound as well. "Your shoulder and your head."

She felt along the top of her head. "Not bad," she said and looked around. "They're gone. I'll go tell the enchantress you're okay. Now close up that wound!"

I nodded and reached for my pouch containing white oak bark. The finely ground powder was a component that made my weak spellcraft a little more effective. That, and the amulet held around my neck by a silver chain helped as well. The marble-sized crystal contained a drop of blood from a fallen angel. Somehow it altered the flow of hidden magical energies, making it easier for me to find and redirect the magical ribbons necessary to heal wounds.

I didn't think about the amulet often, but was glad I had it.

After looking around one more time I limped a few strides back toward camp, to within ten feet of my tent. I sat with my legs outstretched and set my spear aside before opening the slice in my armor to expose the wound. It was deeper than I thought, yet appeared clean, so I sprinkled a handful of the ground white oak bark into it and began my spell.

I quietly chanted the only chant I knew, the only one my older sister had taught me, while opening my mind to the maelstrom of energy that raged beyond the reach of normal senses. I edged closer, seeking a sliver of the swirling energy, a strand that I recognized. One that I could direct.

I continued to chant while energies buffeted my mind as I delved deeper, seeking to draw upon a broad strand, one that might mend my leg enough that I could walk on it.

With strained effort, I peeled a vibrating energy ribbon away from the others and directed it into the wound. There it merged with the oak bark and severed blood vessels and slashed flesh.

A sharp pain formed behind my eyes, but I kept at the spell, realizing I hadn't done enough. I reached out again, this time for a smaller ribbon, one easier to peel away and direct.

It too rippled into the wound, mending blood vessels and flesh, halting most of the bleeding.

Relieved, but under throbbing pain, I slowed my chant as I backed out of the maelstrom, easing my focus, distancing myself from the whorl of magical energies.

When I opened my eyes it was dark. My head still hurt. The magical bonfire was gone, and a shadowy figure stood several paces from me.

I reached for my spear.

"It's okay, Flank Hawk." I recognized Sailor Swigopp's voice. "Captain Flayzin sent me to watch over you while you were crafting your spell."

"Thanks," I said. "Is the enchantress okay?"

"She's okay, but not everybody else is. Thack, Robbins, Delmit and our guide are dead."

Lilly wrapped a cloth around my leg's wound. The black garment she used came from the sleeve of a dead raider. "Think it'll hold?" she asked after tying it. "And won't start bleeding?"

I held up my leather pants. They were stout, but not enough to stop the scimitar that sliced through them. Still, they probably saved me from a crippling wound. "It'll hold as good as the stitching I just finished."

She examined the handiwork I'd just completed on my armor. "Doubt it. Ammond's a better healer than you." The flickering candlelight within our tent caught her grin. "A lot better."

I returned her smile. "That isn't saying much." Ammond had healed Flint's neck wound. Another inch and the hard-edged mercenary's jugular would've been severed. He'd also healed four puncture wounds from arrows, and Storm Claw's broken jaw.

Just about everyone had some cuts and bruises, except Lilly. She'd changed into her beast form, and then returned to her human self after about an hour, repairing her shoulder and scalp in the process. If her wounds had been from fire or silver, she'd have had to wait for Ammond's exhausted spell strength to return, or heal over time like everyone else.

"If we're done," Lilly said, "best we wrap our stuff we aren't taking so it can be buried. The enchantress wants to be after them right quick." She blew out the candle and let me dress.

We'd buried our four fallen and dragged the eleven we'd killed out for the vultures—or whatever scavengers there were—to finish them. Captain Flayzin guessed the desert raiders came after our mounts and hoped to kill most of us in our tents. Luckily Storm Claw had decided to wake Lilly and me a little early. Why? She didn't say. But Enchantress Thulease had Swigopp and Wizard Stok digging graves for Thack, Robbins, Delmit and Ghaiz before their bodies had cooled. They did this while the enchantress plotted our revenge.

I wasn't sure of her motivation, but what she said made sense. They might track and try again, the next time better prepared and possibly in even greater numbers, especially if they wanted to avenge the deaths of their fellow raiders. Dastgir said family ties ran strong in the desert. And they'd still want our mounts, plus whatever else we might have of value. Even if they left us alone for now, odds were we wouldn't be any stronger upon our return trip. What if we crossed them again? We couldn't count on being lucky a second time.

I agreed with the enchantress and so did Captain Flayzin. No one argued the point, especially with avenging our fallen an unmentioned but accepted part of the decision. The desert raiders fled because we were giving them a nasty fight they weren't ready for. Next time they'd expect one. And that was why we had to take it to them first. Not to kill them all outright. Enchantress Thulease's plan was to let the desert elements do that job.

We'd lost our primary guide to the desert raiders' blades, but Enchantress Thulease had something better. She'd marked two of them with her magic before they fled into the darkness. For a week, she'd know their direction and rough distance.

Lilly helped me drop our tent, and we threw what little we had, except our weapons, waterskins and some food onto it. After folding it over several times, Lilly picked it up. "You rest your leg, Flank Hawk. I got this."

I walked over to Enchantress Thulease, taking care not to put too much weight on my wrapped leg. She acknowledged me with a nod and watched Lilly toss our bundled tent in a shallow hole in the rocky sand. Swigopp and Dastgir, breathing heavily, picked up their shovels.

"Here," Lilly said to Dastgir. She took his shovel and began scooping sand from the nearby pile onto our gear. When Swigopp began shoveling, she stepped in his way and said, "I got it."

The sailor wiped his brow and said, "Thanks."

Our fallen guide's son offered the sailor a half-full waterskin. The sailor took it and drank deeply while keeping an eye on Lilly.

I turned my attention from Lilly's anger and frustration, and asked Enchantress Thulease, "Are they still moving?"

She nodded once. "They continue northeast."

"How fast?" I asked.

"Not fast enough to survive."

CHAPTER 13

I'd just finished helping Swigopp and Dastgir water our mounts when Lilly returned from scouting the desert raiders' camp. Enchantress Thulease had sent me to check on their progress with our worn out mules and camels, and I decided to help them finish. There was no telling if we'd need our mounts ready for a quick retreat.

Following the enemy trail wasn't difficult. They weren't expecting us to come after them. With the deaths of our guide, Thack, Robbins and Delmit, I didn't either. At least not as hard as we did. We rode through the remaining night and through the heat of the mid-afternoon sun, continually switching mounts so we didn't fully run down any of them. The decision to carry little of our supplies enabled us to gain on the enemy.

The loss of four comrades in the night's raid didn't strike me as deeply as I expected. That fact weighed on my mind as we pursued the raiders. I'd begun to look forward to hearing Thack's tales. And Delmit, although inexperienced, was a decent, hardworking man. He quietly paid attention and wanted to learn. We now lacked an experienced guide. I wasn't sure if Enchantress Thulease was as concerned as me about that. She was confident that Dastgir was up to the task. He bravely stepped up to take his father's place, but I wasn't confident in his limited knowledge and experience.

Maybe the feeling of loss hadn't hit me because we buried them with haste and immediately began the chase to avenge their deaths. I put such thoughts aside as we sheltered behind a rocky dune, waiting for Lilly to finish her drink before giving us her report.

Lilly wiped her lips and handed the waterskin back to Flayzin. "I couldn't get very close," she said. "They have nine guards posted around their camp. One at each corner. One in between them, and one that wanders out of the tents every ten minutes."

As she spoke she drew the layout in the gritty sand with her finger. "They have three big tents, where most of the people are. Sleeping I'd guess. They set them up like spokes in a wheel so that one side faces the other two. Each has one big door flap and some window flaps tied up for air to go in and out. Next to the tents they have three big canvas shades set up over their animals. They got a lot of them. I couldn't count 'em all, but there's about twenty camels with the same number of horses. And mules too. And there are some sturdy ponies and a few goats too."

From behind us, Swigopp asked, "How do you know they're sleeping?"

Lilly turned and scowled at him. "I looked with this." She held up her spyglass. "And I didn't look so the sun could flash off of it, neither."

Swigopp looked down at the sand. Up until that moment, I'd thought that Lilly had gained some respect for him. He hadn't shirked any duty and fought hard against the raiders.

Flayzin asked, "How close were you able to get?"

"Hundred-twenty yards," Lilly replied. "They picked a flat place to camp. It'll be tough to approach without them seeing."

I asked, "Any estimate on how many there are, Lilly?"

She shrugged. "More than attacked us last night. I saw two or three that looked like women up and moving inside the tents."

"Our goal is not to slay them outright," Enchantress Thulease said. "It is to strand them here. Let the desert do our work." She gazed up at Flint who was peeking over the dune's lip. He must've felt her gaze. He glanced down and shook his head, so she continued. "Wizard Stok determined there is a substantial amount of gold and silver. While some may carry it on their persons, my guess is that the bulk of it will be stored centrally, in a chest or crate. I have been able to determine their water supply is also substantial. Again, some will be dispersed, but the majority of it is probably in barrels."

None of the slain raiders had any gold on them. Of course it might've clanked or jingled while sneaking up on our camp.

The enchantress gestured with a hand to Dastgir. "Our guide believes there is only one oasis within three days riding distance, farther than the well house where we replenished our water supply. If we deprive them of water, mounts, shelter and gold, they will perish." She looked up at Flint again, and he again signaled all was clear. "But we'll have to get closer to know exactly where the water and gold is stored. In which tent or tents, and if the barrels or other containers are together or dispersed."

She looked to Captain Flayzin. "Assessment, Captain?"

He rubbed his red-bearded chin in thought. That and his mustache were no longer neatly trimmed. "First priority would be their water. Then mounts, shelter and last, gold."

She looked to me. "Flank Hawk?"

I shook my head. "Animals priority. Even without water, they still outnumber us. If they give chase they might catch up with us."

"We carry water with us now," Flayzin replied. "And can get more."

I guessed some of what Enchantress Thulease's plan was. "No. Our spellcasters will expend most of their strength getting us close and destroying their supplies. The condition of our mounts and what we have now will have to do for some time." I looked at everyone listening to my opinion. "Who here hasn't been worn down by the heat?" When nobody replied, I finished, saying, "It'll hurt us if it comes to a running fight."

Enchantress Thulease looked from me to Flayzin and back. "Lilly, did you spot any hints of a spellcaster?"

Lilly shook her head. "It'd be hard to tell an earth wizard, with the skin color of the people out here. I didn't see any white hair, red hair or blue skin. I can't scout other spellcasters as good as you, or him sensing them," she finished, making eye contact with Earth Wizard Stok.

"Spellcasters that deal in elements blend in with the environment," Enchantress Thulease said. "Using spellcraft to determine if there are practitioners of any competence in other disciplines will risk revealing our presence."

Flayzin spoke up. "None that I know of participated in the raid. If they had one or two, they'd have used them."

"Maybe that's how they snuck up on Robbins," Lilly said. "Almost got the jump on all of us."

"Whether they have spellcasters or not," Enchantress Thulease said, digging a bit of sand from her thumbnail, "however they managed to successfully close on our camp, our response will be decisively more effective."

"You think leaving your crossbow with that healer will do any good?" Flint asked me. "I hear you're a good shot." He wiped sweat from his brow after helping me strap on my breastplate. "We might need that."

I shook my helmet and knocked some of the gritty sand out of it. It was hot enough, especially with armor on. I didn't need sweat mixed with sand getting in my eyes. "I might get one shot off," I said, knowing I'd rather have my shield. I began strapping on my helmet. "He might need it."

"He's a healer."

"So am I, Flint. You've heard I'm a good shot." I slapped him on the back hard enough that he'd feel it through the metal rings and leather. "It's true. Don't ask me why, especially being a healer—weak one that I am. It might be the distance between healer and violence a crossbow brings."

He looked over at Storm Claw. The dark-skinned mercenary just finished showing Ammond one more time how to step in the stirrup, draw back the string and place the quarrel. The healer hadn't looked so youthful and unsure of himself since escaping from the sinking *Hunchback Maiden.*

The crossbow didn't really matter much. Ammond's real duty was to stay with our mounts while we attacked the desert raiders' camp. Lilly had gone ahead to scout. Once we got as close as we could, remaining unseen, Enchantress Thulease would use her spellcraft to find the enemy's water while Wizard Stok would locate their gold.

The plan was for Enchantress Thulease to mask our approach through the flat open ground with invisibility. Earth Wizard Stok was to sweep the sand flat with his spellcraft so we wouldn't leave a trail. When we got close, we'd try to sneak in between the guards so that we could take them from behind. Lilly was assigned to slay the first guard, the one nearest us between the animals and the tents, and then douse whatever tents she could with the little lantern oil we'd brought with us.

Flint, Flayzin and I were to kill our assigned guards and cut the tents' outer support lines, collapsing their fronts, then fight to keep the enemy from emerging afterwards. Swigopp, Dastgir and Storm Claw were assigned to round up what mounts they could before scattering and killing the rest. Stok was to take one guard from behind and then he and Enchantress Thulease were to back away from the camp and begin their spellcraft. She'd warp the slats in the barrels or sealing caps of any large skins, causing them to leak, while the earth wizard was to do his best to sink their treasure down into the sand. By then Lilly should've used some of the rare matches the enchantress brought along and set fire to the tents.

Lilly wondered at the matches when shown how to use them. I knew Crusaders used them, and had used several myself while traveling with Grand Wizard Seelain. The enchantress's sulfur-tipped matches had been created by a master alchemist—her husband.

We believed burning tents would add to the enemy's fear and confusion and send any remaining animals into a panic. If possible, we'd set fire to the canvas sheltering the enemy's mounts before retreating.

With luck we'd put enough distance between us and the enemy to be beyond effective bowshot before they organized a counter attack.

"Good plan you came up with," Flint said. He checked his gear and shot me a crooked smile, something he rarely did. "Pissed off the captain, but your tactics're better than his."

"We'll see," I said, looking over to the captain and enchantress. They appeared ready to depart. I met Flint's gaze. "Time to go."

We huddled together behind the small dune Lilly said was the closest we could get to the desert raiders' camp. I passed the waterskin to Storm Claw and waited. So much depended on our ability to sneak past the guards before Enchantress Thulease dropped her invisibility spell. Hopefully noise from the animals would mask our boots walking across the sand, and the clinks and scrapes our armor and equipment made.

Enchantress Thulease and Wizard Stok completed their location spells and signaled us to gather close around her. Lilly would lead and Wizard Stok would bring up the rear.

We'd practiced twice before arriving, maneuvering closely packed, trying to remain silent. The closer together we stayed, the less spell energy was required. But too close and we stumbled or bumped into each other, making noise.

We dropped everything in a pile except our weapons. Lilly carried my shield so I could keep one hand on my sword's hilt to keep it and the scabbard still. In my other hand I carried my boar spear. I thought about having left my crossbow behind. It offered one, maybe two shots. I'd need more than that, especially if it came to a fight, and my gut told me it would.

I took my place to Enchantress Thulease's right, with Storm Claw to her left. Ahead of me was Flint and behind Dastgir. To Flint's left was Lilly, and to her left walked Flayzin. Directly behind Enchantress Thulease was Wizard Stok and to his left walked Swigopp, looking wide-eyed but determined as he rested the dull edge of his cutlass's blade against his shoulder.

We gently high stepped, climbing over the dune and toward the camp. The less sand we kicked up, the less likely we'd leave a noticeable trail, despite Journeyman Wizard Stok's efforts.

The enemy's three sleeping tents were on the right side, or eastern half of the camp, and the animals sheltering under three broad canvas covers were on the western half. The tents were big enough to hold at least thirty men each, along with some supplies. They were tan and speckled with black and brown, making them appear more like a small dune from a distance.

I was tasked with the tent whose opening faced farthest to the east. That meant I'd be away from the confusion of the animals nearer the other two tents, but I'd also be on my own. I'd have to take out one guard near my assigned tent entrance and probably the guard standing his post on the camp's northwest corner—after cutting the tent straps. And while doing what I could to keep men from emerging. I didn't think the doorway would be the main concern. Men crawling out from under the edges of the collapsed tent would be.

I thought about whispering over my shoulder to Wizard Stok and suggest he might want to bring down the main tent poles, if possible. In planning it was thought that cutting the ropes would topple the support poles. Looking at the tents, each having one center and four corner poles, I wasn't so sure, especially if they were sunk into the sand.

I gritted my teeth and focused on my responsibility. I was just nervous. We'd be out numbered but surprise would be on our side, just like when Enchantress Thulease and I participated in the assault on Fendra Jolain's main temple. We lost a lot of good men and women that day but, comparing it the current situation, our chances of success were better.

The men standing guard wore white flowing shirts and pants, with black leather belts and white garments wrapped around their heads. They were armed with scimitars and falchions, but didn't look very alert and ready to use them. Whether bored or over confident, it was to our advantage.

I saw what Lilly meant by a lot of animals, and why it was difficult for her to count them all crowded under the tents. There were six barrels, probably filled with water near one edge, but still in the shade. Someone would kick them over and empty them.

The senior guard Lilly had warned us about emerged from one of the tents when we were half way to the camp. He used angry gestures while speaking to a few of the men. All the guards stood at attention and appeared more focused.

We kept on with our approach; they didn't notice. The senior guard returned to his tent, the southwest one, angled toward us and away from the animals.

Our objective was just to the right, or east of the senior guard's tent entrance. That would place us just past and centered between two guards, in the wide angle formed by two tents. We'd huddle down before becoming visible so nobody could spot us through either tent's open window flaps.

By the time we got to within twenty yards I was sure one of the guards would hear us, or at least notice the slight discoloration caused by the partially overturned sand. Just when one guard became alert to something amiss, Lilly chucked a rock into the animal tent, striking a mule, causing it to jostle and bray.

Somehow the guards missed the thrown rock's sudden appearance. The resulting noise from upset animals clustered in the herd's center covered our approach and movement between the two guards. It also revealed two handlers who must've been resting on the far side of the enemy's mounts.

The bent light rays, as I'd once seen while on wyvern back, sometimes caused wavering air, like when intense heat rises from a hot stove. Even though we were under the desert's intense heat where such distortions were common, the two nearest guards looked about, sensing something out of the ordinary. Strain spread across Enchantress Thulease's face as she intensified her near breathless chant.

It worked. Lilly's distraction and the enchantress's increased effort got us past the two nearest guards. Our group reached their flank, in their camp, between them and the tents they guarded.

Everyone except for Lilly squatted down, faced away from the enchantress and waited a second for her to end her spell. When Lilly was halfway to the unsuspecting guard, the enchantress whispered with a hint of exhaustion in her voice, "Go."

Everyone split off. Ahead of me Flint went left, I went right, still crouched below the level of the tent windows. Out of the corner of my eye I saw Wizard Stok slashing his engraved scimitar across the southwest guard's neck.

I came around my assigned tent just as the western guard posted outside the entrance turned to see his comrade fall. As he turned, drawing his falchion and yelling a warning, I thrust my spear's tip deep into his throat, just under the chin.

I ignored his wide eyes and crumpling body as I yanked my spear out. I pivoted and slashed with my spear's blade, severing the two braided cords where they attached to the tent's post-supported corner. I didn't wait to see what happened as I stepped over the fallen guard and strode across the gritty sand, watching as the guard posted at the camp's northwest edge drew his scimitar and shouted a warning in his tongue.

Already other shouts and cries announced our attack so, rather than hurling my spear at my prepared opponent, I continued forward, slashing my weapon's tip, severing one of the two cords anchoring the other half of the tent entrance. The guard rushed me while I side-stepped and slashed the second cord near its stake. That put me on the defensive as I back pedaled from my foe's advance. Better to slow anyone joining him before it came to combat.

The guard charged, hollering his shrill battle cry. I stood my ground, now facing the collapsed tent front. My opponent misjudged my courage, expecting me to flee. He fiercely looked me in the eye and brought his scimitar around to slash my neck. I blocked with my spear's shaft before punching him in the nose. My leather and steel-reinforced fist silenced his battle cry.

He staggered back a step or two. Even before blood began flowing from his broken nose I drove my boot up into his crotch. Stepping past him as he crumpled to the ground, I slammed the butt of my spear across his bearded jaw.

He was down, and none too soon. A wild-haired man halfway out from under the collapsed tent looked up at me. He hadn't drawn his scimitar from its scabbard. Nor had the man lifting the tent's bottom to his left. Lumps moving at their back said they had reinforcements.

The wild-haired man dove to his left, exposing his back to my quick spear thrust. I surprised the second man and caught him with a kick to his face.

Shouts and battle cries continued but mostly toward the middle of camp. Braying and wildly neighing mules and horses nearly drowned them out. I guessed most of the enemy was rushing away from me and trying to reach their panicking mounts.

Returning my attention to the wild-haired raider, I stabbed him again as he crawled away, slicing into his thigh and releasing a fountain of blood. Two more desert raiders emerged, these with bared falchions in hand. I figured I was in for trouble with the face-kicked raider regaining his senses. Yet another raider with long black hair rolled out from underneath the tent to the right of the face-kicked raider who was fumbling to draw his scabbarded scimitar.

I charged the enemy nearest me on the left, causing him to give ground and stumble back onto the fallen tent. The second falchion-wielding raider slashed at me, forcing me to give ground before I could counter. He parried. Burly and bigger than me, he grabbed a hold of my spear's shaft the same moment the scimitar-wielder threw a handful of sand in my face. I closed my eyes in time to avoid being blinded. Rather than tug and fight for control of my spear, I stepped close and snapped my head forward into where I thought the burly raider stood. My helmet's steel *thumped* hard against what had to be the raider's chin. I stepped back, shaking my head to rid my face of sand while yanking my spear away from the big raider's grip.

Dodging right, I avoided a falchion thrust and placed the bigger raider between me and my falchion attacker while I raised my spear to fend off the scimitar-wielder.

Before his scimitar struck the raider collapsed with a grunt. The long-haired raider—a woman still on the ground—had kicked him, driving her sandaled heels into the back of his knees. She rolled away, arms obviously bound by ropes behind her back.

Even as I slashed the blade of my spear across the fallen scimitar-wielder face, the woman shouted in Sea Spittle, "Free me!"

Fear and desperation hung in her voice, but I didn't have time to do anything for her. I pivoted and ducked in time to avoid a blow to my head.

In addition to panicked animals fleeing the camp and continued shouts mixed with shrill battle cries, smoke filled the air. All of this was going on beyond the two falchion-wielding raiders closing on me. Blood dripped into the burly raider's black beard. His bloody grin lacked several bottom teeth, leaving it less menacing. He moved left while the tall, thin raider swung wide right, trying to get behind me.

I gave ground, keeping track of both. They could sidestep faster than I could backpedal, so I charged the burly raider. He stood his ground, earning a gash across his ribs. I got slashed from behind, leaving a deep slice in my right arm just above the elbow. Rather than turn to face the foe attacking me from behind, I pressed my attack on the wounded one in front of me.

A piercing whistle sounded, signaling everyone with Enchantress Thulease to retreat and regroup behind the dune. There was no way I could break off and survive. I ducked while driving forward, earning a falchion cut that *clanged* off my helmet. I dodged, pulling away with more enemy blood on my spear tip—but not fast enough to avoid a second attack from behind. This time the falchion blade bit deep into my hip.

I'd crippled the burly raider, having severed the tendons in his left knee. But I was now bleeding from two wounds and facing an uninjured foe.

The long-haired woman behind me shouted something. My foe ignored her. He didn't ignore the sling stone striking his shoulder. It knocked him enough off balance that I managed to lunge forward and pierce his stomach.

The pain shooting down my wounded arm and hip caused me to stumble, but I continued to drive my spear forward, up to the crossbar, ducking and taking his weak falchion strike across the back of my helmet.

Dropping my spear as I landed on the wounded raider, I drew my boot dirk. He locked his hands around my throat. My high leather collar slowed his stranglehold. We rolled across the hot sand, battling until his grip slackened. Gasping for air, I pulled my thumb from his bloody eye socket and my dirk from his ribs, and staggered to my feet.

An arm's length away stood the long-haired woman, wrists bleeding, gripping a bloody scimitar. "Your people are retreating," she said in Sea Spittle. "Let me help and go with you."

Lilly raced toward me. A bleeding camel limped between us, temporarily blocking her from my sight.

"No, Lilly!" I shouted, picking up my spear. "Go back!"

The young woman, she couldn't have been much older than our healer, held out a blood-covered hand, glancing nervously back toward the nearby tents and fiery chaos.

"Drop your blade," I said in Sea Spittle.

She did without hesitation.

"Okay," I said, looking toward the dune. "That way."

As I started to limp, she put her shoulder under my wounded right arm and took weight off my slashed and bleeding hip.

Lilly sprinted past us, red-stained rapier in hand. She didn't question the woman helping me. I turned to help Lilly, but the woman dragged me forward. I had to keep my legs going or we'd both go down. Swigopp raced toward us, riding bareback on a gray stallion.

"Lilly!" I shouted over my shoulder.

The sailor pulled up in front of us. He hopped off his mount and flung the reins at me. "Go," he said. "I'll get Lilly." Just beyond, behind him charged Flayzin on his own stallion, grim-faced with scarred shield and blood-stained sword held ready. He wasn't going to stop, either.

The woman let go of me and locked the fingers of her hands together. "Step up, soldier," she ordered.

I looked to see Lilly fighting for her life with three raiders surrounding her. Swigopp with his cutlass was almost there and Flayzin right behind.

"Now!" shouted the woman. "They will save your woman."

"No," I said, turning toward the battle.

She yanked my spear from me and slapped me across the face. "We go!"

I reached for my sword with my left hand to draw it.

She grabbed the reins of the nervous horse before it fled and slammed the butt of my spear in the sand next to her feet. "Don't be a fool. They risk their life, so wounded, you might escape."

Being named a fool made me think. Maybe she was right. Flayzin on horseback, with Lilly and the sailor could take three of them without me. "Okay," I said, "help me up."

I didn't realize how weak I was, but we managed. She handed me the reins and slapped the horse's rump. "Ha!" she shouted.

I leaned forward, trying not to fall off and somehow made it to the dune. As my mount climbed it, I looked back. Flayzin rode with Lilly seated in front of him. Flint came about on a sturdy mule, holding the reins of a spare mount trailing behind him. Swigopp and the woman climbed on it and all five galloped through the sand toward the dune. Scattered arrows rose from the camp, sailing their direction. All fell wide or short.

When I made it over the dune, Enchantress Thulease took hold of the reins and looked at me. Stok, next to the enchantress, handed her a bandage. She was tall enough to wrap my arm even though I remained mounted.

The earth wizard examined my hip. "Can you heal this?" he asked me.

I heard him but didn't put meaning to his words.

"He's lost a lot of blood and is going into shock," Enchantress Thulease said. "He carries bark powder in his belt pouch. Spread it in his hip wound."

She reached up, removed my helmet and cupped my face with both hands, looking me straight in the eye. "Now, Mercenary! Stop your bleeding."

What she said made sense to me. My arm ached and stung. So did my hip.

"Now, Flank Hawk. Begin your chant. Heal yourself."

At the barked order, I did. Recalling a summer afternoon, near the brook with my sister, practicing the chant she worked hard to teach me. I did, seeing the whorl of energy beyond normal sight, instinctively knowing which vibrating ribbon to summon, to peel away and direct into my hip.

Sharp pain flashed behind my eyes as the ribbon shot into the wound, binding, healing blood vessels and flesh. The pain I recognized. I was healing and could do more—a little more. I found and peeled away a second, smaller ribbon, sent it into my stinging, aching hip.

I heard Lilly's voice and Flayzin's orders. Slowing my chant, I backed my mind out of the whorl of energy, shook my head and looked around.

Stok examined my hip before tightening a wide wrap, pressing a folded bandage against the wound. While he did so, he said to Enchantress Thulease. "Good enough for now."

I took a drink from a waterskin the enchantress held to my lips.

"Some of them are mounting up," warned Swigopp, sitting on his mule, spying just over the dune's lip.

Healer Ammond had already arrived with our mounts. When he saw the smoke, I recalled, he was supposed to bring our mounts. He sat atop a camel with Storm Claw lying across his knees. Was she unconscious? Or was she dead?

The long-haired desert woman vaulted onto the back of my mount, startling it. She grabbed hold of me before I fell off. "I can ride with him," she said in Sea Spittle. I think she was trying to speak to Enchantress

Thulease. "I won't let him fall."

Flayzin nodded, moving up next to us on his mount, taking the reins from Stok and handing them to her. "No time to argue," he said. "Flank Hawk, hold onto the mane for now."

With that, and everyone mounted, we galloped across the hot sand. Thirty of the enemy pursued us, a quarter mile behind as the late afternoon sun blazed down.

Hard as they rode, we rode harder, not allowing them to gain. My arm and hip hurt, throbbing in tandem with my mount's galloping stride. After fifteen minutes I switched to my saddled mule. Others switched off too, selecting fresher mounts that hadn't carried anyone.

Storm Claw was alive but unconscious. Ammond had done what he could but she was far from fully healed.

After switching mounts we outpaced our pursuers, eventually putting a half mile between us.

After another two hours, they turned back, giving up the chase.

CHAPTER 14

The clear night's moon and stars offered enough light for me to watch Lilly and Wizard Stok dig out our buried equipment. I'd lost a lot of blood and felt weak. Labor like digging would reopen my hip and arm wounds, so I laid on my back about fifteen feet away, listening to them talk.

"You were good at finding where our stuff was buried," Lilly said. "Think ya can find those raiders' gold just as easy?"

Stok leaned on his shovel a second. "Dastgir guided me so that I was close enough."

Lilly grunted, "Uhh, huh," as she continued shoveling.

Our guide had to backtrack once to get back to our camp, but I'd never have found it. I wasn't much of a tracker, and there weren't any landmarks like streams or mountains to focus on. Just rock outcroppings. And for the most part one looked much like any other, especially from a distance. And the small dunes, they changed shape and shifted with the wind.

After scooping out a few more shovel fulls, the earth wizard said, "Wind did obscure our trail as we attempted to backtrack. Even you found retracing our route difficult, Lilly."

"I'm a scout, not a tracker. Maybe we need a better guide."

The journeyman wizard began digging again. "Maybe you should bring that subject up to the enchantress."

"Did already," Lilly said, tossing her shovel full of sand farther than she needed to.

They worked in silence for a moment until Lilly asked, "Flank Hawk, you think we'll set up camp here or move on with our gear?"

I thought a moment. One of the desert raiders Enchantress Thulease magically marked had been part of the group that chased us for a couple of hours. By her latest estimate, he was back at their destroyed camp. The other marked raider had remained at the camp, and hadn't moved any distance since our attack. My guess was that we'd killed him.

Unless they had an enchanter, witch, or seer able to spot the magical marks, we had a huge advantage. The surviving marked raider would likely be among those that would take after our trail tomorrow. If they did, Enchantress Thulease would notice and we'd have a half-day's travel head start.

"They're not after us," I said to Lilly. "I don't know if Storm Claw will make it even if we don't move. We'll camp here, especially if there's water to be had." We were almost out.

Wizard Stok moved to another spot and began widening their hole. "When the enchantress is revitalized, I think we'll be able to draw some water up again."

"So," Lilly said, also working to widen the hole, "if our apprentice guide can get us close enough to the raider camp when we're coming back north, after finding the Sleeping Sage…" She heaved a shovel full of rocky sand and grinned. "Me and you'll be digging for gold, wizard."

The earth wizard shrugged. "It is possible."

"Why?" asked Lilly. "You think they'll find it? How deep did ya bury it?"

"Three feet beneath the surface," he said. "Then I shifted it at least four feet east, under what I believed to be several barrels of water. I also believe the enchantress caused those barrels to drain."

"Ha!" Lilly said. "So they'll have extra trouble finding it, even if they think to dig." After a few more shovel loads, she asked, "So why don't you go work in a mine or something, finding silver or gold?"

"It is far more difficult to isolate such elements beneath the earth, than it is when the elements are resting above ground."

"Maybe when you become tough-enough of a wizard?"

"Am I to assume you will then change your expertise from scouting to mining, and sign on with me?"

"Why not? Flank Hawk could stay a mercenary. You could hire him to guard our finds."

Wizard Stok set his shovel aside and began brushing gritty sand and rocks off a section of canvas he'd uncovered. "And possibly use his skills to heal any minor accidents that might occur while you learn your new trade?"

At the mention of mercenaries and healing, all three of us glanced to where Enchantress Thulease and Healer Ammond stood. At their feet Flint sat on the ground with his back leaning against a saddle. On the ground next to him Storm Claw laid flat out on a blanket, unconscious. The long, hard ride hadn't helped Flint's throat wound any, and it weakened Storm Claw even more.

She'd suffered several cuts equal to mine, but also a chest wound. Ammond said the scimitar thrust had pierced her lung. Although he'd healed some of the tissue around the wound, he said her lung had collapsed and blood remained inside. I'd seen soldiers suffer similar wounds on the battlefield. I'd observed Storm Claw for a few minutes after they laid her down on the ground. Her chest appeared offset and she worked hard for every breath. And the blood that had drained from her nose as we rode, it reminded me of soldiers that died even when a healer as skilled as Ammond was on hand.

There was nothing I could do for Storm Claw so, while Captain Flayzin, Dastgir, Swigopp, and the long-haired woman named Nura unsaddled and worked with our mounts, I decided to join Lilly and Wizard

Stok. Enchantress Thulease and Healer Ammond didn't need to worry about me. Storm Claw's life was the one at risk.

"That scimitar master's the one that got her," Lilly said. "Same one that almost got you, Flank Hawk, when they first attacked and surprised us."

I recalled. He'd cut my leg deep and, if they hadn't retreated when they did, he probably would've finished me.

Lilly said, "I'd just struck a match and lit one of their tents when he came at Storm Claw. Slash, parry—parry, slice—duck, stab, and she was down."

"What happened then?" asked Stok.

"Captain Flayzin saw those of us trying to get the animals scattered were in trouble. He charged over and him and the scimitar guy clashed. I didn't see exactly what happened 'cause I was fighting too, but less than ten seconds later Flayzin had disarmed the scimitar guy and ran him through with his sword." Lilly shook her head. "Took the fight outta the rest of them that saw it."

"I heard Captain Flayzin was an exceptional swordsman," Wizard Stok said.

"I wouldn't wanna fight him," Lilly said. As soon as she said it, her eyes shot over to me.

Reminding me that a fight with Flayzin loomed in my future wasn't really needed.

The next evening, an hour before sundown, we were moving south despite Storm Claw's weakening condition. Wizard Stok said after their last effort to draw up water there wasn't sufficient subsurface moisture in the area to warrant another attempt. While we could travel as little as an hour and possibly find another suitable area to seek water, once we began moving, going farther wouldn't do much to further weaken Storm Claw.

We were too far south to reach Tripoli and seek a more powerful healer for Storm Claw, so the plan was to find a suitable spot for water and allow Enchantress Thulease to rest after combining her magic with Wizard Stok to draw it up. Then she intended to channel what she could of her magical strength to Healer Ammond so that he might attempt to repair Storm Claw's internal wound. While he did this Flayzin would attempt to re-inflate her collapsed lung.

Ammond had spent time examining Storm Claw and magically probing her internal wound. He admitted his limited training and ability in that area wasn't really adequate, but that he'd do whatever he was able.

Enchantress Thulease used a medication on Storm Claw, one of several her husband had prepared. It put Storm Claw to sleep so she wouldn't suffer during our trek in search of water.

Everybody but Nura walked ahead of me. Captain Flayzin had wrapped the head of my spear so that its shaft could be safely used as part of a stretcher. The short tent poles, wrapped and lashed together, made up the other support for the canvas tent half that cradled the slowly dying mercenary.

At the moment, Flayzin and Lilly carried Storm Claw. I couldn't with my arm and hip only partially healed, so I, along with Nura, each led a string of pack and riding mules.

The young native of this region smiled at me. Her teeth were white, like her flowing shirt and sturdy long skirt. Somehow the corner her upper left eye-tooth had been chipped. It was on the same side as a thin scar that ran along her nose down to her lip.

She was younger than me, but her brown eyes didn't hold innocence of youth. Her smile was friendly, yet I wasn't sure it was completely sincere.

"Thank you for your words of support to the enchantress who leads you."

Her command of Sea Spittle was better than mine. Besides Storm Claw, only Flayzin and I spoke the trade tongue. Dastgir and Ammond, along with Storm Claw, spoke Nura's native tongue.

I smiled back at Nura. "I told Enchantress Thulease what happened."

"She respects your opinion, Flank Hawk."

"Captain Flayzin spoke on your behalf as well."

Nura smiled and looked away, toward the setting sun. "She respects his opinion too."

After a few moments of silence, I said, "If you hadn't kicked that man down, and help me onto the mule, I might not have made it." I took a deep breath, recalling the moment, not being able to help Lilly. "As it was, I almost didn't make it."

"I never apologized for striking you." She looked up at me and said before I could say anything, "I am sorry."

I shrugged. The slap across my face got me to think straight. "You shouldn't be."

Nura told us about the desert raiders. She called them marauders. Many of the men from the region's tribes left to fight as mercenaries, mostly for Fendra Jolain. That left an emptiness of good men and allowed the marauder gangs to grow and thrive. One of the marauding gangs had scattered and killed most of her family. She'd just been traded to the marauders we fought. She said a camel was the price, and she didn't have to say what they bought and used her for.

I didn't know what to make of her. It didn't show, but deep down, did their forced bedding—rape—bother her? I thought of my mother and sisters, and how they'd have responded, and if they'd have survived. Lilly, they'd have had to kill her.

If Nura could bury all of that, what else might she feel? What else might she be hiding? Was her story completely true? I figured that was why Flayzin recommended that *if* she joined us, she would do so unarmed. And remain unarmed. I agreed.

"You're a healer and a soldier?"

Nura's question snapped me out of my thoughts. I nodded.

"How is that possible? I've never seen a healer carry, let alone use a weapon. Like Healer Ammond. He carries none."

"I've always been both. I've never really worked at being a healer, other than when my sister taught me, when I was young. Before I joined Pine Ridge's—my home town's—militia. After that I became a mercenary."

"What about the necklace you wear, the crystal with blood in it? You handed it over to Healer Ammond, didn't you? Does that allow you to heal, or to fight? Or to do both?"

It took effort not to reach for the spot on my chest where my amulet containing the fallen angel's blood once again hung. I didn't know she'd observed me lending it to Ammond. The effort failed; the amulet didn't assist his spellcasting.

I looked at her out of the corner of my eye, wondering if Nura secretly understood the Mainland tongue. So I asked her in Mainland, "Why did you choose to stay with us rather than take a mule and water and head north to Tripoli?"

She was silent for a second, then replied in Sea Spittle, "I don't understand what you said."

"Oh, sorry," I said, trying to sound innocent, and repeated my question in Sea Spittle.

"One person traveling is vulnerable. While I don't know why you're traveling south, the enchantress said you'd return to Tripoli's ports. I am thankful you've allowed me to join you, and will eventually get there and seek any of my family who may have escaped and survived."

"Why were you bound with rope?" It'd been asked before, and Dastgir told me her answer.

"I'd gotten a knife and stabbed a guard while attempting to escape. That happened before I was traded for a camel. They warned the marauders who thought I might try it again."

"Why wouldn't they expect you to escape, or at least try?"

She shrugged. "I expected them to kill me. Maybe they were going to, but wanted the camel more."

Nura stared at me while we continued to walk. I watched Lilly and Dastgir mount and ride ahead. She asked, "You don't trust me, do you?"

"More than some I've travelled with."

"The scout, Lilly, doesn't trust me either."

I laughed. "She's suspicious of everyone."

"Not you."

"No, we've seen a lot together. Survived a lot together."

"There's something different about her."

I smiled and looked over my shoulder at the mules plodding along behind us. "There is."

Nura looked over her shoulder and checked her string of mules. "What is it?"

"She'll tell you when she wants to, or Enchantress Thulease tells her to tell you. Or you'll eventually figure it out."

"I didn't think you'd tell me. Of everyone, I can tell you two are the closest, except for maybe Captain Flayzin and the enchantress he serves."

"You're pretty observant."

"It is what's kept me alive."

"You know a lot about deserts too. That's kept you alive."

"I am reasonably certain that's also why the enchantress accepted me as part of her company."

We walked on for several minutes in silence. I began thinking about my family. My father would be walking home after a long day's work at the Royal Stables, expecting a meal. My mother would be finishing up the evening meal, explaining something about preparing it to Katchia. Rin would be racing home from his job at one of the wyvern roosts, trying to think of a way to talk my father into playing a card game later that night. My mind then shifted to Major Jadd and Sergeant Drux. I wondered if they'd returned from their mission supporting the Faxtinian Coalition, driving out remnants of Fendra Jolain's forces. The wars against the Necromancer King and the Goddess of Healing had decimated Keesee's serpent cavalry. It'd take decades of breeding and training new mounts to rebuild. Until then there'd never be enough cavalrymen and their dragon mounts.

Nura interrupted my thoughts with a comment. "For a moment there, you appeared happy. Then a scowl crossed your face. And remained."

I was hesitant to mention my family to Nura; she'd recently lost hers. I did anyway. "I was thinking about what my family would be doing now. And then wondering about Major Jadd and his aft-guard, Sergeant Drux."

"You don't smile often enough. Are you worried about your fellow mercenaries?"

"Jadd and Drux? They're serpent cavalrymen, serving King Tobias. They'll be okay."

"You've seen a lot of death? You and Lilly?"

I nodded. "We have. I'm sure you have, too."

"I've witnessed my share," Nura said. "Not all to the scimitar. This is a hard land. Unforgiving."

"It is," I said. "Do you ever get used to being thirsty?"

"No," she said. "At least I never have. When I'm thirsty I try to think about something else."

"That only works for so long."

"That is true," Nura said. "You're worried about the woman

mercenary on the stretcher? Facing another death?"

I recalled the time a pack of dire wolves surrounded Lilly, and the wounds I suffered saving her. She nearly died, but when she shifted back from her were-muskrat form, most of her injuries healed. It took a week for me to heal. It's different for a healer directing magic into himself as opposed to others. I can do more than stop my own bleeding. Not a lot, but over time my healing ability was enough to make a difference.

Storm Claw wasn't a healer and wasn't Lilly. Her chances weren't good, and odds were I'd be burying yet another comrade.

I didn't want to talk about it, so instead I pointed ahead and said, "Lilly and our guide return." Lilly was riding high in her saddle. "They must've already found someplace where Enchantress Thulease and Wizard Stok might reach water."

Storm Claw wasn't getting better, and wouldn't without taking a risk. Even when she was conscious, she wasn't thinking clearly. The brief instances when she spoke, she rambled in unclear directions. It wasn't like her at all. Some of her confusion might have been the medicine Enchantress Thulease had given her, but some of it was certainly due to her blood loss and weak breathing.

Healer Ammond determined most of her left lung had collapsed—it wouldn't take in air. His examinations, some with magic probing, indicated that there was air pressure outside the lung, keeping it from taking in and holding air. It'd happened either when or shortly after the scimitar pierced Storm Claw's chest and lung.

The plan was simple and straight forward, yet delicate. While Storm Claw was under the last dose of sleep-causing medicine, Enchantress Thulease would insert a hardened leather tube, created and smoothened by her magic, into the cavity around Storm Claw's failing lung. After which she'd draw the air out. My job was to heal the incision as much as I could immediately after the tube was withdrawn. Swigopp would tell me when to begin.

While Enchantress Thulease drew the air out, Ammond was to guide her using his knowledge of internal organs and sensing as best he could with his magic. Flayzin would hold a larger tube in Storm Claw's mouth and pinch her nose shut. Lilly would breathe forcefully into the tube to inflate the failing lung. Its puncture having already been healed, she didn't have to worry about reopening the wound, unless Enchantress Thulease's tube went too far in.

All the while, Flint, Nura and Dastgir would stand guard and watch the animals.

Ammond said the combined effort should take less than fifteen minutes. After that we'd hope for the best.

We had enough water for two days, with the prospect of drawing more from the ground. If Storm Claw didn't recover, we'd move on. Both Dastgir and Nura talked about nomadic tribes that might cross paths with us. Some were violently hostile to anyone using or associated with magic, but even they might have the knowledge and skills to save Storm Claw. Supreme Enchantress Thulease said, "Even if that is a bridge which logic dictates is best uncrossed, if the need remains and the opportunity presents itself, only then will we be in the proper position from which to ascertain the appropriate path. Speculation upon it now only raises unnecessary worry which will consume our thoughts and sap our objectivity, and imperil our survival."

The way the enchantress spoke reminded me of Grand Wizard Seelain, when she was preparing to do something risky and not necessarily in her own self-interest. It surprised me that Enchantress Thulease might risk her life and, by extension, her daughter's life, on a chance to save Storm Claw. Then again, maybe she had no intention of risking her life, or our lives, for Storm Claw, but spoke only to keep our hope intact even if our combined effort failed.

I sat, slowly chanting, my mind's eye observing the ribbons of energy surging around me. It seemed like I'd been there, waiting for at least an hour, but it probably had been less than ten minutes.

A slight pressure on my shoulder and distant-sounding whisper in my ear, "Flank Hawk, time to heal the incision," signaled for me to begin. I peeled away one of the ribbons from the maelstrom of flexing, wavering, ever-moving ribbons and directed it into Storm Claw's fresh wound. The magical energy merged with the white oak bark sprinkled on top of the deep but narrow cut. I managed a second, sending it down into the incision, stemming most of the blood flow. Then I slowed my chant, backed my mind out of the maelstrom, and took a deep breath while trying to ignore the sharp pain behind my eyes.

I looked about, from person to person huddled under the large tent formed by tying the smaller ones together. Healer Ammond's eyes sagged with weariness, but he caught my gaze and smiled, as did Enchantress Thulease.

I listened.

Storm Claw's breathing was steady, and deeper.

Maybe it'd worked.

Time would tell.

CHAPTER 15

The trek south soon fell into a routine, especially after Storm Claw's strength began to return. She quickly got over her anger mixed with embarrassment at being overmatched and easily defeated by the scimitar master.

Flayzin helped the process along. He didn't know much about wielding Storm Claw's fighting sticks, but he practiced with the recovering mercenary, employing the scimitar attacks used against her. That enabled Storm Claw to develop and practice counters to such attacks.

I spent much of our travel time warding the rear of our line. Nura rode next to me when she wasn't assisting Swigopp and Flint with the pack-laden mules, and I wasn't in company with Enchantress Thulease. Instead of arms training, I learned some words and useful phrases in Nura's tongue. In return she learned some Mainland or, as translated in her tongue, North Words.

Lilly did the same with Dastgir. She shared some of the Crusader tongue while he taught her the language of the Southern Continent, or one of its many variations. That occurred when they weren't exchanging knowledge each had of tracking and nature signs.

It was much easier to carry on conversations as the barren drylands gave way to areas with some scrub plants, and occasional thorny bushes and stunted trees. Water became more accessible to Enchantress Thulease and Wizard Stok. The land also provided limited grazing for our horses, mules, and camels.

We did see tracks and signs of several nomadic tribes and swung wide around their paths to avoid any possible conflict. Maybe we passed by unnoticed, or maybe we were simply ignored. It was probably the former as both Dastgir and Nura said the nomadic tribes reacted to spellcasters with swift violence.

Even with the change in habitat, there remained little for us to hunt and we were forced to slaughter the weakest mule. I'd never eaten mule, or horse. It might've been my imagination, but the meat's yellow fat gave it a grimmer taste. Lilly and Nura disagreed, but Flint and Stok stood with me on the issue. Still, Flint, Stok and I ate like everyone else to keep our strength. Storm Claw claimed whatever the taste, that it enabled our survival was of prime importance.

Despite the easing of the dryness, the sun still beat down during the day and limited our travel to early morning and late afternoon until just before dark. Enchantress Thulease did her best to mask her frustration at our plodding pace, a pace that often included walking next to our mounts. But we had to preserve our mounts' strength and health for the return trip. Quick glances and frowns said I wasn't the only one to notice the enchantress's mood, although nobody brought it up, even in quiet conversation beyond the enchantress's earshot.

Once again under a cloudless sky we rode south. An hour after breaking our camp just before sunrise Lilly took her mount up the side of a dune-like hillock in the otherwise flat terrain.

Nura, riding at the rear with me, commented in Sea Spittle, "Although I was prepared, I still found it unnerving to see your scout in the form of a giant rat."

The full moon had shone in the previous night's sky and called out Lilly's beast. Due to the unfamiliar terrain, Lilly in her beast form stayed close to our camp. Far enough away so she didn't unsettle the more high-strung mules, but close enough to be framed by the moon's silvery glow.

I waited a few breaths before replying, recalling my brush with lycanthropy after getting bit while battling a werebat. "Sometimes it still surprises me," I said. "I don't think of her as the beast, yet I know it always lurks within her."

We continued riding in silence. I looked behind and about before returning my gaze to Lilly atop the hillock. She removed her hat and urged her mount to a gallop back toward the front of our line, toward Enchantress Thulease and Flayzin.

I said, "She's spotted something of interest."

Nura said, "Why don't you ride ahead, Flank Hawk, and learn what your friend has seen that excites her so."

I scanned the area. "You're okay back here?"

Nura smirked at me. "I assure you, I am."

Nura's way of saying things sometimes reminded me of Grand Wizard Seelain, hinting that she'd had some formal education. The scrub brush-filled terrain held no apparent danger so I circled around the lines of pack mules and came up next to Flayzin on his mount as he and Enchantress Thulease waited for Lilly to reach them and report.

After hearing what Lilly had to say and listening in on what little discussion there was between Lilly, Dastgir and Enchantress Thulease, I returned to the rear of the march where Nura stood expectantly next to her mule.

"Lilly spotted a swath of green in the distance," I said. "And a bluish-brown expanse just beyond it."

Nura smiled broadly. "The lake you seek?"

I nodded and she remounted her mule.

"Do you think the enchantress will now share with me what you hope to find around the lake?"

I shrugged my shoulders. "Does the lake have a name?"

“Chaad,” she said. “I have heard tell of it, although I’ve never seen it.”

“Looks like you will.” I kicked my stirrups to get Thunder moving south once again, before scanning the terrain behind us, and then glancing at the rising sun. “Lilly estimates sometime after our afternoon rest.”

I thought the terrain would have more shrubs and even more than just two twisted and stunted trees as we approached the lake. But it didn’t, and during our noon rest, Enchantress Thulease and Wizard Stok cast their combination of spells to draw water from beneath the parched, rocky ground. There was enough to refill our waterskins after allowing our mounts to drink their fill.

Standing on the back of his camel, both Dastgir and Lilly were able to see the trees. All I could see from atop my mule was a dark line across the brown landscape. It might’ve been green, but the sun made it hard to tell.

Lilly saw me squint long and hard before shaking my head and wiping the dust from my sweaty brow. She walked back to me and held out her brass spyglass. “Here, Flank Hawk. Stand on your saddle. Me and Nura will hold Thunder.” She rolled her eyes when I shook my head. “After nothing but this,” she said, sweeping her hand to emphasize the barren land, “that lake looks like a fancy dream. ’Least it does to me.”

“I’ll see it soon enough, Lilly.”

She laughed and patted Thunder’s neck. Nura laughed too.

“You better get back to scouting,” I said, looking ahead. “The enchantress will want to reach the lake by suppertime.”

“Two hours, if we push our mounts,” Lilly said, looking over her shoulder toward Enchantress Thulease, consulting with Dastgir and Flayzin. “No reason not to. Just gave all our mounts a good drink. Lake water ahead, and there’s certain to be grass or reeds for them to eat.”

She offered her spyglass to Nura. “You wanna see?”

Nura shook her head. “No, thank you, Scout Lilly,” she said in Mainland, and finished in Sea Spittle, “I am already impatient enough.”

I translated for Lilly, who said, “Okay,” and turned with a puzzled grin to join Dastgir at the head of our march. “Don’t complain later,” she said over her shoulder. “I gave you your chance. Now those riding at the back’ll be sure to see it last.”

The mounts and pack animals must’ve smelled moisture in the air, especially Dastgir’s camel because their plodding pace picked up not long after our noon rest. Soon everyone could see the green tree line, and not long after that the grass and scrub bush terrain leading up to it. Lilly even announced she spotted birds flying beyond the trees.

It was then that the mules, and then Dastgir’s camel slowed, and then stopped. Thunder’s ears perked up, breathing in air with nostrils flared.

“What is it?” Nura asked.

Swigopp and Flint cursed as they fought to keep their strings of pack mules from bolting.

I shrugged and looked about before urging Thunder forward. "Watch our rear," I said.

I couldn't get my mount to go more than a dozen yards forward, so I returned to Nura, gave her the reins and dismounted. I slung my crossbow and proceeded to the front of our line with spear in hand. I didn't don my helmet, thinking I might need my hearing more than its protection.

By the time I got up to Enchantress Thulease and Flayzin, Lilly and Dastgir had already finished speaking with them.

"Shouldn't take me long," Lilly said, dismounting and handing her mount's reins up to Dastgir.

"I'll go with you," I offered.

Lilly grinned, met my gaze and then those of Enchantress Thulease and Captain Flayzin's. "Nahh, Flank Hawk. Your job's to protect the enchantress. Mine's to scout."

I was certain she meant her words as a slight to Flayzin, but what she said was the truth.

"Be careful," I said.

Enchantress Thulease added, "Again, remain wary and take no unnecessary risks."

Lilly turned and trotted off. I heard her mutter, "We've been risking this whole journey." I'm sure the enchantress heard her as well.

Nobody said much as Lilly left the rocky sand and moved into the scrub grass. Enchantress Thulease used Lilly's spyglass to follow our scout's movements as she shifted left and right, occasionally kneeling or hunching over to examine the ground before moving on. Several times Lilly stood still, listening and probably sniffing the air.

After a while Lilly came trotting back carrying something shaped like a quarter moon, maybe a little thicker than my forearm, with a broad knob on one end and what looked like a narrow spike on the other. It was about two feet in length, reddish brown and, from the way Lilly carried it, not as heavy as it looked.

I'd seen plenty of what she carried over the past month—the tail of a scorpion—but none had been larger than half the length of my little finger.

The mules, horses, and camels shied away from Lilly as she lifted the scorpion barb up to show the enchantress.

"Saw two of these. Maybe there's more. There's a claw too, but no body or anything. Can't see where anything dragged'em away. No signs in the grass, and the sand and rocks appear upturned and blown about. It's not exactly like anything I've seen before." She took a few steps back and heaved the tail barb away from us, causing some of the mounts to settle a bit. "Could be they got injured and ran off. Maybe through the grass, at least one from the tracks I saw."

Flayzin commented, "What might be able to disarm and chase them off is of great concern to me."

"Scorpions are normally solitary," Dastgir said. "At least the small ones."

I agreed. "I've seen some of the small ones fight each other. Different types. Maybe that's what happened here?"

Lilly shrugged. Enchantress Thulease looked about and appeared to be deep in thought, then back over her shoulder. "If one or several went straight ahead, we may not want to proceed in that direction."

"What bothers me is the missing bodies," Flayzin said. "I doubt much could, or would, eat their carapace shell."

"If it was one of those trap door spiders," Lilly said, "it'd have to've been awful big."

Nura had convinced me to eat several small scorpions after she'd removed their poisoned tail barbs. They weren't filling, and tasted like burnt pea soup and bitter sassafras bark. Nasty.

"A dragon could eat the bodies," I said. "Maybe fly off with the carcass too."

"That's it," Lilly said. "I smelled something that reminded me of a wyvern a little, but mustier. I thought it might've been one of the giant scorpions." Lilly looked up at Dastgir, still on his camel. "You know of any dragons out here that might eat scorpions?"

"None that fly," he replied. "But there's a lake ahead." He scratched behind his ear in thought. "I've heard of land drakes, but never seen one. For hundreds of miles around Tripoli they were hunted down, and all nests destroyed. None have been sighted for decades."

I pointed to the back of our line. "Maybe ask Nura?"

Enchantress Thulease agreed. "That may be wise, Flank Hawk. Relieve her of watch at the end of our train and send her forward to me." Lilly nodded in agreement while Dastgir squinted his eyes before looking away.

I did as the enchantress requested and waited about ten minutes while she questioned and discussed the situation with Nura. When Nura returned to the rear she said, "It may be a land drake, or it might be a sphinx. In either case, we're going to give this area wide berth before approaching the lake."

I'd encountered a sphinx once, a warden of one of the Colonel of the West's military outposts. It had the wings of an eagle, the face of a man and the body of a lion. Its shoulders stood higher than I could reach with my upraised hand. The sphinx I met was a smart, powerful, arrogant creature. Not one I'd imagine living out in the wilds.

I knew some about dragons—fire-breathing reds, acid-spitting blacks, steam-spewing grays, and a little about frost-breathing whites. I'd never heard of a land drake, which I figured to be a sort of dragon. I wasn't sure which would be worse to encounter, a territorial sphinx or a wild dragon.

"What do you know about land drakes?" I asked Nura as I watched Lilly direct her mount toward the east, leading the way for the rest of us.

Nura settled into her saddle. "Not much, other than they're big, will eat just about anything, and are hard to kill."

"What do they breathe?"

"Air," she said with a straight face, then smiled. "I do not know, but it's said that they can drive both man and beast mad with terror."

"Oh," I said, wondering about what power, maybe even some sort of magic, might do that. Driving man and beast mad with terror? I knew how big, intimidating, and dangerous dragons were—at least those I'd been around. Intimidating size seemed more likely than magic. Wyverns were sort of like dragons, more like a cross between a dragon and a vulture. They didn't breathe fire or spit streams of acid or anything, but the females had barbed tails like scorpions.

After a minute or two of silence, while we rode and observed not only the terrain around us but the sky above as well, I proceeded to tell Nura a little about the sphinx I'd once encountered.

I'd only gotten to describe the sphinx's size and color when the mules at the front of the line stopped and began braying. Thunder's nose flared and ears perked. I held the reins firm and ready, thinking he might try to bolt. Ahead, Lilly's mount bucked and reared, throwing her.

I jumped off my mount. Nura did the same. I handed her my reins as I searched the sky. "Trouble's near," I said.

Nura unstrapped my helmet from my saddlebag and tossed it to me. Donning it and, with spear in hand, I sprinted forward, past Flint and Swigopp, both struggling to calm their lines of pack mules. Storm Claw struggled to calm her mount while Ammond fell to the ground, but kept a firm grip on his mule's reins.

Flint shouted above the din, "What is it, Flank Hawk?"

I didn't slow down but yelled back, "Don't know. Be ready." Ready for what? I had no idea. I just knew my duty was to stand between Enchantress Thulease and whatever was raising panic with our mules and horses.

Wizard Stok stood, holding his mount's reins as it tried to pull away. He shouted to Enchantress Thulease over the panicking mules' neighing and stomping, "I sense earth magic!"

I made it to Enchantress Thulease who was listening to the earth wizard.

"Weak," he said, pointing Lilly's direction. "But out there."

As if his words had summoned power from the earth, sand and rock roiled and mounded up between us and Lilly. Far closer to her. Until that moment she'd been pulling hard against her resisting mount's reins, trying to drag it back our direction.

The beast that emerged from the unsettled earth was a land drake. Its immense size and slate-like brown scales said it couldn't be anything else.

Earth Wizard Stok's feeling of earth magic reminded me of the first time I faced griffins. Grand Wizard Seelain said they held an elemental spirit, weak but a part of them. It was probably the same with the land drake, but with earth instead of air. That meant Journeyman Wizard Stok's magic would be less effective.

I gripped my spear and broke to the right, around the rearing mules gone mad with fear, then charged at the land-bound dragon, giving it a target other than Enchantress Thulease, and also making it impossible to catch us all with any breath weapon it might have.

The land drake reminded me of a thick-scaled brown iguana, except for its size. It must've weighed more than eight prize bulls. Its neck was several times longer than what might be expected for an iguana, but nowhere near as long or serpentine as a red or black dragon's. The land drake's head was massive with three horns. Two were bull-like and swept back with a knob end instead of a pointed tip. The central horn began just behind the land drake's nostrils and thickened as it extended between the beast's onyx-colored eyes, through the top of its skull, curving bowlike eight or ten feet beyond, before tapering sharply to a blunt end. Its reptilian snout and mouth had thick membranous cheeks that stretched tight when opened. The teeth filling the drake's maw reminded me more of jagged flint than yellow ivory.

At first I thought the scaled beast was going to roar, but then I saw its sides expand like a great bellows. The ridge of the central horn that ran between the beast's eyes had to affect its vision straight ahead, so I shouted and shook my spear as I angled toward its left. Little good my voice and action did overcoming the chaos and mule screams as they broke free and scattered. I wasn't sure my boar spear would do much against the land drake's hide, even if I could drive the spearhead into flesh, up to the cross bar.

Other than the drake's eyes and mouth, the only other vulnerable spots might be somewhere along the underside of its low-slung body. A region impossible to get at unless the creature could be goaded into rearing up—something it didn't look built for.

The great beast's neck finished flexing, cocking back its massive head. I knew what that meant—it was ready to exhale. To attempt anything against the land dragon, first I'd have to survive or, better yet, avoid whatever breath weapon it had.

I dove to the ground just as a piercing wail tore through the air around me. Instinctively my hands clamped against my helmet in an effort to cover my ears. Searing pain caused me to curl into a tight ball. When I thought my eardrums would burst, the sound shifted, sending rumbling vibrations through my flesh, rattling my bones. Only once before had I felt something that compared. A bone golem's hellcry.

But this wasn't evil. I forced my eyes open. Through blurring vision I witnessed sand and pebbles vibrate across the ground as if dancing on the head of a rattling drum. I clenched my teeth and struggled to settle my stomach as it churned.

Then it all stopped.

I grabbed my spear and tried to stand. At first my muscles responded like damp sawdust, and my head spun like I'd just tumbled down a steep hill. I had to lean on my spear shaft while climbing to my feet. I wasn't thinking clearly. It was foolish, drawing attention to myself while being nothing more than a helpless target.

I dropped to one knee and shook my head to clear it. Enchanters were powerful spellcasters. They didn't wield destructive elemental forces like wizards—like Grand Wizard Seelain. But Supreme Enchantress Thulease was powerful in her own right, and her subtle magics could be just as deadly. I only had to give her the time to slay, or at least injure and drive off the beast.

I was faring better than most of my companions. And all but two mules were down, some struggling to get back to their feet. The dragon charged past me and pinned Dastgir's camel to the ground with one fore claw while knocking a mule back down. With speed and strength common to dragons, the beast bit down and tore Flayzin's mule in half, swallowing the hind legs, leaving its maw a blood-covered mess.

It might be able to swallow a man whole, a slender woman for sure, but we didn't have any of them and I didn't think the land drake had eaten anybody—yet.

Wild neighing and confusion continued as the land drake moved forward, attempting to slash with claw or jaws any mules in reach. It wanted to down as many as it could before they scattered. It was acting more like an animal predator, confident in its size and brute force, not recognizing that humans might pose a danger. Especially spellcasters.

My head cleared, I got to my feet and charged its left flank as it began it inhale, preparing to sound off again. Enchantress Thulease was alive, sheltered behind a mound of rock and hardened sand Wizard Stok must've raised. Flayzin unsteadily raced to her side with a coil of rope.

The land drake's scales reminded me of oval slats of slate the size of a man's open hand. An armor I wasn't sure my spear could penetrate—unless I could find a vulnerable spot.

Just below the socket of its front leg the scales were smaller where it had to flex to move. I threw myself into the strike, driving the tip of my spear into that spot and penetrated up to the crossbar just as the drake cocked back its head. The blasting roar would surely knock back down any prey in front of it.

Guessing at the land drake's response, I yanked my spear free and retreated before it kicked back with its front claw and turned to attack me. I hurled my spear where I thought its open maw would be, at the last second seeing Lilly atop the beast's back with dagger in hand.

For the moment the land drake ignored her and let loose with its screeching bellow right at me. I covered my head and fell to the ground tucked in a ball, my muscles tightening and then twitching uncontrollably as the sound knocked the wind out of me. The ground rumbled and I was sure the sun disappeared—probably the monster looming over me. Then suddenly everything stopped.

I couldn't move. My arms and legs flexed spasmodically when I tried to reach for my spear and get to my feet. I heard an echoing roar like a waterfall in my head, but it was nothing like the land drake's roar.

Laying on my side I finally was able to draw a breath. The land drake stood about ten yards away. My vision wasn't clear but it was clawing at its neck. Someone grabbed hold of my hands, and began dragging me back, away from the land drake.

"N-nn-o!" I shouted, trying to break free and get to my feet.

Lights burst in the air, silent but blinding me for several seconds.

"It'll stomp you," Nura shouted in Sea Spittle, adjusting her grip and pulling me back again. I could barely hear her above the roaring ocean sound. "Let the enchantress finish the fight."

Enchantress Thulease didn't get the chance. The land drake turned and fled, scuttling fast as a galloping horse. It sank into the grassland before vanishing into the ground. It was difficult to tell from where I sat, but it appeared the beast half dug and half swam into the earth.

Nura let go of my arms and I got to my feet. Lilly was trotting back toward us. She must've still been on the land drake's back when it fled. Wizard Stok stood atop his small earth mound, peering past Lilly to where the land drake had fled. Enchantress Thulease stood at the mound's base, pointing and giving orders to Flayzin. Everyone else was trying to gather and hold whatever mules and horses they could reach, some only then struggling back to their feet. Swigopp and Flint were mounted and riding off to round up those pack mules that had fled back the way we came.

I snapped an order to Nura. "Help round up the mounts." She started to say something, seeing I was still unsteady. I held up a hand. "Go now," I said. "I'm fine. Or will be in a minute."

Lilly trotted up to me and handed me my spear. "Did you see what happened, Flank Hawk?"

I shook my head, slowly. "I saw you on its back."

She smiled. "I saw you get it once with your spear. Thought it was gonna eat you, but roared at you instead."

"That was bad enough," I said.

"I bet," Lilly said. "Good thing for you Thulease blinded that monster. Then she magicked a strangling rope around its neck. It clawed free but that scared it off."

I took a careful step toward Enchantress Thulease, then caught myself from falling by leaning on my spear. Lilly held me up by my arm. "You okay, Flank Hawk?"

"Couldn't hardly stand a moment ago. Its roar rattled my insides pretty hard."

"I can tell. Your armor'll dry pretty fast."

"What?" I asked. Then realized what she meant. "It happened to me once before."

"Really?"

I nodded. The motion didn't make me unsteady and the roaring ocean sound was fading. "When Major Jadd and I stood to a bone golem's hellcry while fighting to save Prince Reveron."

"Road Toad told me about you and him helping the prince and the Crusaders fight that demon." She frowned. "Flint or Flayzin give you a hard time, Flank Hawk, I'll set them straight."

I pointed to where they were stringing some of the gathered mounts together. "Go see if the enchantress needs you to scout, or something. I'll be along in a minute."

Nura and Lilly sat on either side of me in front of our small campfire. Lilly'd just turned the strips of slaughtered mule cooking on the flat rocks next to the fire. Enchantress Thulease, Flayzin, Wizard Stok, and Healer Ammond were sitting around a larger fire about twenty yards away. Swigopp was tending to the animals while Storm Claw, Dastgir and Flint stood watch. The sun was an hour from setting, allowing me to see each of the three watchmen on post a stone's throw from camp.

We'd lost three mules and Dastgir's camel to the land drake. One of them we'd captured from the marauders. The mule we were cooking, the one Delmit named Turd, fell lame while fleeing the land drake's ambush. Building two fires didn't make sense to me. Setting up camp after backtracking only two miles north of where we'd fought the land drake didn't make sense to me either. But Lilly and Nura gathered the wood before building a second fire near my tent. And Enchantress Thulease had confidence that if the land drake should approach our camp, Earth Wizard Stok would sense it.

Two miles didn't seem far enough, even *if* Journeyman Wizard Stok gave ample warning.

Nura stood and said to Lilly in halting Mainland, "When it's cooked, call me. It looks like Swigopp could use some help."

Nura glanced at me and then the three watchmen before striding over to the circle of our tethered mounts. Lilly followed her movements for a moment then asked, "Back to your old self, Flank Hawk?"

The land drake's sounding roar had left me confused and out of sorts.

I stretched my arms and flexed my fingers before nodding. "I think so, Lilly." I grinned and shrugged my shoulders. "There's no more roaring sound in my ears."

She gripped my hand. "You came a hair's breadth from dying."

I looked away from Lilly and stared down into the fire. "I know."

Lilly squeezed my hand. "Do you? It was right over you, ready to bite down and eat you. And it would've except for the coiled rope the enchantress spelled and threw. If she'd've tightened it to strangling a half second later, that monster would've bit in you in half."

I turned back to Lilly. Her eyes held more anger than worry, or concern. "That land drake was more than twice as big as any Nura or Dastgir ever heard of," I said. "Maybe it was set as a guardian—"

Lilly grabbed my other hand and pulled so I faced her directly. "Wasn't for Nura pullin' you out of the fight." She hesitated. "Why'd you charge it like that?"

I twisted my wrists to break her grip. She let go before I had to twist too hard.

"You were on its back," I said.

"Where it couldn't reach me."

"With a dagger that couldn't hurt it."

"I was distracting it, and maybe I could've gotten one of its eyes…maybe, if I got lucky."

"I was distracting it too, Lilly. And I managed to wound it."

Lilly rolled her eyes. "Why?"

"Why do you think, Lilly? I'm Enchantress Thulease's personal guard." I glanced over at the other campfire. Enchantress Thulease and Wizard Stok appeared deep in some discussion, probably about spellcraft. The healer appeared to be nodding at what Enchantress Thulease was saying. But Flayzin might've been listening to us as much as the spellcasters while watching their strips of mule cook. It didn't matter to me if he was listening to us. I stared hard into Lilly's eyes. "It's my duty."

Lilly scooted away from me and around the fire. She used her dagger to turn the cooking meat. "I knew you'd say that."

"It's my responsibility." I leaned in toward her and spoke across the fire. "It's why I'm here, Lilly."

After a moment of silence I added, "Scouting ahead is no less dangerous. That's why you're here."

She scowled back at me across the fire. "I'm here because I'm your friend, Flank Hawk."

"I know, Lilly," I said. "I know." I poked at the fire with a stick. "I'm glad you're here. And yet…I'm not."

"Why?" asked Lilly. "Why not?"

"It's dangerous, Lilly. How many've already died so far on this journey?" The faces of Sledge Fist and Miggs, the blonde witch—I couldn't even recall her name at that moment, and her manservant, Delmit. Robbins and Thack. Pretty much the entire *Hunchback Maiden*'s crew except for Swigopp. And Dastgir's father, dead too. I took a deep breath and forced back all those faces before saying, "And we've not even found the Sleeping Sage."

"You're always like this, Flank Hawk. So worried about your charge dying—so much thinking on your responsibilities, willing to die for your duty, that you miss what's going on around you."

"What do you mean?"

"Nura," Lilly said, her hands shifting to her hips. "She's saved your life twice, you know. Don't cha see how she looks at you? Smiles when you talk, and watches you?"

I thought a moment and shook my head. Then I shrugged. "It doesn't matter."

Lilly sent a nasty glare over her shoulder, toward the other fire, then back into ours. "You still thinking he'll wanna finish that duel?"

"He will," I said.

"Well, he might not make it back," Lilly said quietly.

I stared hard at her.

"Not that," Lilly said. "You know how many we've travelled with that're dead?" It wasn't really a question. Then her eyes became distant. I knew she was thinking about the Crusader, Paul Jedidiah Roos, who'd sacrificed himself so that I might carry Lilly, wounded and unconscious, to safety.

Lilly's hand slid to the rapier at her side. Enchanter Jonas's weapon, slain by a spiteful witch.

I thought on my cousin, Guzzy, killed by an ogre. And the mercenaries, Pops Weasel and Short Two Blades. The king's elite soldiers, Privates Shaws and Zunnert. All dead. There were so many, not counting the battles I'd been in and the nameless hundreds lost in them.

Then there was Prince Reveron. I was too slow in slaying the ogre whose hurled sword cut down the prince's legs from behind as he battled the Goddess Fendra Jolain. The image of the goddess tossing Prince Reveron's broken body, to be snapped up by her venomous hydra…it made me look away from the fire and shudder.

Lilly had moved next to me and put her arm around my shoulder. She must've guessed my thoughts. "Nobody blames you for the prince's death, Flank Hawk. Except for Flayzin over there. Not the king, or even Prince Halgadin. And neither of them even likes you much."

"Grand Wizard Seelain," I said.

Lilly squeezed my shoulder. "She doesn't blame you either."

"But has she forgiven me for failing?"

"They were going to be married, Flank Hawk. That kind of thing may take years. You've saved her life more than once. And you and Road Toad saved the prince's life more than once. And you and me and Roos stopped the Necromancer King. That saved the kingdom, counting Prince Reveron and Wizard Seelain."

Lilly's glare returned to the other campfire. "So, if you ask me, you ain't shirked your duty. You just ain't perfect."

She sprang up and scurried around our fire. "And me neither—letting the meat start burning."

I laughed as Lilly hurried to set the cooked strips on a flat rock away from the fire.

"Do you think I should tell Nura about Flayzin's challenge?"

Lilly shook her head. "I don't know, Flank Hawk. She's got a meanness buried in her. I'll have to think on that."

"Meanness, huh?" I said and pointed at strips of meat still smoking a bit, blackened along the edges that had been nearest the fire. "Then you're taking the blame for part of our dinner getting burnt."

It wasn't that funny, but we both laughed until our eyes filled with tears. I didn't realize Nura had returned until she asked in Sea Spittle, "What's so funny? And who burned the mule?"

I shrugged and pointed to Lilly and we both laughed again.

Nura frowned and tossed a handful of sand at us. In halting Mainland she said, "It is good to see you smile, Flank Hawk. You don't do that enough. You too, Lilly. Even if it means we must eat burned meat."

CHAPTER 16

I stood calf-deep in Lake Chaad's gentle surf. The water was fresh but colored with bits of algae. My boots sank only a fraction of an inch into the tan-colored sand. My gaze remained focused on the gentle waves as they approached, and any danger they might conceal.

Lilly had climbed a nearby tree to get a better view. Flint scouted the shoreline to the right while Storm Claw went to the left, both staying within earshot. Dastgir, Flint, Nura and Swigopp kept control of our mounts and pack mules as they edged into the surf and drank. Flayzin watched back into the wooded area while Wizard Stok, Healer Ammond, and Enchantress Thulease tended to their individual mounts.

I caught a glimpse of Nura's grin when the first wave washed over her sandaled feet. I had to step further out into the water so the mules wouldn't block my view, and so I could better keep track of Flint and Storm Claw. There appeared to be a sandbar just below the surface about forty yards out, causing me to wonder how deep the lake might get near its center? Lake Chaad was big. The distant shorelines to the left and right didn't appear to curve inward, and I couldn't see anything but the skyline meeting water out across the lake.

Nura was better with the animals than Swigopp. I listened to her tell him what to do in a mixture of Mainland and Sea Spittle. She'd picked up a lot of Mainland, far faster than I'd expected. She was smart, and I guessed Enchantress Thulease thought so too. The enchantress sometimes called Nura over when discussing plans with Dastgir and Lilly. Flayzin's scowl, I'd seen it although he tried to keep it hidden, told me it annoyed him. I wasn't sure why. Enchantress Thulease asked my opinion too, but about where to camp and establishing watches. I knew that annoyed Guard Captain Flayzin as well.

What Lilly had said to me about Nura occasionally crept into my thoughts. Once or twice I did catch her watching me from a distance. I wasn't sure it meant what Lilly seemed to think it meant.

Was Lilly right? I didn't look at life and people like my friend did, so maybe Lilly recognized something I didn't. It didn't matter, I decided. I couldn't afford any emotional attachments. Duty and responsibility came first. Nura was a comrade, one whose company I enjoyed. And we each had a part to play in the mission's success. Enchantress Thulease's mission to revive her daughter. We'd crossed the Mediterranean, and the harsh desert, and reached the lake in the middle of the Southern Continent. Now we had to find the Sleeping Sage, who Enchantress Thulease believed resided somewhere along Lake Chaad's shore.

I glanced up over my shoulder at Lilly. She waved back at me from her perch about fifty feet up a smooth-barked tree. Its broad leaves flickered gently in the breeze blowing off the lake.

After all the blazing sun and heat and dry sand, the cool breeze, the moisture it carried, and shade the trees offered was welcome. That thought snapped me back to alertness. What else might be lurking nearby, also taking advantage of what the calm lake offered?

After watering our mules and resting we travelled about a quarter of a mile to our left which, by the sun's position, was mainly south and a little east. The area Lilly and Flayzin found was flat, elevated about ten feet above the lake shore and about forty yards back. It held a few small trees, and was largely covered by tufts of thick grass trying to survive in the sandy soil. Wizard Stok sensed the foundation of an ancient structure, possibly a fortress underneath. The wooded area around the small plateau wasn't nearly as dense as other places along the shore. That offered some measure of security should any creature or people attempt to sneak up on us. Even so, there was plenty of available firewood nearby.

While Nura and Swigopp tended to our tethered mounts, Flint and Wizard Stok began digging a fire pit. I knew Swigopp had talked to Lilly about fishing and, moving quickly among the mules, he appeared anxious to be at it.

Flayzin spoke quietly with Enchantress Thulease, ignoring Dastgir and Ammond setting up our small A-Frame sleeping tents. Lilly and Storm Claw paced around the camp's outskirts, watching for possible danger. After adding my armful of driftwood to the pile near the growing fire pit, I moved to help erect the final tent when Enchantress Thulease dismissed Flayzin and signaled me over.

I grabbed my spear before hurrying over to her. "Yes, Enchantress?"

"A moment, Flank Hawk. Once Scout Lilly joins us, it is my intention to take a short walk and I would like for both you and her to attend me."

"Okay," I said, seeing that Flayzin had relieved Lilly of her watch duty.

Lilly trotted up next to me and said while pointing her thumb back over her shoulder, "Guard Captain Flayzin said you're wanting to see me, Enchantress?" Lilly had to crane her neck even more than I did to look up and meet the tall Enchantress's gaze.

"Indeed I do, Scout Lilly." Enchantress Thulease smiled before making eye contact with me and then once again with Lilly. "Please, accompany me."

Enchantress Thulease led us away from our camp and down along the shore. I placed myself between the enchantress and the lake. Its waves lapped against the shore twenty feet to my right. Lilly stayed alert on the enchantress's left. The spellcaster was far more dangerous than either of us. Still, it was our responsibility to protect her.

Once we were out of earshot from anyone in the camp, our pace slowed and the enchantress began to speak. "We have reached Lake Chaad, my friends. Despite all we have endured to get here, I believe the peril yet to be risked as we seek consultation with the Sleeping Sage will be far greater." She slowed in stride and glanced down at me. "Imperial Seer Lochelle believes so as well." The enchantress's green eyes held a grim stare.

I was about to ask a question but Enchantress Thulease raised a hand, signaling me to remain silent. "All that have ventured with me have performed well, even in the face of savage violence and unexpected danger. However, except for the land drake, the threats have been largely…" She paused, looking for the right words. "Of a lesser magnitude, one might say."

The enchantress stopped and stared back at the camp. Flayzin was watching us, but everyone else appeared focused on their various tasks. "Even my loyal guard captain," said the enchantress, "hesitated a fraction of a second before taking action when the land drake revealed itself. You, my friends, did not."

That she repeatedly named me a friend, and Lilly too, took me aback, somewhat. Still, I stood straight and continued to listen.

She placed a hand on each of our shoulders. "We faced, and battled a goddess, and her host of minions, both magical and mighty. We did this in support of two princes of Keesee, and survived. And each of us emerged..." Her voice became distant and she turned her face away from camp, staring unfocused, out over the lake. "Yet, scarred."

She was quiet for a moment. Lilly and I waited, and watched around us. Me toward the water, and Lilly, inland.

Finally the enchantress removed her hands from our shoulders and broke the silence. "Ever wary, both of you, my friends. For that I am thankful. And also for your experience in facing creatures of great power. Hard won experience which far exceeds mine. You have confronted a fallen angel, a great sphinx. A greater elf, the Colonel of the West. You've battled the goddess of the sea's Kraken, and survived."

"It survived, too," Lilly muttered, shuffled a moment and then remained silent.

Enchantress Thulease must've stirred up hard memories in Lilly. Her words were doing so in me. Memories of impossible dangers and of comrades lost.

The enchantress said to Lilly, "You survived, and witnessed firsthand the Kraken's retreat. I, on the other hand, have only been told." Then she turned to me. "You had a question for me, Flank Hawk?"

"I was interested to know, Enchantress, if the Sleeping Sage is an immortal blood, like the Colonel of the West?" Immortal blood was the term the Crusaders used. I figured Enchantress Thulease knew what I meant. Even so, I clarified, repeating her words. "A greater elf?"

The enchantress stared off in thought a half a moment before answering. "A greater elf? No, I suspect that is not the case. Is he, or possibly it, immortal? To some measure or extent, I believe so. And so does the king's Prime Counselor, Imperial Seer Lochelle." She gazed from me to Lilly and back. "What I do know is that the Sleeping Sage is powerful."

The fact that he was powerful wasn't a surprise to me. The concern in Enchantress Thulease's eyes did surprise me.

The enchantress lifted her dusty robes. While the garment's bottom edge had long ago succumbed to the tattering ravages of travel, her high boots remained in fine condition. I guessed she could've used magic to mend and repair light robes. Maybe she had? From a sheath sewn along the inner calf of her right boot, the enchantress pulled a stiletto. Although the narrow stabbing weapon's leather-wrapped grip was dust-covered, it showed little wear. The large amethyst set into the pommel looked freshly cut and polished. Even so, the stiletto wasn't a ceremonial piece. The delicate runes carved along the oddly colored steel blade spoke of magical properties.

She held it out for me to take.

As I did and examined it, she explained, "Although a weapon, it is also similar to the brass rod given to Lilly by Belinda the Cursed, daughter of the Colonel of the West. It can be used as a guide to a place by dropping it and proceeding in the direction it points."

I held the magical weapon out for Lilly to examine while I scanned the area around us for danger. I caught the enchantress suppressing a smile. Then her mouth turned down into a frown as her gaze hardened.

"Flank Hawk, I desire that it would be you who drops it."

I nodded once. "I will, enchantress, as you direct."

"Are you not curious as to why I have requested it of you, as opposed to myself, or even Scout Lilly, who has had experience wielding similar magic?"

In truth, I was. But being a personal guard meant accepting risks on behalf of my ward. I shrugged and handed the stiletto back to the enchantress.

Lilly huffed and spoke up. "He'd like to know, Enchantress. He just won't admit it."

"Scout, I shall trust to your long and enduring camaraderie with the mercenary, and answer his question." She returned the stiletto to its sheath and began walking along the shore again, slowly putting more distance between us and the camp.

"While there are a number of minstrel ballads about the Sleeping Sage, the content of such are often lacking in accuracy, especially when handed down over the years from one minstrel to another." She paused. "In this case, apparent centuries. Nevertheless, I collected what was available through them, endeavoring to discover any possible grain of truth. Coupled, of course, with exhaustive research in Keesee's Royal Library."

It looked like she suppressed a sigh before continuing. "The effort revealed little about the Sleeping Sage. Five instances of recorded histories, spanning eighteen centuries, support his existence. The most recent I obtained from the traveling diary of an astrologer. This particular practitioner utilized his expertise in observing significant dates and events and tying them to the movement celestial bodies. This provided accurate predictions such that he could reliably track fugitives and traitors. Apparently he and a partner accumulated a small fortune through the collection of bounties."

The enchantress once again stopped walking. "Although I did not delve further, cursory evidence suggests he retired to an estate and composed volumes of poetry over the course of his remaining years.

"As recorded in his diary, erroneously catalogued as containing largely incomprehensible content, this astrologer-bounty hunter tracked an earth wizard believed to have participated in the assassination of a duke. This wizard escaped capture and fled to the Southern Continent. I was able to determine the Sleeping Sage's approximate historical location based upon notations related to travel and where the astrologer caught up with the fleeing earth wizard. Along the shores of a large freshwater lake."

Enchantress Thulease again frowned. "The astrologer bartered with the 'Awakened Sage' for possession of the accomplice in the duke's assassination, only to obtain the earth wizard's desiccated body."

I wanted to ask the enchantress how far behind the astrologer had been when trailing the earth wizard. It was possible the earth wizard had died in the desert, but then why wouldn't scavengers have gotten his body? And why would the Sleeping, or the Awakened Sage, have the dried-out corpse?

Placing a finger to her chin, Enchantress Thulease said, "Perhaps I should reiterate while adding to what I have previously shared. The Royal Library and other sources I was able to access failed to offer a solution to my Thereese's deteriorating condition. Imperial Seer Lochelle's spellcraft offered a direction where a remedy might be obtained. The Sleeping Sage. Historical records yielded little on this sage. Both I and Lochelle believe he exists. During our efforts he managed to shroud himself from much of our combined spellcraft. Also a factor, powerful beings are difficult to divine. The more powerful one is, the more difficult the process, resulting in severely limited…results."

I nodded, having learned this through observing war councils where King Tobias strove to ascertain where and how the Necromancer King might deploy and maneuver his forces during the war. It was like playing chess and getting to see an opponent's moves ahead of time. Powerful seers enabled a peek at the board several moves ahead. That was countered by magics to confound such divinations and having competent or better seers working against you, and just being powerful. How the last factor worked, I wasn't sure, but Imperial Seer Lochelle and Grand Wizard Seelain took it as fact. So either the Sleeping Sage was a powerful seer, or enchanter, or had one on hand to counter Imperial Seer Lochelle and Supreme Enchantress Thulease. Or he was a powerful creature. Or maybe even all three combined.

Hearing my name snapped me out of pondering what I'd learned while standing in Imperial Seer Lochelle's dark, rune-scribed chamber far below the Royal Palace. Enchantress Thulease had addressed me. I focused on recalling what she'd just said in addition to my name.

"That brings me to you, Mercenary Flank Hawk." That's what she'd said, but in a halting voice.

I scanned the lake's surface before looking up to meet her gaze.

She offered me a wry, knowing smile. "Many bear such a look while reflecting upon their experience within the Imperial Seer's spell chamber." She rested a hand on my shoulder. "The fact that you have a history with Lochelle, and that she has used her spellcraft to draw out some of your memories has provided for the contingency I proposed and you have accepted."

She removed her hand from my shoulder and signaled for us to continue back toward the camp. "That amulet you carry around your neck, Flank Hawk. The one containing the blood of a fallen angel. You know it alters the pattern of magical energies that surround you."

I nodded. "It affects the ribbons of energy I'm able to see when I cast healing spells. I've been told by Belinda the Cursed that it makes it difficult for seers, and maybe even immortal bloods, to track, and even anticipate my actions."

It was her turn to nod. "I believe that the Sleeping Sage has somehow been tracking our, or should I say, my progress toward his…abode. I imagine my magic combined with Wizard Stok's, in our regular drawing of water, could be magically observed. Our path has largely been linear from the coast toward Lake Chaad."

Lilly asked, "How did he even know to look for the magic?"

Enchantress Thulease didn't appear annoyed at Lilly's interruption. "How does Imperial Seer Lochelle warn King Tobias of an otherwise unanticipated danger?"

"So, the Sleeping Sage sent that dragon after us. To stop you?"

"I am not convinced of that, Scout Lilly. But that possibility has lingered in my thoughts."

"Maybe them pirates?"

Enchantress Thulease shook her head. "I believe we might trace the roots of that particular scourge back to Keesee. Or possibly Vinchie, once the seat of power of fallen Fendra Jolain."

A moment of silence followed. I guessed they were both remembering the moment of Prince Reveron's death, and the death of Fendra Jolain that occurred moments later. At least that's what stood foremost in my mind.

I pushed that image back and scanned for danger. Nothing. Ahead, Flayzin was pointing around the camp, directing Flint to take care of something.

"So," I said to Enchantress Thulease. "If I, instead of you, drop the magical stiletto, you believe my amulet might mask it?"

"It may," she said. "Or at least introduce an element of doubt. I carry a split crystal. Lochelle holds the other half. In addition, she carries the twin of my dagger, both forged from metal of the same meteorite."

Lilly squinted her eyes in a confused look, so the enchantress explained, "What you might call a fallen star."

Lilly's eyes widened.

"I thought the blade's steel looked different," I said.

"My husband would inform you the blade contains a combination of nickel and iron, and several rare earth elements."

"Earth elements?" Lilly asked, and shrugged. The enchantress didn't explain that, to Lilly, or to me.

But I knew how message crystals worked. When one half was destroyed, the other half simultaneously shattered. It was a method to send coded messages, especially if you carried several. The prearranged sequence and time between breaking them was key. "That means," I said, "Imperial Seer Lochelle will cast the spell, and the direction her stiletto falls will govern the way yours falls when I drop it?"

Enchantress Thulease nodded. "Lochelle and I discussed this contingency. She will be prepared for it."

Later that night, after the campfire had burned down to coals, I did as Enchantress Thulease instructed. I smashed the smoky quartz crystal between two rocks and immediately rested my hand upon the shattered bits.

In addition to the enchantress, Wizard Stok, Captain Flayzin and Lilly stood around me, silently watching. Out of the corner of my eye, I spotted Nura observing from her tent. Everyone else, except Flint, who stood guard, was asleep.

We waited for what must've been an hour, until the amethyst in the stiletto's pommel glowed. When it did, I immediately stood, held it between my thumb and index finger, extended my arm, counted to ten and dropped it. The pommel struck the sandy ground. The blade fell, pointing northwest. The amethyst flared for several seconds, and then faded, its faceted edges reflecting the glow of the campfire's embers.

"We must retrace some of our steps," Enchantress Thulease said. "The glow was both brief and bright. Our search *may* be near an end."

For some reason, the way the enchantress stressed 'may' didn't rest well with my stomach. Lilly looked from the enchantress to me, and frowned, too.

CHAPTER 17

I'd never been attacked by biting flies as bad as that night, despite crowding near the fire fed with green leaves to create more smoke. Breezeless air near a lake, especially after another hot day, didn't seem right to most of us, including Enchantress Thulease.

Lilly knew plant oils and waxes she found in leaves and bark that could ward people from most biting bugs, but she didn't recognize most of the nearby plants. Even her heightened muskrat senses didn't help her locate anything.

Tempting as it was, seeking shelter in the lake wasn't an option. Earlier that day we witnessed a large antelope caught in the long jaws of a thirty foot water reptile that shot from concealment under the water. Dastgir called the long, low-slung beast a crocodile. Its attack reinforced our efforts to select *very* shallow areas, and redouble our watches with Lilly perched in a nearby tree, when we watered our horses, mules, and ourselves.

The only relief from the bugs came when Enchantress Thulease finally expended magic to protect us, and our mounts and pack animals. It was something she'd told me, Lilly and Flayzin she was loath to do, especially because she felt the intense insect swarm might've been magically summoned. To determine if it was, however, would've risked further revealing our presence to the one who sent it—if anyone sent it. Lilly and I weren't sure why it would matter, either way, but neither of us were enchanters.

Before she slept, Enchantress Thulease shared with me and Lilly that the insect swarm had been a magically summoned event, but no attempt to resist her dispersal magic was made. Rather, the summoning spell simply collapsed.

It was only an hour after we'd broke camp. Trying to ignore the itching of bites on my neck, I was about to ask Nura what she thought about the insect swarm Enchantress Thulease had driven off when we both spotted Lilly racing back toward the front of our march. She'd gone to scout ahead and wouldn't ride her mule so hard without a reason.

Before I said anything, Nura urged, "Go on and see what Lilly found. I will watch back here."

I nodded and urged Thunder ahead and around the pack mules, riding ten yards distant from the lapping waves. Both I and my mount kept one eye on the lake.

I caught Lilly saying to the enchantress, "I'd bet you anything it's what we've been looking for."

Fifteen minutes later everyone could see that Lilly's hasty description was on target. A broad, squat hillock that looked like it was formed from narrow streams of pond muck that had dried immediately upon being poured—except on a larger scale. Instead of dried mud, it appeared to me made out of a rust-colored limestone splattered with patches of crust-hardened desert sand. Twisted bushes and tufts of tall, half-dead grass sprouted from crevices and other seemingly random spots, giving the hillock-mound a mottled look. It didn't quite reach the height of the abnormally tall wall of trees that grew into thick woods extending away from the lake.

The mound looked to be a little over one hundred yards across. It reminded me of an upturned bowl, with steep sides that might not be too difficult to climb. A lot might depend on how fractured and crumbling the rock face was. Counting on the stunted bushes and tufts of grass for a solid grip or support didn't seem like a good idea. That was if we had to climb it—to find an entrance.

As we approached, I realized the mound's color combination and the scattered trees between it and the lake might break up its outline. That would make it hard to spot if someone was in a boat out on the lake. And the wall of tall trees behind the stone mound would hide it from view if someone approached from opposite the lake.

Enchantress Thulease raised a hand, signaling everyone to stop. We were between the mound and the lake shore, about eighty yards distant from each. The scattered trees offered some shade in the morning sun that hung a good measure above the mound.

Everyone dismounted.

I looked up at the mound, wondering if this was where we'd find the Sleeping Sage. If so, could Lilly find an entrance? Or could Earth Wizard Stok, or Enchantress Thulease? Would we be welcomed in?

I slung my shield across my back, donned my helmet, and took my spear from Nura, who was holding it for me. She pointed to my crossbow and quiver tied next to a saddlebag.

I glanced at the stone mound again, weighing the likelihood of engaging a foe at a distance. My job was to ward the enchantress. I wore my breast and backplate over my leather armor, prepared for combat inside the mound—if that was where we'd find the Sleeping Sage. Would he be hostile? Does he not want to be found? It was already getting hot, and my crossbow was just another thing to carry and hinder my movement. Instead I took a drink from my waterskin and handed it to Nura. "If needed, you're welcome to use my crossbow."

She smiled and took a drink from my waterskin. "I wish you good luck," she said in Sea Spittle. "Remain safe, Flank Hawk, even as you guard the enchantress."

"Take care, yourself," I said, sounding more serious than I intended.

"Of course," she said, this time in Mainland. She looked away while taking a halting breath. "The return trip north would be empty without your company."

I took her left hand in my gauntleted right and squeezed gently. "You've listened to too many of Lilly's tales."

Nothing left to say, I marched up to where Lilly, Flint, Wizard Stok and Flayzin, all armed and prepared, were gathering around the enchantress.

"Where's you crossbow?" Flayzin asked me sharply.

"It was that or my spear," I said, meeting his narrow gaze. When he opened his mouth to say something else, I added, "Lilly has her bow. And if we have to retreat, Nura is competent to provide covering fire." I'd given her a few lessons. She'd do well enough.

Enchantress Thulease cut off whatever else her guard captain intended to say. "Captain, Wizard, lead the way. Flank Hawk with me. Flint, ward our rear. Scout, prepare your bow, and give special attention to the rock face above as we approach."

Lilly nodded with a grunt and scowled at Flayzin as she nocked an arrow.

I couldn't allow Flayzin's question to distract me. I shot a glance at Lilly. She winked back at me, then began a methodical scan of the rock mound as we approached its western face.

We hadn't closed more than a dozen yards when Lilly signaled for us to stop. She backed toward us without altering her hawk-like gaze focused on a spot about halfway up the mound, a little toward the northern face.

About the same time, Earth Wizard Stok stepped back to Enchantress Thulease's left, and whispered up to her, "I see it too. A statue." He pointed to where Lilly watched.

She nodded.

"And there is a second," Stok added, "nearer the apex, partially obscured by vegetation."

"Me and Flank Hawk's seen one of them before," Lilly said. "They aren't statues. They're rock goblins—gargoyles."

I spotted the second one Wizard Stok located. It blended in well, but its outline became apparent when I knew what to look for. I saw the folded wings, the long pair of tusks thrusting upward from the bottom jaw of its menacing face. It was built like a muscular baboon, except instead of flesh, it was made out of stone. It sat motionless, a silent sentinel, nearly invisible with patches of sand and rocky debris resting on its shoulders.

"Maybe they *are* statues," said Flint.

Lilly asked, "You think we're that lucky?"

We stood in place while Enchantress Thulease thought, and then conferred quietly with the earth wizard.

"Wizard Stok believes he can handle one of them," the enchantress said quietly. "I believe that I might overcome up to three. More, if given time."

"How do you stop 'em?" Flint asked Lilly. He was probably trying to decide if his cudgel would work better than his thick short sword, that he wielded like a cudgel.

"Not with a crossbow," she said, bending over to pick up a fist-sized rock, and weighed its use against her sling and its smaller stone."

Gargoyles were creatures of legend and nightmares. Nasty and evil. Most that chance to cross one don't live to tell about it.

"They can be broken," I said, recalling my time spent with Dr. Mindebee, the Colonel of the West's long-time companion. "But their clawed fists will hit like a morning star. And their tusks will tear through flesh good as any bear."

"They exist primarily as guardians," Enchantress Thulease said. "If it comes to combat, it is they who will regret it."

Her confident words put a grim smile on Flint's angular face. Wizard Stok and Captain Flayzin stood a bit more erect.

Enchantress Thulease took the lead, and I stayed to her right, boar spear held ready. As we circled around to the north face seeking an entrance, the heads of the gargoyles slowly turned, tracking our movements. No other body part moved. Eventually we spotted three more of the rock goblins, as Lilly named them, making a total of five.

Once along the north face Enchantress Thulease motioned for us to stop. She gazed intently at a section of the rock face.

"Enchantress," I warned as three of the gargoyles nimbly climbed toward us. Where their claws didn't find purchase in minor crevices, it appeared they could grasp bare flat stone like a magnet to iron.

Lilly hissed, then said, "Them other two rock goblins are on the ground."

I shot a glance to my left, spotting one just around the curve of the rock mound, sitting on its haunches, observing us with a curious tilt of its head.

"I got that one, Flank Hawk," Lilly whispered. "You watch above."

"I have the one down on the left," Flayzin added in a low, even voice.

Enchantress Thulease stood up straight with shoulders thrown back, resting one hand on the hilt of her saber. "I am Supreme Enchantress Thulease, daughter of Imperial Enchantress Theenine, granddaughter of Supreme Enchantress Thareene, and great granddaughter of Grand Enchantress Thoolah. I have travelled far to barter knowledge with one named Elevenzor Stimm, colloquially referred to as the Sleeping Sage." She directed her words at no one in particular. "I await an audience."

That Enchantress Thulease drew her lineage along her mother's, grandmother's and great grandmother's side caught my attention—and all *very* powerful enchanters. I began to wonder if they were still alive. I didn't recall hearing any of their names while serving as Grand Wizard Seelain's personal guard, in Prince Reveron's war council meetings, or even by Enchantress Thereese during the brief times I'd spent with her.

My attention snapped back to watching the gargoyles. As a mercenary and personal guard, wondering about bloodlines and what relative might be still alive? Any delay in action or reaction, even a split second, could mean injury to or the death of my charge.

The three gargoyles perched above hadn't moved. Nobody had moved in those few heartbeats.

Enchantress Thulease took a step back. I followed suit. Her gaze remained ahead, seemingly focused somewhere beyond the rock face.

After a moment Enchantress Thulease said to me, barely above a whisper, "There is a stirring within."

Lilly's keen hearing certainly heard the enchantress's statement. If Flint, Flayzin and Wizard Stok heard, I couldn't tell for sure. They remained tense and, like me, poised for action.

With a jerk of sudden motion, the uppermost gargoyle stood upright and released a gravel-grating bellow into the sky.

Enchantress Thulease motioned for all of us to step back. As we did so the two gargoyles on the ground moved toward where we stood, and faced the rock mound. With less than a cursory examination, the two stone creatures each slapped a hand against the rock and simultaneously thrust forward with arm and shoulder.

Sand and bits of gravelly debris dropped away as some sort of rock doorway fell downward like a drawbridge, the base or bottom pivoting inward where the gargoyles had thrust. Ill-balanced as it appeared, the long, narrow stone plank smoothly lowered to touch the ground several paces in front of Enchantress Thulease.

I involuntarily shivered as a chill ran through me, like an icy breeze whisking through both flesh and bone. It reminded me of an instance when a ghost, one that I'd summoned through a talisman, passed through me while battling a lamenting soul trying to possess me.

Flint's grunt and Flayzin's sharp intake of breath told me I wasn't the only one who felt it.

"Flank Hawk?" Lilly asked in a muffled tone.

I didn't need to reply. Her gaze must have followed mine. From the dark narrow hollow revealed in the rock mound a gray, ghost-like figure came into view. Frosty mist swirled around the figure's feet, obscuring its form up to its knees.

"Wraith," Enchantress Thulease said as if simply stating a fact.

The chilling figure neared but didn't advance to where the sun's rays reached into the mound's tunnel.

My knowledge of wraiths was minimal. I'd heard it said their touch could decay flesh so that it shriveled and fell away from the bone, all the while freezing their target's soul. Whether that was true or not, I didn't know. But I recalled Old Lowell once saying: "People tell ghost stories to scare each other. Ghosts tell wraith stories to scare other ghosts."

The gaunt-looking figure must've been twisted and old in life, maybe he'd been a sorcerer. The wraith's ragged tunic and breeches were also colored shades of gray, as if they were a part its being. Even so, the normally dull color contrasted with the blackness of the mound's tunnel like a pile of damp ash resting on a polished onyx plate.

The undead creature observed us through dark, empty eye sockets before raising a hand, painfully twisted by arthritis in life, and pointed a crooked finger at Enchantress Thulease. "You," the wraith said, its voice sounding as if spoken from the bottom of a crumbling well. Even so, the words reverberated with icy power. "Follow. The Sleeping Sage awaits your presence."

The wraith, which I initially thought might be the Sleeping Sage, was a servant. The cold evil emanating from the servant wraith wasn't as powerful as that of a bone golem, a creature which held the beating heart of a demon. Yet it suggested the considerable strength its master must wield.

Enchantress Thulease nodded once. Without looking back, she said, "Flank Hawk, attend."

The wraith halted in mid turn and craned its neck to fix its empty stare on the enchantress. "Which of your servants is, Flank Hawk?"

I stepped forward, doing my best to keep a stern look on my face.

The cold gaze shifted to me and remained there a moment. I couldn't tell for sure where the wraith's dark, hollow sockets focused. They appeared to start at my face and maybe dropped to my breastplate. Then its gaze shifted back to the enchantress. "If you desire the accompaniment of a servant, choose another."

Captain Flayzin shifted his stance, drawing attention to himself.

I remained still, thinking if Flayzin truly desired to escort Enchantress Thulease into the darkness instead of me, he was a little slow in volunteering, despite his restrained yet less-than-subtle action.

That was my initial thought.

Then I reconsidered. Although it was my responsibility—my duty—did I really want to enter the cold darkness? Enchantress Thulease selected me, told me months ago I'd accompany her. But Flayzin had stepped up, demonstrating his willingness to face whatever dangers there might be within the mound. Follow a wraith into darkness.

Enchantress Thulease cocked her head as if in disbelief. "I have an established history and trust with this mercenary," she said, gesturing with a hand toward me. "I will not insult him by selecting another." She then moved her hand to place a finger along the side of her chin. "Is it your ultimate intention to offer me harm?"

"You have many servants which might accompany you," the wraith replied, only its shadowy mouth moving. "Choose one of them instead."

"Why?" asked Enchantress Thulease.

"It is you who desires entry into my master's domain. It is you who seeks to barter with him."

"While that may be true, it does not address my question." Enchantress Thulease shifted position, again resting a hand on her saber's hilt. "I ask again. Why?"

Silence hung in the air. I heard Lilly release a breath and sharply intake another. Would Enchantress Thulease risk being denied an audience with the Sleeping Sage over my accompaniment? Risk the survival of her daughter? Was her insistence based upon one of Imperial Seer Lochelle's visions? Even more, what greater threat did I offer than anyone else, including Enchantress Thulease? What caused the wraith's silence? Was it thinking up a lie? Or was it indecisiveness? Or something else?

The wraith hissed before saying, "As the one insisted upon is your servant, you are responsible for his actions."

"As it should be," Enchantress Thulease replied after offering a grim smile. She turned her head. "Captain Flayzin, await our return."

With that the wraith fully turned and faded into the tunnel's gaping darkness. Enchantress Thulease strode up the plank-like ramp and through the doorway. I followed, watching the gargoyle perched above the entrance until I'd passed beyond its immediate grasp.

Several steps beyond the threshold the passage turned left and widened enough that I could walk alongside the enchantress, so I moved up to keep pace on her right. I was beginning to worry about the lack of light as the darkness closed in about us after the turn. As if anticipating my concern, the wraith stopped and pointed back to a hook set in the wall holding a tarnished lantern covered in dust.

I reached up and lifted it from the rusted hook. Liquid sloshed in the lantern's base, telling me it contained oil. Before I could wipe the dust away, Enchantress Thulease spoke a brief enchantment, cleaning the glass cover and sparking the wick to flame.

That finished, the wraith turned and continued leading us down the stone corridor.

The air was stale and heavy and the floor smooth and grime-covered. Our boots left prints. The wraith didn't.

The corridor's arched ceiling was almost eight feet high. I stepped ahead of the enchantress because her height required her to tilt her head and shoulders if we walked side by side. I spotted runes carved in vertical patterns up the walls to the peak of the ceiling. Sometimes they extended across the floor, their power apparently barring any dirt and dust from covering them. I couldn't read any of the black markings, let alone guess their purpose. I was careful not to step on any of them, especially as they reminded me of the runes set in the walls of Imperial Seer Lochelle's dark chamber.

The corridor's gentle curve made me think we were walking near the outer edge of the rock mound, and the path seemed to be level. This near the lake, I didn't think the Sleeping Sage would dwell very far below the ground where water might seep in. I sniffed, confirming the air wasn't heavy with moisture, like in a cellar after a strong rain would be.

I kept my distance at five paces behind the wraith, allowing me time to react should it turn. I didn't think my spear could do anything to it. My sword was infused with silver, and I knew that silver sometimes affected magical creatures, but I wasn't sure about the ghostly wraith. I really didn't have any magic to use against it should it turn on me and the enchantress. Maybe the blood of the fallen angel held in my amulet might affect it, but I wasn't sure—even if there might be a way to wield it against the wraith. If it came to combat, Enchantress Thulease's magic would be needed, although I couldn't be sure what spell she might have to undo or destroy a wraith. The undead creature avoided the sunlight. I'd seen her and other enchanters summon magical light.

I cleared my thoughts and refocused on watching and listening for potential danger. Enchantress Thulease knew her spellcraft and how to employ it far better than me. Except for the noise of our boots and the rattle of my weapons and gear, all was quiet as a tomb.

And that's exactly what the inner mound appeared to be.

After what I guessed might be up to two circuits of the mound, maybe spiraling inward, all the while the air becoming heavier and more stale, a sharp turn right and several paces forward revealed a domed, circular chamber so large that I guessed it encompassed a good portion of the rocky mound.

The wraith faded from view, taking with it its soul-chilling aura. Less than a moment later it reappeared across the chamber, at the base of a three-step dais, upon which rested a broad, dust-covered throne.

The lantern I held carved a yellow glare into the silent room that appeared to be bathed in bluish-silver, like moonlight. Along the walls, beginning immediately to our right and left were three tiers of stone bench seats, the first tier elevated eight feet above the smooth, dust-covered floor crisscrossed with wispy, tracks. The seats reminded me of a coliseum, and were occupied by hundreds of brownish-gray, mummified corpses, appearing as if they'd been been preserved by the desert's dry, relentless heat. Some bore full heads of straw-like hair. Others held only patches. All slumped with eyelids closed, leaning back, or against each other as if they'd died in their sleep, dressed in an array of garments, all now moth-eaten and tattered. Some bore jewelry. On others I saw the hilts of scabbarded swords and daggers. A few clutched a dust and grime-covered staff while others had one resting alongside them.

I hesitated to draw a breath, but when I did, the cloying scent of rotting leather and fleshy decay filled my nostrils. The silvery light, I noticed, emanated from patches of fungus, a peculiar form of foxfire I guessed, scattered among the seated corpses, domed ceiling, and around the base of the dais where the wraith had reappeared. Crawling over and among the corpses I spotted cockroaches, some the size of my fist. A centipede the size of my forearm skittered along the base of the eight-foot wall to our left. They and the cockroaches must've been the creatures that left the swirling tracks across the chamber's dusty floor.

Atop the circular dais, leaning back and slumped to the right upon the worm-eaten wooden throne rested another desiccated corpse. This one gripped an ornate rod, bejeweled and magical. I could tell even from the fifty yard distance as several of the blood-red rubies and blue sapphires set into the metal glowed, casting an eerie, mottled purple aura on and around the robed corpse.

The Sleeping Sage? When the light in the rod faded and the corpse began to stir, I somehow knew it was the sage, and began to look around with concern. Hundreds of corpses. Were they undead, like the sage? Instinctively I felt for my salt pouch, then recalled shoving it into Sledge Fist's hands so that he might salt his death wound and not be raised as a zombie to row aboard the *Bone Yard*.

The lantern in my hand offered fire, useful against two, maybe three of the undead creatures. I had my sword, infused with silver. It might prove effective. But what did I have to wield against a wraith, should it come to combat?

CHAPTER 18

Even as the leathery form upon the throne sat up straight, Enchantress Thulease strode across the chamber. I kept to her left, one pace behind, watching for movement among the rows of corpses and trying to keep an eye on the wraith standing dark and motionless near the bottom of the dais. I figured Enchantress Thulease would be paying attention to the undead sage upon the throne.

The sound of our boots on stone didn't echo as I expected. Quickly glancing up, after tilting the lantern slightly, I saw that there were runes carved into the curved ceiling. I didn't bother to study them. They were beyond my comprehension, but knowing they were there cautioned me to be doubly wary of the magical powers the undead sage likely possessed.

I also reminded myself Enchantress Thulease didn't seek it—or him—out, intent on conflict, but to obtain knowledge which might save her daughter. Maybe it was my inborn mistrust of undead speaking, but I didn't believe things would end well. That, added to the axiom, as Grand Wizard Seelain called it, which stated that powerful spellcasters, even those working for a mutual cause, rarely cooperate without incident. And, although Enchantress Thulease mentioned bartering, it was unlikely their cause would be mutual.

Enchantress Thulease stopped three long strides from the bottom of the dais. The only movement, other than the undead sage, had been several of the oversized cockroaches scurrying away from the reach of my lantern's light.

I chanced a glance up at the sage. He stared down at Enchantress Thulease with remarkably life-like brown eyes. They were the only thing that appeared alive in him. His hands, one gripping the arm of his throne, carved to resemble an eagle's head, and the other clutching the jeweled rod, were both claw-like, sheathed in brittle skin. His face was drawn and leathery, as were his lips. Yellow teeth ground against each other as the undead sage's jaw slowly slid left to right, and then left again. The eyes and jaw were the only parts animated, showing movement. At least for the moment.

The wraith stood unmoving, its black form seeming to absorb both the lantern's yellow light and the scattered foxfire's silvery glow.

Enchantress Thulease tipped her head slightly. "Thank you for granting an audience, Elevenzor Stimm, renown sage and seer. Although you undoubtedly know, I am Supreme Enchantress Thulease. I have journeyed far, to your secluded fortress of silent dwelling, so that I might barter knowledge with you."

I listened but didn't trust only my ears to detect possible movement from the corpses in the gallery. For two dozen heartbeats there was no reply to the enchantress's greeting.

Then, as if air were being drawn into a dry-rotted bellows, the undead sage's chest rose before he spoke. The words, although heavy with expired air, sounded remarkably clear. Magic had to be involved. His jaw and lips moved, as did a dried, prune-leathered tongue, but all were ill-formed to produce such accurate speech.

Although the words were clearly spoken, I couldn't understand them. They were in the High Tongue, the language royalty and nobles spoke among themselves, especially when they didn't want commoners to understand. I'd heard it spoken by Grand Wizard Seelain and Prince Reveron, and some powerful and influential spellcasters. Over time I'd picked up a few words in the oddly staccato tongue, and I strongly suspected Supreme Enchantress Thulease was fluent in it. Even so, she responded in Mainland.

"I would prefer," she said, "that our exchange be held in Mainland, so that my personal guard might be able to fully comprehend."

The undead sage's reply was short, and in the High Tongue. "*Ta*," was followed by several other words. I recognized the initial word as meaning, "No."

Enchantress Thulease tilted her head to the right and smiled. "I regret that you are of that opinion. However much it may interfere, where I deem necessary, I shall take the time to restate your words, such that my personal guard may be kept abreast, before I endeavor to reply."

The undead sage emitted a long raspy exhalation that sounded like an autumn corn stalk dragged across dried fish scales. Still, only the sage's eyes and jaws moved. The rest of his body remained motionless, just like a long-dead corpse should. A brief utterance followed, again in the High Tongue. This time tinged with a hint of agitation. Or anger.

Enchantress Thulease said, "You state that the discussion is between us alone." With a sweeping gesture of her left hand, Enchantress Thulease gestured toward the wraith. "You would feign to imply that your personal guard is ignorant of the High Tongue?"

Enchantress Thulease interrupted the sage's harsh reply, sharply sweeping her right hand in front of her. "It will take much to convince me that the primary purpose of a necromancer, of any measurable competence, having summoned a wraith and maintaining its attendance is other than for protection." She then shifted her words to Sea Spittle. "That debate is not..." she paused, and said, "germane," in Mainland, then finished in Sea Spittle, "to my purpose. And will be certain to prove a waste of both our time." Saying that, she lifted her robes and drew the jeweled and rune-scribed stiletto from its boot sheath.

The wraith stirred, reacting to her action.

In response, I set the lantern on the floor and adjusted my grip upon my boar spear's shaft. I knew the weapon would have no effect on the wraith, but hurling it at the sage, knocking the rod from his grip could hinder any magic he might attempt, and benefit Enchantress Thulease should it come to that. I could then draw my broad-bladed short sword and discover if its silver held any worth combating the undead creatures dwelling within the domed chamber.

The sage drew in like a bellows and released another raspy, rattling breath. At the same time the left hand gripping the throne's arm flexed, and relaxed. The rest of his limbs remained still, causing the brief reflexive movement stand out.

"Ahhsss yhhooo, desihhherrr, Enchanntrrrhhis," the sage said, his voice resounding with excessive breath. "Ahhh mhhooomeent ahhsss ahh-eye, ahhh-jahhhhst."

Enchantress Thulease altered her stance, spreading her feet apart an additional few inches. At the same time she placed her arms behind her back, the left holding her right hand's wrist while the right retained a firm grip on the stiletto.

The undead sage's eyelids closed while he mumbled some incantation. When he spoke again, the hollow breath remained heavy in his words, but they were spoken more clearly.

In that short time I decided upon three things. The sage's voice was indeed magically supplemented, if not produced, and that it was unlikely the wraith understood Sea Spittle. And that Enchantress Thulease must have gained a working knowledge of the Trade Tongue during our long trek south.

Slowly, with apparent stiffness, the Sleeping Sage shifted position until he sat erect upon his throne. A faint suppleness returned to his leathery skin as his hand shifted along the shaft of his bejeweled rod. Finally, he gripped it with both hands while resting it upon his dust-covered lap.

I recalled the souled zombies I'd seen, standing dormant within a mountainside cave. Their clothing had decayed and their armor and weapons had rusted, but they remained physically like other souled zombies I'd fought. Private Shaws estimated by the markings on their shields that they'd been holed up for almost a hundred years. I looked at the undead sage and wondered if he were some sort of souled zombie, but a spellcasting one far older than a century. If he was, my weapons, my spear, sword and dirk would be effective against him.

But the wraith. I thought about Roos's saint-blessed saber, and wished I had it sheathed at my hip. I shifted my stance so that my muscles wouldn't stiffen. Wishing for something like a blessed saber was a fanciful waste of time.

The Sleeping Sage gestured with a hand toward Enchantress Thulease before speaking in Mainland. "You have come seeking knowledge." He slumped in his throne, or maybe relaxed, although I couldn't imagine why an undead creature would need to relax. The move was clumsy, and maybe meant to put the enchantress at ease. "Tell me, what knowledge have you trekked so far to obtain, and what you intend to barter for such knowledge." He again gestured with his right hand before returning it to once again join its partner in gripping the rod. "It must be obscure to have eluded one of such intellect, skill, stature, and resources."

"My intellect, skill, and resources directed me to you, Renown Sage Elevenzor Stimm, as the most direct route to obtain what I seek."

His teeth locked together and his dried lips spread. Maybe it was a smile. Even on a living face it wouldn't have been a friendly one. "Tell me, Supreme Enchantress, of your daughter."

I stiffened at the mention of Thereese, but Enchantress Thulease did not. Instead, she nodded. "I appreciate your foreknowledge of my desire, yet I will relay to you her condition and issue my request."

At this the wraith's form appeared to flutter, becoming even darker, and colder. Or maybe it was my imagination. Maybe some of the glow of the nearby fungus clumps had dimmed. Even so, the lamp's flame remained strong and steady. I stood, attempting to mimic the lantern's flame and ignored the knowledge of how fast its flame could be snuffed out.

Enchantress Thulease then explained how she wielded the Shard Staff against the forces of Fendra Jolain, and directly against the goddess, and that she drew upon magical energy of the holders of the staff's shards, slaying four holders and leaving two, including her daughter Thereese, with only a fleeting ember of life.

The Sleeping Sage demonstrated his knowledge of the Shard Staff and its magical effects through stiff head nods, and brief comments and requests for clarification during the enchantress's tale.

Since I knew the tale, I focused on the wraith and keeping an eye on the gallery of dried corpses. The talk of magic made me think of what magic I had, neophyte healing ability and the amulet containing fallen angel blood, and how I might be able to employ them against the wraith and the undead sage.

At the end of her tale, Enchantress Thulease took a half step back. The sage leaned back on his throne, and a moment of deep silence filled the gallery. Nothing, except for steady breaths—those of my charge and me, which had fallen into an identical rhythm—and the quiet scuffling of the oversized cockroaches as they climbed and skittered about could be heard.

The Sleeping Sage sucked in a deep, raspy breath. "You desire of me, the knowledge to revive your ailing daughter." He slid to an erect posture upon his throne. "I am not only well-versed in the history of the Shard Staff, the device's magic and intricacies. I am also holder of a practicable solution to your daughter's dilemma."

Enchantress Thulease nodded. "My research, Renown Sage Elevenzor Stimm, indicates that you trade a knowledge for a knowledge. I believe that I have a rare knowledge to exchange for that which I seek."

At the same moment the undead sage began to raise his bejeweled rod, out of the corner of my eye I caught motion in the gallery. One of the mummified corpses in the gallery's second tier, surrounded by others of its kind, shifted and wobbled to its feet. The figure's brittle and dust-covered hair had been pulled into a ball atop its head. Its tattered robes crumbled as it attempted to lift an arm before tottering, and falling back. I expected the ancient corpse to crumble, but it didn't.

I flashed a look around but other than scattering cockroaches, nothing else moved.

The now still corpse caused more than me to turn my head. Enchantress Thulease, the undead sage, and even the wraith were looking toward the gallery's second tier.

Enchantress Thulease bit her lower lip with a look of uncertainty in her eyes. That was something I wasn't used to seeing. I'd seen it only once in her, just after she'd narrowly escaped death while struggling against the magic that held closed the gates to Fendra Jolain's main temple. Then, I stood by her when other raiding soldiers shied away. Now, I intended to do the same. I moved a step ahead and closer, both to the undead sage and his wraith. But this also placed me directly between the enchantress and the corpse that had moved.

I met her gaze, telling her that I was there, with her no matter what.

The Sleeping Sage sucked in another hollow breath. "Your concern demonstrates wisdom, Enchantress," he said. "For if you do not fulfill your end of the exchange, the price will be steep, far more than you might imagine." His head slowly traversed from left to right, as if examining each corpse in the gallery. It reminded me of a marionette's head turning, with the rest of the brittle toy remaining absolutely still. "Or," he added, "possibly not."

Enchantress Thulease nodded once. "The parameters of our potential exchange of knowledge are?"

"As you may have surmised, Enchantress, I bear a curse. Acquisition of knowledge will lift it, for a span of years. Possibly decades." He slowly lifted his hand and pointed at the enchantress. "I will provide you with the knowledge you seek. However, if in exchange, you provide me a knowledge of which heretofore I am aware, my curse will fall upon your shoulders, freeing me of it for a time."

He opened his hand and gestured to the gallery. "Many have borne my curse over the centuries. They wrongly believed their knowledge was both rare and unique." He sucked in a deep breath. "Yet, there have been those that did provide a knowledge, and departed with that which they sought."

After a pause, he continued, saying, "Lastly, I must caution you,

Enchantress, the knowledge you intend to impart mustn't be trivial, inconsequential. The scale must be balanced to that which you seek."

His head shifted toward the gallery, the direction of the corpse that had moved. He nodded once. "Your suspicion is correct, Enchantress Thulease. Grand Enchantress Thoolah is a member of my court."

That name, I thought. Enchantress Thulease's great grandmother?

"After seven score years," continued the Sleeping Sage. "Retaining the strength to animate her bones speaks well of her fortitude, and of her bloodline."

"Release her consciousness. Her soul," Enchantress Thulease demanded. Her tall frame leaned forward while tightly gripping her stiletto.

"The curse," the undead sage rattled, as a reminder. Even as he spoke those two words the wraith flowed to interpose itself between my ward and its master. At the same time I stepped forward, hefting my spear, preparing to hurl it.

The sage said, "Through *her* failure, because of the curse, *she* has bound herself to me."

A moment of silence hung in the stale air. Even the cockroaches halted their movements, or went into hiding. Could they sense impending violence? Maybe it was the wraith's sudden movement, or something new or more powerful emanating from it? I pushed thoughts of uncertainty aside and focused, ready to take action.

Enchantress Thulease broke the silence. "Is there a benefit to you, Sage Elevenzor Stimm, should what I share prove novel to your collection of knowledge?"

"You depart with what you seek, Enchantress, and the curse long ago laid upon me will retreat for one score minus two years."

"What about those who serve me?" Enchantress Thulease asked. "Whether my portion of the exchange proves to be novel or not?"

My mind flashed to Lilly, even as the enchantress spoke, facing the arrayed gargoyles near the mound's entrance. And to Nura, and the others waiting nearby with our animals and equipment.

Gargoyles, beasts of living stone, would be hard to defeat with sword and club. Stok was only a journeyman earth wizard.

"I am not an evil man," the undead sage said. "Long centuries of bearing this curse have taught me the hard lessons of patience and humility. Yet, even in this wretched state, I carry hope of revitalization, albeit temporary."

The sage's gaze shifted to me. Despite his noble words, his eyes appeared sinister. What person of good heart would be served by a wraith?

"Those who enter my domain will have memory of it removed from their thoughts. Such is but one of the warding powers I have scribed into the walls to protect both me and my domain."

His eyes then moved to observe the entrance beyond our shoulders, and then back to Enchantress Thulease. "Those outside will have their memories altered and replaced with the belief that you, Enchantress, perished and had been devoured when the land drake attacked. A persistent disbelief that my abode ever existed will be planted."

I did not trust him. Even if he didn't set the land drake on us, the fact that he knew about the attack and had a plan to use it to his own best interest made me trust him even less.

He wasn't telling the full truth, if any of what he said was truth.

Enchantress Thulease felt much the same as she said with confidence, "My people are certain to resist."

"Those that resist capture to be enspelled with new memories, to the point of death, will perish. Where any injuries sustained can be associated with the land drake's attack, they will. As will any deaths, just as yours, Enchantress. So much the better for history to be rewritten. For my domain to remain obscure and hidden. Fodder for campfire stories."

"And should my shared knowledge prove novel? What then?"

"Why, Enchantress, we shall depart together, and then go our separate ways. Upon my departure, my domain will crumble to bits of rubble and dust. Or so it will appear. And you *will* be bound to keep my secret."

"The wards will not affect my memories?"

"They will not. What would be the point of your venturing to risk bearing my curse? However, your personal guard will require a consistent story between us to instill an appropriate recollection."

The sage's shoulders lifted as if in an awkward shrug. "It was you who insisted upon a companion, and this one in particular."

"And my great grandmother?"

"Her fate can be discussed, should you be successful."

"Even if I am not, might Flank Hawk, my personal guard, carry with him, if not in mind, then in written form, the knowledge to save my daughter?"

"No." Having said that with echoing finality, the undead sage leaned back in his throne. "Now, you, Supreme Enchantress, must decide."

Enchantress Thulease hadn't explored the option of simply turning back. But I suspected deep down in my heart that turning away from this one chance to save Thereese was never one of the choices.

Even so, I said, "Enchantress, as you are my ward, I urge caution."

She turned her head slightly my direction, so I continued, keeping an eye on the wraith as it flowed back to its original position along the dais. "Your great grandmother was ensnared in this undead sage's trap. Or curse. They are one in the same. I can't imagine that you don't know, or at least suspect what caused her to seek out this undead sage. Give that, and the result of her quest, due weight in your decision."

I recalled Imperial Seer Lochelle had once used a spell upon Grand Wizard Seelain that affected the perception of truthful words when they strayed from truth. Seer Lochelle and Enchantress Thulease had combined efforts for many months while preparing for this journey. Maybe such a spell effort was in play.

It didn't matter. Enchantress Thulease was brilliant, powerful, and wise in many ways. But she was also a mother and would risk all to save her child.

The undead sage knew this too.

I don't believe anyone within the chamber was surprised when Enchantress Thulease said, "Renown Sage Elevenzor Stimm, let us proceed."

Chapter 19

The Sleeping Sage sat erect upon his throne. "Step forward, Supreme Enchantress Thulease." He stiffly extended his right hand, the one that gripped the bejeweled rod. "Approach and place a hand upon my scepter, and receive the long-sought answer to reverse your daughter's demise."

Enchantress Thulease slid the rune-carved stiletto into her belt so that it hung angled above her left hip. She then strode toward and up the dais with confidence. She stopped one step from the top. The undead sage rose to his feet, an action that again reminded me of a marionette.

I stepped forward, not quite interposing myself between the wraith and the enchantress, guessing that the undead spirit could move faster than it had shown thus far. Such close proximity raised the hair along the back of my neck and across my forearms. The wraith didn't respond to my movement. Still, a sinister cold, intertwined with dread, seeped into my bones.

I took a moment to prepare myself mentally should I need to enter the invisible maelstrom where I might summon the ribbons of spell energy used to heal.

Enchantress Thulease gripped the rod and nodded once. With her height she looked down at the undead sage even though he was atop the dais and she stood one step below. The rod's blood-red rubies and blue sapphires began to glow with increased intensity as several long moments passed.

Enchantress Thulease broke the silence. "The Soul Forge of the Dark Elves."

That was all she said, maybe for my benefit, to know that knowledge had indeed been provided. Or as a statement, a direction to somehow take with me and share should she not survive what was to come. Giving me a path to pursue and save her daughter, Thereeese.

The undead sage sucked in a raspy breath. "Are you satisfied, Enchantress?"

She released her grip on the rod and nodded once. In response, he tipped his head forward. "I await what you have brought to share, Supreme Enchantress."

Enchantress Thulease's jaw tightened as she once again gripped the rod. Long moments of silence settled within the chamber. Then, her body shuddered and she grunted, like she'd been kicked in the gut. She staggered back down the steps, somehow not tumbling to the floor.

I rushed next to my ward with my boar spear held poised between the undead sage and his wraith servant. Thulease began chanting a spell. Vibrant power emanated from her even as the smell of sulfur, searing iron, and the stench of a rotting goat carcass tossed onto a bonfire filled my nostrils.

Keeping my attention split between the wraith and the undead sage, I asked, "What is happening?"

Without hesitation, the undead sage said, "The knowledge the enchantress offered for exchange was already a part of my vast repertoire. Thus, as openly agreed at the onset, the curse is falling upon her shoulders."

Although I suspected, I asked, "What will happen to her?"

As the undead sage responded, I could see a change in his skin. Where it was once hard and leathery, there seemed to be a suppleness around his eyes and mouth as he spoke. "She will join my court."

I looked down at the enchantress who had fallen to one knee, strain across her face and urgency in her voice as she continued to chant what had to be protective spells. Guessing by the confidence held in the Sleeping Sage's words and the vast number in the gallery, despite her spell strength and knowledge, Enchantress Thulease would eventually succumb to the curse's overwhelming power. The smell of burning and sulfur, I'd smelled its like before. The curse's origin had to be demonic.

Whatever happened, I couldn't let it take her. I was betting that the sage and his wraith were waiting for me to make a move, but the longer I waited, the weaker Thulease became. Already I could see a graying in her hair that hadn't been there before.

Her eyes met mine. Despite her continued chant between now clenched teeth, I saw in her eyes and the shake of her head, urging me not to do what she knew I must. Without taking time to look, I hurled my spear where the undead sage stood, pulled the stiletto from Enchantress Thulease's belt, and put her between me and the wraith. There was no reason for the undead spirit to attack her and the distance would give me vital seconds to prepare.

Demons had captured and imprisoned the fallen angel whose blood I wore around my neck. So I began my own chanting, the seven syllables I knew, opening my senses to the realm of whirling energy. Even as I did this, I backed away, and unshouldered my shield, for whatever protection it might provide.

The undead sage had cast a spell that slowed my spear's flight and he easily dodged it. He directed his wraith, "Slay him!"

The wraith flowed toward me and I knew its touch would be icy cold, deadly. While Thulease's rune-scribed blade might deflect his attack, my best hope was my feeble magic. I summoned one of the long vibrating strands of silver energy, and took a chance, directing it through the blood-filled crystal that hung over my chest, and then to my left arm as I brought up my shield to block.

A shock of pain knifed behind my eyes as I rushed the spell.

The wraith was already upon me, a ghostly arm swiping down at my head. My shield offered no protection as a numbing cold fell upon my left arm, causing me to lower and then drop my shield. It broke into halves when it struck the floor.

If front of me the wraith's hand and arm flared silvery gray and then dissolved, leaving it with only one arm and screeching like a tormented eagle. As it flowed back and away from me I tried to flip the stiletto in my right hand to throw it at the retreating creature but dropped the weapon as I fumbled the effort.

My left arm ached. I couldn't lift it but I was able to move my thumb.

I looked up at the undead sage whose body now resembled a cross between a souled zombie and a wretched old man, seemingly caught somewhere between life and the grave. His clear and confident eyes met mine.

"Violence cannot undo what is falling upon your master," the sage said.

I picked up the stiletto and stepped toward him. "We'll see what your death might accomplish," I said, figuring that Enchantress Thulease's only hope was that the curse might die along with its original bearer. I had to get to the sage before the receding curse returned his full physical strength. With a deadened arm, I had little hope to best him if he had that added to his formidable magical power.

The wraith's wailing ceased and it stood poised to charge me once again.

The Sleeping Sage raised his left hand and from behind the throne a rapier rose and flew into his hand. It looked tarnished with age but still deadly. I looked at the stiletto. Against both the wraith and sage, I couldn't win. I glanced back at the enchantress. She continued chanting, but at a more measured pace. The gray was more pronounced in her hair, as were the crow's feet around her eyes.

Every moment of delay hurt the enchantress that much more. The sage now appeared nothing more than a hunched old man. "You cannot prevail," he said.

Did he read my thoughts? No, I decided. It was a logical assumption.

"I may not win, and the enchantress may receive the full force of the curse, but that doesn't mean you get to survive." I stepped forward again. He thrust his rod my direction and a force, like a huge pillow slammed me several strides back. At the same time the wraith charged me. I ducked under its arm swipe and slashed with the stiletto. I felt some resistance. It backed away with a shimmering across its left thigh that quickly faded.

Then I heard rapid clapping of stone upon stone. I glanced over my shoulder and spotted two gargoyles enter the far end of the chamber.

I was rapidly running out of choices. I looked at the stiletto again and then to Enchantress Thulease. If its magic worked against a wraith, and threatened the Sleeping Sage, it would surely kill her, curse notwithstanding. Anything would be better than becoming a member of his gallery.

I had another card to play before that final option. My left arm was still heavy as lead and useless, so I slipped the stiletto into my belt and lifted the necklace bearing the crystal holding the fallen angel's blood.

I'd used a similar talisman given to me to summon a ghost to fight on my behalf. Whether I could actually do it or not, I said, "This holds the blood of an angel, fallen yet not demonic. Release Enchantress Thulease from the curse or I will break the crystal, mix the blood with my own and summon him to do *my* bidding."

The Sleeping Sage scoffed, now appearing to be about as old as my father. "Even with his blood you have not the power to compel a purgatory angel to do violence on your behalf, and if you hope he might be of sufficient strength to dispell the curse and free your enchantress. She would die in the effort and her soul would be condemned to the Abyss."

I smiled, hoping my eyes didn't hold the despair I felt knowing what might happen to Enchantress Thulease upon death. "The angel will free me from this gallery with knowledge of its existence intact. I will spread word to the nomads, to whom your magic means the same as it would to the Crusaders of the Reunited Kingdom." I didn't need to tell him how they responded to users of magic.

"If you were to succeed in such a bid," the Sleeping Sage said, the change in his appearance having stopped, "your enchantress would then be condemned to the Abyss."

"She is already condemned." I glanced at the enchantress. She seemed to be holding her own, but her voice sounded weaker. The gargoyles had stopped a few paces from the entrance, resting on their haunches. "I see no reason you should enjoy any continued reprieve from your long-waiting reward."

"Mercenary, if you believe you can successfully effect such an end, go ahead. It will not, in the end, alter the fate of your enchantress."

I was poised for action but something tugged at me. My chance of success, against the sage, the wounded wraith and two gargoyles was very slim. I could slay the enchantress before the curse fell upon her, but I didn't know if that would free her, or if the magical curse would cling to her soul despite her death.

I didn't have sufficient knowledge to make an informed choice.

I took a breath. The sage couldn't get any magical insight on me because of the blood-filled crystal, especially without an intense magical effort. And, although I wasn't fully bluffing about an attempt to summon the fallen angel—even though it was likely he himself was imprisoned in the Abyss—or attempt to kill the sage with my own hand, my charge, the enchantress, would remain condemned to suffering as an undead husk, or possibly even to the sulfury Abyss. And no matter the result I'd probably die in the effort.

I didn't think the Sleeping Sage was lying. Actually it would be better for survivors to return home with tales of the Sleeping Sage's abode not found and determined to be a myth, than all of us who sought it not returning, resulting in a rescue party sent to find out what had happened. The enchantress's husband would surely do that.

Such secrecy ran against new victims to bear the Sleeping Sage's curse, but he probably had a method to get word out in a controlled and limited fashion.

Those thoughts ran through my mind in a split second, pointing me toward my next and possibly final decision of my life.

I slid the stiletto into my belt next to my sheathed sword. "I bear a knowledge which you do not," I said, placing as much confidence in my voice as I could muster. "If I give it to you, will that lift your curse falling upon the enchantress?"

The sage raised a hand to his mouth to stifle the laughter seeking to erupt from his lips. He shook his head. "Flank Hawk, is it? You're a mercenary, and a fledgling spellcaster of some variety." He paused for a breath. "My knowledge is vast, collected over centuries. Those in my court," he said, gesturing with a sweep of his now pudgy, living hand, "have shared *all* their knowledge with me. The chance of you bearing a knowledge which is unfamiliar to me is so insignificant as to count as nonexistent. The curse will fall upon you as it is now doing with respect to the supreme enchantress. Your commendable yet foolish gesture of loyalty will result in your doom. Beyond that, two individuals simultaneously bearing my curse will be of no benefit to me."

Enchantress Thulease's voice was becoming weaker and strained.

Meeting the sage's eyes, I said, "Either you accept my knowledge, if its uniqueness will lift the curse. Or I will do my utmost, as stated a moment ago, to bring you down. Despite what you say, it is possible that the curse will end the moment your life ends—and before it defeats Thulease."

"While I could easily point out the flaws in your logic, loyal mercenary, I urge you to step forward and share what you believe is both rare and unique. If it proves novel, while not being pointless or trivial, it will lift my curse falling upon your enchantress. But do it with haste, for she does not have much time." Saying that, he extended the bejeweled rod.

I stepped forward. Just before I gripped the rod the round-faced sage looked me in the eye. "Your purgatory angel's blood will not avail you in any struggle against the curse which will slam down upon you and overcome your resistance within twelve beats of your racing heart."

He'd thrown water on the one hope I'd held in the back of my mind. I looked back down at Enchantress Thulease, still struggling to fend off the curse. The stench of sulfur, searing iron and smoldering rotted flesh becoming even stronger.

She jerked her head back and forth, looking up at me, telling me, 'No.'

I turned, strode up the dais steps, closed my eyes and grabbed ahold of the bejeweled rod.

CHAPTER 20

Within my mind's eye I saw the Sleeping Sage's court, but not as dried, leathery husks. They appeared alive and breathing. I sensed that outside the stone gallery, sulfury smoke and ancient fires burned, lashing at some magical barrier, seeking entry.

With my eyes I sought out the court member who was Enchantress Thulease's great grandmother. She closely resembled Enchantress Thulease, looking like she might be and older sister. The older enchantress held her hands clasped against her chest while biting her lower lip.

Within my mind the sage's authoritative voice said, "Share your knowledge with me, loyal mercenary. If it is heretofore unfamiliar to me, the curse will be lifted, not from me but from the one who is about to bear it for a span of time in my place."

I imagined what words Grand Wizard Seelain would use and how she would phrase what I was about to share. Then I responded. "While it is known that the faith of a Crusader priest and ingestion of silver nitrate combined can ward off the beast of lycanthropy, having been bitten and surviving until the first full moon following, a neophyte ability with healing magic, combined with ingestion of silver nitrate, an amulet containing the blood of a fallen angel, and a strong will to resist, can also overcome the werebeast striving to emerge when the first full moon after the individual has been bitten, rises."

The sage responded, "While you may *believe* that to be true, mercenary, how can I have confidence in the veracity of your assertion?"

"Because, Elevenzor Stimm, renown sage and seer, I was bitten by a werebat and the beast had settled within me and grew in strength, peaking at the full moon. It was those elements which I stated that enabled me to defeat the rising werebeast within me.

"Examine my heart and mind, and know I speak the truth."

CHAPTER 21

Healer Ammond asked me, "Flank Hawk, do you have the strength to bend your elbow yet?"

It was the second time he'd asked. I was too busy watching Enchantress Thulease's contemplating face caught in our campfire's glow. Her shoulders continued to slump in exhaustion but, like me, she found it difficult to sleep.

I was able to move my left hand's thumb, fingers, and wrist, which was an improvement over my arm hanging like a piece of cold meat. Despite the crippling of my arm, I'd managed to lead Enchantress Thulease out of the Sleeping Sage's gallery with her using my spear as a staff and leaning on my good shoulder. We'd moved at little more than a hobbling pace, but it was enough.

A powerful spell of reluctance fell upon me while I'd gripped the Sleeping Sage's bejeweled rod. I didn't recognize it until we emerged from the mound. It established a barrier, stopping me from forming words to describe my experience in the Sleeping Sage's gallery. I guessed it might extend to writing and drawing, as it did to spoken words. Even so, with concentrated effort, I believed I might one day manage to discuss it. Maybe it was due to the fact that my amulet affected magical energies around me, and protected me from spellcraft. Or maybe it was part of the sage's plan, so that someday I might release information that might lead others seeking knowledge to his abode. I wondered if Imperial Seer Lochelle could draw the experience from my memories.

The same enchantment had been placed on Enchantress Thulease. I knew because she didn't answer Guard Captain Flayzin's questions, other than to say she'd obtained the information sought.

Just before we left the gallery, the Sleeping Sage informed us that he intended to use his temporary freedom to continue his quest—to escape his curse. If he did so, he assured Enchantress Thulease that her great grandmother would find safe release as well.

Flayzin didn't have much time to question Enchantress Thulease upon our emerging, or tell her of their fight against the three remaining gargoyles to gain entrance when two of the tusked creatures abandoned their post and bounded inside the mound—probably after I'd fought off the wraith. Flayzin and Storm Claw hadn't helped us get twenty yards away before the mound began to crack, crumble and finally collapse. Within minutes the remains were consumed by the earth when a great sinkhole opened. It then filled with water.

I wasn't so sure that the mound had been destroyed, but rather some sort of illusion had occurred, created for the benefit of keeping the place elusive and secret. What would Captain Flayzin or Lilly, or anyone in Enchantress Thulease's traveling company say when questioned? What tale would they tell?

And that led to where Lilly had gone. Now that the moon had risen, it was easier for her to change to her beast form, enabling her broken ribs, arm and shoulder to reform and heal. Flayzin, on the other hand, was next to Enchantress Thulease, trying to work out the damage while sharpening his sword. He'd chipped and scarred one of the gargoyles before being knocked unconscious. Stok had bound the legs of a gargoyle together, limiting its ability to move and fight. And Lilly had taken on the third gargoyle and gotten the worse end of the deal.

Nura and the others had rushed forward to help, but by that time the gargoyles had retreated into the mound and closed the door. It must've magically sealed because they, including Earth Wizard Stok, couldn't get it open. They were hard at it when the ramp-like door dropped and Enchantress Thulease and I emerged.

"Has strength enough returned to bend your elbow?" Ammond patiently asked me a third time.

I glanced at him before attempting to flex my arm. It moved a little.

"Good. That is better," he said, examining my arm once again. Without me saying, Ammond surmised that my injury was inflicted by the wraith. The gray and scaly skin where the ghostly hand had struck, he'd said, was superficial and would slough off and heal in time. He was amazed that my arm hadn't entirely withered. His studies said that withering resulted when a limb was exposed to the touch of a wraith. Heart, head or other vital organs resulted in withering, followed by death.

I signaled with my good arm and Ammond helped me to gently lie on my back. "Tomorrow," I said, "if my arm isn't better, I might have the strength to try healing it myself. If the enchantress is ready to move by then, you can always tie it in a sling for me."

He nodded and smiled. "Having seen you attack a land drake, and having fended off a wraith, and yet live, it's easy to believe some of the stories minstrels tell about you."

"Stories retold again and again are always more grand than what actually happened," I assured him, and closed my eyes.

The next day we were retracing our path north. My arm was weak but I'd regained full movement after using some of my healing magic. Actually the healing magic only took away some of the ache. That helped. Despite the improvement, Ammond put it in a cloth sling. I took my usual position, riding in the back of our line, next to Nura.

"Thank you for patching my armor," I said. She'd sewn a leather strip over the area where the wraith had struck my forearm. That part of my armor had turned black and brittle. I guess that's what happened to my shield and could've happened to my arm. I was able to think that but forming those words would've been challenging. Even hinting at what had occurred within the mound left me unable to translate such thoughts to words.

"It needed to be," she said, now that you don't have a shield. "The healer says you'll be able to wield your spear in a few days."

"Maybe," I said, scanning the trail behind us. We were already several miles from the lake's shore and the plant life was becoming more scattered.

Nura asked, "Where do you think the enchantress will get all of those components? And how will she find the Soul Forge?"

I grinned. "She's determined and resourceful."

"I know someone else like that. I believe she will request you accompany her." Then Nura frowned. "Lilly told me about the challenge Captain Flayzin made against you? Naming you a coward and the reason the prince died." She turned away and spat. "How can anyone believe such words are true?"

I shrugged, mostly with my right shoulder. I figured Nura would eventually find out. "It's what he believes."

"Lilly says he wasn't even there. You'd think he'd have a better measure of you by now."

"Guard Captain Flayzin is stubborn."

"You think he'll follow through, after all of this?"

I nodded. "I believe so."

"He's better with a sword than you."

"He is," I agreed.

"Maybe something will happen to him before we make it to Keesee?"

I looked at her questioningly. "You're going all the way to Keesee with us?"

It was her turn to grin. "Yes. Enchantress Thulease told me this morning she'd like for me to accompany her all the way back. When I was helping her dress. She said I am reliable, smart, and a quick learner of languages. She said that meant I had aptitude and her husband could train me as an assistant. Plus, there wouldn't be any concerns about me having political or other loyalty entanglements."

Her gaze wandered back toward the middle of the line where Enchantress Thulease and Flayzin rode. A frown set across her face. "Too bad that gargoyle didn't finish him."

"If the challenge comes, I'll face it as I do all other things. I've faced worse than him."

That didn't seem to convince Nura. In truth, it didn't convince me either. "Well, if you consider it to be an execution rather than a challenge,"

I said, putting as much mirth as I could in my voice. "If you're correct and Enchantress Thulease brings me along in her search for the dark elves and their Soul Forge, she might send me out to recover one of the items she needs to bring with her. Both of those reasons should stay Flayzin's sword for a while, at least."

Nura looked over at me then stared ahead. "You could always depart and avoid the fight."

"No, Nura, I couldn't."

There was a long silence between us. I broke it by saying, "Let's see if Enchantress Thulease is correct in her assessment. You being smart enough to serve as an alchemist's assistant. Recite the six elements Enchantress Thulease must collect to revive her daughter."

Enchantress Thulease had shared this information with all in her service so that if she didn't make it back, the knowledge of how her daughter might be saved could still be carried forth to the King's City in Keessee.

Nura laughed. "That is hardly a challenge." At the word *challenge*, she frowned again.

"Unsure?" I asked. "Can't quite remember? How about reciting it in Mainland?"

She recited with her eyes locked facing forward. "The breath of a fish. The core of a unicorn's horn. The blood of an immortal being. The yolk of an unfertilized dragon's egg. A lodestone that has never seen the light of day. The tears of a giant."

"Maybe the enchantress is right about you."

Nura smiled and then looked away.

As we rode on, I thought about the blood contained within the crystal around my neck. The fallen angel Tyegerial's blood. Blood of an immortal creature had to be a rare thing, and hard to come by. If she needed it to revive her daughter, I resolved to give it to her.

CHAPTER 22

Our trek northward was slow, but equal to what our pace southward had been. The daytime heat was more intense. And, despite the absence of the baking sun, the evenings and nights remained warm. This further sapped our strength and that of our mounts. But, since we knew the route and where Enchantress Thulease and Wizard Stok might access water, our path was more direct and less advance scouting by Lilly and Dastgir was needed.

Before striking out north, we'd moved away from the site of the Sleeping Sage's collapsed mound. For three days, while Enchantress Thulease and I recovered our strength, Lilly, Flint, Dastgir, Storm Claw, Nura and Swigopp caught, cleaned and sundried fish, and gathered and bundled grasses for our return trip. Flint and Lilly even used my boar spear to kill a twelve-foot crocodile. They smoked most of it over a fire, but the rest we ate.

Lilly said the crocodile tasted like chicken. To me it was more like duck with a hint of snake, tougher and more gamey.

Two weeks into our return trip Enchantress Thulease called a meeting. I huddled in the narrow shade of a rock outcropping thirty yards from our main camp, along with Lilly, Dastgir and Flayzin, waiting for Enchantress Thulease and Earth Wizard Stok to join us. Nura was tending to the mounts and Storm Claw was on watch while Swigopp and Healer Ammond tried to get some sleep despite the rising heat.

Guard Captain Flayzin leaned his back against the rock face and asked, "How's the arm, Flank Hawk?"

Lilly shot him an unfriendly sideways glance. I took a drink from my waterskin and handed it to her.

I bent my elbow and twisted my forearm. "Mostly. It's still a little weak. Healer Ammond said there was some tissue damage that may take months to heal on its own. Or it may never." I shrugged and looked back toward the camp. Enchantress Thulease and Wizard Stok had filled another bucket for Nura to water the mules. It looked like their last as they completed their spellcasting and began to withdraw the leather hose from the ground.

"Was it the wraith that got you?" Flayzin asked. "Like the healer said?"

With great effort I nodded once, in a jerky motion. Even that little caused me to see gray and feel light headed.

"I figured he was right," Flayzin said. "He's pretty smart for as young as he is."

Dastgir nodded in agreement while Lilly scowled.

Flayzin ignored them both. He and I didn't talk much, other than about the condition of the mounts, assigning watch duties and things like that. Enchantress Thulease was obviously trying to keep us away from each other as much as possible during the return trip. I wondered what she might do to accomplish our separation if we got stuck on a small vessel travelling back across the Mediterranean. Separate watches, sleep routines and places in the trek north would work well enough until then.

I guessed we both agreed with her efforts. Even though I didn't care for Flayzin and he had a strong hating of me, after Enchantress Thulease and I emerged from the Sleeping Sage's abode, he struggled more to keep the hate out of his voice and expressions.

At the moment, however, he seemed to be doing pretty well. Maybe it was because Lilly was sitting next to me. Although Lilly never voiced her opinion of Flayzin, other than to me, she never tried to mask what she thought of him. Even so, she followed his orders without question.

I knew it would come to steel between us, one day. But we were both professional soldiers and right then focused on our commitment to ensure Enchantress Thulease's safe return so that she could revive her daughter.

During the long hours of travel I'd set my mind to figuring a way I might best Flayzin in combat, but hadn't come up with one yet. Major Jadd was the best sword fighter I knew. He might know something I could use. A rare or unexpected move that might give me a momentary advantage over Flayzin. Sergeant Drux, however, might be a better source. He'd know something underhanded or what some might call dirty fighting. But, when it came to life and death, what mattered was winning.

"Well," Flayzin said, rubbing the red beard stubble on his chin. "I can't say I agree with the enchantress taking you in there with her, but as you both came out…barely…I guess it was wise enough. Barely."

"What could you've done against a wraith?" Lilly asked. "Except die. You couldn't even handle a rock goblin."

"Haven't heard anybody say it was Flank Hawk that dealt with the wraith. My money's on the enchantress saving your mercenary friend and getting them both out." Flayzin rested a forearm on his knee. "Besides, it was your gargoyle that got behind me."

"I never said I could take a wraith, but two rock goblins would be easier than a wraith any morning, noon, or night."

"Flayzin," I said.

He interrupted, saying, "Captain Flayzin."

"You aren't my captain," I replied.

"Mine neither," added Lilly.

I held up my hand to silence her. "Imperial Seer Lochelle advised Enchantress Thulease that both of us were necessary for her mission's success. You proved your sword's worth aboard the *Hunchback Maiden* and against desert raiders. I proved my worth..." The next words came with great difficulty. "…in the…sage's…mound."

"So says you, and nobody else."

I leaned back, taking several deep, steadying breaths to clear my head. While I did, Lilly said, "I do. The healer does. Nura does. Everybody thinks so but you, Flayzin."

Flayzin started to say something to Lilly, but glanced over and saw Enchantress Thulease and Wizard Stok approaching.

Lilly sneered, saying, "Don't forget that big land dragon. Didn't see you anywhere around when Flank Hawk was charging it."

"That's true," added Dastgir, in a halting voice.

I'd almost forgotten our guide was sitting with us. In a low voice I said, "We can settle this anytime you like, Flayzin."

He smiled. "I won't break my vow to the enchantress," he said. "Your time will come, Mercenary."

"Flank Hawk dealt with a wraith, Flayzin," Lilly said. "Don't think he can't deal with you." She followed her statement with a nasty grin.

We all stood as Enchantress Thulease strode up to us, Wizard Stok a half step behind.

"Gentlemen," she said in a harsh voice. "I trust civility will continue to reign in my camp."

"It will, Enchantress," I said, the same time Flayzin said, "Without a doubt, Enchantress."

"Scout Lilly," Enchantress Thulease said, "there is no doubt where your loyalty lies. Do I have your word civility will continue its reign within my camp?"

Lilly bowed her head. "You do, Enchantress."

She then gazed down at Dastgir, our young guide.

He bowed his head. "No troubles from me, Enchantress."

It struck me then how much the young man had matured since his father's death at the hands of the desert raiders.

"Then I expect no further words of discord. We have yet a long and arduous leg of our journey facing us. That is what I have assembled you to discuss with me."

At her signal we all sat, huddled close to take advantage of the rock outcropping's shade.

I handed the enchantress my waterskin. She took a drink and passed it to the earth wizard on her right.

"Let me share my thoughts." With her hand Enchantress Thulease brushed smooth the pebbly sand in front of her. With her finger she drew a small oval and pressed three small divots into the sand moving away from it. Along the last she drew a jagged line that hooked away. She pointed at the oval. "Lake Chaad, and we are here." She point to the other divots as she spoke. "Vulture's Foot Crossing where we first ran afoul of the desert raiders. And this is Tripoli along the coast."

She met the eyes of all around the circle, assessing our understanding before continuing. "I believe that agents set the pirates upon us as we crossed the Mediterranean. Their origin or motivation has yet to be discovered. However, if my belief is accurate, they logically will have individuals awaiting our return to Tripoli. If they are present, with certainty the White Doors Inn will be watched, as will the sea port where we would be expected to depart the Southern Continent for the King's City."

"Will you be signaling through message crystals for our pickup?" I asked.

She nodded once. "It is a possibility, Flank Hawk. Lochelle and I believed it would be more secure than having a ship in port awaiting our return to Tripoli, and more reliable than seeking to purchase a return passage to the King's City."

Flayzin said, "You have prepared codes for alternatives, then."

"We have, Captain."

The enchantress waited a moment before continuing. "I propose that instead of the primary route, we abandon the plan and use of the message crystals. Instead we shall employ an alternate, unanticipated route of return."

She pointed and drew a line in the sand from the divot indicating where we currently were toward the Vulture's Foot Crossing. Before reaching it, she veered west and continued northward, up long the hooked coast and stopped. "Along the coast there are a variety of towns with small ports and fishing villages. Our objective will be to reach one of them where we can secure passage back to Keesee. I do not propose sea travel directly to the King's City. We will put ashore along Keesee's coast and travel overland."

She paused. "I am fully cognizant that any and every delay further jeopardizes my daughter's chance of recovery. However, intuition tells me the unplanned choice is the superlative option."

She indicated with a deliberate hand gesture. "The main concern with respect to the alternate route is the scarcity of water. Through experience, Journeyman Earth Wizard Stok and I have become more adept at securing water."

She made eye contact with our guide, Dastgir and then Lilly. "The three relevant questions are one, will our improved ability to obtain water suffice for the route I hope to take? Two, can you, Guide Dastgir and Scout Lilly, successfully lead us along this unplanned route? And three, will you be able to guide us such that we might avoid conflict with the nomadic tribes?"

Lilly's and Dastgir's eyes locked for a brief moment. Then Lilly said with confidence, "Yes, Enchantress, we will get you there. Get all of us there."

Then Lilly added, "Don't forget the desert raiders' gold Wizard Stok buried."

Enchantress Thulease smiled down at my friend. "That, I have not, Scout Lilly. If convenient, we will retrieve it. Yet, no amount of gold and silver are worth a delay which might further risk my Thereese's life."

CHAPTER 23

We'd just skirted wide around a nomadic tribe's temporary camp and pressed on, putting additional distance between us and them, despite the rising sun. We weren't really in any shape to continue on in the rising heat. Water had proven scarce, and we'd gone through most of the dried grass that barely kept our mounts going, and our store of dried fish. All we had left was crocodile jerky added to the rare scorpion, desert rat or other vermin we came across.

Even so, enduring the heat was better than risking a confrontation. Worn down as we were, a fight would go hard on us, especially if Enchantress Thulease's magic proved weak or ineffective. It would falter against Crusaders, and logic said it would falter against the tribesmen as well.

Just before noon, we made camp after walking next to our mounts the final hour. Lilly had rejoined us after using a spare mount. She confirmed that we weren't being followed.

Enchantress Thulease and Wizard Stok settled near the base of a nearby boulder to use their magic to draw up water. I worked with Flint, and Storm Claw, setting up the canvas fly to provide shade for some of our mounts. Swigopp and Nura started unsaddling our mounts and unloading the horses and pack mules. As always, first off was our A-frame tents, which Healer Ammond and Lilly worked to set up. That left Dastgir and Flayzin for watch duty.

After the canvas fly was set up, I started helping Nura with the mounts.

She handed me a saddle and I moved it under the canvas's shade. She followed with Enchantress Thulease's mount and held him while I attached the bridle to the saddle.

Swigopp said, "Nura, I'll get the buckets over to the enchantress."

"Okay," she said to him. Then said to me, "Your friend Lilly looks exhausted."

"*My* friend?"

Nura smiled at me as we went to get another saddle and mount. We didn't have to worry that Swigopp had left the mounts unattended. They were too hot and worn to wander anywhere.

"She talks to you—likes you," I said. "That makes you and her friends. Unless you're thinking about buddying up with Captain Flayzin." It was my turn to grin at her.

"You know what I mean. You two have a bond like no one else here has."

"Okay. I'll give you that."

We secured another mount to its saddle to keep it in place should something startle it, and went back for a third.

Nura whispered, "I wouldn't be surprised if she knifed the captain in his sleep."

"I don't think so," I said. "She's not like that."

"I wouldn't be so sure, Flank Hawk. I might even attempt it…if it comes to that."

I wasn't grinning any longer. "Lilly knows I'd never forgive her. Nor would I forgive you."

She looked around to be sure nobody was listening. Her voice remained low. "I know how honor works, with a mercenary, and especially among men. Life is better than honor. And I don't really think he could stain your reputation with his words, and a challenge that you should decline because it's based on something that didn't occur."

I shook my head. "You mean run. Won't happen." I picked up another saddle. "Let's talk about something else."

After a pause, she said, "Okay. Back to your friend. Lilly."

"What about her?"

"How does she get along in the king's palace? She works there as a gardener. Studies and lives there too?"

"She has mastered her beast," I said. "But what Lilly is has caused her grief."

"Not that, exactly," Nura said. "She seems more than common. Wild and unfettered. Her language doesn't come close to the enchantress's or the wizard's. Is her tutor any good?"

I laughed. "Actually, no. Tutor Roeth is better than good. She's excellent. She's taught Lilly proper courtly manners, in addition to reading and speaking the Crusader tongue."

"She seems to have forgotten the manners, or the words that would allow her to fit in."

"No," I said. "Lilly is able to change her words and behavior depending on her company, better than I am by far." I tied the mount to the saddle while I thought about Lilly.

"Maybe it's from years of practice, hiding her beast. She's done it from childhood. Blending into palace life probably isn't that hard for her."

Nura gave me a look of disbelief.

"Not that she dines and dances among royalty, or the lords and ladies, on a regular basis. But she does just fine when they visit the gardens."

After we got the next mount tethered to its saddle, Nura said, "Lilly mentioned that you used to serve a grand wizard. A friend of Enchantress Thulease. She was to wed the prince that died."

"I did serve as Grand Wizard Seelain's personal guard," I said. "But things changed."

"Does she blame you for the prince's death?"

"She says she doesn't."

"That isn't an answer, Flank Hawk."

"I'd rather talk about something else," I said. "Or not at all."

"Okay," Nura said. "But you should think on this. Understand the grand wizard's emotions. You served her and must know her, if not well then well enough." Nura held up a hand, signaling me not to interrupt. "She has selected others to serve as her personal guard, but she doesn't blame you for the death of her loved one. That could offer a window into the captain's anger and hatred. Why did she turn away from blame when he hasn't?"

"Because Grand Wizard Seelain was there when the prince died. Flayzin wasn't."

"Is that all, Flank Hawk?"

"Yes, Nura, it is."

She frowned. "Give it some more thought." Then she pointed to Flayzin who was waving his hand, signaling me over to him.

"Time to organize the watch," I said.

"Think on it, Flank Hawk. Do it for me."

"Since you ask, Nura, I will. When I'm not so tired."

Nura replied, "You might as well have said, 'Never.'" Then she laughed and lightly shoved me toward the awaiting guard captain.

Three days after our conversation Nura and Dastgir had gone into a town that the young guide and Lilly had located. Having been deprived of water for so long, it seemed like I could smell the salty sea on the breeze, even if it was a half-day's travel north. It might've been only a third of a day's travel if we were in better condition.

I'd just come off my nighttime watch shared with Enchantress Thulease. It wasn't her regular routine but, being short two people in camp, she took Dastgir's place.

It was after midnight with no moon, but a lot of stars and a few clouds hung in the sky. Lilly had killed three birds that resembled quail just before sunset. Storm Claw flushed them and Lilly brought them down with her sling. There weren't many trees about but some woody shrubs and brush afforded us a small fire.

Lilly had gotten up early and finished cooking half of a long-feathered quail for me and the enchantress.

As we sat by the fire waiting for our late meal to cool on its stick, I commented to the enchantress, "Guess you'll have some stories to tell your husband. Dining on skinned desert rats and sun-dried grubs."

She scrunched her nose and tightened her lips. "Beyond a doubt,

Flank Hawk, I will appreciate what my cooks set before me far more than I have in the past. But we have yet to cross the Mediterranean Sea to reach the Tyrrhenian Sea and travel up the coast of Keesee, as far as we think prudent."

I laughed a little under my breath. We kept our voices low so we didn't disturb those asleep. "I used to think winter campaigning with bitter winds, snow and ice was the worst." I shook my head and picked at a piece of quail meat. "Unending sun and heat, and scarce water is worse. Even worse than the harsh food we've had to survive on. If the ship has plenty of fresh water and a cool sea breeze and a bit of shade, that'd be plenty enough for me."

"It remains unfortunate that I have no method of contacting my husband. He has resources and connections." Enchantress Thulease paused to take a bite of her meal. "I will need to research what is known of the Soul Forge, and how best to locate and contact the dark elves. I have a general knowledge where they might be found but quite limited knowledge regarding them."

I finished another bite and then said, "Gathering the six things for the Soul Forge and dark elves will take time. I have one of them. My amulet carries the blood of a fallen angel. An immortal being. Using it will save time."

"I have thought on that, Flank Hawk. However, the blood your amulet holds exhibits a penchant to disrupt many types of magic. Attempting its use in combination with the necessary elements, especially the core of a unicorn horn, may unnecessarily complicate, if not nullify the required spellcraft.

"Nevertheless, I appreciate your offer and will keep it in mind should circumstances necessitate its use."

In a way I was relieved, but also disappointed.

"Flank Hawk," she said. "Gathering the elements may end up resembling a bizarre scavenger hunt." The dim firelight caught her teeth when she smiled. "I would like to reserve your services, should I need to send either a seeker or an emissary to obtain one or more of the necessary items."

"I'd be happy to do what I can, Enchantress." My gaze turned away from the fire, toward where Flayzin stood watch. "But I may not be available."

"Ah," she said. "Captain Flayzin has given me his word that his challenge will remain postponed until the situation with my Thereese is resolved, one way or the other."

Looking at Flayzin standing poised, slowly moving his hand to his sword's grip, the grim thought settled in my mind: My fate being tied to Enchantress Thereese's life…or death.

Then, my mind focused on what Flayzin was doing. "Enchantress," I said, just above a whisper. "Set a few more branches on the fire and then slowly back away from it."

I heard the rustle of her picking up twigs. She whispered, "What is it?"

"Maybe nothing," I replied. "Your captain is trying to decide."

I scooted a little away from the fire and to my right so I didn't have to watch over my shoulder and to let my eyes better adjust to the dark. It could be danger, or it could be vermin moving around in the brush.

I pulled my gauntlets from by belt and slipped them on.

Then I saw it—something maybe an eye or bit of metal about four feet above the ground that caught the flaring campfire light. It was behind some brush about twenty feet from Flayzin. His head was turned, searching the wrong direction. Or were there two threats out there?

Without a sound a dark shadow about the size of a horse shifted, moving closer to Flayzin. Enchantress Thulease might've seen it too as she began chanting.

Grabbing my spear, I shouted, "Behind you, Flayzin!"

The shadow shot through the brush and fell upon Flayzin in an instant. A glow, like a blazing campfire, appeared in the air above the guard captain, with the creature bearing him to the ground.

"Wolf spider!" I charged toward Flayzin. The guard captain's draw cut managed to clip one of the horse-sized spider's legs before it flattened him on his back. Lilly tore through the brambles, following the spider's path and leapt onto its back, driving her broad-bladed dagger into it again and again.

Behind me Enchantress Thulease shouted orders. "Swigopp, Ammond, the mules! Stok, watch our back!"

At the same time, Storm Claw called, "Flint, with me!"

Flayzin's cursing turned shrill just before the giant wolf spider reared up and then rolled over, trying to crush Lilly. She leapt clear.

With lighting speed the spider righted itself, spinning to face me. I knew it'd be stronger than a bear and nearly impossible to kill with one blow, like an ogre. I—we'd have to cripple it before taking it down.

I shouted, "Hhaaa!" Extending my spear, its tip struck but only scratched its remaining front leg. Facing me it reared up again as Flayzin rolled away, out of range and Lilly got to her feet.

The spider's eight dark eyes reflected Enchantress Thulease's flaring magical light. Glistening venom dripped from its fangs, flexing and clicking, ready to bite.

I took a step back, wary of its spine-covered legs, thick as my thigh at the base and equal to my forearm at their hooked end. It followed me, using its four hind legs to move. I did my best to ignore its acrid stench.

Lilly, back on her feet, closed on it. "How do we take it, Flank Hawk?"

"Cripple it first," I said.

Storm Claw shouted, "Surround it! Captain, back off." She moved up to my left, her fighting sticks held ready before her. Flayzin was on my right. Lilly was behind it, stalking forward and Flint was circling wide around. The big mercenary gripped a sword in one hand and his cudgel in the other.

I didn't take my eyes off the spider to see how steady Flayzin was. If he'd been bit, the venom would be working on him fast. The spider was an instinctive hunting creature. No fear. Even if we drove it off now, it'd probably come back again. To it, we and our mules were prey. Food.

A bucket flew above the spider, aided by magic, and dumped its load of water. That didn't distract our foe. It lunged toward me. I set the butt of my spear and braced for the charge.

My spearhead bit just under the fangs as the spider dropped on me, driving forward. The rocks on the hard-packed dirt ground gave way under my spear's butt. I retreated, twisting my spearhead in the wound while trying to keep my feet. Flayzin lunged forward, driving his sword into a joint where a leg sprouted from the spider's body.

Storm Claw attacked and sparks erupted where her sticks struck home. I heard Lilly shout and Flint's battle cry but couldn't see their attacks.

The spider leapt forward, dislodging my spear. It came down on me. Somehow I managed to keep my head from slamming against the ground. Releasing my spear, I grabbed onto the bottom of the spider's carapace. It had overshot, leaving its fangs twitching a foot beyond my scalp.

I had my breast and backplate on so if the spider slammed its body down, it might not crush me. Clicking and hissing, it scuttled backwards, extending and snapping its fangs in an attempt to get me. I hung on, its course under hair scratching my face. As I was dragged across the ground, my legs hooked on a big rock, knocking my torso to the left.

Viscous blood drained on my neck and breastplate from where I'd wounded it with my spear.

The wolf spider began to spin, dragging me over one of its legs that someone had severed. A jolt of energy shot through me. It must've been Storm Claw's clubs. I hung on despite the shock.

Then the spider slammed down upon me. I did my best to protect my head as it knocked the wind out of me. Then the spider was off of me. It'd leapt, out of the reach of our swords and clubs and scrambled on its six remaining legs, one of them dragging, into the darkness. It left a trail of dark blood glistening in Enchantress Thulease's magical light.

Lilly began to give chase but stopped when Enchantress Thulease ordered, "Scout, stop! Let it go."

My own blood trickled down the left side of my face from cuts and scrapes. My right thigh throbbed, deeply bruised from striking a half-buried rock. It hurt to stand but not enough to keep me from grabbing my spear and getting to my feet.

Flayzin sat on the ground, his sword at his side. He grunted sharply as Flint tightened a leather strap below his bicep. Enchantress Thulease shouted for Ammond while removing Flayzin's gauntlet before folding up his leather sleeve.

I limped toward them while Lilly came up to my side, wiping spider blood from the length of her rapier. "You okay?" she asked.

"Just scraped and bruised," I said. "You?"

"A few bumps. Those rocks are hard."

Flayzin's wound, two deep punctures looked red and inflamed. Despite the immense pain, he grimaced but didn't cry out. Everyone else looked unhurt. Stok and Swigopp had the unsettled horses and mules under control.

Healer Ammond sprinted toward our group. Enchantress Thulease said, "Giant arachnid. Flank Hawk said it was a wolf spider."

That's what it looked like to me, just a thousand times bigger than those I remembered around our farm outside Pine Ridge. Nobody from this continent, Dastgir or Nura, was here to verify my assessment. Lilly nodded her head, agreeing with the enchantress, then stepped back to give Ammond room.

The healer looked worried. It hung in his words. "I am not well versed in nullifying toxins."

Flayzin said, "It's not hurting much but I'm losing feeling in my fingers. It's getting hard to move them. Lifting my arm too."

"I can only stop a little of his bleeding, and maybe a little tissue damage," I said.

"I will detoxify what I can before it spreads further," Ammond said, rolling up his shirt sleeves."

Flint asked Enchantress Thulease, "Why not suck it out like you do with the water from the ground?"

"I am unable to separate the venom from the blood and other fluids," she replied.

"I got a tourniquet on tight, but if it gets to his heart or lungs he's done for. Just take what ya can outta his arm and let the healer detoxify what's left in is arm?"

Ammond said, "Any way around it, the less toxin the better. But he'll lose a lot of blood."

Enchantress Thulease looked to Flayzin. "I am willing to attempt it. Are you?"

He clenched his teeth and nodded.

She immediately withdrew her stiletto and its sheath fitted along her boot. "Lilly, your dagger."

Lilly gave the enchantress her dagger. The spellcaster then sliced the leather sheath, creating a stubby tube while ordering, "Lay him flat. Hold him in place. I suspect this will be painful."

Flint helped the guard captain to lay back and then made room for Storm Claw to hold Flayzin's right shoulder. I held down his left leg. Lilly held down the other. Ammond pinned his left hand to the ground.

Enchantress Thulease placed the makeshift tubes over one of the fang wounds and immediately began chanting. Seconds later Flayzin's body tensed. Storm Claw put the long end of the discarded sheath over the guard captain's mouth for him to bite down on. He did, grunting.

Then blood mixed with dark fluid began to fill the stubby tube and overflow out of it, covering the enchantress's fingers as she held it in place.

Flayzin tried to kick a little, then passed out.

The enchantress kept her spell going while Storm Claw put her head to Flayzin's chest and listened to his heart. "It's sounding wrong, not normal," she said.

Ammond said, "You had better stop, Enchantress."

She did. The blood stopped flowing over her fingers. She slid back away from the guard captain and Healer Ammond took her place. He looked at Storm Claw who listened to Flayzin's heart and then nodded. Lilly, Flint and I let go and stepped back.

The healer then began his magic to counter the poison still in the wounded arm. After several minutes the sound and cadence of the spell shifted. He began healing up the wound. During this time Lilly gave me a damp cloth for my bleeding cheek and forehead.

"It's mostly stopped," she said.

I thanked her with a smile before leaning close to the healer. "If you're spent, I can do a little for the wound. Not much, but some."

He nodded but didn't stop his spell for another minute. "There are still some blood vessels that need mending," he said. "He is weak and halting any blood loss will help."

I then switched places with the healer.

Lilly turned and walked away. Everyone else except Ammond looked surprised, including Enchantress Thulease.

I didn't know what to say, so I began my spell. Distantly I heard Ammond say, "Deep down, I believe the mercenary has the true heart of a healer."

Flayzin survived the night, and was sitting up with his back against a rock. Flint and Ammond watched over him while he ate a piece of the snake Lilly and Storm Claw had killed just south of camp.

After I'd cut a piece of the cooked snake on a rock near the fire, Lilly caught my attention and signaled me over to her at the edge of camp. She was in one of her scowl-faced moods and I knew why.

I bit a piece of snake from the ribs and chewed on it while walking over to Lilly. My leg still hurt from last night's fight, so I was limping a little. I walked past Lilly, going further away from camp. I knew she'd follow and tell me what was on her mind. The extra distance would help keep it between us. Actually us, and maybe Enchantress Thulease who was standing watch along the south edge of camp.

Either way, Lilly didn't care. "You know what, Flank Hawk?" she said, barely able to control her temper.

"I can guess, Lilly. If you can keep to a talking voice, I'll listen."

We continued walking, both looking ahead and around. Anywhere but at each other.

"I betcha don't," she finally said. "You know what that Flayzin said?"

"No, I don't, Lilly," I replied, a little curious.

"He was talking to Flint this morning. Flint told him what happened after he passed out last night. After the enchantress pulled the poison out of him. And Flayzin said, 'It appears the gods intend for us to fight on equal terms.' That's what he said. He said more but he was talking about his arm. And about your arm, Flank Hawk."

When I didn't say anything she added, "And you went and healed him, knowing he wants ta kill you." She clenched her left hand into a fist. "Why'd you even help him?"

"Because, Lilly, we haven't made it back to Keesee. Enchantress Thulease may—we may need his sword arm on the way home." I looked at the uneaten snake in my hand. "I promised to do all I can to help ensure Enchantress Thereese is revived. Flayzin, like it or not, is a part of the enchantress's team."

Lilly just scowled at me.

"If Flayzin is so bad, why were you there first. On the spider's back, stabbing it?" Then I thought a moment. "Why were you on that side of the camp?"

"I smelled something," she said. "Didn't quite know what it was. Smelled near like that trapdoor spider's lair we got kind of near a long time back. But wasn't exactly the same."

She looked at the half-eaten piece of snake in her right hand. "You're just lucky I got to it before you. It'd've took you down same as it did Flayzin, but we all wouldn't've been there to get it off you."

"So, Lilly, if I hadn't seen the spider. Warned Flayzin, you would've let it get him?"

Lilly met my gaze with a hard stare of her own. "Maybe," she said.

"That's not right, Lilly!"

"Him naming you a coward ain't right, Flank Hawk. And you know it." She threw her hands up in the air, almost losing her piece of snake. "Everybody knows it. Everybody but him!"

"Lilly, when you're on watch, you're on watch for *everyone*, including Flayzin. If I was out there and he saw that spider, would he have warned me?" When she didn't say anything, I answered for her. "Yes, Lilly. Yes he would have."

She looked down at the ground, stirring a pebble around with the toe of her boot. "I'd just spotted it when you did. I was fixing to chuck a rock at it before yelling. I could've thought faster, I suppose."

"I suppose?" I said and handed her my piece of snake. "You're a better person than that."

She squeezed both pieces of snake in her fists. "Sorry, Flank Hawk."

As she walked away to circle around the camp I heard her muttering to herself, "You're a better person than that? That's what I'll be saying over your grave."

I stayed where I was for a few minutes, thinking things through. What Lilly said made sense. What Nura said made sense. Not the part about running. The part about how Grand Wizard Seelain thought about Prince Reveron's death.

On the way back to camp, Enchantress Thulease moved to intercept me. In a low voice she said, "It might be best if our scout is not assigned a watch paired with Captain Flayzin."

I nodded. When she didn't say more I continued toward camp. Before going two steps, I stopped and turned. "Enchantress, you're friends with Grand Wizard Seelain."

She nodded once. "I am."

I knew she was. And she knew that I knew, having served as both her and Grand Wizard Seelain's personal guard. "If I may, I'd like to talk to you some time about her."

"I would not mind that at all, Flank Hawk. Whenever you believe the time is appropriate."

"Thank you, Enchantress."

"You're welcome, my friend."

CHAPTER 24

Enchantress Thulease sat at a long table made of mismatched planks grayed by age. I sat to her right and Dastgir sat to her left. Our three-legged stools looked rickety but turned out to be sturdy. Across from the enchantress sat a cargo ship's dark-skinned, balding captain. To his right sat his middle-aged first mate. Both wore canvas breeches, wool vests and brown knit caps. The captain had a long curved dagger hanging in a belt sheath. The first mate had one on each hip, and a throwing knife sheathed along the small of his back.

The warehouse where we met smelled of fish and exotic spices, the kind that if tasted would make my eyes water. The breeze carried the salty smell of the sea through the wide doors propped open with small wooden crates. Just outside Earth Wizard Stok stood as requested by Enchantress Thulease.

The sun hadn't risen yet, so a lantern on the left end of the table provided light.

"We seek passage north, to a city along the western coast of Keesee," Enchantress Thulease said in Sea Spittle. "Fort Benemere Cove would be my first choice."

I was there as her personal guard and to assist her with the trade tongue. Dastgir knew the local tongue and had made the initial contact with Khaahz, captain of the *Mule of the Waves*. That was how Dastgir translated the two-masted ship's name into Mainland.

"Old Salerno, twenty leagues north, has a larger port and would be a better place to offload cargo to be auctioned off, since I do not have a merchant contract. The owner of this warehouse has a small load of trade items that I could take off his hands and possibly turn a small profit."

"How much trouble would it be to dock in Fort Benemere Cove and then continue north the half day's sailing at most to the more…" She paused, and whispered for the word that she wanted to use in my ear. Giving it to her, she finished, "more lucrative port in Old Salerno."

I wasn't sure why the enchantress didn't prefer Old Salerno. I knew that Grand Wizard Seelain's estate was there, and her family held sway there. Her uncle, Baron Zimmerman, ruled the city and had command of the garrison. Certainly it'd be a safe port and city once reached—or safer than most.

"No," said the captain. "I must sail wide out to sea. The coastal waters are treacherous and unknown to me." Then he made eye contact with his first mate. "This will require two additional days. Unless you will pay for the added time and work of my crew. I may not earn a profit even sailing directly to Old Salerno."

Enchantress Thulease smiled at this. "I have a proposal for you to consider, Captain Khaahz." Then she said to Dastgir, "Would you relieve Stok and ask him to join us?"

Dastgir stood. "Yes, Lady Thulain," he said, giving the title we'd been instructed to use before any of us approached the city. I was to be called by my name, Krish, and Flayzin named only as captain. It was believed that none others among our group would be notable, whatever name was used. I didn't understand why we didn't all use false names. It would, however, stand out if we got caught up, calling each other by different names. Even with innkeepers or merchants it would attract suspicion, and make us stand out even more than we already did.

Before Dastgir made it through the propped open doors, Enchantress Thulease said over her shoulder, "And ask him to bring a handful of sand."

I did not know what Enchantress Thulease wanted the earth wizard for and her request earned the enchantress raised eyebrows from the captain and his first mate.

Once Wizard Stok was seated, Enchantress Thulease said to the captain, "Please observe." Then she said to Stok, "Please spread the sand thinly over the second board and we shall attempt as we have practiced."

Stok sprinkled the handful of sand along one of the weathered boards making up the tabletop. While he did, Enchantress Thulease stood. I pulled the stools on our side of the table back to give the two spellcasters room.

"On three, Stok, we shall attempt the combined spellcraft."

I thought her statement was for the benefit of the two sailors.

Both began chanting. Stok's palm resting on the top of the enchantress's hand, they held them no more than an inch from the tabletop, and moved them over the sand.

They worked very slowly, and Enchantress Thulease showed more strain in her face and voice than I thought was necessary. Before, when I'd been equally close to her and saw such strain, I'd felt the radiating magical energy. There was none that I could sense at that moment.

After their hands passed over, about half of the sand was gone, or at least no longer visible.

The captain and first mate had leaned back, yet watched with interest.

Enchantress Thulease and Wizard Stok stopped their spell a half foot from the lantern. He stepped back, both breathing heavily.

With her hand she brushed the remaining sand to the floor. "Captain, I'd ask you to have your first mate pull his dagger and stick its tip into the center board, and then the board we just affected with our spellcraft."

The first mate's narrow dagger easily stuck in the first weathered board about the width of a finger. When he attempted the same with the spelled board, it went in only half as far.

"Together our spellcraft has fused the sand into the wood's fiber," Enchantress Thulease explained. "About one tenth of the wood's flexibility is lost yet the strength is increased by nearly half. It is a spell used to strengthen clubs and cudgels, and a more powerful version can be used to buttress the strength of a wooden palisade. Although not proof against fire, wood altered through such spellcraft resists it. Even if set to fire by oil, the wood is consumed at a slower rate."

"An interesting demonstration," the captain said. "And this table will endure for many more years, or at least part of it will." He rapped it with his right hand's knuckles. "But what has this to do with the destination of your passage?"

Enchantress Thulease smiled. "In exchange for our passage and departing for Fort Benemere Cove as soon as is practical, foregoing obtaining cargo for trade, I and my fellow spellcaster will bring along sufficient sand to reinforce the keel of your ship during the journey. Depending on how fatiguing that is, we will attempt to strengthen the deck as well."

The captain scratched his short beard in thought. "More strength, loss of flexibility. Resistance to fire." Then he stepped toward the lantern. "Do you mind me examining the effectiveness of this spell fending off fire?"

"Of course not," she said, and took one step back from the table.

The captain nodded to his first mate, who then poured two narrow lines of oil from the lantern's tank, one along the spelled board and a second along an unspelled board next to it. Then, from the lantern's flame he lit a long piece of straw and set the spilled oil to flame.

After about twenty seconds, he used a nearby rag to snuff out the flames. It was clear to see that the spelled board showed some blackening, but less than the normal board.

Captain Khaahz asked, "How much sand, how much weight would this add to my ship?"

Swigopp had accompanied Enchantress Thulease, me and Dastgir in looking over the ship before our meeting with the captain. We'd boarded, and examined the two passenger cabins and the cargo hold. Swigopp said it looked sea worthy.

Enchantress Thulease said, "With the keel, one hundred pounds of sand. With the deck, we would only infuse the very top layer of the wood, so an additional two hundred pounds."

The captain nodded. "If you agree also to reinforce several key planks in the bow, Lady Thulain, we can be ready to depart two hours after noon today."

They shook and I exchanged details with First Mate Dukkan, such as the exact number of passengers and gear, and the request to keep silent on the fact that there were spellcasters among us until after we departed.

The *Mule of* *the Waves* sailed short a few crewmen because of our quick departure. So, Swigopp threw in to help, along with me, Storm Claw and Lilly, being familiar with life aboard a ship.

I was making my way back to the ship's bow to stand watch when Enchantress Thulease emerged from the empty cargo hold. Earth Wizard Stok followed. He headed to one of the two cabins the nine of us shared. Enchantress Thulease walked over to join me.

Dastgir remained ashore, intent on returning to his home. Enchantress Thulease paid our guide with gold coins and our mules and horses, sorry lot that they were. But with food and care, and time, they'd be fine mounts and pack animals once again. Nura had taken the enchantress up on her offer to serve as one of her husband's assistants, and I was glad of that. I'd come to enjoy her company, as much as Lilly's, but in a different way. It would've been difficult to say goodbye.

"It is a clear night," Enchantress Thulease said.

"It is, Lady Thulain," I replied, quietly so that my voice wouldn't carry far on the breeze that filled the sails. Although the sailor at the wheel and the one sitting near him watching aft didn't speak Mainland, I used her false title. "Have you and Stok finished the task?"

"We have, my mercenary friend. Normally it takes a greater earth wizard to accomplish such a spell. My spell ability and our long practice working together drawing water from beneath the dry earth has made it possible."

"Has it worn you out?" I asked. "You should get some sleep. The ship's captain says we'll reach port several hours after sunrise."

"It will be later than previously estimated," she said. "I spoke with the captain and we have altered our course. We are going to Old Salerno, Krish. If there were spies in the port town we departed, the ruse may offer some frustration. Although I do not believe that it is a legitimate concern."

It remained odd, the enchantress and the others calling me by my given name, instead of my mercenary name. "Baron Zimmerman will provide us mounts and additional guards. Loyal ones," I said, nodding in agreement at the change of plan. The baron led a powerful cavalry and still had a sizeable force despite fighting in Keesee's two wars.

"He will provide mounts for all that intend to return to the King's City," the enchantress said. "Except for you and for me."

That got my attention. "We're departing directly from the port to seek the six items?"

"No, Krish. You shall accompany me as Seelain flies us upon her gray dragon. I believe she named her Balooga?"

Grand Wizard Seelain, I thought. I wasn't sure she'd be too happy with the plan. I know she didn't hate me, but it had become clear she no longer cared for my service as a personal guard, or my company. "Will she be there, at her estate?"

"Without a doubt," Enchantress Thulease said. "That reminds me, Krish. Were you not interested in my ability to answer questions about our mutual friend?"

"Grand Wizard Seelain? I cannot say that we're friends."

She scoffed at my words. "Krish, you are a rare individual. You are able to serve, yet form a lasting bond of respect and friendship. You assert the risks you take and the dangers you have faced on our behalf, are merely associated with your duty."

I noted strain in the enchantress's voice. It could've been a hesitancy to share a personal opinion. More likely the cause was the same spell I was under. Her indirect reference to what had happened within the Sleeping Sage's gallery triggered a surge from the otherwise latent spell.

She continued after a long, steadying breath. "I say with you, Krish, it is loyalty to a friend. Duty is present, but loyalty and friendship bolster your sense of duty." She gazed out at the dark sea. "But I stray."

Before I could say anything, she lifted a finger, signaling for my silence.

"Did you know that my guard captain is Seelain's cousin? They are hardly more than acquaintances, but well-disposed to each other when Seelain would occasionally visit my home in Keesee. I imagine this grows from a shared childhood experience as daughter and son of lords and ladies around Old Salerno.

"The guard captain harbors a fierce love for family, and that encompasses Seelain. His duty to them. Seelain's devastation at Prince Reveron's death, was his devastation. Beyond that, the guard captain saw the marriage of Seelain to a prince, even though not the crown prince, as a vital chapter in his family's history to be written. That chapter was burned before it was written. The guard captain does not envision you as lighting the flame, Krish. Rather, to him, you are the one who was in position to, do what was necessary to snuff that flame, and failed. Shirked your duty to the prince. Preserved your life instead of Reveron's. The fiancé of his cousin."

She sighed. "Failed the prince in your duty. Failed Seelain in your duty."

As Enchantress Thulease spoke, the fateful moment replayed in my mind's eye.

From behind me Otis yelled, "Take'em, Flank Hawk."

The ogre ignored me and cocked his arm back, preparing to throw his sword up the dais at the prince, in a desperate bid to help his goddess.

The two fan-bearing servants lay at the bottom of the dais, dying from bloody wounds inflicted by the prince's sword. Prince Reveron stood a step below the goddess, the Blood Sword's ruby flaring red being so near to the healing goddess. At least eight feet tall, she towered over him, raining down sharp blows with her white staff. Despite an arrow in his calf, Prince Reveron parried and deflected the goddess's attacks. He'd managed at least one successful strike as the goddess's white robe showed blood around a split in the fabric below her hip.

They exchanged words as they fought, but with the sounds of battle echoing in the chamber, what they said couldn't be heard but by them.

Even as I took the ogre in the chin, driving my spear into his throat up to the crossbar, he followed through with his throw. With a twist I yanked my spear free and leapt back to avoid the collapsing ogre. He didn't clutch at his throat as he fell. His eyes remained locked on the goddess. I turned in time to see his sword strike Prince Reveron across his calves.

The prince toppled back while taking a blow to the head from Fendra Jolain's staff. The Blood Sword flew from his hand and clattered down the dais steps. The prince lay unmoving where he fell, a dent creasing his steel helmet.

"NO!" I shouted and hurled my spear at the goddess. It pierced her robe and stuck in her chest. She pulled it free, clean of blood and smiled as she tossed the weapon aside. An arrow pierced her arm. Otis had killed a balcony archer. She ignored the shaft and stepped down, picking up the prince with ease.

Drux came up next to me, wheezing with blood dripping from his nose and mouth.

"Surrender, and he lives," the goddess announced. "Lay down your weapons."

"The sword," Drux whispered to me as the sounds of battle dropped off. "Fight her with me."

It didn't even look like Prince Reveron was alive, and Drux was in no condition to fight.

"Never!" Prince Halgadin shouted from the far end of the chamber.

"It matters not," Fendra Jolain said. "My worshipers are but moments away. Your king's gambit has failed and your lives are forfeit." With that she tossed Prince Reveron down the steps, to the awaiting hydra.

Wizard Seelain attempted a spell to save her fiancé, but she lacked the strength and only slowed his descent into the snapping, venomous jaws.

A silence had fallen between us until my unfocused gaze rose to meet her eyes.

She rested a hand on my shoulder. "I can see in your eyes, the reliving of that horrible moment."

"War has offered me many horrible moments," I said. "Moments that intrude upon my quiet times. Haunt my dreams."

It was the enchantress's turn to stare unfocused, out to sea. "I would venture to guess my most horrible moment occurred moments after yours with the prince." Her hand slid from my shoulder. "Where your spear thrust was a second too late and where Seelain failed her fiancé through lack of spell strength, failing to deflect him from the hydra's venomous jaws."

My mind's eye recalled that moment.

Regally, the healing goddess descended the steps toward the Blood Sword.

I dove for it, but with a flick of her wrist, the sword lifted off the floor toward her hand.

Supreme Enchantress Thulease must've used the Shard Staff, shouting a spell that countered Fendra Jolain's. The Blood Sword fell and I caught it by the grip.

The ruby flared. I looked up and saw fear in the goddess's eyes as the evil spirit contained within the sword flowed into my arm.

Catching the moonlight, it was my turn to see the regret and despair in Enchantress Thulease's eyes. That was the moment, having completely exhausted her own magical energies, she had to summon more through the Shard Staff, to keep the sword from the goddess's hands. And that energy came from those holding the shards of the staff, including her daughter. Draining her daughter's life in a bid to defeat the goddess.

"Seelain endures the same regret as you, Krish, believing somehow she should have mustered the strength for just one more spell. If she had, her love mightn't have died. Flayzin recognizes her anguish. No matter what she says, or I or the baron says, or anyone says, my guard captain intends to act upon that anguish."

A thought crept into my mind. Flayzin lay in the cabin, weak, recovering from the wolf spider's poison. It would be easy to overpower him, kill him, drop him over the side. I didn't think anyone would stop me. Then I thought further. Maybe Healer Ammond. I wasn't sure about Earth Wizard Stok, and even fully sure about Enchantress Thulease. Flayzin had loyally served years as a trusted household guard before rising to the captain of her guard.

I knew Lilly would cheer me on, should I move to end Flayzin's life—she'd jump to assist.

I shook my head. No, that was something I could never do.

"Is there any logic to loyalty?" Enchantress Thulease asked. "Or to duty?"

"There is," I said. "It's what motivates us. Binds us together."

"And love?" she asked.

"And love," I replied, not knowing what else to say, thinking on the loss Grand Wizard Seelain must have felt. She had become hardened to loss, but not to the extent I had. And she'd lost the love of her life.

That I had failed didn't make me a coward. But, for right or for wrong, loyalty, duty and love bound Flayzin to act.

I gripped the gunwale. "Acting upon a belief and prevailing are two different things," I mumbled to myself.

Enchantress Thulease must've heard. "I agree, Flank Hawk," she said, intentionally using my mercenary name. "I agree."

CHAPTER 25

"Getting away from Flayzin makes sense," Lilly said. "Splitting up so it's just you and the enchantress doesn't."

We'd disembarked from the *Mule of the Waves* and Enchantress Thulease shared her intention with the rest of the group, except for Swigopp who'd hired on to sail with Captain Khaahz. Why he did that I wasn't sure. He could've crewed on a better ship. The enchantress paid him in silver and some gold and told him that if he ever needed work in the King's City, she would find something for him.

Lilly and I were standing just off the street next to the corner of a warehouse, drawing some attention in the busy port city. She didn't seem to care. Enchantress Thulease was thirty yards away, across the narrow street, standing under the awning outside a fish market to avoid the rain. She was giving instructions to Flayzin. He was to obtain mounts and supplies from Baron Zimmerman and proceed to the King's City at the best pace manageable.

From what I could see, he was just as upset as Lilly. He was just more restrained in his expression.

"Colonel Ibrahim's gift can only carry three," I said to Lilly.

"What?"

I stared her in the eye. I couldn't risk mentioning Grand Wizard Seelain or her gray dragon mount. Lilly'd catch on if she took a moment to think. The Colonel of the West had gifted the gray dragon to Grand Wizard Seelain.

Then she mouthed, "Balooga?" She crossed her arms and huffed, before saying, "Okay."

I'd warned Enchantress Thulease that Lilly might object. The enchantress figured Lilly was reliable enough to know a sliver of her plan. Travel by serpent would save time. It was the fastest way to reach the King's City. It was also a route difficult for Flayzin to argue, that it was his place to escort Enchantress Thulease the final leg to the King's City. He knew nothing about riding a serpent, wasn't fully recovered yet, and his duty leading the rest of the group north to the King's City made logical sense.

Lilly's frown turned to a smile. "I'll try not ta'kill Flayzin."

I pulled the brim of her hat down, causing water to drip from it. "Just do your job and scout ahead."

"Flayzin knows the route between here and there better than me. I'll watch out for Nura for you, though. Good as you."

"Thanks, Lilly."

"Just do your duty like always." She slugged me in the shoulder. "And get things worked out with…" She looked around. People were hurrying along the muddy street, trying to get out of the rain. "You know who."

Enchantress Thulease hired a carriage to take us to Grand Wizard Seelain's estate fifteen miles north of Old Salerno. The enchantress quickly nodded off as the rain pattered against the carriage roof. I stayed awake, sitting across from her and watching for potential danger.

The driver and his pair of sturdy horses made steady progress along the curved roads that cut through the hilly and rock-strewn countryside.

After turning off the main road and traveling up a narrow, winding trail the driver announced, "We approach the grand wizard's estate."

His words didn't stir the enchantress from her sleep. I leaned across and gently gripped her forearm. "Enchantress, we're almost there."

She startled awake, nodded with a tight smile and began to examine her white cotton shirt, green vest and brown trousers tucked into her worn leather boots. She'd sent Nura and Lilly to purchase the clothing prior to our boarding the *Mule of the Waves*. It wasn't a perfect fit. The sleeves were a little short for her arms. Enchantress Thulease frowned and tugged at them in annoyance.

"Enchantress," I said. "The grand wizard has endured wilderness missions. She'll understand."

"I suppose," she said. "In comparison to you, I must appear as a rough emerald to a jagged shard of granite." She held a tight smile and a gleam in her eye.

My leather armor had been mended so many times it reminded me of a quilt patchwork. My breastplate looked equally dull and battered. I shrugged. "I've looked much worse."

"That you have, Flank Hawk. That we both have." She gazed out one of the carriage's windows. "Keesee. We are nearly home."

Grand Wizard Seelain's estate wasn't large by a lord's standards. Fifteen or so acres that included a hillside vineyard and what I guessed to be a small wooden winery situated below. The winery was easily the oldest building on the property. A whitewashed cottage near a reed-filled pond stood a distance from an eight-foot stone wall that encompassed a two-story brick home with a slate-tiled roof. It was tucked in front of a square tower that stood at least eighty feet tall. To the tower's right sat a row of small log cabins that probably housed her servants. Behind them stood two large barns, one with a fenced area holding six horses. The second barn, newer and far more stout with a large water trough next to it probably housed Balooga, her gray dragon mount.

A guard stood in front of the wall's open gate and signaled for the carriage driver to stop. A second guard on the wall held a crossbow ready, but not aimed at us. Both appeared well-trained, but young. No more than sixteen summers.

I stepped out of the carriage. At my appearance, the guards became more wary. "Please notify Grand Wizard Seelain that Supreme Enchantress Thulease requests a consultation."

I'd never been to Grand Wizard Seelain's estate. She'd lived in the White Wing of King Tobias's palace when I served as her personal guard. I didn't know if Enchantress Thulease had ever visited here, but the two guards on duty were probably new hires. With the losses suffered during the war, men with the necessary training were difficult to find.

The guard on the ground called to a gardener and ordered her to run to the house with the message. The young girl shot off, sprinting the entire way. Another guard arrived, dressed in leather armor with rings sewn into it, like the other guards, but this mustached man looked to be in his late thirties. He nodded to me before looking through the carriage's glass.

"Enchantress," he said in recognition. "Grand Wizard Seelain will be most pleased to see you."

"Koleno," she replied, "when did you put aside the ledger and take up the sword?"

"When the Necromancer King's forces marched on Keesee, Enchantress."

"And now you serve as Wizard Seelain's Captain of the Guard?"

"I do, Enchantress, and keep her books by candlelight," he said with a smile beaming beneath his thick mustache. "We'll have you up to the house in a moment."

"Please, Guard Captain Koleno, step inside with Flank Hawk and myself and relay to me how events have progressed around Seelain's estate."

"That's okay, Enchantress," I said, stepping back. "I'll ride up top with the driver."

The guard captain met my eyes. While his lips smiled, his observant brown eyes didn't.

Enchantress Thulease might know the guard captain and be comfortable with his security team, but her safety was my responsibility. Not his. He climbed into the carriage while I rode the short distance to the estate seated next to the carriage driver.

The two-story brick home looked unremarkable but sturdy. The two columns that supported the porch's roof were covered by flowering vines. I thought they were morning glories. Lilly would've known for sure but, even though the pink and purple flowers were closed, I was fairly confident.

I'd seen the gardener rush into the white double doors after I'd climbed up next to the driver. From that vantage I was able to observe a woman working among the grape vines and an additional guard walking the property inside the wall. He made his way to the porch and stood with a nervous hand fidgeting as he gripped his short sword's hilt. He looked as young and innocent as the two gate guards.

Of course, Grand Wizard Seelain was no longer in line to become royalty, become a princess. But she was a powerful air wizard, more than capable of defending herself and her estate.

Then a servant, I guessed a maid by her white bonnet and long brown dress, opened the double doors from within.

I hopped down when the carriage stopped and took my spear from where it had been secured with leather thongs to the back of the coach. Then I assisted Enchantress Thulease from the carriage, having waved off the driver. She had to duck low through the carriage door, but was used to that.

The guard captain followed her out and said, "I must return to my duties, Enchantress. I hope you enjoy your visit."

"Thank you, Guard Captain Koleno. And give my regards to the baron, when the opportunity presents itself."

He smiled and nodded. "I will, Enchantress." Shooting me a glance, as if to say he was trusting me to remain armed while in the presence of Grand Wizard Seelain, he turned and departed with purpose-filled strides.

Enchantress Thulease turned back to the carriage and said, "Driver, please remain on the grounds of the estate until I release you from service. I anticipate a possible return trip. I shall request the lady of the household provide water and oats for your horses and refreshments for yourself."

When the enchantress turned back to the porch the maid said, "I shall see to it, Enchantress."

I followed Enchantress Thulease up the steps. "Thank you, Pamellia," she said to the elderly maid before crossing the threshold.

The maid bowed low. "You're welcome, Enchantress."

At the far end of the marble-floored entrance hall Grand Wizard Seelain was speaking to another of her servants, then noticed we'd entered. The young man dressed in a gray cotton shirt and tan pants bowed quickly before hurrying off.

Then the air wizard turned to greet us. "Thulease, I was fully unaware you had returned to Keesee, let alone intended to visit me here."

The wizard was dressed in a sky blue silk dress with intricate white stitching along the bottom, just above her white-sandaled feet. The threading reminded me of wispy clouds. She had thumbnail sized pearl buttons running from the V of her neckline down to a white leather belt lined with silver. She wore an intricate silver chain necklace with a sparkling blue sapphire teardrop pendant. On her hip hung a sheathed dagger, long and narrow with an ivory grip.

Her white hair, with hints of translucence, reached well beyond her shoulders, longer than I remembered her wearing it. Her eyes were blue, her left a shade darker than her right, reminding me of a time I'd nearly failed in my duty to protect her when a sorcerer's spell had ruptured her left eye. Fortunately, a powerful healer was able to regenerate it, but not to its wizard-altered color.

Like all wizards, as she became more powerful, she took on the color of her element. As an air wizard, her eyes grew lighter blue, and eventually her irises would become cloud white. Her hair had already turned white, before starting to lose even that coloration. Her complexion was, of course, quite fair, not quite milky, yet.

Enchantress Thulease and Wizard Seelain embraced and then stood apart.

"I know, Seelain, and I apologize. But even if notice had not been near to impossible, it remained unwise."

"And that, I imagine, is why you have Flank Hawk at your side." As she said that, Grand Wizard Seelain turned and stepped forward to embrace me. "It is good to see you as well, Flank Hawk."

I wasn't prepared for such a greeting and returned her embrace awkwardly. "It is good to see you too, Grand Wizard."

She stepped back and gestured with a sweep of her hand. "Please, Thulease, Flank Hawk, join me in my parlor while we await the meal my people are preparing. I hope you will find it acceptable."

As we followed Wizard Seelain into her parlor filled with elegant shelves containing a mixture of books and wooden carvings depicting deer, dragons and great elks, she directed us to sit in chairs of padded blue fabric and polished oak.

"You may guest here in my home or in the cottage by the pond. I will see that whichever you choose, the rooms are prepared."

Enchantress Thulease's voice rang flat when she said, "We will not remain so long, Seelain. Not much beyond your hospitality of a fine meal." She leaned close. "If we might retire to somewhere more secure, I will explain."

A smile remained on the wizard's face, but her eyes took on a serious tone. "Of course, Thulease."

"Flank Hawk," the enchantress said, "please accompany us." The setting of her jaw and curt nod told me without uttering the words that I was to ensure that no one overheard.

I followed two paces behind the women as they made their way to the back of the house, through a heavy oak door reinforced with steel, down a steep set of stone stairs, along a short underground hallway built of brick and stout oak support timbers, and then back up a stairway to an identical door.

Once we were in Wizard Seelain's tower, she introduced us to Abigail, a student apprentice studying to become an air wizard. The girl was probably thirteen or fourteen summers, slim and awkward with thin smiling lips, large teeth and penetrating brown eyes. Each part separately might be off-putting, but together they formed a friendly, attractive appearance, especially her face framed by dark curly locks that barely brushed her shoulders.

Wizard Seelain and Enchantress Thulease stopped at a heavy oak door. As the wizard opened it, revealing a cast iron spiral staircase, the enchantress said, "Flank Hawk, please see that we are neither interrupted nor overheard."

I nodded and closed the door behind them. The sound of both a lock clicking and a wooden crossbar dropping into place, probably rune-scribed, said they didn't need me to stop any intrusion. Nevertheless, it was what I was directed to do.

I turned to observe that I was in a rectangular room lacking windows but illuminated magically through recessed lighting along the ceiling near the four corners. In addition, two lit candles sat on a sturdy wooden table in the middle of the room next to several large tomes, one opened. A matching pair of high-backed chairs sat at the table. One chair in front of the open book was pulled out. Abigail must have been reading it.

The granite walls held shelves filled with rolled scrolls, leather-bound books, spare candles, a lap-sized chalk board, and other minor items. It seemed an odd place to study air wizardry, housed in a room surrounded by stone.

In one corner I noticed a wooden stand holding several sheets of paper filled with lines and musical notes, and a flute resting on a nearby cabinet. To the best of my recollection, Grand Wizard Seelain didn't play a musical instrument. Either she was learning, or the flute was her student apprentice's.

There was a third door in the room, another wooden one, but not impressively sturdy. On either side of it sat two steel-reinforced trunks. Both had large iron locks.

I moved to stand two steps to the left of the door the enchantress had gone through and rested the butt of my spear on the polished granite floor, next to a small but ornate, circular steel grate set into it.

Hesitantly, Abigail walked toward one of the chairs and pulled it out. "Would you care to sit?"

It wasn't difficult to guess what the enchantress would tell Grand Wizard Seelain. Her urgency meant it was unlikely I would be waiting long. In any case, standing watch for ten minutes or two hours, or ten hours wasn't a problem.

I shook my head.

My mind shifted to thinking why Grand Wizard Seelain had hugged me. The only other time she'd done that was after Prince Reveron's memorial service. If Flayzin were with us, which of us would she have hugged after Enchantress Thulease, if either of us? What if Lilly had been with us too?

I wiped such thoughts from my mind. They were distracting me from my duty. My purpose for being there. Such thoughts would confuse responsibilities and priorities, and could result in my charge's injury or even death.

The thought of death reminded me that so many people I'd known and travelled with were dead. Many times I should've died myself. More than one died in my place.

My life didn't have room for attachments, like the one that I felt budding between Nura and myself. I'd have to trim it before it had a chance to bloom. To do otherwise would be selfish and ultimately unfair, especially with my eventual crossing of blades with Guard Captain Flayzin. It wasn't that far down the road. Enchantress Thereese's hold on life would swing one way or the other all too soon.

Student Apprentice Abigail stood with her eyes averted and holding her hands clasped.

"If you were studying," I said, "please return to it."

She moved around the table but didn't sit. "The enchantress...called you Flank Hawk?"

I nodded once. "I am Enchantress Thulease's personal guard." It wasn't my place to discuss our journey and its purpose.

"I know who you are," she said, her voice cracking a bit. It was youthful and reminded me of my younger sister, Katchia. "You have served the grand wizard. Wielded the Blood Sword. Travelled across the Western Ocean. Battled giants and ogres. It's said you slew the goddess, Fendra Jolain."

"Did Grand Wizard Seelain tell you that?"

"No," the young apprentice said, gaining confidence. "But everyone says it was you who took up the Blood Sword when the prince fell. I have asked Grand Wizard Seelain, and she does not deny it to be true."

The girl looked from floor to ceiling, as if searching for words to say. "She's never spoken to me of that day. But she did tell me how you fought off three griffins while she ran ahead to camp to ready your wyvern mounts to escape."

I smiled. "Did she tell you that she sent magic to aid me?"

"Of course the grand wizard did. But you stood against them, on the wooded mountainside alone, with only sword and spear. And how, once aloft and still outnumbered you took the fight to them, getting your wyvern to battle against the beasts that normally prey upon it."

"It was the grand wizard's spellcraft that enabled us to survive."

Abigail shook her head and smiled. "Grand Wizard Seelain said it was your combined effort that enabled the both of you to not only survive but to emerge victorious. The story was a lesson to me. No matter how powerful I *might* someday become—*if* I study long and hard. Never dismiss the skill and courage of others."

"Has she told you a lot about me?"

"No, she has not—may I address you as Flank Hawk?"

I laughed. "That is who I am. How might I address you, Student Apprentice Abigail?"

"Just Abigail." She smiled and briefly looked away. "She only talks about people like you to illustrate a point, Flank Hawk."

"Really?" I asked, trying to draw her out and get her to relax. I was just a normal person, nobody to be intimated by.

"Like when she tells me to rely on whatever skills I have," Abigail said. "Grand Wizard Seelain said you're not the best spearman or swordsman, and know your limitations. As such, you employ what skills you have wisely. Just like Guard Captain Koleno. She says he is competent with a sword. She counts on his analytical thinking and sense of duty to supplement his average ability with a sword. That is why she hired him to be her guard captain."

"And that he can also serve," I said, "keeping her gold and silver accounted for."

Abigail giggled. "That is true." She leaned back against the table. "I believe they have known each other a long time."

She clasped her hands in front of her chest. "Can you tell me one of your adventures?"

I looked around the room. "Where does that door lead?"

"To my sleeping room."

"Is that all? Are there any windows?"

She shook her head.

"Well, if you will block the door leading to the grand wizard's house."

She looked at me, confused.

"I have been assigned to watch. If I am telling a story, I will be distracted. Blocking the door would give me ample time to recover and assess the situation."

"No one would attack us here," she said.

I shrugged. "My duty as a personal guard calls for me to be prepared, small chance of danger that there might be."

I could tell she was judging how serious I was.

"Would you expect me to shirk my responsibility?"

"No," she said before carrying her wooden chair to the door and wedging its back under the latch. She then returned and sat upon the other chair.

"I will tell you a tale," I said, and pointed to the flute. "If you promise to play me a tune."

She nodded eagerly. "Only if it's a true tale."

I grinned. "Only if you promise to play your best."

I briefly told her about the time Lilly, the Crusader Paul Jedidiah Roos, and I confronted the fallen angel Tyegerial, the Warden of Outpost 4, along with his host of troglodytes and lamenting souls, so that we might contact the Colonel of the West.

Abigail missed the point of my lesson: Sometimes you have to be willing to lose, yet bar the enemy from succeeding through loss. She wanted to hear more about Outpost 4, the skyscraper preserved from the time of First Civilization's fall. Of the reflective blue windows, its grand ballroom and hallways lined with seemingly endless doors. But I insisted on hearing her music first.

Enchantress Thulease and Grand Wizard Seelain's return interrupted Abigail's flute melody. They, however, encouraged her to finish, which she did, a bit more nervous than she had been with just me as her audience.

We sat at a table in Grand Wizard Seelain's dining room. It was large enough for twelve, so we sat together. Grand Wizard Seelain sat on the end with Enchantress Thulease to her right followed by me, and Student Apprentice Abigail to her left.

Like the rest of the house, the room was conservatively decorated, with white curtains framing a large picture window overlooking a small flower garden. Pictures of various ships in harbor or at sea decorated the walls. Our meal included bread, several types of cheese, walnuts, dried apples and strips of salted beef, and was served on highly polished steel plates. We were each poured a half goblet of red wine from Wizard Seelain's own winery, and a tall cup of cinnamon spiced apple cider.

It was a hastily prepared meal, during which Guard Captain Koleno and the serpent handler prepared and saddled Balooga for travel.

Wizard Seelain instructed her student apprentice on what she was to study, and to assist the guard captain as needed. They were not to speak of us visiting, and the carriage driver would be housed over night before returning. The guard captain would see to his bunking and payment.

There was little talk during the meal, except for Enchantress Thulease remarking upon Abigail's excellent music, and the student apprentice commenting upon the story I'd shared with her, and how, even as a child, she'd dreamed of being part of such an adventure.

I started to explain the danger, and fear involved in such an adventure, but stopped. I didn't mention what had stung my heart so many times and left a lasting darkness lurking there, my witnessing the deaths of so many. Although I was no more than seven or eight years older than the student apprentice, her youthful enthusiasm brimming with hope and anticipation made me feel far older. I didn't want to chance smothering even a fraction of her envisioned future. It's what would carry her through the long years of relentless study, learning the base knowledge and skills to perform her chosen spellcraft.

Instead I reached behind my breastplate and tugged out the cotton cap Lilly had talked me into buying for the desert portion of our trip. It was sweat-stained, tattered and frayed, especially the flap that had shaded my neck. "Here," I said to Abigail and slid it across the table. "I wore this to the center of the Southern Continent and back. Something to remember our visit, and to wear when you're assigned to work under the sun in the vineyard and flower gardens."

"How did you know that was part of my duties?"

"Having spent time serving as Grand Wizard Seelain's personal guard, I guessed she'd have you spending time out in the sun and fresh air, away from those dusty tomes." I grinned and then wiped my mouth with a cloth napkin.

Both the supreme enchantress and the grand wizard smiled while sipping their wine.

"Thank you, Flank Hawk. I will wear it." She admired it a half a moment and said, "Someday, after my student apprenticeship is complete, I will gift to you something that I bore on one of my travels."

"I very much look forward to that, Air Wizard Student Apprentice Abigail." I don't think she saw that my smile was forced, my mind reminding me that my odds of living until that occasion might occur were impossibly long.

Both Enchantress Thulease and Grand Wizard Seelain stared at their empty goblets. They recognized my forced smile, and certainly guessed at its reason.

We'd put two hours between us and Old Salerno, Balooga flying fast as a strong horse's canter. Unlike the carnivorous red and black dragons I'd ridden upon, gray dragons were herbivorous. Balooga's horned head reminded me more of a bull than a reptilian serpent. She ate any and all vegetable matter with horse-like incisors and molars, and the splay-hooves on her hind feet emphasized that she wasn't a predator. That didn't mean the broad-winged beast was defenseless. Balooga's three-foot curved horns were sharp and she had the ability to spout streams of scalding steam more than her body length, head to tail. That was only half the reach of a red dragon's fiery breath, but more than enough to fend off most creatures.

Of course, I rode aft guard with a new crossbow drawn from Grand Wizard Seelain's small armory and gifted to me. Although I was an excellent shot by most measures, the spell strength of a grand air wizard and a supreme enchantress, and the breath weapon of a gray dragon…in comparison my offensive firepower was feeble.

Even on the ground, unless caught unprepared, we were more than a match for any group of brigands. But they weren't the reason we travelled until dawn and stayed to the less travelled rural areas and wild regions. It was the concern of assassins, possibly with poison, and spellcraft of their own, somehow informed of our return to Keesee and having guessed or divined our route to the King's City.

We slept through the day in coppice of oaks and timed our approach to the King's City for dawn, arriving just as the sun was rising.

Chapter 26

Ice Gale, Major Jadd's serpent mount, was one of four stabled in the northern royal serpent cavalry roost. Jadd was one of five serpent cavalryman assigned a white dragon captured from the Necromancer King's bevies. The war had severely depleted Keesee's serpent cavalry to a shadow of its former strength.

The white dragon's presence meant Jadd and Sergeant Drux had been rotated to local patrols. The serpent cavalry's numbers were too few to afford leave from duty.

Several serpent handlers recognized Grand Wizard Seelain, especially because of her mount. One, Kayjay, recognized me. Supreme Enchantress Thulease didn't frequent the stables. In addition, she often wore a scarf to mask her face when in public. So it was possible she wasn't recognized while waiting for a runner to bring back a carriage to take us to the enchantress's grand tower.

Grand Wizard Seelain's conversation with the stablemaster resulted in a request taken as an order not to discuss or share who arrived with her. If those in the stable remained silent, it might give the enchantress a day to begin her search to gather the six items that might revive her daughter. And time to discover who'd plotted to stop us from reaching the Southern Continent.

The supreme enchantress's husband appeared surprised at our arrival. He immediately shared that Thereese's condition had slowly worsened. He'd resorted to a chemical stimulant to keep her breathing and elevate her heart rate and blood pressure.

To me, Enchantress Thereese's face appeared sunken and her muscle tone more slack, like what happened to bed-ridden elders. She'd further weakened during our mission to discover the means to revive her.

Alchemist Butlir directed a servant to prepare a room for me while Enchantress Thulease prepared a written message for delivery to Imperial Seer Lochelle. Grand Wizard Seelain's reluctance to visit the royal palace melted away. She was one of the few who might enter the palace without questions and be granted immediate access to the ancient passages and dark rooms below the main floors.

"Swiftly as I may," Grand Wizard Seelain said to Enchantress Thulease, "I will deliver your words to the Imperial Seer and return, come nightfall. Together we shall make our way to the Royal Library and begin our research of the dark elves."

"In the meantime," Enchantress Thulease said, "my husband and I shall initiate contacts to obtain the necessary elements."

Then she turned to me. "Flank Hawk, we have completed a long journey." Then her eyes met those of a servant while still speaking to me. "After you have eaten, I recommend you retire to your prepared room and sleep. If you are willing to continue your service, I anticipate another mission. Soon."

That evening, when I entered the enchantress's kitchen, a servant came to fetch me, saying the master alchemist requested my presence in his research laboratory upon my awakening.

After drinking a ladle full of water, I followed the servant to Alchemist Butlir's work room. It was filled with glass vials, some suspended by clamps over oil-lit flames. Others were lined next to each other on tables and shelves, many of them in wooden racks.

Ceramic jars and casks filled several long, knee-high tables under shelves along the far wall.

The stocky alchemist stood next to a tall table, holding up and examining the milky contents of an odd, fluted vial. He was dressed in a brown shirt and pants with a gray apron splotched with stains. He had a pair of goggles settled over his eyes, which he lifted after placing the fluted vial on a narrow rack.

"Mercenary Flank Hawk," he said while removing a pair of close-fitting leather gloves. "You appear at least somewhat recovered from your travels."

I raised my eyebrows. "Ten hours of uninterrupted sleep on a feather mattress is better than twenty outside on the rocky ground."

He leaned a hip against the table. "I will get directly as to why I summoned you, Flank Hawk. I have learned that you have a relative who, among other trades, is an accomplished fey trapper?"

I thought a moment. Then it came to me. "My Uncle Garrin. One of my mother's older brothers. I haven't seen him in ten summers."

I recalled the last time he visited. He talked my mother into cutting my older sister's hair. Later my father told me my uncle needed the locks of a virgin to weave a net. To catch something. I never learned what.

"According to my sources," the alchemist said, "Garrin, son of Naxton, served as an auxiliary scout and tracker for the king's light cavalry during the war. Most recently he and several like-minded compatriots have been hunting goblins in northeastern Keesee. They are currently in the King's City to claim their bounty."

I wondered who a master alchemist's sources might be. I looked around his workroom. Probably glass blowers. Dealers in herbs and merchants trading in similar things. And the maybe individuals known to his wife.

"It is my understanding that he frequents the One-Eyed Pelican, a rather unsavory tavern in the lower city." He squinted. "Are you familiar with it, Flank Hawk? Mercenaries are said to frequent it."

"I've been there," I said. "Rats scramble through the rafters. The food is terrible, and the ale is harsh." I laughed. "It's one of Major Jadd's favorite places."

"I have met Major Jadd. Why would he favor such a place?"

"He doesn't mind the food. And those that eat or celebrate there don't listen to what's said beyond their own table." I shrugged. "It's not my favorite place, but it sort of grows on you. I could see if my uncle's there tonight. What did you want to speak with him about?"

"His services as a fey trapper. They are immortal beings, and the blood of one of their number is an element necessary to revive Thereese."

"I'll visit the One-Eyed Pelican tonight, then. And the next few nights if you're not able to locate my uncle another way." I rubbed my chin while thinking. "Your new carriage driver, Pault. If you could spare him tonight, I'd like him to go with me."

Visiting the lower city at night alone wasn't wise. I'd weapons sparred with Pault several times. He wielded his long-handled mace well enough—just like Miggs who'd served as the enchantress's carriage driver before dying on the *Hunchback Maiden*'s deck.

Alchemist Butlir nodded sagely. "It is a place known for crime and violence after nightfall. Safety in numbers." He began to untie his stained apron. "I should accompany you as well. I shall direct Guardsman Pault to prepare the carriage right away."

"No," I said. "Pault can handle himself well enough. And he already knows Enchantress Thulease has returned, so inviting him wouldn't increase that circle."

The alchemist frowned. "You are quite correct, Flank Hawk. I would stand out in such an establishment, and am not known for my combat prowess. But thank you all the same for not saying it directly."

His frowning face shifted to one of concern. "I imagine you know how gossip travels within the palace. It is likely a noble or a servant, or a library assistant has seen the enchantress. Word there travels like ripples spread after a pebble's been tossed into a glassy pond."

"More like a brick," I said.

He smiled and rubbed his hands together. "Nevertheless, I shall have the carriage prepared. What manner of coin would be appropriate?"

I shook my head. "Not necessary, Alchemist Butlir. I'm still in your wife's service. Until your daughter is revived. And the tunnel down to the docks closes at sunset. Pault and I will have to use the stairs to descend the cliff face."

"Well, someone should at least drive you through Brown District. And the coin is to reimburse you in advance for the meal. How many silver?"

"I'm sure Pault'll appreciate the ride there," I said. "As for coin? Not much. It *is* the One-Eyed Pelican."

I spotted my uncle right off, sitting at a round table with two other men. He was tall and lanky, with a sharp nose and strong chin, just like I remembered. But he now had more gray in his shaggy hair. He had the same leather band, decorated with a tarnished copper coin, trying to hold some of it in place. Like the stocky man on his right, my uncle was wearing leather pants stuffed into his boots. My Uncle Garrin had a soft leather jacket, unbuttoned to show a green and black plaid shirt. The stocky, bearded man with short curly hair wore a deerskin vest over a faded green shirt, and a wool cap that was almost the same color as his shirt.

The third man at the table was sitting with a full mug of beer, listening to the other two argue about something. This man had a medium build, short salt and pepper hair, with a square, beardless chin. He was wearing sturdy cotton breeches and shirt, both mottled brown, the pants a bit darker. He had a heavy leather jacket with finger-wide strips of blackened steel sewn into it, and decorated with what had to be turkey feathers along his forearms.

They each had a short sword sheathed on their left hip and a long straight dagger on their right. My uncle had a second, curved dagger on his belt behind the straight one.

The One-Eyed Pelican was a shack of a place, actually several wooden buildings, each attached and expanding upon the initial structure. When Pault and I entered, the place was only half full, mostly sailors, with a couple of soldiers and mercenaries scattered among them. But it was full of smoke and laughter, talking and occasional shouts.

I looked up and pointed out to Pault a gray rat creeping across a rafter. He looked up and shook his head. He'd never been in a place like the Pelican before.

"You say that Major Jadd favors this…this place?" Pault asked. "Over what?"

"Anywhere, I think." I shrugged and picked up a short-backed chair. "Come on, I see my uncle over there."

Pault picked up a chair and followed. He had his mace slid into his belt, and I had my short sword and dirk should we run into any problems.

I stopped a pace away from the table and waited for the men to look my direction.

The third man saw me first and reached over to bump my uncle, interrupting his conversation. From what I gathered, it was about hunting turkeys.

Uncle Garrin looked over at the third man then followed his gaze over to me. After half a second my uncle stood with a broad grin. He was almost half a head taller than me. "Krish! What the hell're you doing in here?"

"Looking for you, Uncle."

"Really?" He slapped me on the back. "Who's your friend?"

"Pault. He's a guardsman, animal handler, and coachman for one of the local spellcasters."

The stocky man looked up from where he was sitting with a grin. "Is he now?" His voice was deep but held a measure of mirth.

"Well, I see you've brought over your own chairs," my uncle said. "Sit down and join us."

The stocky man slid his chair around the table to the right and my father scooted his chair left, giving Pault and myself room for our chairs at the table.

"Gentlemen, this is my nephew, Krish. You might have heard of him."

The stocky man shook his head with a grin. "Krish? Not that I recall. What about you, Ashman?"

The other man said, "Can't say that I have either."

"He's a mercenary," my uncle said. "Goes by the name of Flank Hawk."

The third man's eyes widened just a bit. "Really. Hmmm."

The stocky man grinned and extended his hand. "They call me Grouch."

"His given name's too hard to remember," Uncle Garrin said, and laughed.

"That's because I associate with people like you," Grouch said.

My uncle scoffed and drank a gulp of his ale.

"Say," Grouch said, still a bit of relaxed mirth in his voice. "You really killed a goddess like they say?"

"I was there, and a part of the doing," I said. "But probably not like *they* say."

Then Grouch released a loud belly laugh and signaled over a waitress. Uncle Garrin pointed to the serious man next to him. "This here is Ralph, but he goes by Ashman."

I reached across the table and shook Ashman's hand, and then Grouch's. I put my right hand on Pault's shoulder and introduced him. After everyone shook his hand the waitress arrived and my uncle ordered everyone except Ashman a drink. His mug had remained untouched.

I ordered the fish soup, red and greasy, but something I could tolerate. Pault had the same. He scrunched his nose every time he took a spoonful. Grouch thought that was pretty funny.

We talked a while. I told my uncle and his bounty partners the true story how the goddess Fendra Jolain died. I didn't like to tell that story, but it was my uncle.

After I finished, Uncle Garrin asked, "You look like you're meaning to tell me something. Is my sister well?"

"Yeah," I said, not knowing for sure. I hadn't gone to see her since my return that morning. "I know you trap fey, Uncle. Or used to. I know an enchantress that would like to hire you do just that, if you still do."

"Any particular kind?"

"I'm not exactly sure. She needs the blood of one. You'd have to get the details from her. I know she pays fair coin."

To that statement, Pault nodded.

"Well," Uncle Garrin said. "I got an idea where I might trap one or two of the lesser sort. Fairies."

He looked to the man on his left. "Ashman?"

The man held his hands out in front of him and said in a calm voice, "No thanks. Messing with the fey isn't something I aspire to."

"Grouch?" my uncle asked.

The stocky man finished his mug of bitter ale. "Goblins and ogres and the odd troll here and there, I have no problem with that. Even hunted werewolves with you, Garrin. But I'm with Ashman on this one."

"Okay," my uncle said. I hear you both with full understanding. Nephew, it's more than a one man job." He shifted his gaze to Pault. "Really needs three."

Both Ashman and Grouch looked pretty battle-hardened. That gave me pause.

"You faced hydras and a goddess," Uncle Garrin said. "Nothing compared to lesser fey."

"I'm in," I said, knowing if I said no, my uncle would too. How long might it take the enchantress to find someone else?

Pault said, "If Flank Hawk's in, I'll be your third."

CHAPTER 27

Clipper, my bay gelding had a bit of an ornery streak, but he had nothing on Wick, my mount while serving a year of the war as a wyvern scout.

My Uncle Garrin was nothing like my mother. He was boisterous and talked a lot. Pault figured my uncle just liked to hear his own voice. At least he was entertaining, some of the time.

"That Rin," Uncle Garrin said. "Fine boy. You could've backed me up on him going with us, Krish."

Uncle Garrin had joined Lilly and Nura at my father's home for an evening meal. I knew my father didn't like Garrin much, but they tolerated each other. My sister Katchia liked Nura almost as much as she liked Lilly. She'd finally gotten over Lilly being a lycanthrope and the two laughed and talked with smiles on their faces. I guessed a lot of it was that my mother became comfortable with Lilly and that reflected in my little sister, who wasn't so little any more. She was growing into a young woman.

I think my mother felt Nura was too worldly for me, forgetting I'd traveled to the heart of two distant continents and faced beasts from legend.

"Like my dad told you, Uncle Garrin, Rin's got a job in the royal stables. When he isn't caring for cavalry mounts, he's looking after the wyverns. Might be a serpent handler, and even the stablemaster someday."

"You think your friend Major Jadd has that kind of influence? Jobs like them are hard to come by, especially as the king don't have many of his dragons left."

After a pause he continued, "You say he's got some sword training under his belt. No reason he couldn't apprentice under me. Being a bounty man isn't a bad life."

Uncle Garrin tugged on the rope leading his cantankerous old mule. Or that's what he said about Bucky. Maybe that's why the mule and Clipper seemed to get along. But my uncle's mule, just like his horse, responded to odd commands better than most dogs. They knew when to neigh, or quietly slink into deep brush on their own after a hushed command.

The old mule carried plenty of scars, as did the gray horse, Slate, my uncle rode. Probably due to close scrapes with goblins or trolls, or werewolves. The same might happen to Rin. That's why me and dad worked so hard at getting him a good trade. So that he wouldn't take up as a mercenary, like me, and get scarred up. Or worse.

"Uncle, how much does that storage merchant charge you?"

"Why, Krish?"

"I go on long missions but keep a room at a boarding house. Keep some of my belongings there. A locked storage room could do the same, maybe better and for less coin."

He stared back over his shoulder at me, considering his words. "You got a decent boarding house room, probably what you carry with you, your armor, silvered sword is what you got of real value. For that, a boarding house is cheaper."

The storage room my uncle had rented in a guarded, two-story warehouse, built of granite blocks and filled with rooms shut up with locked steel doors, seemed like a small fortress. Painted gray, its wooden exterior made it blend in with nearby buildings in the Blue District.

He had a half dozen swords of various types, several spears and crossbows, and at least twenty crates and trunks filled with skins, silver and iron trinkets, and some jars filled with liquids and powders that reminded me of Alchemist Butlir's workroom.

While there he'd dug out a crate and handed me three pairs of iron mesh gauntlets, each wrapped tightly in an oil cloth to keep them from rusting. And he grabbed a smaller wooden box filled with several hundred iron treble hooks of various sizes.

From a cedar trunk he pulled out two stuffed goblin heads. Each was mounted on a two foot stick. Another head had been skinned off the skull with lacing so that it could be slipped over a man's head and tied to hold it tight, like a gruesome mask. All three looked a little shriveled but life-like enough, with coarse hair and copper earrings. The eyes had been left out of the skinned mask, but the heads on sticks had yellow cat-like glass eyes identical to goblin foes I'd faced.

"A little oil and they'll almost look to be living," Uncle Garrin had said. I didn't doubt him.

Finally, from a large clay pot my uncle pulled a tall jar. After breaking the lid's wax seal, he counted out forty-five white hairs. They were silky and white as freshly fallen snow. He had plenty left in the jar when he resealed it with candle drippings.

"From a real unicorn I managed to shoot back my youth," he'd explained. "Sold the pelt, hooves, bones, and the blood, but kept hair from its mane and tail. Good for making certain garments that're handy for my trade. Makes nets of woven virgins' hair especially potent. We'll need that for what we're after."

"You wouldn't happen to still have the horn," I asked.

"Why? Krish. You know those are pretty rare. Pretty near unheard of."

"I know, Uncle," I'd told him. "But I know someone who'd pay you a fair price, especially for something so rare."

"Won't be coming out of your pocket," he replied. "Mercenaries don't earn near enough coin. Not even in a lifetime."

I looked up at the sky as we passed through the broken terrain on what was little more than an old goat trail. Clipper nickered and shook his head. Bucky followed suit.

"You're right, Uncle Garrin. I don't have much of value, other than a few things gathered over the years, and my experience."

Uncle Garrin pointed to his head and laughed. He looked past me to Pault. "You've got knowledge and skills, Krish. Or should I say, Flank Hawk. You've got friends. Good ones. Influential ones."

Uncle Garrin did like to talk, about the weather, towns he'd visited, how many trolls he'd killed, the current bounty paid for goblins, ogres and souled zombies. He said Keesee paid the highest bounties. The Doran Confederacy, Faxtinian Coalition, and the Lesser Kingdoms were more focused on rebuilding and less interested in spending their coin on bounties. Short sighted, my uncle explained. Not keeping their citizens safe.

One thing bounty men like my uncle did was free up the soldiers and militias to do things they were better at rather than tracking individual and small bands of creatures that were almost certain to cause trouble of one kind or another. In the past few years I'd met a few mercenaries that were bounty men. They always remained silent on their trade and techniques.

Like them, Uncle Garrin wasn't interested in talking about his bounty trade secrets. How to hunt goblins, trolls, werewolves, basilisks and even a catoblepas, which I'd once been told by Lesser Enchanter Jonas was an extinct species.

I thought it wasn't that he didn't want to tell me. He didn't want to share more than he had to with Pault. Maybe that was why he wanted Rin to accompany us as the third person instead of Pault, and keep his hard-learned secrets in the family.

But he'd eventually have to tell me *and* Pault something, especially why Grouch and Ashman didn't want anything to do with hunting and trapping lesser fey. Pault thought my uncle intended to get us so far out in the wilderness that we'd be less likely to back out.

Pault took my uncle's gruffness pretty well, and that spoke of the new coachman's loyalty to the enchantress.

About two hours before sundown Uncle Garrin turned off the trail to stop near a coppice of red pines. It was our second day traveling southeast, away from the King's City. "We'll make camp here and get ready for tonight."

"Tonight? What about it?" Pault asked, a shade of anger in his voice.

My uncle ignored him. "Cold camp. We won't be here most of the night anyway."

"Tie, or hobble the horses?" I asked.

"Tie Clipper and Roof Run to a pine. Slate and Bucky should be fine hobbled."

Pault handed me the reins to his mount, Roof Run. She was an obedient appaloosa and wouldn't wander, or so I thought. Being white with only a few spots on her neck and flank, she'd be easy to spot after dark if she wandered a little. Of course, she might be just as ornery as Clipper and Pault handled his mount better than me.

Spirited is how Pault described Clipper. Of course, he spent the better part of his days around horses, so who was I to argue.

Uncle Garrin signaled for me and Pault to gather near the birch trunk reinforced by steel bands, and two tightly packed leather sacks he'd unstrapped from Bucky. "Okay, Pault, here's what you've been itching to know. You too, Krish." He grinned. "You've just been less griping about it."

Pault nodded and watched as my uncle undid the latches that held the trunk shut. "The reason Grouch and Ashman weren't interested in trapping fey is because you got to get them all. All in their pod. Every last one. Even one gets away, you're done for. We'll all be dead."

"What do you mean?" Pault asked. "What if there's a hundred and one and we only get a hundred? Can't you just kill the one that got away? Flank Hawk's darn good with his crossbow."

"First off, there ain't more than seven in a fairy pod. They ain't what you might call overly gregarious types. Usually three, maybe four."

He began laying out the filled sacks from the tightly packed trunk. "Second, even if they don't charm ya, they're too fast. Like a humming bird dipped in lighting. How might you be shooting at something like that, Krish?"

Hitting a flitting humming bird was more than a challenge, and getting one at a distance required luck, not skill. I shook my head, saying, "I'd need more luck than all three of us could imagine."

I'd never seen one of the lesser types of elves, or as my uncle called them, fey. But like everyone, I'd heard tales from childhood. Magical creatures, invisible to mortal eyes. They lived deep in forest glens, sharing them with unicorns and frolicking with dryads and satyrs. I'd once fought alongside a company of satyrs. They were sturdy as any burly man, and wise in the ways of the forest and nature, and the predicting of weather. But they weren't immortal.

I thought about the tightness of the nets he'd woven. I asked my uncle, "Are you saying that they're the size of humming birds?"

Pault added, "I thought fairies and sprites aren't violent and don't favor carrying weapons."

My uncle continued to unpack the trunk's contents, including a sack of cold iron beads, twine bundles made from flexible vines, an iron whistle and two gadget whistles that were actually three iron whistles attached to a single blow tube, a bunch of screws, clamps and braces that he said went with his pine rods precut to varying lengths and bundled together, four coiled metal springs, and more.

"They're bigger than a humming bird," my uncle said. "More like the size of a crow. They have translucent wings, sort of clear like a dragonfly's, and they beat like that too. But they're cut more like a butterfly's. Don't let that fool ya. They're rigid as steel slats. And fairies, they're beautiful beyond anything you can imagine. Anything. And they'll use that against ya if you give'em the chance."

Pault scowled at that, but I knew the power of magic, even subtle magic like charms and glamors.

"They'll charm, you," my uncle warned. "Mesmerize. Next thing you know, they're gone."

"That doesn't seem so dire," Pault said, but with concern in his voice. "What aren't you telling me? Why aren't your bounty partners here instead of me and Flank Hawk?"

My uncle held up his pointing finger. "I'll say again. If even one gets away, you will die." A ring of doom curled tight to his words. "We all will die."

He waited a moment for that to sink in. "How would you die?" He shrugged. "They can affect all things in nature. A tree limb may break and land on you. If you pass near a hornet nest, they may swarm you. The mud in a streambed may give way, trapping you and then the hornets get ya. Maybe the mud'll suck you down like a bog. I've heard tell they can influence mountain trolls. If one of them begins stalking you, you won't know it till you're tied to a spit, being cooked for supper. And even if you do see it coming…even ogres don't dare mess with a troll."

I recalled my only brush with a mountain troll. I'd been gutting a goat with Enchanter Jonas when a bear came snuffing around. Without warning a troll hurled its crude spear, skewering the bear through its rib cage. The spear was a twelve-foot limb thick as my bicep, bark peeled away and hacked sharp.

Tall as two men and broad-shouldered, everything on the mountain troll's face seemed pointed. Its ears, its long nose, chin and especially its double rows of dagger-sharp teeth.

"I don't blame them," I said, thinking about the ogres I'd faced. "It'd be like pitting a hound against a wolverine."

"So how do you plan on catching *all* of them?" Pault asked. "You only have three nets. What if there's more than three?" He sounded agitated.

"They're fast and got magic," Uncle Garrin said, and grinned. "But they're predictable. Knowing that, I set this venture up eight summers past."

That got my attention. It'd take a powerful seer to predict Enchantress Thulease's need. So much time, so many variables, and powerful individuals involved in the sequence of events, including a goddess and the secretive

Sleeping Sage.

My uncle answered my unspoken questions.

"I picked the spot nine summers ago, did the planting and landscaping eight years ago. I used what I know about them. They winter hibernate in the root systems of daylilies, flit and hide among their greens and blooms, especially during sunny spring and summer days. Sleep in them at night. They favor small spots with springs or ponds, if possible." He grinned, but his eyes were serious as jagged steel. "Fairies. Daylilies to them is like a rotting carcass to bloat flies."

Beautiful fairies and carrion flies didn't seem to fit—but I knew what my uncle meant. Maybe that said something about him?

"Haven't been back to see it since today."

"We passed through it?" I asked.

Uncle Garrin nodded while untying the cords holding the leather bags closed. "Yes, a little over an hour ago."

I closed my eyes, trying to recall passing by a spring with daylilies nearby. "Where the trail narrowed," I said, "with the ironweed covering those dead trees, up into their low-hanging canopy. There was a spring draining from the rocks and it formed a small pool. I thought it was a perfect place to stop and water the horses, and get a drink ourselves."

"I thought that too," Pault said. "Especially as we had to dismounted to avoid the press of ironweed vines. But right there, Garrin, your mule and horse both crapped."

I laughed. "One of your commands, Uncle. That's what you muttered. Right?"

Uncle Garrin returned my laugh, turning into snorts. "Yeah, it'll mask, or at least compete with our scent when we go back there close to midnight. "That's when the fairies are least active, deepest in their sleep. They're most active around dusk and dawn."

My uncle carefully pulled one of the nets I'd watched him weave out of hair, from virgin girls I was willing to bet, and the white strands from a unicorn's mane. Evenly spread throughout the net he'd strung iron treble hooks and cold iron beads. He used a canvas tarp set on top so that when folded the hooks wouldn't tangle the net. Only a few of the hooks had snagged the canvas.

"Okay, you both remember the place of our ambush to trap them fairies. I didn't tell you about it till now because I didn't want either of you looking suspicious. They were certainly watching us when we passed through. They can detect subtle things in men like us. An overlong glance or fixing of the eyes on something, and facial expressions hinting at study, familiarity, or planning. Any of those would doom my plan. Doom us."

Pault frowned, showing disapproval, changing to disappointment.

I agreed with my uncle's caution. "He knew what to look for, Pault, and could do it best without giving away our purpose." Then I said to my uncle, "Okay, so what habits do they have that can be used against them? What part do Pault and I have to play in your trapping scheme?"

After that, Pault said, "You never answered how many there are. And even if we do catch them all, unless the enchantress kills them—they can be killed, right?"

"Yes," Uncle Garrin said. "Using cold iron."

"Well," Pault continued, "if fairies are as dangerous as you say, Garrin, it'd be her death too if she didn't exterminate those we bring her. Then they'll come after us." He crossed his arms, gazing intently at the nets. "Both she and her husband aren't the blood killing types."

The guardsman was right. They weren't ice-hearted killers. But I figured he'd never seen either of them in a fight.

Pault sighed. "It is their daughter's life at stake, though. What parent wouldn't kill to save their daughter? And themselves, if it came to that?"

"That's the thing, Pault," my uncle said, authority of experience filling his words. "Predictability is on our side. Fairies are immortal, but it's as though they live only in the moment. When we hand them off to someone else, they'll hold them new folks responsible for their captivity. Not us. We're safe from their wrath."

"What about the enchantress?" I asked.

My uncle shrugged. "She's smart and'll figure something out, or extinguish them and their magic with cold iron." Everything unpacked, he leaned back. "That last time I visited you and your family back in Pine Ridge, Krish. You remember that?"

"I do," I said. "You took my sister's hair."

"Paid good coin for it too. Helped your family through a rough time, you know."

"Well, not long after that I trapped and handed two lesser fey off to an enchanter. I don't think he ended them." My uncle let out a long breath. "He's dead now. Not through fairy magic. Company he was attached to during the war, one of Lord Hingroar's, got overrun by a troop of ogres and goblins."

My uncle paused. "Probably the same night your cousin Guzzy died."

Why my uncle brought that up, I wasn't sure. I didn't like to think about that night, Guzzy's death. I clenched my teeth and nodded. That's all.

He then shot Pault a glance. "There's probably two fairies. You can tell by the flowers. The color that should be there is orange. That's what I planted. There's two other colors, purple and yellow, and in even numbers. Maybe four, but probably two, since there's still a bunch of orange."

"So how do we drop the nets on them?" Pault asked. "And what do we do with them after that?"

"Okay. First of all, cold iron mutes their magic, and its touch is like a dozen bee stings. Stuns them only for a few seconds, though.

"Second of all, certain pitch noises confuse them. That's what the whistles are for.

"Third of all, goblins hunt fairies. For some reason fey magic is weak against goblins. Like how some owls hunt skunks. The spray don't seem to bother them.

"Fourth of all, when fairies flee, they don't go up. They fly along the ground. That's how we'll catch them.

"Fifth, yellow fairies, you can tell by the dominant sheen when they flap their wings, can go invisible.

"What about the purple?" I asked.

"Don't know," he said. "Never trapped that color fairy before, or heard tell from anyone who has." He reached for the bundles of pine rods. "Now, help me put these frames together for the nets."

The sun was up, but it hadn't reached over the steep hill to my right. Anytime, I thought, waiting for the first fairy to show. If we sprang the ambush before they were up, they might burrow down into the roots instead of taking flight. We'd never catch them.

I was hiding behind a low-growing pine shrub. My job was to start blowing my triple whistle gadget to set the ambush in motion. Pault had the other triple whistle. They'd make us sound like six goblins instead of just two.

About twenty yards ahead of me was the pool fed from a hillside spring. It had a few reeds and cattails growing opposite the rocky hillside. On the side across from me was the bed of daylilies and just beyond the flowers was a wall of white pines infested with ironweed. Those twisting vines were tough as leather and the rust-colored leaves were small but jagged, and rigid enough to tear flesh. That and their curved, inch-long thorns would discourage any fairies from trying to fly through them. Or so my uncle said.

A little to the left of the vine-entangled pines stood the dead trees where the trap was to be sprung. My uncle had poisoned the tree's roots eight years ago. A slow poison that ironweed was immune to, and the invasive vines had grown up the dying trees and into the canopy above. The trail we'd ridden yesterday passed through the path walled in by the ironweed. A twenty-yard tunnel walled in by thorny vines. Pault and I had to appear threatening, and move fast. Get the lesser fey to take flight before thinking, fleeing through the ironweed tunnel.

Even though my uncle said my blood-filled pendant wouldn't be noticed by the fey, and might even be handy to be wearing during the ambush, I wasn't so sure. Still, I trusted in his experience.

Then, I saw it. A group of yellow blossoms rustled, and it wasn't due to a morning breeze. Pault was off to my left, and my uncle hidden inside the far end of the tunnel. It was up to me to decide when to set things off. I slid the triple whistle in my mouth, holding it with my teeth and grabbed a handful of cold iron beads from a belt pouch where I normally carried salt when facing zombies. With my left hand I gripped the stick stuck into a stuffed goblin's head lying next to me.

I spotted a slender human-like figure the size of a crow, like my uncle said. It appeared male, long wavy hair the color of dandelions and dressed in a green shirt and yellow pants that must've been made from daylily leaves and petals, but somehow spellcraft had given the clothing a wispy silk texture. I avoided his face, although my glimpse told me he had yellow eyes and lips. His wings fluttered faster than a butterfly's but not as fast as a humming bird's. He rose from the flowerbed and stretched his arms just as the sun's first morning rays reached the pond and flowers.

The wings were just as my uncle described. Lobed like a butterfly's and translucent, with shimmering rainbow colors, but dominated by yellow.

If the fairies didn't rise together, we were in trouble. Even if we backed off and fled, the fairies would find the two framed nets set to spring up and close off the ironweed tunnel, and the loose net suspended along the tunnel's ceiling. It wouldn't be hard for them to decide upon our intention.

Then the violet flowers rustled a few feet from the yellow fairy. As soon as I saw the tips of fluttering purple wingtips I flung my handful of iron beads at the flower bed and grabbed a second handful, sending it just as the first beads rained down on the unsuspecting fairies. I had to hope there were only two because the yellow fairy looked ready to flit away from the flowerbed.

After releasing the second handful, I ducked fully behind the pine shrub and blew hard on the triple whistle. It sounded like a trio of dog whistles, almost too high-pitched to hear. I lifted the stuffed and mounted goblin head above the shrub, twisting and moving it from side to side. Then I lifted the other goblin head with my now free hand.

I blew the whistles again but, between breaths, I heard the second triple whistle sound off. At the same time I heard piercing screams of surprise. They sounded like a cross between a screeching violin and a squeaking clarinet, both stuck on high notes.

Some of the beads must've struck the two fairies—unless there were more than two. And those beads that fell among the flowers would block them from burrowing back into the ground and hide among the daylily roots. How they'd even do that with their wings, I wasn't sure. Maybe with magic, but it didn't matter. I pumped the goblin heads up and down one more time just above the pine shrub and then dropped them. Continuing to blow my whistle, I raced around the shrub and charged toward the tunnel, trying to slip on the iron mesh gloves quick as I could manage.

Pault, wearing the goblin mask over his head and blowing his triple whistle, hurled handfuls of iron beads with one hand and shook a two-tined, forged iron spear in his other. He stomped forward, causing the two fairies to stop their flight and spin about. I dropped one of the gloves, grabbed another handful of beads and whipping a wide scatter at them. Several beads struck. Maybe they were mine or maybe Pault's. I couldn't tell and it didn't matter. The fey turned and fled, wings a blur of flaps, and shot into the ironweed tunnel.

I slowed a little while glancing over at the flower bed. Nothing. No third or fourth fairies. I realized I'd stopped blowing my whistle and started again.

Then I heard my uncle's single, piercing whistle sound. At the same time the framed net lying flat on my side of the tunnel sprung up into place, covering my side of the tunnel.

Working quietly, last night we'd managed to place the nets with leather ties and stakes, and springs, set to snap up like a ponderous mousetrap. The frogs in the reeds and along the pool's edge, while serving as a warning to the slumbering fairies should the croakers fall silent, provided cover noise as we'd worked for an hour, finishing shortly after midnight.

Actually, my uncle did most of the work. We hauled and held parts in place as he constructed the trap with only glimpses of moonlight to assist.

Both framed nets snapped up simultaneously, and the hanging net fell just after. My uncle rose from his shallow dug hole, the leaves scattered over him sloughing away.

One of the fairies, the yellow one, was caught beneath the dropped net. It screeched in agony, but somehow managed the magic to disappear. My uncle dove forward, grasping where the net bulged with his iron mesh gloves. The invisible yellow fey's screeching intensified.

The purple fairy avoided the dropping net and reversed direction. It must've seen the far framed net spring into place. However, it retreated too fast to notice the net on our side blocking its retreat.

It flew right into the net, caught like a moth in a spider web, several of the iron treble hooks digging into flesh as it tried to fly out.

She screamed—I could tell it was female, looking like a miniature maiden of beauty swathed in a purple gossamer tunic. Her wild violet eyes and high-pitch squeal of terror and pain dug at my emotions. For some reason I'd discounted the effect of the barbs woven into the net. I accepted my uncle's words, what cold iron would do, but didn't translate the consequences to a living being of such beauty. Mute their magic, yes, but also cause surges of stinging pain. I'd set aside the consequences and focused on getting the job done.

Until that moment.

The haunting sounds of agony tugged at my heart. What would happen when I gripped the fairy with my iron gloves?

I pushed all that aside. I was far from innocent. I'd killed before. There was blood on my hands, not only of undead, monsters and beasts, but blood of men and women as well.

Duty. It was my duty, my promise to Enchantress Thulease. Life for her daughter, Thereese.

In the second or two it took to throw off the emotion and guilt, Pault had made it to the framed net. He'd sloughed off his mesh gloves and was carefully removing barbs from the caught purple fairy, ignoring my uncle's shouts and curses. Rather, he gazed down into the ravishing fey's purple eyes.

I stepped forward and struck him from behind, catching him in the jaw with a roundhouse punch. Having knocked him aside, I thrust my left hand forward, into the net, grabbing the purple fairy by her legs.

She screamed, so piercing that I thought my ears would bleed.

Then she fell silent.

My uncle's two iron-mesh gauntlets held the yellow fairy pinned to the ground. "Get the cages, Pault!" he shouted.

Dazed, both from residual magic and my blow, the guardsman removed his goblin mask and staggered to his feet.

"Look away!" I ordered. "Get the cages. Now, Pault! Get them now, now, NOW!"

Breaking into an unsteady trot, the guardsman headed toward the pair of fallen logs where we'd hidden three cold iron cages, each lined with dangling, iron treble hooks.

I asked my uncle, "What would've happened if there'd been more than two?"

We'd ridden hard after caging the fairies and dismantling and packing up the nets. The towers and walls of the King's City were in sight. We'd reach them not long after nightfall.

Slowing his mount from a canter along the hard-packed trade road leading to the city, he glanced back over his shoulder after we passed an empty wagon pulled by a team of oxen. His eyes focused on Pault, who looked away. "We'd be dead," he said to me.

Uncle Garrin and I pieced together that purple fairies must have spellcraft that could influence feelings and emotion. She'd ensnared Pault with it. And it was nearly our undoing.

"But there weren't, Krish. If I'd've thought there was, I have two other sites planted and waiting. Both far from here, though. One in the western Doran Expanse, the other along the Faxtinian Coalition's northern reaches."

My uncle released a throaty laugh. "Pault," he said, a little mirth lingering in his voice. "You're not the only man ever to be mesmerized by fairy magic. Just the only one I've ever heard tell to still be taking breaths." Then his voice became low and threatening. "You won't hunt or trap with me again. Ever."

He paused until Pault looked him in the eye. "You won't tell my trapping secrets to anyone. Ever."

"I won't," Pault said. "I swear. It'll never happen."

"Then we'll say goodbye on good terms, Guardsman. Once we deliver our cargo to your lady." He rested a hand on the ball-like cage covered by leather, suspended in a lashed wooden frame on the rump of his horse.

I turned and checked the rigging holding an identical cage and frame to the rump of Clipper. The fragrance of a hundred daylilies emanated from it.

The yellow fairy was quiet, crouching and holding tight to a thin slat of lead. The cage's only piece not constructed of the fey's bane, cold iron.

CHAPTER 28

"Thank you, Flank Hawk, for such a fine meal."

"You're welcome," I said to Nura as we made our way from Koko's Bistro back to Enchantress Thulease's tower. Nura had already begun to work with Alchemist Butlir, and shared a room with one of the servants there.

I'd long remember the fine white wine, halibut cooked with exotic spices and sauces, and the salty, deep fried shredded potatoes. Nura dined on orange squid and broiled broccoli. Lilly had selected lobster, saying she wanted to see how Chef Mangus would prepare it. She couldn't talk Sergeant Drux into trying what he named the "Cockroach of the Sea." Instead, he chose deep sea eel.

I'd thought about doing something with Nura after she got settled. She'd never actually been in Tripoli and a big city like the King's City was a new experience. She felt a lot like I did the first time Major Jadd had taken me out of the palace to explore the city's streets, mostly wondering how to not get lost.

I figured Lilly had set up the dinner to get me and Nura time together outside of a mission. Lilly had Sergeant Drux reserve a table at Koko's Bistro. Since he was in the serpent cavalry, he had the connections to do that.

Drux wore his dress military uniform. Lilly borrowed a dress from her tutor. I had to buy a fancy silk shirt and wool pants, but had my new pair of boots polished to a glossy shine. Lilly's tutor had accompanied Lilly and Nura to find a green evening dress with a black shawl to match my green shirt and black pants.

Lilly thought it was hilarious—the look on my face when I arrived at the enchantress's tower and saw how close to the same our outfits were. Getting into the carriage, driven by Pault, I was worried about the ride with Lilly and Drux sitting next to each other, let alone attending a fine dinner together. They'd always had sharp words for each other, especially during our mission to slay Fendra Jolain.

But they actually seemed to enjoy each other's company, especially during the meal. And when we three—Lilly, Drux and me—told Nura the full story of the assault on Fendra Jolain's main temple, some sort of binding seemed to form between the pair. A shared experience, one both desperate and horrific, gave them common ground.

Nura asked, "Did you know the nobles and rich merchants were listening to you, Sergeant Drux, and Lilly tell your tale?"

"Not at first," I said. "I think Drux did. Maybe it was part of his plan, because they paid for our meal, just like patrons do for storytelling bards and minstrels."

"As well they should," Nura said. "They were getting a telling from firsthand accounts. From three perspectives."

In truth, I was a little nervous when those folks sitting near us discovered it was Lilly seated near them. One table did move away to another, owing I suspected to her being a lycanthrope, gossip released by the king's nobles. And wrongly naming her a werewolf, one of the most vile and violent of the werebeasts.

I didn't share that with Nura. Instead I said, "We're going to be leaving soon, I think."

"Lilly thinks so, too, Flank Hawk."

She reached out and I took her hand. We continued walking, keeping to one of the main east-west streets through Blue District. They were well lit by street lanterns.

"I know, Flank Hawk." She squeezed. "One morning I'll wake up and you all will be gone."

"I'm glad we let Lilly and Drux take the carriage," I said.

"Last two missions," Nura said, "you haven't been able to talk about what happened."

She was right, I couldn't tell her or anyone else what had happened in the Sleeping Sage's gallery because of spellcraft, and I couldn't tell about the fairy trapping because of a promise to my uncle.

"I know," I said and paused at an intersection. "It's a nice night out, Nura. Will you be able to get up for your reading and study if we turn here and take our time getting you back to your room?" Having traveled the Southern Continent with her, sometimes worn out and with little sleep, I knew the answer. But I wanted to give her an opportunity to end the evening, if she wanted to.

She grinned and leaned close. "Only if you promise to take me to the One-Eyed Pelican when you return."

I shook my head and laughed. "I don't see what Lilly and Major Jadd see in that place. She told you about it, right?"

"Yes, Lilly did. Ale that makes you want to spit. Food prepared by a half-blind cook with no sense of smell, and you'd fit in better if you don't bathe for a season."

"Yeah, she described it pretty close." Like Lilly, Nura could handle herself. Lilly told me Nura had a sheathed knife strapped to her leg under her dress. "But it'd be only fair if Jadd and Lilly accompany us."

Nura cocked her head and met my gaze.

"It isn't a place for just a couple like us," I said. I swept my hand in front of us, from me to her. "Especially dressed like this."

She smiled and laughed. "So I've been told."

I didn't care in the least for the One-Eyed Pelican. But if it meant spending an evening in Nura's company, with her smile and laugh, I'd go. No question about it.

It was almost enough to make me forget what loomed in my future. Flayzin and his sword arm.

CHAPTER 29

The pair of guards nodded to us and stepped aside as we made our way through the palace. They knew who I was, but it was Enchantress Thulease's presence that opened palace doors without question.

We made our way along the main floor in a secondary hallway decorated with tapestries and sculpted statues on pedestals, depicting mainly dragons and soldiers. Each had a small bronze plate with an etching that stated who or what the statue depicted. I'd traversed this hallway thrice before when making my way to Imperial Seer Lochelle's chambers below. The hallway was one rarely used by nobles and forbidden to most servants. I'd never stopped to look at or consider any of the pieces of art. I supposed some nobles did.

Enchantress Thulease noted that I'd turned my head while passing several of the statues. "It is possible that King Tobias may commission a sculpture of you, Flank Hawk."

I almost laughed, but didn't know if she meant it as a joke. She wasn't a person that tended toward mirth. The king appreciated what I'd done to help preserve the Kingdom of Keesee, but he wasn't fond of me. "I believe that's unlikely, Enchantress."

"Possibly Prince Halgadin, then?"

I looked up to meet her eyes as we turned a corner, our boots clapping on the polished marble floor. "I am not so sure he is overly fond of me either, Enchantress." I was friends with Major Jadd, who'd once been exiled by the crown prince. Although they'd settled the issue between them prior to our assault on the Fendra Jolain's Main Temple, I'm not sure all of their bad blood had ended. It was Prince Reveron who favored Major Jadd, and me. He was dead.

"Is there a statue of Prince Reveron?" I asked.

Indeed. There are two. A bust in the Gold Hall leading to King Tobais's personal chamber. A three-foot statue along a corridor nearly above where we now walk. There is also an oil painting of the fallen prince with his serpent steed, Night Shard. I believe that was the beast's name."

After I nodded once in agreement, recalling Prince Reveron charging, thrusting the red-glowing Blood Sword deep into the flank of a white dragon that had its jaws locked on Night Shard's throat. The prince's steed refused to die peacefully and tore into the white's belly with its hawk-like talons.

Both mortally wounded beasts rolled down the hill, fighting to the last. The prince turned from them and ran toward the crest of the hill where

Private Shaws dodged and traded blows with a pair of ogres.

The enchantress interrupted that memory, saying, "I believe Dame Christine Griffin was commissioned for the work." The enchantress slowed the pace of her long strides. "Five years have passed since its unveiling. I believe it now hangs in the Queen's bower where she may look upon it privately and remember.

"I do miss him," she said, her voice quieting and losing its normal air of authority.

"As do I, Enchantress. And you knew him far longer than me."

She stopped walking for a heartbeat or two, prepared to say something else. She then looked forward and continued down the hallway, approaching two heavy oak doors guarded by a single soldier, halberd and breastplate both brightly polished.

Once past the guard and going down the iron spiral staircase and the door above was closed, Enchantress Thulease stopped and turned to face me. "I believe it appropriate that I inform you, Flank Hawk. Grand Wizard Seelain spoke with her cousin, Guard Captain Flayzin. She was unable to dissuade him from his intended challenge."

The dim light rising up from a lantern hanging near the bottom of the stairwell failed to pierce the gloom of her words. "I spoke with my guard captain as well. I mistakenly believed that his experience with both you and him serving me side by side would shed light on your character and adherence to duty. It is most unfortunate that he…" Enchantress Thulease took a deep breath before forcing out the next words. "W-was not witness to your actions…as it…p-pp-ertainss to what hhapp…"

I placed a hand on her shoulder. "I know, what you mean…Enchantress. No need to say more." Even those few words from me were difficult to utter.

She took a steadying breath, loosening her grip on the metal railing. "Although my husband does not agree, should Flayzin press his challenge, he will be released from service to me. He knows this and also that I will use my influence to ensure that he is unable to sell his sword and skills within the King's City, and anywhere in Keesee where my desire holds sway. I am cognizant that it may ultimately be of little comfort to you, Flank Hawk."

"No, Enchantress, it does mean a lot to me."

"I will also share that the guard captain has prevailed upon my husband to provide an alchemical remedy for the fireweed resin which you are known to coat your blades with." She sighed heavily, regret hanging in her voice. "He and my husband have a long history, and—"

I raised a hand to interrupt the enchantress. "That's okay, Enchantress. I have prevailed upon my Uncle Garrin to offer insight into what I might employ to increase my odds of survival."

"Both Seelain and I believe you both relentless and resourceful, and likely to, in the end, prevail."

"I would not be so certain," I said, and set a grin across my face. "I also intend to speak with Sergeant Drux. His long years of experience as a city guard in some of the most dangerous parts of the King's City may offer me something of use."

She pursed her lips and nodded once in approval. "The sergeant has a reputation based on some of the unsavory individuals among his circle of associates. Yet, I trust him."

The enchantress ran her long-fingered hand across her cheek, down to her chin. "Coachman Pault," she said, disapproval in her tone. "Does he know of the tactics gleaned from your bounty man uncle?"

"No," I said.

"That is good. Guard Captain Flayzin is sure to question him, and the new coachman does not lie well. Even so, I do not believe he would attempt to do so on your behalf."

She turned and continued down the stairwell. "I learned how he almost brought you all to ruin," she said. "Jizzereena, the purple lesser fey, relayed to me how she and her pod mate were captured and how Pault proved a weak link that nearly doomed the trap."

Even so, my uncle paid Pault fourteen gold coins, which I thought was more than fair. He'd paid me twice that amount. That suggested how much he'd earned for the task. But what was better was what he'd given me when I asked him for ideas to defeat Flayzin in a duel. My uncle'd met Flayzin once and remembered him as an arrogant ass. He had two of what he called "troll stoppers." Rare pods of some carnivorous vine flower found far out east of Keesee. The spore cloud, even though dried out, would lock up any muscles under the skin they contacted. "Worse'n lockjaw," he'd said.

The enchantress stopped at the bottom and said, "Your uncle is very clever. Such a trait runs through family lines and rarely skips a generation, or so I have been led to believe."

It took me a second to get her meaning. Probably because I was thinking of the scaly walnut-sized spore pod sealed in a padded tin box, tucked deep in my satchel. "Thank you, Enchantress."

Before she opened the heavy oak door leading out of the staircase, I asked, "My clever uncle said that fairies live in the moment, and once we handed them off to you, we wouldn't need to worry about retribution. That their ire for being captured would be passed from us to you. How did you avoid that?"

"Trade," Enchantress Thulease said. "I learned the secret of casting invisibility from a yellow fairy many years ago. This time I traded for their blood. Your uncle is right. They do mentally reside in the present far more than most immortal beings I've encountered. They are quick to forgive, as long as one offers compensation for their captivity."

I'd pondered life spans and mortality, especially when it came to the shorter life spans of lycanthropes, and the nearly three thousand years the Colonel of the West had lived, and would continue to live, unless somehow he was slain.

"Several days of captivity," I said, "would be like a child waiting between flashes of a firefly. It may seem like a long time at that moment, but in comparison, when the new flash returns, the wait's forgotten."

She opened the door into the gray, damp hallway that eventually led to Imperial Seer Lochelle's dark chamber. "I believe you have come upon an accurate comparison, Flank Hawk. Let us hope you are equally perceptive as we delve to understand the mysterious Dark Elves of the North."

CHAPTER 30

A dozen flickering lamps hung from the domed ceiling, lighting Imperial Seer Lochelle's octagonal chamber. The rune-scribed pillars and walls made it appear even more ancient than it probably was. I wondered who, before Imperial Seer Lochelle, resided and wielded their spellcraft within the foreboding chamber. I couldn't imagine a more powerful seer than Imperial Seer Lochelle.

I guessed Enchantress Thulease and I were the last to arrive. Grand Wizard Seelain, Major Jadd, Sergeant Drux, Lilly and Captain Bray, a fellow serpent cavalryman to Major Jadd, sat on high stools around an oval table. Along the left wall stood two women in long gray dresses. One of them I recognized. Lilly's tutor. Between the two middle-aged women stood a table covered with stacks of thick, leather-bound tomes and a partitioned box holding yellowing scrolls.

Major Jadd's pock-marked face offered a friendly smile beneath his mustache, but he didn't say anything. Sergeant Drux to his left winked and grinned at me, making the scar along the right side of his chin stand out. Lilly looked my direction but was scowling for some reason. Captain Bray turned on his stool to face me and Enchantress Thulease. His eyes were a little wide, probably like mine were the first time I'd been in this chamber.

Directly across from him sat Imperial Seer Lochelle, Prime Counselor to the King. Until that moment she hadn't looked up, hiding her face behind long strands of stringy brunette hair. Imperial was the highest rank, denoting supreme and unsurpassed skill in the magical arts. Her eyes were pure white. No pupil, no iris. That always unsettled me.

Everyone at the table stood at our approach.

For an instant echoing whispers filled the chamber. Except for Supreme Enchantress Thulease, everyone's back stiffened at the sound. Tutor Roeth and her partner looked about, momentarily unsettled. The tutor adjusted her wire-rimmed glasses while her partner clasped her hands together.

As we sat my attention refocused on Seer Lochelle. I always thought gray or white hair would better match the seer's gaunt, creased face. Her youthful hands, adorned with jeweled rings, stood in stark contrast to her aged and haggard face. "Welcome, Thulease, Flank Hawk," she said, her quiet voice amplified within the chamber. "Mercenary, would you please close the doors so that we may begin?"

I stood and quickly strode toward the heavy doors and pulled them closed. Silver runes set into their metal bands glowed when I released them.

I noticed a bar with magical symbols burned into it resting on the floor to the right of the doors. Before I could turn to ask, the seer said, "Bar the door as well, Mercenary."

More than gravity pulled the oak plank into place. Instantly the chamber seemed somehow muffled.

Enchantress Thulease had taken a stool to Seer Lochelle's right. I returned to my seat on her right, between the enchantress and Lilly, who was sitting next to Captain Bray. Across from me, to the seer's left sat Wizard Seelain. Major Jadd and Sergeant Drux were seated to the wizard's left. A large silver disk had been placed over the table's recessed bowl.

Imperial Seer Lochelle turned to her right. "The chamber is secure, Thulease. Proceed as you deem appropriate."

"Thank you, Lochelle," the enchantress said. "I am always appreciative of your hospitality, support, and insight."

Enchantress Thulease made eye contact with each person around the table as she spoke. "I have individually invited each of you to this meeting as you have agreed to assist in my effort to locate the Dark Elves of the North with the intent of reviving my daughter.

"Each of you is aware of Thereese's condition. Her health and strength continue to deteriorate. The king's healers believe she has a month of strength remaining. A month at most.

"Upon my request, King Tobias graciously released Major Jadd and Sergeant Drux, and their serpent mount from patrol to bear my daughter north."

That got my attention. Lilly's and Captain Bray's as well. I'd figured Jadd and Drux were here at King Tobias's leave. But that Thereese would accompany us during our search was unexpected.

"Lochelle and I believe that we have located the distant mountain range, and the particular mountain side located in the Land of the Midnight Sun, as it's called during the summer months, and the Land of the Noontime Moon during its winter season. My daughter simply does not have the time remaining for me to locate and negotiate with the dark elves before retrieving her to be revived upon their Soul Forge.

"For a myriad of reasons the decision is fraught with risk. I am cognizant of that, but the decision has been made, thus, interjecting or enumerating the risks in an effort to suggest recklessness is unwelcome."

She took a deep breath before turning upon her stool. With a short sweep of her hand she gestured toward the two women still standing, with hands clasped in front of them. "I have invited Senior Research Assistant Parmer." The taller of the two women with short dark hair stepped forward and bowed slightly. "She is an expert on the contents of ancient tomes and scrolls that reference obscure peoples and cultures."

When the researcher stepped back, Enchantress Thulease introduced the shorter, light-haired woman with wire-rimmed glasses. "This is Royal

Tutor Roeth, who is knowledgeable in linguistic translation of older languages." Lilly's tutor stepped forward and bowed slightly. "In addition, she is well versed in rituals and customs of both modern and ancient races and their cultures."

Lilly's wide eyes announced she was more surprised than me that her tutor's education and knowledge was so vast. Lilly'd only told me that her tutor had taught her how to read, write and speak the language of the Reunited Kingdom. That, and proper courtly manners. King Tobias offered a boon to Lilly for her part in locating the Colonel of the West, and placing the destructive weapon secured in trade for the royal family's Blood Sword which turned the tide of war against the Necromancer King. The boon Lilly requested was to be taught how to read Crusader Paul Jedidiah Roos's book of scripture. King Tobias honored Lilly's request to a higher degree than either of us realized. Assigning a tutor far more qualified than he or anyone ever let on, including Royal Tutor Roeth herself, said as much. Her depth of knowledge was far more than that required to meet Lilly's request.

I wondered if this revelation might alter Lilly's view of the king. What it did do was emphasize how far outside the noble circles Lilly and I were, and would continue to be.

Enchantress Thulease nodded once and the two women stepped back and took a seat upon the stools provided for them. "Both women assisted Grand Wizard Seelain and I in our research of the dark elves, the Soul Forge, and the elements required to revive my daughter. They are sworn never to reveal what is discussed here today within the Imperial Seer's chamber."

She then turned to Imperial Seer Lochelle. "Would you please speak to the dangers posed by those who desire both my death and possibly that of my daughter?"

"I shall," Imperial Seer Lochelle said, her voice smooth, brimming with power, yet seeming somehow distant. "King Tobias has signed an armistice with Supreme General Gorjan, de facto ruler of the Vinchie Empire, as have the Doran Confederacy's Council of Lords, and the Elected Prime Minister of the Faxtinian Coalition. The Lesser Kingdoms have refused to sign such an agreement.

"General Mzali, the Ancient Dictator and Necromancer King, has been defeated and has fled the field."

The seer paused. "It is believed that this armistice is little more than an extended breath before the resumption of hostilities. Uplersh, the sea goddess, remains belligerent to those who risk venturing within her domain. General Gorjan is a puppet of the resurgent Cult of the Long Tooth Tiger. We have not heard the last of the Necromancer King, while his son, Corradin the Conjurer, continues to build his, as of yet, largely untested strength.

"The fact that war still rages upon the Western Continent, where the

Colonel of the West fights on two fronts against forces of the Pantheon of Sky Color Gods, and those of the Az-Texas Empire, and the recent news that war between powers to the east of Keesee appears imminent, lends credence to the believe that hostilities will once again commence, with Keesee again in the middle of the fray.

"The only question? What will spark the remaining tinder, and fan the flames of war?"

The seer lifted her sightless face. "As for those who set into motion the effort to intercept and capture or kill Enchantress Thulease and those of her party while aboard the *Hunchback Maiden*? My spellcraft points to the Cult of the Long Tooth Tigers."

Enchantress Thulease frowned, but nodded once in agreement.

"Beyond my magic, the logic supporting this belief is threefold," Imperial Seer Lochelle explained. "Retribution for the part Thulease played, not only in slaying the Goddess of Healing, but also in tracking down insurgents and their Long Tooth support within the King's City, foiling their attempt to spread strife and terror. Finally, her daughter Thereese, has the potential—I believe is destined—to surpass her mother in both skill and power of enchantment. Like her mother, she will prove to be a powerful ally to the current and any future kings of Keesee."

The seer paused, then added, "Should she survive."

"That is why," Enchantress Thulease said, "we are meeting within Lochelle's chamber and in secret. It is my desire to evade any threat or interference the Long Tooth Tiger Cult might attempt."

She gazed at everyone around the table. When nobody commented or asked a question, she continued. "Now, we shall proceed to what has been learned of the dark elves and where we hope to find them."

Lilly sat in the only chair in my boarding room and watched me as I sat on my bed and examined my equipment. My new helmet, a gift from Enchantress Thulease, was a finely crafted steel marion. Its narrow crest and broad brim was supposed to deflect not only weapons, but possible stones or debris from above, as we were expected to spend a good amount of time underground. It also had perforated ear flaps that added protection without hindering hearing, much. It wouldn't be ideal for flight aboard a wyvern or serpent because its brim would catch the wind when I looked up, but I'd never gotten used to the nose guard of my old helmet. I decided to take the new one instead of my old one, with its battle scars and dents, and specks of rust.

In about an hour a runner from the palace would arrive and announce the king's request that I patrol the western frontier along the Pyrenees Mountains. I was then to proceed to the Second Royal Wyvern Roost where my mount, Wick, would be waiting.

Wick had been my mount when I served the king as a wyvern scout. One of my first missions had been to watch a pass through the Pyrenees along with Grand Wizard Seelain. We'd spotted the advance invasion force of Fendra Jolain, and barely escaped a flight of griffins controlled by a beastmaster so that we might return and report.

Captain Bray would be waiting, to lead our paired patrol. He'd lost his serpent mount Flint Spitter when the Kraken attacked us outside of the Colonel of the West's skyscraper outpost. With the shortage of mounts and his experience as a serpent handler, he'd been assigned a female griffin. Among the wyvern species, which resembled a cross between a vulture and a dragon, females were dominant over the males. Not only were they larger than the males, but they had a poisonous barb much like a scorpion's on the end of their serpentine tail.

Lilly'd joined me since her room was in the palace and she always had her gear packed and ready to go. The plan was to ask her, within earshot of the king's runner, to tell Enchantress Thulease that King Tobias requested my service as a wyvern scout. She'd make her way to the enchantress's tower and then return to her room and prepare for departure with Grand Wizard Seelain under cover of darkness.

Enchantress Thulease should have already left her tower in a rented carriage along with her ailing daughter. Both Flayzin and Storm Claw were to accompany them for protection. They were to meet Jadd and Drux, waiting with their white dragon mount in a secluded grove.

We all had a rendezvous point along the rocky coast nineteen miles north of the King's City. I wasn't sure the ruse would work, but it was the best Enchantress Thulease could arrange under such a strict timeframe.

Lilly crept over to the door and listened. Once satisfied nobody was nearby or listening, she said quietly, "Can you believe what Enchantress Thulease said? Those dark elves'll turn to stone if sunlight touches them?"

"Moonlight can transform you, Lilly," I replied, keeping my voice just above a whisper.

Lilly whispered, "Yeah, but that's different. At least the moonlight can give them back their flesh. Or so the old books said."

While I was checking the buckles to connect the shoulders of my breast and backplate, Lilly asked, "Why do you think they don't use their real names?"

"Part of their magic, I guess."

"Makes sense then we can't call each other by our real names. Except for you and Road Toad."

"Flank Hawk's not my real name, Lilly," I said, grinning. "You know that."

"It is to me. Just like Major Jadd will always be Road Toad to me." She gave me a mischievous grin. "Nura thinks of you as Flank Hawk too."

I shrugged and set my breastplate aside. "It's a good mercenary name."

"I'll say goodbye to her for you, Flank Hawk. If I can. It's not like she won't figure it out when the enchantress isn't around and her daughter is gone too."

"Thanks, Lilly."

I pulled out my short sword and examined it. The silver infused in the blade caused it to lose its edge more quickly. It didn't need any work.

After sheathing my sword, I said, "I don't like that they might try to challenge us. The dark elves," I explained while examining my boar spear's tip and crossbar. "Maybe try to enslave us."

"I'd like to see them try that against Enchantress Thulease," Lilly said. "They won't take me for a slave, or thrall or whatever they call slaves. I can tell you that."

I signaled Lilly to keep her voice down. "I won't go that way without a fight either, Lilly. None of us will." I set my spear aside. "If it comes to that."

Enchantress Thulease made sure we knew that the dark elves were said to be both crafty and cruel.

"I know, Flank Hawk. I just don't like walking into something like that."

She went and pulled the chair up next to the door and listened again before saying, "Won't you feel weird with me being the enchantress's personal guard while you're watching over her daughter. Being *her* body guard? At least until we're under the mountains and I'm helping Sergeant Drux carry the young enchantress on her stretcher."

I shrugged and got out my tin of fireweed resin. "Duty is duty, Lilly. It says a lot that she trusts you, over Drux or Jadd."

"Maybe," she said, trying to hide the pride in her voice. "They need to be free to act. They're better with swords than me with Jonas's rapier."

"True, Lilly. But you're quicker than any of us. Sensing things before any of us can. Even the enchantress. It's a good plan."

"As good a plan as she and that seer could figure." Lilly shifted in the chair and scowled. "She sends shivers like ice down through my bones. She do that to you too, Flank Hawk?"

"Did the first time I met her, Lilly." I took a strip of leather and began to spread the fireweed resin over the blade of my dirk. "But not anymore."

"Not even a little?"

"Not even a little," I replied.

She stood up and walked over to the bed where I sat. She bent down, putting her hands on her knees and stared me in the eye. "You. Are. Such. A. Liar."

While waiting for Grand Wizard Seelain and Lilly to arrive I spent time reacquainting with Wick. I'd moved him away from Ice Gale, Major Jadd's white dragon steed.

Jadd had warned me that his serpent mount, and whites in general, were more temperamental than either blacks or reds.

I'd been around black and red dragons and served a short stint as Major Jadd's aft guard. Black dragons had jaws that most resembled a giant snapping turtle and spit streams of acid. Red dragons were larger and stronger, with dagger-like serrated teeth. They breathed gouts of flame. I'd been Jadd's aft guard when ambushed by forces of the Necromancer King riding white serpent steeds. They spewed streams of liquid nitrogen that could freeze flesh upon contact. White dragon mounts were longer, with narrower wings than other dragons. They were faster than both blacks and reds, but couldn't turn as sharply. They had a long bony crest extending back from their skull and their honking bellows sounded like angry giant geese.

Ice Gale's snorting and wing ruffling intimidated Wick. I'd been around serpents enough to know it was intentional. Ice Gale's greater size and belligerent display didn't bother Cruelty's Cousin, Captain Bray's female wyvern mount. I knew this not only by the wyvern's threatening tail flicks, but the fact that Cruelty's Cousin had shifted to the color white. Wyverns could shift colors much like chameleon lizards and white was their color of aggression.

Wick had shifted to the camouflage color of black, matching the night. It was also the color showing submission or fear. The gurgling rumble in Wick's throat confirmed he was unsettled. The fact that Cruelty's Cousin was around and that Major Jadd and Sergeant Drux had taken action to quell their serpent mount's aggressive threats helped Wick maintain reasonable calm. The arrival of Balooga, a herbivorous dragon would confuse the situation more. At least temporarily. Mixed bevies always took a day or two to settle.

Wick took pretty well to my return as his rider. Although I'm a competent wyvern scout, the fact that Wick followed the lead of Captain Bray's mount made my initial return to the saddle easier. Wick's current master, a m'unicorn cavalrywoman whose mount had been killed in battle, was on temporary leave. She was soon to deliver a child.

It'd take some time for Wick to regain confidence with me as his rider. Cruelty's Cousin and Ice Gale weren't making that transition easy. However, Balooga and Wick had travelled together and got along pretty well. Their history might make things easier.

I hoped so. The plan, once we located the dark elves somewhere under the mountains of the cold north, was for Grand Wizard Seelain and Captain Bray to stay behind, guarding our mounts. Both knew their way around serpents, especially Captain Bray, but we'd be in unfamiliar territory, likely dangerous as well.

"Flank Hawk," called Enchantress Thulease. "Please attend."

I double-checked the hobbling tether woven of leather and metal that ran from Wick's neck to his right leg before trotting over to the hammock strung between two walnut trees upon which the unconscious Thereese lay. Both the enchantress and Major Jadd stood over the extremely tall and very frail spellcaster.

"Yes, Enchantress?"

She signaled for me to follow as she strode away from her daughter. "Healing magic provided no positive effect upon my Thereese. Even so, I would have preferred to have a healer accompany us on this mission."

There was a shortage of both healers and serpent mounts. Far more missions than the number available of each. Adding to the shortage, the female dragons were being rotated out of patrol duty and, through magic, were being brought into season so that they might lay eggs sooner and begin the long process of rebuilding the royal bevy. The unexpected stress of forced season pregnancies grounded the dragons through the gestation period and up to six weeks beyond. Wyverns, useful in their own right, were poor replacements for true serpent steeds. The king just didn't have more than a single serpent and two wyverns to spare. If it had been anyone other than Enchantress Thulease requesting such assistance, not a single serpent steed would've been lent to the mission.

"I understand, Enchantress."

We walked past the small campfire tended to by Bray. He gazed up at us before turning back to poking the glowing coals with a crooked stick, creating a small flicker of light.

"Flank Hawk, I realize your healing ability is limited. However, that ability coupled with your familiarity with my daughter may enable you be attuned to any subtle changes and anticipate a precipitous deterioration."

She held up a hand before I could respond. "You and Major Jadd have the most combat experience, and have witnessed those near death more than others among us."

"I agree, Enchantress, except that I am not sure *familiar* is how I'd explain the relationship between me and your daughter."

"You saved her from an assassin's poisoned blade."

"And broke her leg in the effort."

As we reached the edge of the grove Enchantress Thulease's face caught the moonlight, revealing a broad smile. "Despite that, she has remained, shall I say, quite fetched with you?"

I shrugged. During my time serving as Grand Wizard Seelain's personal guard, I'd been afforded the opportunity to spend small amounts of time with Enchantress Thereese. We'd played several games of checkers and she tried to teach me chess, twice. We shared four lunches together in the palace's Stickley Dining Hall.

The first time I'd met the young enchantress, it was her first visit to the palace. While escorting Thereese to her room in the palace at her mother's request, the apprentice enchantress tried to cast an enamor enchantment on me, and lure me into her room. I was lucky to have resisted, and it was foolish for her to have tried. How could it have ended well, for either of us?

The confession to her mother, the Supreme Enchantress, must've been horribly embarrassing for a young girl.

It was good to see Enchantress Thulease smile. A true smile, remembering her daughter.

Then she frowned. "Seelain should be here soon."

"You'll succeed, Enchantress. Thereese will recover."

"When she does," she said, "*we* will have succeeded." Then she pointed at a shadow passing in front of the stars as it approached. "It appears Seelain and Lilly have arrived."

"Lilly's senses are keener than any full human's," I said. "She'll watch over your daughter too."

We travelled through most of the night, rested a few hours before dawn, and then travelled north the rest of the day. Enchantress Thulease said the objective was to outdistance any effort to disrupt our mission. Unless the Cult of the Long Tooth Tigers were somehow able to determine through seer spellcraft, divine through astrologers, or had somehow obtained our intended destination through spying, betrayal, or similar means, distance from the King's City offered greater security.

Major Jadd's serpent steed was the strongest flier and led our V formation. Sergeant Drux served as his aft guard with Supreme Enchantress Thulease between them. If there was trouble, they'd be our primary offence. The dragon's freezing breath and the enchantress's spellcraft would prove formidable.

Following on the left rode Captain Bray on Cruelty's Cousin. He would serve as Jadd's wingman, should we encounter an aerial threat. Grand Wizard Seelain flew upon Balooga with Lilly as her aft guard, armed with a short bow. The gray dragon steed's scalding steam didn't have the range of Ice Gale's. And the serpent's maneuverability was hindered with the comatose Thereese slung tightly beneath her.

I, on Wick, would serve as their wingman, doing what I could to assist Air Wizard Seelain's formidable spells.

Wick was more than happy to trail on the left, behind Cruelty's Cousin, with Balooga, in view, trailing on Ice Gale's right.

Four days of traveling north left us in the heart of the territory once controlled by the Necromancer King. Bray and I directed our mounts to slowly spiral down toward the boulder-strewn hills below.

The only hint of a settlement was a goblin tribe's camp along the edge of a narrow river. Our aerial view showed thin wisps of campfire smoke sifting up through the sheltering trees which betrayed their presence. Lilly's spyglass confirmed it was a goblin camp.

At the moment the goblin tribe was almost two hours south of us. Too far away to concern us.

Wick seemed tense as we got closer to the ground. I scanned the hillside to my right while a gurgling rumble began in my mount's throat. Wick's color shifted from gray to a mottled gray and black just as Cruelty's Cousin ten yards ahead became white except for a few spots of gray on her wings.

"Something's down there," Bray shouted back over his left shoulder, the direction he was scanning. We were about a hundred yards above the hillsides, flying over a trickling gully clogged with boulders.

"Wick agrees," I shouted back. "Let's pull up. Maybe Lilly's spyglass can spot what it is."

Captain Bray tugged on his reins, shouting a command for Cruelty's Cousin to climb. She wasn't interested and resisted for two heartbeats before giving in and flapping hard to gain altitude.

I spotted movement halfway up the hillside the same instant Wick screeched out a cry of alarm. From behind a crop of boulders a dark figure, which I thought upon first glance was a lion with a black folded tent strapped to its back, leapt atop the jumble of boulders. Without slowing the big lion leapt from the boulders, launching its muscular body into the air. Black bat-like wings spread and began flapping.

I banked right, shouting, "Manticore! On the right!"

Back when I was seven summers old a carnival travelled through Pine Ridge. What haunted my dreams through that summer and following winter was the caged manticore.

My father was very careful with his hard-earned coin, but spent a few of them and took me and my older sister into the big gray tent to see the rare legendary beast. Lying stretched out, it filled the wagon lined with steel bars that were thick as my forearm, watching us gawking townsfolk with its fierce blue eyes.

The mane-less female made a wolf seem like a young pup. The carnival barker explained how they'd chopped off its scorpion tail to keep us spectators safe from deadly poison. I wondered why they hadn't pulled its three rows of pointed teeth. It had the body of a lion with leathery wings that were too big to spread wide in its cage. Its face was like a woman's but twice as big, with a jutting jaw and malicious sneer.

Even as a child I recognized the monster's intelligence, but not a human's. More feral. It watched people. It watched me and my sister as we walked past, half hidden behind my father. The deep blue eyes, they followed us like a barn cat watching a baby mouse, waiting for it to wander just close enough to pounce upon. Eager to tear the mouse apart while devouring it.

What scared me the most was looking up at my father and seeing him look away from the manticore's fierce gaze. Nobody could endure it. Not one grown man or woman in the tent met the manticore's predatory stare for long, even though it was caged behind thick steel bars.

"Two on the left," Bray shouted. "Coming up at us!"

Cruelty's Cousin loosed a screeching challenge that sounded like a cross between a crow's *caw* and a hawk's piercing cry. Wick echoed her, but where her tail flicked in anticipation and her head twisted left and right, seeking to meet a challenge, Wick's eyes were wide, like a horse being chased by a wolf pack.

Wick wasn't defenseless. His beak was sharp and powerful, but his clawed feet were more like a vulture's than a predatory eagle's. And he didn't have a poison-barbed tail.

I checked right. There were two manticores in the air, pursuing us, and more among the hillside boulders launching to join the chase. The same was happening on our left. Over a dozen manticores responded to our mounts' challenge with roars sounding like a chorus of deep trumpets reverberating throughout the hillside valley.

That caused both our wyvern mounts to flap even harder to escape. Checking behind and on my right, I knew it wouldn't be enough. The man-faced beast to our rear on the left was flapping faster and getting closer. The wild black mane said it was a male, and its tail didn't end in a barb. Instead the male wielded a morning star ball packed with foot-long spikes.

I recalled Jadd once telling me about aerial threats, including manticores. The males could shoot their venom-covered spikes. Not far and not with enough force to pierce a dragon's hide. But a wyvern's hide couldn't match a dragon's armor-like scales. If the male manticores got above us, they could rain their spikes down on man and wyvern alike.

I shoved on my new helmet and tightened the strap while urging Wick on. Our only hope was to reach the dragons and spellcasters circling far above.

My boar spear was tied along Wick's right side. It had good reach, but if a manticore was close enough that I could pierce it, teeth and claws, barbed and spike tails would be bringing us down. Instead I reached for one of my javelins. Unless I got a lucky eye or throat strike, it wouldn't stop a six-hundred pound beast. Ahead, Bray gripped a javelin as well.

Wick called out again, more shrill than challenging, wings beating for distance and altitude, straining to escape. Maybe if he didn't have a rider. Wick wasn't as strong as the dominant female, but Bray held his mount back a little, letting us pull up alongside on his right. Looking over my shoulder, the nearest manticore, a male, was less than fifty yards behind. The next, maybe sixty yards. There were at least two dozen fanned out behind them, the farthest no more than a hundred yards back.

I looked up. Jadd and Wizard Seelain couldn't have missed the calls of our mounts and the manticore pride's roars. Ice Gale was in a dive, wings folded back. Balooga was in a spiraling dive, falling behind Ice Gale but still coming on fast.

It wouldn't be fast enough. The manticore pride would be all over us before the dragons were in range of their breath weapons. We'd be sure to get caught in the streams of liquid nitrogen and scalding gouts of steam.

Bray shouted, "We can't out climb them. Let's dive!"

Even though Wick would follow Bray's mount, I commanded, "Down, Wick," kicking my heels in the stirrups. "Dive!"

Initially the manticores gained, but then we held our own, even pulling away a little. Trading altitude for speed. The problem was we didn't have a lot of altitude to trade.

Hunched down, I looked back. Thirty yards. The nearest manticore's black mane swept back, blue eyes wide, triple rows of teeth bared. He was curling his tail up, lining it up above his head. No way I could twist around to throw my javelin, even if I loosened the leg straps holding me in the saddle. Looking over his shoulder and gripping his own javelin, Bray came to the same conclusion.

A small thunderclap sounded. With a trumpeting snarl cut short the lead manticore tumbled from the sky. Grand Wizard Seelain's spell had destroyed the air around the beast. The impact of the air rushing in to fill the void slammed against the wizard's target like a trio of sledgehammers.

A second small thunderclap sounded and the next nearest manticore fell. A stream of vaporous liquid from above raked across the wings and backs of three females. A whirlwind caught up one that angled up to close with the dragons above. A fifteen foot length of rope shot down from the white dragon's middle rider, entangling and tightening around the wings of another woman-faced lion, sending it tumbling like some of its sisters, their backs snapped like icicles and frozen wings shattered to pieces.

Balooga bellowed and snorted like a raging bull. Ice Gale's snarling honk reverberated off the hillsides, breaking the manticore pride's morale. They broke off pursuit and scattered, seeking cover among the hillside boulders and deep in the ravine's shadow.

Bray and I pulled up on our mounts, leveling out thirty yards above the ravine's floor, stubby trees and jagged rocks covering the hillsides racing by. Ice Gale shot past overhead, her serpentine neck craned back, tracking several of the fleeing manticores.

Sergeant Drux, facing aft on the white dragon, shook a fist above his head. "That'll learn'em to mess with the king's serpent cavalry!"

CHAPTER 31

"I thought they were gonna get you, Flank Hawk."

"Lilly, that concern crossed my mind, too." She was helping me remove Wick's saddle. Without it, he'd be able to fully blend into the background. It'd help him sleep.

"Road Toad said those manticores probably got loose when the Crusaders defeated the Necromancer King." She handed me the leather and steel tether to hobble Wick. "What else do you think is running loose?"

After securing one end of the tether to Wick's leg, I swatted at a mosquito hovering around my face. "Goblins, giants, maybe a few souled zombies."

"Well, I guess those things," Lilly said. She scratched and patted Wick along his neck while I secured the tether behind where her hand rested.

Wick released a deep breath and settled down, leaning against a pair of red pines. The flickering campfire wasn't bright enough to tell me if my mount was a solid black, or mixed with dark greens and browns to blend in with the trees. It'd say a lot about his mood after escaping the manticore ambush a little over an hour ago.

"You think those manticores will try to get us again? They looked pretty fierce."

"Until Wizard Seelain and Ice Gale scattered them," I said. "They'll think twice about coming after us."

"Then what do you think they eat?"

"Besides what regular lions might hunt? Goblins, giants. Maybe even zombies, if they don't care what their meat tastes like."

She scrunched up her nose. "Ugh, why'd I even ask?"

"That wasn't the first time I came face to face with a manticore, Lilly."

"Really?" She stepped back and signaled with a flick of her head, suggesting we gather around the fire. Jadd and Enchantress Thulease had just secured the mosquito net around Thereese, lying wrapped in a wool blanket on her hammock.

I rested a hand on Lilly's shoulder. "I'll tell you about it while supper's cooking."

Drux was squatting near the fire, waiting for me, Lilly and Grand Wizard Seelain. What helped us decide upon where to establish our camp was a small herd of deer gathered near a stream to drink at sunset. Their presence suggested there probably wasn't a manticore pride in the area. It also provided the opportunity for meat, not only for us, but for our white dragon and wyverns. Balooga had swept down on the small herd and caught them by surprise. The gray dragon's scalding breath downed the five of them, and Wizard Seelain dispatched them with small thunderclaps centered one by one on the heads of the fallen deer, quickly putting them out of their misery.

While Balooga ate branches and leaves, the wyverns needed meat. The white dragon could survive on organic matter like rotting logs, but preferred fresh meat. We harvested a leg to cook over the fire and dine upon, and boil a broth mixed with flour to make gravy for Thereese. The rest we'd toss to our mounts to replenish their strength.

I didn't understand exactly how a sextant worked. I'd seen seafaring captains and first mates use them to navigate the oceans and seas. Enchantress Thulease was using one to find the exact location of the dark elves. Not just any clan of dark elves, but the particular one that had the Soul Forge.

I'd used the sun and stars to navigate not only cross country on foot but also as a wyvern scout. Still, I used landmarks such as towns, cities and rivers.

Enchantress Thulease and Imperial Seer Lochelle had consulted a master astrologer before reviewing the Royal Library's ancient scrolls to determine an approximate location based upon the day and season, patterns of the sun crossing the sky, and the location of certain stars in the night sky on a certain date. The thing was, the further north we went, the longer the days seemed to be.

After listening to the young enchantress's shallow breathing and slow, faint heartbeat I looked up at her mother. "She's weakening."

"It is as I feared," Enchantress Thulease said.

Grand Wizard Seelain wrapped an arm around her friend's waist. "We are nearly there. Possibly before noon tomorrow."

We were to watch for signs of a settlement, in a deep east-west valley, near the base on the southern face of a mountain. Enchantress Thulease said that during the winter, the sun wouldn't rise high enough, leaving that side of the mountain without direct sunlight for months at a time.

I couldn't imagine that. But, if the touch of sunlight would turn me to stone, it sounded like a good solution. Still, I'd been among mountains before. Those we were traveling through, the ice and snow and bitter winds and cold? I think I'd stay under ground just to escape it.

Then I recalled the relentless sun, endless heat and thirst of the Southern Continent. It made me realize how few people had travelled as far and seen as much as I had. I better understood why Rin always wanted to hear me tell about the places I'd been and the people and creatures I'd encountered. Given the chance it's exactly what I would've done at his age.

"We'll find them, Enchantress," I said. "She'll pull through."

For some reason my words seemed to comfort her more so than those of Grand Wizard Seelain.

After breakfast and before the appearance of sunrise, Jadd signaled me over to where he was inspecting his mount's harness and the leather cinch, and other straps securing the saddle to the dragon. They showed some wear but didn't appear to be a problem.

Jadd frowned while patting Ice Gale along her serpentine neck. "I expect we'll locate the clan that owns the Soul Forge," he said. "If not today, then tomorrow."

I nodded in agreement. Jadd had taken me under his wing after my militia company had been overrun by the Necromancer King's forces. Zombies, ogres and goblins. He taught me how to be a mercenary, how to fight and how to survive. He looked out for me, gave me my mercenary name, vouched for me, and bolstered my confidence when I needed it. Without Jadd I'd have been dead long ago.

I respected his opinion more than any other man's, except my father's.

He gazed back toward camp. Enchantress Thulease and Lilly were preparing Thereese for travel. Drux and Bray were saddling the wyverns. Wizard Seelain was down by the stream with Balooga.

"You know the enchantress better than me, Flank Hawk. I suspect any negotiations will take place underground. Wizard Seelain will remain behind with Captain Bray, watching the dragons. So she won't have her long-time friend for guidance. For emotional support."

I knew the plan. Wizard Seelain's command of the air, her spell strength would be greatly diminished underground. Considering her experience with serpent steeds and spell strength, it made tactical sense for her to remain behind, guarding our mounts and stand prepared should we need a fast retreat from the area.

Jadd continued, saying, "I believe the dark elves will attempt to use the enchantress's maternal instincts against her."

That made sense. They weren't allies, and their reported history of cruel and manipulative ways? "I agree."

"Good," Major Jadd said. "Be prepared, then. We may have to intervene during the negotiations. It may take the both of us to convince her…to remind her of what is right and proper for both her and her daughter."

I took a hard swallow. There was a lot I didn't know, such as what the enchantress had brought to offer the dark elves to entice them to use their Soul Forge to revive Thereese. I suspected the enchantress herself didn't know what would be asked.

"Life," I said. "Survival at any cost? For any price?" I looked past Ice Gale to where Enchantress Thulease and Lilly had finished wrapping

Thereese in wool blankets, like a brown cocoon. "There are worse things than death, Road Toad."

I stepped back as he took Ice Gale's reins and led her down toward the stream. Wizard Seelain's mount was finished and they were moving back up hill. Although Jadd and Drux did a good job of keeping control of their mount, the white dragon did her best to intimidate the gray dragon whenever an opportunity presented itself. For the most part Balooga ignored the larger white's growls, wing ruffling, and jaw snapping, especially when in close company with the wyverns.

"The sergeant told me you and Nura dined at Koko's Bistro."

"Yeah. He went with our scout, which kind of surprised me." I thought about how they'd gotten along this trip thus far, then added. "At least at the time."

Jadd glanced at me with a crooked smile.

"You'll like Nura," I said. "Made me promise to take her to the One-Eyed Pelican when we return."

He laughed a deep laugh. "And you believe that's my measure of a woman? A willingness to visit the Pelican?"

I laughed and shrugged. "Your aft guard said you've got your eye on a m'unicorn cavalry officer. Think you could talk her into joining us?"

"If she's not out on patrol, I'll ask her."

"If she says, yes," I said, "what'll that say about her?"

Jadd snapped Ice Gale's reins tight. "Whoa, girl," he said. The beast responded by sitting on her haunches and sniffed the air. Jadd watched her for any sign of danger. When the dragon turned her attention to Cruelty's Cousin, Jadd continued our conversation. "Saying yes to the Pelican? Maybe that she'll have no problem finding common ground with Nura and Lilly."

I shook my head. "Maybe, Nura. But not our scout."

Jadd cocked his head in surprise. "Why not our scout?"

I glanced over toward Lilly. I knew she heard our discussion, especially as it included her. "Because," I said, "our scout went back to the One-Eyed Pelican. Willingly."

Jadd laughed. Out of the corner of my eye, I caught a huge grin on Lilly's face as she helped Enchantress Thulease and Sergeant Drux secure the leather straps to hold Enchantress Thereese in place once again for sling-bound travel.

CHAPTER 32

We made a second pass over the deep, east-west valley. Lilly'd shouted after the second pass, saying that she smelled traces of burnt metal and fire. During our third pass Sergeant Drux spotted movement, so Bray and I took our mounts down in a sharp spiraling descent.

It takes practice to search the ground below while riding on a dragon or wyvern. Observing around the neck, head, outspread wings, and even the tail can be tricky. Even so, Captain Bray pointed to a scattered stand of spruce trees that stretched for almost a quarter mile along the southern rise of the mountain valley. The trees didn't quite reach down to what looked like a dry streambed and only extended about two-thirds of the way up.

Bray motioned to me, signaling he spotted something along the bottom of the valley. I relayed Bray's message to the serpent riders above, confirming Drux's initial sighting.

As planned and rehearsed, Drux took out his bugle. The trumpeting call he made was close to one I learned while serving in Lord Hingroar's militia before becoming a mercenary. If it didn't have an extra *Ta-Taaah* after the first four notes, it would've been the signal to fall back to prepared defenses. What the call said, or what the sergeant was attempting to do, was announce our presence, and a desire to meet and trade. It was one of many things the enchantress's research uncovered.

But the records were old. What if the call had changed? Or maybe it was different from clan to clan? When I'd asked Jadd this the night before our run in with the manticores, he smiled and said, "They're long lived, and probably don't change much." After I agreed with that, he asked, "If they used different bugle calls, wouldn't one clan need to know the proper way to signal other clans?"

I agreed, mostly. I wasn't sure such calls were expected of fellow dark elves. But Enchantress Thulease and Major Jadd were more experienced in such things than me.

A figure wearing a gray wide-brimmed hat stepped out from the base of the large spruce coppice and waved up at us, one hand further shielding his face from the cloud-filled afternoon sky.

Captain Bray signaled for me to land, so I brought Wick around and landed fifty yards east of the spindly figure.

As I unstrapped my legs and dismounted, the man stiffly walked toward me and Wick. Bray, on his mount, circled about two hundred yards above, with those on the two dragons casually circling at an altitude equal to the mountain tops.

The man approaching had a brown scarf covering his face starting just below his eyes. He wore leather gloves, a wolfskin vest over a long-sleeved brown sweater. He had green pants tucked into knee-high black boots and what looked like a gun, more primitive than a Crusader revolver, in a holster on his belt. Opposite the firearm, on his left hip, hung a rapier in a steel scabbard.

I scanned the tree line above and spotted a figure kneeling behind a stump with a rifle pointing my direction. I made a point of looking that direction as a signal to Captain Bray. Without urging, Wick gurgled a hiss, his color shifting from gray to mottled gray and black. I made a show of keeping a firm grip on his reins.

The spindly figure pulled the scarf below his chin, revealing a long, crooked nose. His green eyes stood out against his ashy brown skin. As best I could tell the man was bald with only hints of dark eyebrows. His left cheek bore a tattoo of sixteen black circles in the shape of a box. Nine of them were filled in.

He waved again and smiled, showing gray teeth.

I waved back, pointed to myself, and said in Sea Spittle, "I am Flank Hawk."

"You speak Trade," the man said. "They call me Barkey."

I guessed Barkey wasn't a dark elf because sunlight, even though it was blocked by clouds, was touching his skin. He looked a little older than me but moved like a man that had seen seventy winters.

I pointed over to the man with the rifle barrel resting on the stump, aimed my direction. "We're not looking for a fight. The enchantress I serve seeks to meet with your clan chief."

"She does, hunh?" The man put his hands on his hips. "You know the call to meet and trade, but you don't know the time to establish trade is midwinter."

"Little is known about your people by my people," I said. "The enchantress I serve—"

The spindly man swung his arm, level across his body, cutting me off, saying, "Not my people." Then he tipped his head from side to side while his eyes glanced upward. "*Well*, sort of not my people."

I neither understood what he meant nor what his statement meant. "Are you a thrall?" I asked.

He pointed to the dots on his cheek. "These say so." Then let out a sharp, chorting laugh.

"So, you're not a dark elf?"

"Svartálfar? Me?" He laughed again, then said, "Well, sort of." He rested his hands on his hips again. "What'd you say the name of your master was, Flank Hawk?"

"I didn't give her name," I said. "Just like I didn't give mine, and you didn't give yours."

He gave me a crooked smile. "Well, you all do know something, about Svartals, then." He gazed up at the wyvern and dragons circling, again holding a hand before his eyes to supplement his hat's wide brim. "Where did you travel here from?"

"The Kingdom of Keesee."

"Keesee, hunh?" He rubbed his pointing finger under his long nose. "That's some portion of travel south of here. You say the enchantress you serve has something important to trade with the clan chief?"

I nodded once. "That she does."

"I don't suppose she'd want to return this upcoming winter season?"

"She would not."

He scratched the back of his neck without moving the scarf out of the way. "Tell you what, Flank Hawk. I'll deliver your mistress's request. Return here a smidge before midnight. Just to warn you though, the clan chief is mighty short of temper during the sunny months."

With that, Barkey turned and walked, stiff-jointed, back into the woods.

"That firearm the half-breed thrall carried sounds like a flintlock," Major Jadd said after taking a sip of his lukewarm tea. "Not as advanced as Crusader guns, but might be just as accurate. Unless it's smoothbore."

Major Jadd had learned a lot, especially about Crusaders, during his exile from Keesee and living the life of a wandering mercenary.

I sat near our campfire, finishing off several strips of mountain goat Lilly'd cooked for me during my watch.

We'd flown about twenty miles east to await nightfall. This far north, the sun hung in the sky far longer than it did in Keesee. I'd experienced long days before while travelling across Iceland and the ice-covered land whose ancient name translated to Greenland. Then, it was early spring and not as noticeable. And we never sat around, waiting for a meeting, one fraught with peril, as Enchantress Thulease described it.

A stiff breeze whipping around the boulder partially sheltering our campfire kept the ashes stirred up. I could taste them in the broiled goat meat.

"If these dark elves are as plotting and cruel as the enchantress warns," I said, "it's bad that they've got a chance to prepare for our return."

"It won't work to our advantage," Jadd agreed. He looked around our camp, a relative clearing on a level portion of the boulder-strewn mountainside. Enchantress Thulease was sleeping next to her daughter in the shadow of a squat boulder with a broad overhang. Lilly sat a few paces away, watching over them while sewing up hole in one of her gray socks. Drux was asleep as well, the small A-frame tent he sheltered under rippled with the wind gusts. Captain Bray was examining one of Balooga's outstretched wings while Wizard Seelain stood watch, posted near a pair of boulders just outside of camp.

"That thrall," I said. "I'm not sure what to think about him." Enchantress Thulease explained that the small circles tattooed on his face showed how many years of indentured service he owed, with those filled in indicating how many he'd served. Each dot meant seven years, according to Enchantress Thulease's research. That meant human-dark elf crossbreeds had long lifespans. He looked about my age. But the nine of the sixteen circles on his cheek filled in meant he'd already seen at least sixty-three winters.

"That one you spoke with, called Barkey," Jadd said, "tried to get you to reveal names."

I nodded. "I still don't get what difference it makes if they're freely given, obtained through trickery, or even overheard, instead of researched or gotten through torture."

Jadd finished his tea and said, as he wiped out the tin cup with a rag, "You'd do better directing that question to the wizard or enchantress." He grinned. "We only know a fraction of their story, true. But how much of our story do the dark elves know?"

I agreed. "It could stand as an advantage."

Preparing for the mission to revive her daughter, Enchantress Thulease consulted and worked with a lot of powerful people in the King's City. Wizards, enchanters, seers, witches and more. Maybe even a sorcerer, from what I'd heard.

"The only person I can think of that might be worse to cross than the enchantress," I said, "would be Belinda the Cursed."

"You won't get any argument from me on that point, Flank Hawk." Jadd slapped his knees before getting to his feet. "I'd add the Imperial Seer to that list of people to avoid crossing."

Neither Belinda Ice Heart nor Imperial Seer Lochelle would be with us under the mountain, in the caves of the dark elves. Something told me that the dark elven clan chief was high on a similar list, for those who'd met him.

While chewing on what was left of my last slice of broiled goat, I watched Jadd make his way back to our mounts. I no longer noticed the broiled goat's taste, or the specks of ash stuck to it.

I glanced back up over my shoulder and could just make out Ice Gale, near the bottom of the spruce tree line. The moonlight reflected off her scales. I knew from this distance I'd never see Wick, almost certainly camouflaged by shifting to black. I didn't spend more than a quick second looking. As planned, Grand Wizard Seelain and Captain Bray remained with our mounts. My duty was to keep alert and watch over Enchantress

Thereese.

Positioned to her right, I strode up the steep mountainside as we cut back and forth along a well-disguised trail carved into the stone and rocky soil. It was wide enough for two horses to ride side by side.

Lilly carried the front end of Enchantress Thereese's stretcher. Drux carried the rear. When the mountainside was on my right, the thrall, Barkey ambled along to the stretcher's left, seemingly unconcerned with his footing along the narrow edge. Maybe it was because he held one of the three lanterns lighting our way.

Barkey no longer walked like an old man. He winked at Lilly once, causing her to scowl. But most of the time he just grinned, shooting a glance my way from time to time.

Whenever a switch in our ascent put me on the outside, Barkey hustled to get ahead of Lilly and occasionally pointed out a rock or fissure that might cause trouble.

Ahead of us walked Enchantress Thulease, with Major Jadd a half step behind, shifting sides, always leaving the enchantress along the mountainside. Ahead of them strode what I guessed were full-blooded dark elves. They were shorter than Barkey, who was a half head shorter than me. Their faces were drawn and thin with long, pointed noses. From their tight gloves and boots, and their narrow shoulders draped over by their black hooded cloaks, the dark elves revealed their slight build. Their skin was black, reminding me of coal. Their eyes were red where mine were white, and each held a slate-gray iris encompassing a large black pupil. Their teeth were even and black, like glistening chips of onyx. Both of them were males, completely bald heads, thin, ash-gray eyebrows, eyelashes, and lips.

Both carried a lantern and both were armed with a rapier. Unlike Barkey, neither had a flintlock pistol. At least not that I could tell. A lot could be hidden under their flowing, ankle-length cloaks.

After a twenty minute hike upward we came to a boulder formation framing a fissure in the mountainside. Flying overhead, we hadn't noticed it. Like the trail leading to it, the entrance blended in unless someone knew what to look for.

A gritty sound, like rocks grinding over sand, emanated from the fissure as we approached. One of the dark elves led us in. The other waited and trailed behind.

The fissure was about six feet tall and four feet wide near the base, forcing Enchantress Thulease to duck her head before following Jadd in. Lilly and Drux carrying Thereese entered next, followed by Barkey and me, and then the dark elf with the lantern.

My satchel held a short torch and two candles. I even had three Crusader matches in a steel tube topped with a screw cap. Going underground without a quick source of light seemed like a bad idea. I'd brought my spear even though I knew we were going underground. Maybe it wouldn't be of use but, like the torch and candles, I'd rather not be caught in a situation where I wish I'd brought it. Instead of carrying my crossbow, Captain Bray had secured a javelin to my back with leather straps from Wick's rigging.

The ceiling remained about six feet high and the natural rock corridor widened to about seven feet before we reached a set of stairs heading downward.

A half human, half dark elf thrall stood guard along the steps. He was dressed much like Barkey, in green, gray and black, but he stood with a flintlock rifle, barrel in hand with its butt resting on the smooth stone floor.

Upon reaching the steps, the elf behind me muttered something I guessed to be a spell. I turned in time to see and hear a large stone door slide across the fissure's opening. It felt like a coffin's lid had just creaked shut, sealing a stifling darkness around us that threatened to snuff out the flickering lanterns at any moment.

The cave was dryer than the last one I'd entered, where Lilly and I fought a cornered werebat. The smell of smoke and hot iron, like in a blacksmith's shop, reached my nose.

The guard with the rifle near the steps pointed at the floor and said in Sea Spittle, "Step over, not on the runes."

Ahead of me, Enchantress Thulease looked cramped and uncomfortable as she ducked even lower to get through the doorway.

Fortunately Wizard Seelain had added an additional strap to hold Enchantress Thereese's head in place as the steps Lilly and Drux carried her down were wide but steep. On the floor at the threshold I spotted runes carved into the floor, and along the sides and above my head. The light wasn't good, but it appeared that a door was set to slide down, sealing off the steps much like the tunnels leading from the upper portion of the King's City down to the ports. I'd have wagered a lot of coin that the runes were magical and would hold the door in place.

The long staircase leveled out every seventy steps to a thirty-foot landing. After the third landing, each thereafter gently curved to the left before descending another seventy steps. Each stairway narrowed to about three feet in width and each ended with runes carved into channels where a five-inch thick slab of granite was poised to drop, sealing off the passage from the level landing area.

I didn't get the feeling that we were descending through a primary entrance. The entire time the smooth texture of the gray stone walls and steps didn't change and the arched ceiling showed no sign of soot from oil lanterns or torches. The only thing that did change was the stronger hint of forge smoke in the air. Twice I spotted circular holes along the ceiling. They seemed to be ventilation shafts with the stale air rising out rather than flowing down and in.

If the dark elves, or Svartálfar, were secretive and dwelled underground, sheltered from sunlight, maybe all the routes down into their sunless domain were narrow and cramped, and easy to conceal.

Still, it didn't fit. The haughty attitude and swaggering stride of the full-blooded Svartálfar almost demanded a grand entryway.

Being forced to walk hunched forward, as Enchantress Thulease's towering height required to navigate the cramped stairwells and passages, had to be wearing on her. While it was close for me most of the time, both Drux and Jadd had to duck their heads to avoid bumping the arched stone ceiling. That added to the sergeant's difficulty bearing Thereese's stretcher. Both he and Lilly were physically stronger than me, yet I began to note hints of strain building in their breathing and the increased adjustments in their gripping the ends of the stretcher's poles.

Carrying my boar spear in the confining space required more of my attention that I cared to spare.

Finally we emerged into a large oval chamber fifty feet long and half as wide. Half way up the fifteen foot walls were six balconies, three on each side, each encompassed by a three-foot iron latticework and railing. A pair of iron doors stood closed at the chamber's far end.

From each balcony a sneering Svartálfar looked down at us.

"Not good." The faint words, spoken in Mainland, reached my ear. I realized they were Barkey's words. Unless the dark elves had hearing equal to Lilly's, only she, me, and Drux heard what I took to be a warning.

I gripped my spear and turned to see the Svartal behind me step back, into the staircase's doorway. His right hand fell to his rapier's hilt. I gripped my spear and shouted a warning. "Ambush!"

At the same instant all six Svartálfar shouted, "Surrender!" Their sharp voices echoed off the chamber walls.

Out of the corner of my eye I caught Barkey ducking with arms covering his head, shielding it. Lilly had dropped her end of the stretcher while Drux was lowering his end to the floor. The dark elves above lifted flintlock pistols, one in each hand, cocking the hammers back with their thumbs.

Lowering the tip of my spear, I lunged and thrust it forward, releasing it in an underhanded throw. There wasn't much force behind it, but I caught the grinning, lantern-bearing Svartálfar in midstride, leaving him unable to dodge. He grunted as my spear tip bit finger deep into his gut.

I stepped back, avoiding Barkey as he scampered toward the left wall. I placed myself with sword drawn along Enchantress Thereese's right side and faced up toward the balconies. Drux stood opposite, his sword and shield held ready. Lilly and Jadd flanked Enchantress Thulease, their weapons drawn. His shield held high and ready. Despite my attack, the Svartálfar hadn't fired yet.

"Lay your weapons aside," the dark elf at the front of our march ordered. His voice was both grating and sinister. "Or perish where you stand."

"Is this how it is to be?" Enchantress Thulease said, authority ringing in her voice.

I watched the Svartálfar I'd wounded carefully set the lantern to the floor so that he could plug his bleeding stomach while still gripping his rapier.

"There is no other ending," the dark elf menacingly replied.

Suddenly, a flash of light filled the room, leaving me only able to see a white spot before my eyes. I turned right and thrust, believing the only one behind me would be the wounded Svartálfar. My blade found only air.

Enchantress Thulease's voice cut through the clattering confusion, after the single gunshot. "Incorrect assumption, arrogant fool." She must have shouted it. Even so, I could barely hear her words because my ears rang with the reverberating sound of the gunshot.

My vision quickly cleared as did my hearing.

Where the wounded Svartálfar once stood, the nearby flickering lantern revealed his rapier and black robe crumpled on a pile of slate-gray gravel. Lying next to the robe, his toppled boots and black leather gloves overflowed with identical stones ranging from the size of a grape down to a kernel of corn.

Scattered pebbles and leather gauntlets lay beneath each of the balconies, along with several flintlock pistols, one of which must have discharged when it struck the floor.

Enchantress Thulease examined the room with a satisfied look on her face. It was easy to determine her magic triggered the transformation of the threatening Svartálfar into stone.

I strode toward Barkey with sword held ready. The half-elf used the wall to lever himself stiffly to his feet.

"What happened?" I asked him. "Why weren't you affected?"

"I was," he said, standing hunched like an old man. "I can hardly move, but it'll pass." He feebly pointed at Enchantress Thulease as she stood over her daughter, watching the right-side balconies for possible danger. "She must have released true sunlight trapped in a locket. 'Least that's the device she appeared to hold over her head and flick open."

Enchantress Thulease met my eyes and nodded once in agreement with the thrall's statement before returning her attention to the balconies. Major Jadd moved to examine the pile of robes and rock debris that had been the Svartálfar leader, while Drux watched the left-hand balconies.

"She's okay," Lilly said after feeling Thereese's wrist for a pulse while holding a finger under her nose to ensure she was breathing.

Barkey straightened his back and stretched his arms out to his side, and then above his head, while flexing his fingers. "As you might guess, my Svartálfar blood doesn't mix well with sunlight."

"Road Toad," Enchantress Thulease said. "Step back so that I might attempt the doors."

Barkey unsteadily strode toward the enchantress, his hands extended palms up. "No, no."

I stepped between him and the enchantress.

He stopped and pointed to a balcony nearest the double doors. "Boost me up and I'll go around and down and open the doors." Before Enchantress Thulease could answer, he added, "You, the one called Road Toad. Pick out Gadzill's teeth." He turned to me and pointed to the pile of pebbles and rumpled clothing near the chamber's entrance. "Get Jander's, Flank Hawk."

"To what purpose?" asked Enchantress Thulease.

"Why?" Barkey replied. Then he set to laughing. "Only takes a glimmer of moonlight to touch any of their stones to reform their body, good as new. Even will repair wounds, like you did with your spear. All except their teeth. 'Least not if someone possesses their original choppers."

He extended his hands, again palms up. "It's a reminder to all that someone got the better of them. Plus, Gadzill and Jander are wielders of the arcane arts. Having no teeth will mess with their power, not being able to properly state the spell words. 'Least until their choppers grow back in about four thrallspans."

Enchantress Thulease asked, "Thrallspan? Seven winters?"

Barkey looked up in thought. "Three-hundred and fifty moon cycles," he said before nodding vigorously. "Yes, about twenty eight of your years by the seasons—yes, winters."

"Is it necessary for the teeth to be in contact with the holder's flesh?"

"No. A pouch or box carried on your body will do."

I moved to the left of the entrance and watched while the discussion between Barkey and Enchantress Thulease continued.

The enchantress asked, "For the full span of three hundred fifty moon cycles?"

"No. Only when they're reformed by the moon's rays. After, ummm." The Svartálfar thrall gazed up in thought. "After seven winters it won't matter no more. They'll have nub teeth by then."

"What is your interest in this, thrall? Might you not suffer repercussions by informing and by assisting us?"

He shook his head quickly. "No. The clan chief's son is not my master. Clan Chief is. His son told Gadzill to disarm and enthrall you. My master desires to meet with you. I heard his desire spoken. I was sent because I had been the one you spoke with first."

"Would they have killed us?" Jadd asked.

"Yes. If you fought. They'd say you failed to follow a reasonable order."

Lilly jumped to her feet. "Reasonable?"

Enchantress Thulease signaled for Lilly's silence with a quick hand gesture.

"Yes, reasonable," Barkey said. "You were surrounded by two effective users of the arcane and under the aim of twelve hand muskets." He grinned. "And me."

"Might collected teeth prove useful as leverage?" Enchantress Thulease asked.

Gadzill is the henchman of the clan chief's son. Jander is Gadzill's henchman. Barkey gazed up at the balconies. "Don't know who all was up there. But I could guess."

Drux, volunteered, "Enchantress, I'm guessing one can never have enough teeth in his pocket." He grinned broadly, causing the scar on his chin to stand out. "Or her pocket."

"How much time do you estimate we have to obtain our potential leverage, Thrall Barkey?"

"Enchantress," he said cautiously. When she didn't object, he continued. "I would estimate at least two hours before Gadzill is sorely missed. A little over two hours before anyone makes it here looking for him."

"Might you be trusted to guide me and my associates to this clan's chief?"

"I am more trustworthy than any Svartal under this mountain. Far more."

While Enchantress Thulease considered the thrall's words, Major Jadd commented, "Not much of a standard to measure by."

Barkey stuck out his lower lip and nodded. "Well, my master desires to meet with you."

"You have yet to speak up, Flank Hawk."

I met the enchantress's gaze. I didn't really have a good question, so I asked, "Why are you called Barkey?"

"Well, best I can say is I like to bark out orders. When given the chance—which ain't too often."

"Sergeant," Enchantress Thulease said and pointed to the balcony opposite the entrance from me. "Assist our scout up there. Take a lantern and begin collecting teeth. Road Toad, collect teeth as well. Flank Hawk, stand watch. Barkey, remove your rapier and flintlock pistol, then stand over there." She pointed right in front of the double doors. "Where I might keep an eye on you until we are finished."

After Drux had boosted Lilly up, Jadd said, "Scout, get me a couple of those flintlocks along with their holsters. There should be a reloading kit with bullets and patches, and a horn with powder."

She nodded. "What about you, Sergeant?"

"Don't know how to use one," he said.

"Me neither." She looked down at the enchantress who declined with a slight shake of her head. "Flank Hawk, what about you?"

I'd seen Roos point and pull the trigger of his cap and ball revolver. "Get one for me. If it comes to it, Road Toad can reload it for me."

Ten minutes later, Enchantress Thulease had possession of the two spellcasting Svartálfar's teeth. Lilly, Jadd and I each had possession of teeth from two balcony Svartálfar. They resembled the shape of human teeth except they looked to be made of pitch-black onyx. The teeth I had were jumbled together in the bottom of my satchel, in a small leather pouch next to the steel case holding the core of a unicorn horn. Removing my satchel would've been tricky if I'd had my old helmet tied to my belt on the back of my hip. Like my spear, I might end up needing a helmet, and wearing the new one did little to hinder hearing a potential underground ambush. It did block my natural view above without tipping my head back but Jadd said, like my breastplate, it might deflect a flintlock pistol's bullet.

Jadd checked my flintlock pistol, reviewed with me how to cock, point and shoot it, and helped me affix its holster to my belt on the right hand side, opposite my sword. It felt awkward but manageable.

Barkey opened the iron double-doors and stepped through, followed by Lilly.

"Road Toad," Enchantress Thulease said. "With your newfound firepower, I would prefer you watching our rear. Flank Hawk, you will stay in the front with our new found…acquaintance."

I handed Jadd the lantern as we switched positions. Drux and Lilly lifted Enchantress Thereese.

"Barkey," said the enchantress, handing him the other lantern. "Guide us to this clan's chief, if you would?"

The dark elves were immortal, or close to it, and had dwelt underground since First Civilization's Fall, so I thought there'd be more of them. Maybe Barkey led us through the back alleys of the Svartálfar's underground domain. We descended more often than climbing stairs, and once a ladder with great difficulty. I knew Drux was strong, but helping him haul the rope secured to Thereese's stretcher? It was mostly him and a little me.

Early on, most of the corridors allowed Enchantress Thulease to walk erect. Maybe that was intentional. Then we passed through several levels of thrall quarters that reminded me of the skyscraper that served as the Colonel of the West's Outpost 4. Except these were underground, damp and dark, and smelled of stale urine. Closer to a dungeon than any type of home.

"Why this way?" I asked Barkey. "It's been almost an hour."

"To avoid any more henchmen of the clan chief's son."

We received a lot of stares from the half-breed thralls. There appeared to be two types: Human Svartálfar and goblin Svartálfar crossbreeds. The former looked much like Barkey, although some more heavily favored dark elven traits, and others less. Those with goblin blood had ears with both pointed tips at the top and the bottom lobe, whereas the dark elves only had narrow lobes pointing down. The goblin bloods also retained their yellow, catlike eyes.

Two other things I noticed. In my experience, humans and goblins rarely got along but there seemed to be no problem among the thralls, goblin or human blood mixed with Svartálfar. Maybe it was because each had tattooed rows of circles on their left cheek. The other thing I noticed was all the thralls were male.

Faces covered in ash and grime stared at us as we walked past. They wiped calloused hands on their sweaty shirts and trousers and shuffled aside, some making eye contact with Barkey, their eyebrows raised. I couldn't catch his silent response.

After we'd passed through the barracks area, I asked Barkey, "All the thralls are men?"

My question caught him off guard. "Well, ahh, yeah. The Svarts call us mules. A molly? Well, I think there's two of them here in the Iron Hoard Clan Chief's Mountainhold."

The thought that mules weren't a crossbreed that gave offspring must've shown on my face or maybe he'd had this discussion before because he shrugged and said, "You're thinking right that you won't see none of us raising kids." When I didn't say anything he slugged me in the arm. "There's them kids of ours that won't ever exist, plus no goats down here neither." He paused, taking a breath. "They don't do so well under mountains, you know."

"Oh," I said. He laughed. I smiled back and added, "That makes sense. Before I took up as a mercenary, I worked as a farmhand."

He nodded as if that made perfect sense.

"What do you do down here?" I tipped my head back to the left. "What do they do down here?"

"Well, you might recall, Flank Hawk, I stand watch. Us mules can endure sunlight, even though it stiffens up my joints. Affects all of us like that. We're the army that defends the mountains." He laughed. "Dig in and defend during daylight, advance and attack at night."

"Who do you war against?"

"You've fought your share as a mercenary, right?" When I nodded he continued, asking, "Who do you fight?"

"Most recently, the forces of Fendra Jolain. Mainly facing Long Tooth warriors. I've fought against mercenary forces of the Sky Color Gods, and against the Necromancer King's invasion."

Barkey spat down where the smooth carved rock wall met the damp floor. The hall was still wide enough for two to walk side by side but the ceiling had crept down to where I had to duck a little bit, especially where the tunnel dog-legged to the left or right every fifty or so paces. It felt like we were going up a shallow slope, but the faint lantern light didn't offer much beyond thirty or so feet, making visual assessment hard. Every so often a tunnel branched off to the left or right, but never a cross tunnel. There might've been a reason to that.

I glanced back, and saw Jadd mark the wall with a piece of chalk. He'd suggested that tactic back while making preparations in Keesee. Although not assured, should we have to find our own way out, it offered a possibility.

A few steps after spitting, Barkey said, "Walking dead. Hate'em, 'specially those with the spark of thinking in their eyes and their actions."

"You've fought them too?"

"More like stopping them from getting in down here. Never heard of any Sky Colored Gods."

"I hadn't either until I'd was on a mission that took me to the Western Continent."

"Where you say?"

"Across the Western Ocean," I said. "I've heard some call it the Atlantic."

"Well, whew. I've never been much beyond this mountain range. But when I'm done serving." He paused while pointing to the dots on his cheek. "I'll go east, like all of us do."

"Do you have any brothers?" I asked.

"Oh, two half-brothers, but my thrall cropper—my mother you would say—earns most of her coinage through harvesting her fungus caverns. She just had us to gather enough to get her started."

"She earns coin through growing fungus?"

"Food, don't you know? Hard to come by underground and trade isn't always reliable."

I was going to ask who they traded with, but I knew that Enchantress Thulease was listening and it'd be more important to learn about how things worked with the Svartálfar, under the mountain.

"Do you trade things constructed or created using the Soul Forge?" It wasn't a very subtle question, but Barkey seemed to be talking and had been around a while. The way the other thralls looked at him, he was someone respected, at least among them. And I saw some light ahead. Maybe it was another set of thrall barracks. Or maybe not.

Barkey laughed. "That's why you're here with her." He pointed his thumb over his shoulder. "She dying?"

"She is," I said, figuring the clan chief or whoever hammered out the Soul Forge's magic, if a hammer was even a part of it, would know soon enough. I gazed back a moment, past Lilly to the young enchantress. "A slow magical death."

The din of clomping boots, scraping and clanking and dozens of conversations in a foreign tongue became apparent as the light down the tunnel neared.

"Up against the right wall," Barkey said, tersely barking out what sounded like an order. I was used to orders. Enchantress Thulease wasn't. Making room for the approaching dark elves or thralls, or both as they passed by made sense and I followed Barkey's example. So did everyone else in our line of march.

After the seventy or so thralls passed us by, we continued our trek.

I'd been correct in my spotting light beyond the several lanterns the thralls had been carrying. Before we got much closer Barkey signaled for us to halt and for us to remain silent. He closed his eyes and appeared to be listening.

Sixty or so heartbeats later he turned and looked up at Enchantress Thulease. "I'm figuring that you're pretty accomplished as an enchantress?"

Keeping a straight face, she replied, "I am."

"Do you sense any magic around us?"

"What type? Elemental, witchcraft, an enchantment?"

"Well." He looked around and licked his lips, then whispered in Mainland, "The type that can ear in on my words."

Enchantress Thulease pinched her chin with a thumb and forefinger. Then she mumbled what was certainly a spell and closed her eyes. I watched down the tunnel and listened for possible danger. The way Barkey rubbed his hands and then held them clutched together told me he was nervous. Besides, there was little reason for me to watch behind us. Enchantress Thulease knew her business, and Major Jadd was watching our rear.

The enchantress replied to the thrall's question in Mainland. "I detect ambient magic ahead. Nothing in our immediate vicinity."

"You're sure, now?" Concern, or more probably worry, reverberated in his words.

"There are few equally accomplished as I in my chosen art. At least in the Kingdom of Keesee, and across the Doran Confederacy and the Faxtinian Coalition. Among the Lesser Kingdoms, there is only one that surpasses me."

That was news to me—about a powerful enchanter in the Lesser Kingdoms.

"Well, then," Barkey said. "I'll say my piece while I can."

He looked over his shoulder warily before gazing up at the enchantress again. "You seem like good folk who don't know there's very little good down here." He swept his left hand wide, gesturing as he spoke.

"The clan chief is cruel and crafty, but will bargain trade if he thinks he'll come out ahead. His word, once given, is reliable as stone."

Then Barkey shook his head. "His son. Now, he's petty. He's vile, and will trick you anyway he can if he gets a word in. And he will, 'cause…well, he just will." Barkey nodded sharply. "To get something for himself."

Barkey scratched the back of his neck. "Now, if you manage access to the Forge Master, well, he'll trade services or magic or something. I'm figuring you've got something to barter?"

Enchantress Thulease tipped her head with a smile. "That I have." Then her smile faded. "I assure you, friend, that I…that we, are many things. Novices in the art of exchange is not among them." She tipped her head toward me. "My daughter's personal guard, the one you call Flank Hawk, has bartered with the one some call Belinda the Cursed, and also negotiated with Colonel of the West on behalf of our king."

She turned and gestured toward Major Jadd. "My personal guard, Road Toad, has stood before the Parliament of the Reunited Kingdom, successfully negotiating for the right of passage of both serpent steeds and spellcasters through their lands and holdings. I might go on, but I imagine my point has been made." She crossed her arms. "With that in mind, what anticipated payment might you have fancied for your cautionary words?"

"Ohh, well," said Barkey, a mischievous grin spreading across his face. "By rights, any wealth, goods, or property I might obtain is obtained in the name of my master, the Clan Chief of the Svarts dwelling here in the Iron Hoard Mountainhold. He's more than capable of bartering for his own wealth, property and goods without me contributing on his behalf."

Enchantress Thulease stared down at Barkey. Her left eye squinted as she tilted her head, clearly showing her skepticism.

"A half-shovel of times I've seen your type enter down here," the thrall said. "Sometimes they get taken in the Balcony Room. It's constructed to trap trespassers, but it's used to ambush traders. Of course, you noticed that.

"Myself? I've never seen anyone get past like you did. Once I heard about a fight. Most everyone got killed."

He shrugged. "Depends on the clan chief's mood, or if his son is around, whether traders like you are allowed to pass through unchallenged. But that's only half the concern, Enchantress. That you've got experience and you not trusting me?" He clapped his hands and rubbed them together. "You might get what you've come down here looking for."

"Your confidence is most encouraging," Enchantress Thulease said. I didn't know how to interpret the flat tone in her words.

"Well," Barkey said, apparently unsure about Enchantress Thulease's final view as well. "Hope you end atop the coal pile and not under it."

After twenty minutes of marching we left the narrow tunnels and travelled through increasingly grandiose passages, some lined with drawings and words scripted in silver and gold. Before we continued, we exchanged our lanterns with two of the forty hanging on two rows of iron hooks set into the stone wall. Barkey placed our nearly spent lanterns on the bottom row and took two fresh ones from the top row.

While we did this, Enchantress Thulease knelt next to her daughter. Gripping Thereese's hand, Enchantress Thulease whispered into her daughter's ear. Before she stood to continue our trek, she wiped a tear from her eye.

Lilly rested a hand on the supreme enchantress's shoulder. "I've been watching her close when you can't. Whispering reminders to her that you're near."

"I know and I thank you for that, my scout."

"She'll make it," Lilly said. "Flank Hawk and me'll see to that, while you do all you must do to get her to the Svartálfar's magic forge."

CHAPTER 33

A twelve-foot tall and equally wide set of double doors covered in a mosaic of thumb-sized gold, silver, and copper squares stood a short distance ahead of us.

"The Clan Chief's Hall," Barkey announced. I stepped aside so that Enchantress Thulease could take the lead. Major Jadd moved up to her right. I prepared to walk along side Enchantress Thereese on her left. Lilly met my gaze. She wanted to say something but bit her lip, thinking better of it.

As Barkey stepped off to the side, Enchantress Thulease, said, "Barkey, as our guide, I believe it proper for you to accompany us into the Clan Chief's Hall." I pointed for him to walk with us on Drux's right.

Flanked by Major Jadd, the enchantress led the way past the mumbling and pointing dark elves that lined the hallway leading up to the meeting hall's ornate double doors. As we approached, the huge doors opened with half-goblin thralls grunting as they hauled back on silver chains. The thralls then leaned their shoulders against the doors, pushing them closed after we passed them, striding into the huge rectangular hall.

Forty-foot pillars carved from black marble stretched up to support the arched ceiling. Inlaid silver, stylized to look like wrapping ivy vines, decorated each of the twenty pillars and extended into a web across the ceiling. The pillars stood ten feet in from the side walls which were lined with tiered rows of benches. They reminded me of the Sleeping Sage's gallery except black and gray-clad dark elves filled these seats, instead of desiccated corpses. There were at least two hundred murmuring spectators on each side. Silver-haired female Svartálfar, a little taller and leaner than the males, filled the top row along both walls.

The hall appeared to be lit through magic that maintained hardly more than a murky twilight. The dark elves and their attending thralls probably saw more clearly than we did in the meeting hall, their eyes being used to underground darkness. Enchanters could magically enhance their vision to see with very little light, but I didn't think it was dark enough that Enchantress Thulease required it, especially with our lanterns.

Looking about I realized the faint glow of light that filled the hall emanated from the silver ivy. Lilly's head movement, following the silver ivy up to the ceiling, said she'd determined the source of light too.

Ahead, at the hall's far end rose two narrow stairways, also carved from black marble and covered with the magical silver ivy. The pair of stairways angled up, like an upside down V and converged on two chairs, the larger of the two on the right. The ornate chairs were carved from white marble instead of black, with the heads of yawning marble gargoyles supporting each leg. Each chair also had smaller gargoyle heads carved into the arms and two perched atop the backrests.

Both male Svartálfar occupying the seats were dressed primarily in black. The one on the right appeared far older. His left hand and arm rested motionless in his lap. Even from a distance it appeared twisted and withered. The older dark elf had a large gold medallion hanging from a thick gold chain. Pitted as it was, it must've represented a full moon. But what stood out most was his brimless hat made of leopard fur, except it was white with only black spots, and ringed with large, blood-red rubies.

He held an angry expression with bushy gray eyebrows drawn close. His unblinking eyes stared at us as we approached.

The younger dark elf on the left, whose seat was one step lower, wore a vest made from some sort of thick white fur and also had a gold medallion that looked like a partial moon, half way through its cycle.

The older Svartálfar, the clan chief, had a flanged mace leaning against his seat, or throne. The dark elf on the left, I guessed to be the chief's son, caressed the hilt of a rapier hanging over the gargoyle armrest. Its jewel-encrusted scabbard and silver-studded belt caught and reflected the dim magical light. More than seemed normal.

I gazed back at the rows of seated dark elves. All of them were armed, some with swords or axes, and a few with flintlock pistols but, from what I could see, all carried at least a dagger. In the King's City, beyond those soldiers serving King Tobias, few were armed in his presence, especially within his meeting hall. Only those deemed the most loyal carried weapons with a range, such as a crossbow.

Although virtually all in the Svartálfar chief's hall were armed, few reminded me of soldiers.

From the little I knew, or thought I knew based on a brief encounter and what Barkey had said, I didn't think they were armed because the clan chief trusted them all. If anything, it spoke of a mistrusting, violent race.

Enchantress Thulease regally walked around a fifty foot diameter pit set into the hall's floor two thirds of the way across. Curved red granite blocks the size of bricks made up the brim. Three-foot long strips, each one-foot wide and draped over each other like a shingled roof, lined the pit's steeply angled sides. It was ten feet deep with a flat bottom made of polished red granite.

Major Jadd strode confidently with his hand resting on his sword's hilt. I did my best to match his bearing and stride. Out of the corner of my eye I caught the image of Enchantress Thereese. The eerie gray light gave her a corpse-like visage. I swallowed hard, reminding myself that it was the light causing the appearance. Having come so far, Thereese had to hold onto life just a little longer.

Even though it didn't make sense to do so, I brushed my fingers across her hand. The touch of my leather gauntlets might still remind her that we were there. That I was there. After a deep breath I decided that the jostling movement as Drux and Lilly bore the young enchantress on her stretcher was a stronger reminder of our presence than my brush of leather. But it also served to remind me that she was still with us. Why I was there—why we were there—in that echoing, twilight chamber.

Once around the pit Enchantress Thulease angled back toward the hall's center and stopped midway between the narrow staircases. She bowed her head once and looked up at the older dark elf. When he nodded in return, Jadd set his lantern on the smooth stone floor. Drux and Lilly carefully did the same with the stretcher bearing the weakening enchantress.

From our left a half-goblin thrall scurried up to Enchantress Thulease and beckoned with his hand for her to bend low so that he might speak to her. After a quiet exchange, the thrall stepped forward and looked up to the clan chief.

After taking a deep breath the thrall shouted in Sea Spittle, "Clan Chief of the Iron Hoard Mountainhold, I present to you the Supreme Enchantress and a portion of her party, from the Kingdom of Keesee." His screechy voice echoed off the ceiling and walls, but quickly faded to silence.

The son of the clan chief yawned, leaned back and rubbed his long crooked nose. He gazed every direction but at us.

The clan chief dismissed the thrall with a wave of his hand. After the half-goblin scurried away, the Svartálfar leader leaned forward. "Who are you?" His voice was gravelly and his words measured. "You who have entered my domain, requesting an audience?"

"The thrall that announced us identified me accurately," Enchantress Thulease said.

She was cut off by the clan chief's son. His demeanor transformed to one of fury. "Where are my men, sent to escort you to my father's grand hall?" His voice was also gravelly, but his words were fast and insistent. He pointed down at Major Jadd. "Keeseeans are not known for carrying firearms. The Svartálfar who serve me are."

"In addition to the full-blooded Svartálfar that met us above ground," Enchantress Thulease explained, "we encountered a number of Svartálfar in a subterranean balcony room. Ultimately they remained in that room while we proceeded here."

His eyes shot to Barkey, but the clan chief's son continued to address Enchantress Thulease. "You would dare infringe upon my father's hospitality by offering violence to the Svartálfar of this, his mountainhold?" He ended with a harsh hand-sweeping gesture, indicating the hall, and presumably the subterranean areas beyond.

Enchantress Thulease shifted her hands from her sides to behind her back, clasping her left with her right hand. "I do not stand before your father to play a pointless game of accusation. Those you have certainly dispatched by now will deliver the answer to your question in due time." She then turned to address the clan chief. "If you are prepared, I shall endeavor to address why I have ventured to speak with you, Clan Chief of this Mountainhold."

Halfway through Enchantress Thulease's statement, the clan chief's son leaned forward and shouted, "I asked you a question. Answer!"

It was easy to see Enchantress Thulease determined that offering words akin to biscuits smothered in honey wouldn't further her cause. But it invited threats that promised violence. I observed the crowd. All were quiet and attentive, eager to see what would happen. I'd have wagered plenty of coin that very few insulted the Clan Chief's Son, and even fewer without retribution.

"Clan Chief of the Iron Hoard Mountainhold," Enchantress Thulease said. "If your son held more than indifferent concern for those who serve him, he would not have sent them to intercept and attempt to disarm and enthrall one of my power, stature, resources, accompanied by loyal and capable followers."

The clan chief's son began to speak but his father silenced him with a gesture of his good hand.

I was impressed with the enchantress's command of Sea Spittle gained over a short span of months. She continued addressing the clan chief. "Is it your desire that your son subvert our discussion based upon this pretense?"

The clan chief smiled, but it didn't reach his eyes. Even so, it stood in stark contrast to his son, whose face was twisted in anger.

The clan chief leaned back in his chair. "If, as you say, the answer to my son's question is forthcoming, moving on to your purpose is my desire."

Enchantress Thulease nodded once. "I have journeyed far, seeking the magic of the Soul Forge so that it might revive my daughter. Through my research, I learned that my path to the Soul Forge goes through the Svartálfar clan chief who rules the mountainhold where the magical forge resides. I believe you, Clan Chief of the Iron Hoard Mountainhold, to be that individual."

The clan chief revealed his black teeth in an unusually wide grin. "*Resides*, is an interesting choice of words, Supreme Enchantress. Nevertheless, you are correct. It is *I* who will grant or deny you access to the mysterious and mighty Soul Forge."

He extended his good hand and pointed down at Enchantress Thereese. "That would be your daughter? She does not appear well." The false concern in the clan chief's statement was easy to recognize.

"Supreme Enchantress, I am quite certain that the blood bondlove for a child is as strong among your kind as it is among my kind." Moving his hand to his chest and then back to resting upon his lap, the clan chief continued, saying, "Possibly even more so for those of both authority and magical prowess.

"What gift do you offer for access, realizing that even if sufficient, you must entice the forge master to attempt the magic you desire?"

"As you ask this question in open court, then it is your desire I answer this in open court for all to hear as well?"

The clan chief laughed loud and long, attempting to make some sort of point. "In such matters, Supreme Enchantress, I do not negotiate through side alcove deals."

"Very good. A little over seven-hundred moon cycles ago, according to my research, your clan was in conflict with the Necromancer King." She gestured toward the clan chief's arm. "In honorable combat you defeated the Necromancer King's champion, a necromancer of undeniable strength and knowledge in his dark arcane art. During the final throes of his struggle, the Necromancer King's Champion channeled spell energy directly from his master, resulting in the curse of the undead arm you have since endured."

The clan chief's eyebrows rose, apparently impressed with Enchantress Thulease's knowledge.

"If my source of knowledge is correct, should sunlight fall upon your skin, Clan Chief, you would be transformed to stone, including your cursed arm, until moonlight restores you, undead arm intact."

Enchantress Thulease gripped her chin between her bent forefinger and thumb. "That leaves you in a quandary." She then began to walk from left to right, in front of the clan chief's seat, and then back as she continued. "Among the many Svartálfar traditions, is one that states a clan chief must not be permanently crippled if he hopes to remain in his seat of authority. I would imagine your victory to have left you in a vexing and precarious position."

The clan chief's gray eyebrows pinched downward. He wasn't happy with Enchantress Thulease's words. Where there had been a background of hushed conversations, the entire hall fell silent—so silent that my breathing felt like bull's nose flaring and blowing out a threat.

Before the clan chief responded, Enchantress Thulease held her hand before her, index finger raised. "Add to that a second logical concern," she said. "What might happen to the arm in question if you found yourself within the spell range, let alone in the presence of a powerful necromancer?"

If all that Enchantress Thulease said was true, how powerful and ruthless and feared was the clan chief to have retained power? His son, assuredly in line for the high seat, seemed like the type to challenge given a reasonable chance of victory. Maybe it was because of the blood lovebond mentioned? And his son propping up his father? I didn't think so. More likely using his father as a sort of stalking horse.

The clan chief grunted and shifted positions in his seat before leaning forward. "Ignoring and setting aside your erroneous, ignorant assumptions, Enchantress, you have said nothing to entice me. Rather…"

Enchantress Thulease again held up her right hand, long index finger extended. "If I may interrupt and complete my proposal?"

The clan chief said nothing. Instead he signaled to two squads of guards seated among the spectators to our left and right. I gripped my spear and prepared for whatever was to come.

Enchantress Thulease said boldly, "Clan Chief, wouldn't you rather once again direct and dismiss those who serve you with whichever hand you desire? Your impatient actions indicate that is not the case."

The clan chief held up his hand, his index finger raised, signaling his rapier and pistol-armed soldiers to hold in place. His stiff movement and pursed lips said he wasn't happy how the discussion had gone thus far. I wasn't either, but trusted Enchantress Thulease. The clan chief would've done better to barter with her in private.

He once again laughed loud and long. "What makes you believe your magic is superior to mine and that of my magicians?"

"Because, Clan Chief, I am a learned and powerful enchanter." She held up a finger as she finished, "And I have access to a resource largely antithetical to necromancy that you and your magicians do not. Sunlight."

The clan chief cocked his head. A broad grin followed. "Step forward, Supreme Enchantress, so that we might discuss your proposal in conversational instead of proclamational voices." He gestured with his hand, sending the soldiers back to their seats. "Those in attendance have heard the essence of your proposal. At least those familiar with the Trade Tongue."

The fierce scowl the clan chief's son directed at Enchantress Thulease could've scorched steel. That she ignored him, as did his father as they spoke, only stoked the raging fire within him.

I overheard Barkey whisper up to Sergeant Drux standing next to him. "His wrath's going to hammer someone." After a pause, he finished, his voice trailing off, "I'm worse than doomed."

After the clan chief had summoned the forge master by sending a runner, he offered us bench seats carried in by several of his soldiers and placed near the circular pit. The Svartálfar crowd wandered in and out of the hall and ignored us for the most part. The clan chief and his son remained on their high seats. They'd spoken, or rather argued, in hushed tones for a few minutes. After that, they ignored each other while drinking what I guessed to be some sort of ale from tall mugs.

I stood watch, making a point to appear alert with boar spear ready in an effort to deter any dark elves that might consider wandering too close. Barkey sat with us and watched as Sergeant Drux held Enchantress

Thereese in a sitting position and Lilly poured a thin, cherry-colored gruel slowly into her mouth. She helped the unconscious enchantress to swallow by massaging her throat. Thereese's alchemist father had created the mixture which had sustained his daughter over the long months.

Enchantress Thulease was hesitant to speak much with some of the Svartálfar seated within earshot, and especially with Barkey among us. Whenever the thrall glanced toward the high seats, he'd take in a sharp breath, wide-eyed, before looking away or down at his boots.

Lilly was talking to Drux, lamenting that she didn't get one of the flint-lock pistols. He was explaining to her that they weren't allowed in the King's City. Furthermore, blacksmiths were forbidden to forge gun barrels and alchemists from making the powder that enabled the guns to fire their bullets.

I'd learned as a child that in trade for Algaan's and M'Kishmael's protection from other gods encroaching, the first kings of Keesee and some of the other leaders on the Mainland swore never to pursue development of the weapons that precipitated First Civilization's fall. Instead they were granted insight into spellcraft, which grew and flourished over the centuries and kept the realms safe.

Still paying attention to movements around us, I told Lilly what I'd learned before reaching ten summers.

Major Jadd added, "Don't neglect to mention the fact that assassinations of nobles through use of firearms would be far easier for the common man to enact, creating instability."

"That's not how it happened, Flank Hawk," Lilly said. "The Colonel of the West showed me and you different."

"Maybe," Jadd said. "Maybe not. What I do know is that it takes far less training for a man to become competent with a gun than with a sword. It would lead to anarchy."

Lilly's eyebrows furrowed as she thought about that. "I don't know. But him having that pistol on his hip? It sure would solve Flank Hawk's problem with Flayzin."

My hand fell to the holstered flintlock.

Barkey shook his head. "Any magician worth anything can spark off the powder with a spell, unless the gun's rune-warded 'gainst it. Your guns are, but with personal rune-warding. Magic you can't summon to action." He tipped his head up at Enchantress Thulease who was sitting quietly, listening. "She could, I expect."

Enchantress Thulease didn't respond to the thrall's statement. Instead she asked in Mainland, "How long might we wait for the forge master to arrive?"

He responded in Mainland, "He won't dawdle. But if you brought any food with you, you have time enough for that."

"Any insight into how I might negotiate with him?"

Barkey shrugged. "He's pretty confident in his skill. Anything you might have to supplement it. That *might* work." His eyes shot over toward the high chairs before he whispered. "Him and the clan chief's son, well, they're not friends. Close as the clan chief's son has to one, though."

As we got out some of the cheese and bread we'd brought, Lilly mumbled, "Well, Flayzin, he's not a magician. That, even I know."

Twenty minutes later a stocky Svartálfar wearing leather coveralls and a burn-marked leather apron swaggered into the hall. He gazed our direction as we stood but continued on his way toward the high chairs. About thirty Svartálfar strode into the meeting hall behind him and moved toward their waiting seats.

"That's him," Barkey whispered.

Enchantress Thulease gazed at the forge master intently as he climbed the stairs and exchanged words with the clan chief. "He will be far more difficult to negotiate with."

Before anyone had a chance to agree or disagree, the clan chief summoned us over. "Supreme Enchantress, the forge master has arrived for you to barter with."

Major Jadd walked a half-stride behind Enchantress Thulease, on her right. Lilly and Drux bore Thereese behind her, with me on the young enchantress's left. Barkey again stuck next to Sergeant Drux, which the clan chief, his master, didn't object to.

Enchantress Thulease stopped next to the far shorter forge master who'd descended the steps. He smelled of sweat and coal smoke. Pulling his black braided beard out from beneath his apron, he smiled up at the enchantress. Lines creased his soot-smeared face.

"I've been informed that you have a proposition for me, Tall Enchantress." The forge master's voice sounded scratchy, like he'd breathed in too much smoke over the years. Like many of the Svartálfar, he spoke Sea Spittle.

"That I do, Forge Master."

The clan chief leaned forward on his perched seat. "Enchantress, I have delivered my end of the agreement."

She bowed her head once. "You have," she said, and reached into her satchel and withdrew a loosely woven mesh gauntlet made from intertwining threads of delicate copper and silver links. From a pocket she pulled out a silver locket identical to the one she opened in the Balcony Room and released a burst of sunlight. "May I approach?"

After he nodded, she climbed the narrow steps, three at a time.

"Extend your afflicted hand and arm," she ordered.

The clan chief did, his son watching warily, hand resting on his rapier's hilt. I saw how tense Major Jadd had become, ready to spring into action.

Even so, he'd never close the distance fast enough, and the narrow steps offered almost no chance for Enchantress Thulease to maneuver out of the way.

The clan chief pulled back his black sleeve and extended his unmoving arm and hand. It was gray and withered, the skin looking like that from a mummified corpse.

She carefully straitened each of the curled fingers before slipping the mesh gauntlet over the hand and up the clan chief's dead arm. After she did, she pulled a leather cord from her pocket and strung it through eyelets near the elbow before tying it tight to hold the gauntlet in place.

The clan chief watched each movement with interest, as did the forge master, stepping closer to get a better view from below. The clan chief's son watched with suspicion.

She then attached the locket to four latches across the top of his hand.

"Clan Chief," she said. "Upon speaking the activation word, pain thrice that you experienced when the curse fell upon your hand and arm will course through it, after the curse is overwhelmed and neutralized."

He nodded, accepting the revelation. "How long will it take?"

"Sixty heartbeats. Upon completion, the locket will most certainly be drained. I have another which I will affix. I have not had the time to study the curse laid upon your arm—"

He cut her off. "Then how can I be assured it will work?"

Enchantress Thulease took a deep, patient breath. "I have not had the opportunity to study the curse laid upon your arm, and thus, I do not know its strength. It may even require the second locket to complete the transformation."

He glared at her.

She shrugged. "There are multiple factors. The strength of the necromancer served as the conduit through which the curse was inflicted. Your strength as a magician, influencing your ability to resist, among others."

"What if two is not enough?"

"They will be."

He frowned, unconvinced. Sitting back in his seat and gripping a carved gargoyle head, he said, "Proceed, Supreme Enchantress."

Before she did, she asked, "Do you wish for your son to overhear and possess the word of activation?"

He replied after a breath of hesitation. "It matters not."

His son stood and emptied a leather pouch of several rubies. He tossed them down to the forge master. After twisting the pouch he offered it to his father. "Bite down on this."

When the clan chief did, Enchantress Thulease whispered a word. The clan chief grunted, stiffened and bit down. The muscles in his jaws and neck bulged and his right hand snapped off the throne arm's gargoyle head.

After half a moment his jaw relaxed and he spit out the twisted pouch. He then raised and flexed his black-skinned, living left hand.

He grinned, observing it as a cheer arose from the dark elves in the hall. I wasn't able to hear what Enchantress Thulease said to the clan chief as she handed him the locket in her hand and then another from her pocket, this one open—the one from the Balcony Room.

Lilly looked over her shoulder and said, "She's telling him he needs to get the lockets recharged with direct sunlight." After a pause, listening she continued. "Each one'll take twelve hours to fill on cloudless days. More with clouds, and more with the sun at a low angle in the sky."

After another pause, Lilly added, "She estimated that each locket'll last about forty hours, except the one that broke the curse's grip. It'll only last twelve and, as it is now nearly drained, only about an hour."

Finally, Lilly added, "And if the glove ever goes more than three hundred heartbeats without a sun-filled locket, the curse will reassert itself."

The clan chief had listened intently, probably considering where to place the lockets, who to entrust, how much sunlight could be obtained during the shorter winter days, and all sorts of other concerns.

After Enchantress Thulease turned and descended the steps, his son leaned back in his high seat, deep in thought.

For some reason I got the idea that the clan chief's son was trying to determine if Enchantress Thulease had any more sunlight-filled lockets in her pocket. And if so, how many? It was a good question—one I wanted to know the answer to. But that moment wasn't the right time to ask.

CHAPTER 34

Enchantress Thulease and the Forge Master of the Iron Hoard Mountainhold stood in the V formed by the steps leading up to the clan chief and his son's high seats, facing each other. He craned his neck, gazing up at the far taller enchantress. Even so, he was anything but intimidated, confident in his own magic and abilities.

Enchantress Thereese laid upon her stretcher to their left, her shallow breathing was weaker than before we ventured underground. I stood over the young enchantress, opposite the two negotiating spellcasters, while Major Jadd stood ready, observing the situation from two steps to my right.

"You believe my magic, channeled through and amplified by the Soul Forge, will revive your ailing daughter?" The forge master glanced toward Major Jadd. "Based on your research and, as your Sword Arm there explained a few moments ago when you hesitated, the Sleeping Sage's advice."

Enchantress Thulease grimaced when he said the name, in reference to what had happened inside the Sleeping Sage's abode. I'd felt a powerful urge to turn and walk away as Jadd finished his explanation to the Svartálfar blacksmith that the enchantress's knowledge and belief stemmed from her journey to the Southern Continent where she consulted with the Sleeping Sage.

The forge master observed Enchantress Thulease, gritting her teeth and clenching her hands into fists. He'd turned his head to glance at me, then asked Jadd, "The mercenary accompanied the enchantress?"

The blacksmith tugged on his beard's two braids as he spoke half to Enchantress Thulease and half to himself. "Few know much about the Svartálfar and where to find us, and even fewer dare venture into our lands. And the very few that venture among our mountain ranges ever enter one of our mountainholds." He gazed back up at the enchantress. "Based on your experience, you might guess how many emerge to return home."

While waiting for the forge master, a servant had raced into the hall. After being granted permission he rushed up and spoke, leaning close to the clan chief's son. I'd have wagered a lot of coin that was the moment the clan chief's son learned the men he sent to disarm us, or worse, were piles of stones. Piles lacking obsidian teeth. The effect was like shoveling hot coals under an already boiling cauldron. By the time the forge master arrived, I couldn't imagine that even one Svartálfar or thrall in the meeting hall didn't have some idea what had happened.

Were we going to be those of the very, very few? Not if the fuming clan chief's son had anything to say about it.

The forge master released his beard's braids and clasped his powerful hands together. "I have evidence of the boon offered Clan Chief, to grant our meeting and even access to the Soul Forge's magic, should I be persuaded. What will you offer for my labor in hopes that I might revive your daughter?"

Enchantress Thulease bowed her head once. "I thank you, Forge Master, for setting aside your work to hear and consider my proposal.

"First, I have brought with me magical components necessary to assist your spellcraft."

The forge master grunted and placed his hands on his hips. "You would presume to know my work? Have knowledge of its needs?"

Enchantress Thulease responded in an even tone. "Road Toad has spoken to you on my behalf." She gestured to Major Jadd. "One as knowledgeable as you certainly recognizes the reason I am unable to elucidate…further."

"What have you brought to ease my task, should I undertake it?"

"The breath of a fish. The core of a unicorn's horn. The blood of an immortal being. The yoke of an unfertilized dragon's egg. A lodestone that has never seen the light of day. The tears of a giant."

The forge master's eyebrows rose as he ran a thick, scarred finger along the sooty ends of his mustache. "Not the elements I would've chosen," he said in deep consideration. His unfocused gaze wandered down to Enchantress Thereese. "Yet, they might suffice." He nodded slowly as he pulled at his beard. "Yes, they just might."

"What I have to offer," Enchantress Thulease said, "is a tome of alchemical formulas, many of which focus on metallurgy. My husband is a master alchemist. The most knowledgeable and respected in the King's City. In the Kingdom of Keesee."

The forge master grunted again. "Master alchemist or no, his knowledge of metals compared to mine. A cub to a bear. He wouldn't trade his life's research secrets with me."

Enchantress Thulease pulled a steel scroll case wrapped in leather. From that she pulled a rolled vellum scroll and handed it to the blacksmith. "Although the tome in question is written in Mainland, symbols and numbers used in alchemy straddle many languages. What you are looking at is a sample with relevant parts translated into the written language of the Svartálfar."

The hall remained silent, all struggling to hear the exchange. The clan chief and his son also watched and listened with interest.

The forge master spent several long minutes reading and studying the scroll's contents. He then rolled up the vellum scroll and handed it back to Enchantress Thulease. "Your daughter will remain with me for a thrallspan."

At the mention of this the clan chief's son sat up in interest, a smile creasing his face.

"Unacceptable," Enchantress Thulease said, her face losing all expression. "Better she dies than serve as anyone's slave."

"Not as a thrall. She will remain and serve as my apprentice while learning the Svartálfar tongue. Then she can transcribe her father's tome so that it will be useful to me."

Like me, Enchantress Thulease must have sensed there was more—something deeper to his request. "I will provide a competent and reliable translator."

"Who better?" the Svartálfar blacksmith said, gesturing to the young enchantress. "No. I do not intend to share these secrets with anyone other than her—if she survives." He folded his arms across his chest. "She certainly can read, and can decipher her father's script. And from him she must have learned at least the basics of his trade. Enough to reliably transcribe. She is an enchantress. Serving as my apprentice, I would learn secrets from her, magics I would not otherwise have access to. *And* she would learn magics and secrets from me, a Svartálfar Forge Master."

The din of muffled discussions rose from the benches in the hall. The clan chief frowned down from his high seat. His son, he continued to grin. His anger had transformed into something sinister. Something evil. If Enchantress Thereese remained, she'd suffer his wrath.

The forge master was certainly powerful among his people, but I didn't think equal to the clan chief's son. And Barkey said the forge master and the clan chief's son weren't friends, but close to it, giving him further access and leverage to enact whatever scheme he was devising.

Barkey. I thought about him. What he'd said about his mother. The lower place women held in the Svartálfar culture, some having to birth half-breed thralls for coin to prosper, or even live.

"I would rather my daughter die," Enchantress Thulease said, "than allow her to endure winters as a…a broodmare. She would choose death. Will choose death."

Enchantress Thulease must've been thinking along the same lines as me.

Eyebrows raised, the forge master asked, "Choose death?"

Either the forge master hadn't considered that fate for Enchantress Thereese. Or he didn't anticipate Enchantress Thulease recognizing the threat to her daughter, and objecting to it.

Enchantress Thulease slid a half step closer to her daughter. "Yes. Death."

Whatever happened wouldn't matter to the clan chief. He sat and watched with interest, but he'd already obtained his payment—or bribe. His son was harder to read, his face set in a grin as he watched. Then it struck me. As long as someone, somehow suffered, he'd be satisfied. And the more suffering, the more satisfied.

The death of Thereese, knowing that a supreme enchantress from Keesee, someone so powerful having risked so much, sacrificed so much, travelled so far, only to fail when potential life was at hand. That was the desire of the clan chief's son.

"You then realize," the forge master said, "that human witches, earth wizards and enchanters are the only ones who can survive bearing a half-Svartálfar thrall. Those that such human females birth, through their magical nature, are destined to be talented thralls, often with magical potential. In front of all, I now oathspeak. I will not take your daughter such that she might bear offspring. As my apprentice, I will shield her from others who might wish to create thralls through her, despite the gained riches such action would set aside, both for myself and for her. Powerful the offspring would be, able to endure direct sunlight, and benefit the defense of this mountainhold."

After a moment of consideration, Enchantress Thulease replied. "*Shield*," she said, crossing her arms, "has a different meaning than *prevent.* My limited understanding of your culture and traditions suggest that with a word or public proclamation, such as your oath just stated, you prevent anyone of equal or of lesser prestige or standing than you. Am I correct?"

Indignation rumbled in his response. "You are correct."

Enchantress Thulease pointed at the clan chief's son. "What if he decides to impregnate my daughter? Will you stop him?"

The forge master stared at the floor and didn't answer. Licking his lips, he turned and looked up at the clan chief.

The clan chief stood. "I choose not to shield her, least of all from my son whose right it is to take any unbonded female, be she Svartálfar, goblin, or human." A wide grin crossed his face before he finished. "Or troll."

His statement drew laughter from the Svartálfar audience in the hall.

Although Enchantress Thulease held her head high, her shoulder slumped, knowing her daughter's fate was sealed. Inside her heart had to be breaking. I couldn't allow that to happen.

I stepped forward, over Thereese and locked eyes with the clan chief. "The young enchantress is *not* unbonded," I said. "She is to be my wife."

CHAPTER 35

The words were out before I realized their implications—or some of them. But just as Enchantress Thulease couldn't allow her daughter to be ravaged and raped, I couldn't just let her die. Not when the long sought instrument that could revive her was so near at hand.

I heard Lilly, just above a whisper, say, "Flank Hawk." Her voice hung between a question and surprise. Major Jadd didn't turn or say anything. He pushed his shoulders back and stood a bit straighter.

"By unbonded," Enchantress Thulease said to the forge master, "my daughter's personal guard and fiancé interprets to mean married. In our culture, husband and wife."

The smoothness in which the enchantress latched onto her daughter's lifeline and named me as her daughter's chosen suitor surprised me. Had she anticipated it? Might Imperial Seer Lochelle have seen it happen in a magical vision?

The clan chief cleared his throat before speaking. "Then, to be clear, the dying young enchantress is yet unbonded."

I started to speak, but Enchantress Thulease silenced me with a stern look and hand gesture. "It is best if negotiations proceed through one voice, Flank Hawk."

I stood at attention, like Major Jadd. Maybe Enchantress Thulease had anticipated this too? Whether she had or not, one negotiator made sense.

"As she is unbonded," the clan chief's son said, a violent edge in his tone, "I shall claim her to bear my child into thrall service, as is my right. That is *if* the Soul Forge's magic can revive her. I might even add her to my string of bondmates."

Enchantress Thulease focused her gaze on the forge master. "The price for my daughter's life is seven winters as your apprentice, where she will be subjected to rape and giving life to infants that would be indentured from birth? There is nothing else you would have in trade for you to kindle the Soul Forge's magic on her behalf?"

The forge master didn't have to turn to identify the source of the threatening gaze boring down upon him. He wouldn't dare cross the clan chief's son, not for Enchantress Thulease and her daughter. Not for anyone.

"Nay, Enchantress," the forge master said. "The tome of alchemical secrets, and a thrallspan of your daughter's service as an apprentice, during which she will learn our tongue, and then transcribe. As she proves capable, she will also learn some secrets of my craft. To become a forge master would require more thrallspans of study and practice than most humans have in their life."

"There you have it," the clan chief said to Enchantress Thulease. "Allow the forge master standing before you to return your daughter to vitality, in exchange for the tome and her service. Or depart."

There it was. A death sentence for young Enchantress Thereese.

I met the clan chief's son's leering grin. Strength and a willingness to employ violence seemed to be the coin in this underground realm. It wasn't far from the mercenary code. And that code demanded that an insult must be challenged, even onto death.

I strode forward, past Jadd and placed myself between Enchantress Thulease and the clan chief and his son. "The Young Enchantress is to be my wife. Mine, not to be sullied or abused by anyone." I pointed with the tip of my spear at the Clan Chief's Son. "I dispute your claim."

For a span of several breaths silence fell throughout the meeting hall, followed by a rising ruckus. Shouts, jeers, laughs, slapping of steel blades against stone.

The clan chief stood, raising both hands, signaling for silence. Once the din fell to a hushed murmur, he turned to his son. "This mercenary guard stands in defiance of your right of choosing. What do you say?"

The clan chief's son stood, chest puffed out, hands on his hips. "I am a magician, an ur-master magician. By clan law and tradition, the sun-dwelling mercenary has no standing to defy me in this hall or anywhere within this mountainhold. His words and challenge are hollow, empty, nothing I need address. My claim stands, unchallenged."

He was a bully, not used to being challenged. But he was also powerful. I didn't know clan law—law that he would claim and use against me, to thwart my attempt to protect Thereese from him. With no idea how to counter his claim based on Svartálfar law and tradition, I'd have to fight him…force him into a fight is what I had to. Thinking it through again, it'd come to crossing blades. He had to maintain his reputation. Was he trying to give me a way to save my reputation and to back out? Because there was no way he could back down.

I wouldn't. I couldn't. It meant Thereese's life.

I rested my spear's butt on the stone floor. "I wield magic, rare and valuable among my people. My words are not empty, not hollow." I took a breath. "Your words ring of cowardice. They ring of fear."

From behind me I heard Barkey whisper, probably to Sergeant Drux. "He can beat the clan chief's son? He's an ur-master magician, and damn good with his rapier."

To my right, Major Jadd stepped forward. "Clan Chief, may I address you before you speak a ruling?"

The clan chief turned his head and squinted down at Jadd. "As your enchantress master has not objected, I will listen to your words, Serpent

Cavalryman. Major."

Major? It wasn't hard to guess the dress of a serpent cavalryman. We arrived on dragons. And there was his armor's insignia. The clan chief was also showing that he recognized the marks on Major Jadd's sleeve, that he knew more about us, or at least more about Keeseans than we might've guessed.

"Clan Chief of this Mountainhold," Jadd said. "I believe your son mistakenly assumes that the mercenary, Flank Hawk, is young and an easy mark." He gestured from the clan chief's son to me. "If you know of Keesee's most recent battle alongside the Crusaders of the Reunited Kingdom against the Necromancer King, you must know that Flank Hawk is the mercenary that delivered the blow which turned the tide of the war.

"He has slain all manner of beasts, from griffins to land raptors, and foes from wizards and necromancers to sorcerers and witches. He's withstood bone golem hellcries and survived direct combat with a fallen angel, once a servant of the Crusader's One True God. He drove off the Kraken, and lived to tell about it. When the Young Prince fell, it was Flank Hawk who took up the Young Prince's sword and defeated Fendra Jolain, goddess of healing."

The clan chief's son said disdainfully, "That isn't the Blood Sword on his hip."

After holding up a hand to silence his son, the clan chief asked, "Do you have any more words, Major? Any more grand boasts about your fellow soldier?"

"None," Jadd said with a smile. "I didn't want you to be surprised by the result after you sanction what is about to occur."

"So, you believe my son will be slaughtered, by this young mercenary?"

Jadd shrugged. "You know your son, Clan Chief. More than once I have fought alongside Flank Hawk. I know where I'd place my coin in a bet."

Well, I thought, Jadd's effort to deter a challenge meant the clan chief's son would be less likely to underestimate me. Even so, I agreed with Jadd's ploy. It might make the clan chief's son uncertain and overly cautious, giving me more time to find an opening.

The clan chief shook his head. "Do know this. While almost always deadly, a blood duel allows for one to yield. So, should my son's desire for the young enchantress not fade, you just might return with your fellow soldier. Maimed, most likely."

Taking a quick breath, the clan chief addressed me. "Demonstrate your claim, Mercenary, that you possess skill in the arcane arts."

I reached over and pulled Major Jadd's dagger and nicked my cheek with its blade. I didn't want to use either of my blades as they were covered with fireweed resin. Once I felt the drip of blood I handed the dagger back to Major Jadd and closed my eyes, chanting and opening my mind to the maelstrom of energy that raged beyond the reach of normal senses. I quickly edged closer, seeking a sliver of the swirling energy. One that I could direct. While doing so, I reached into my satchel and withdrew a pouch that held finely ground white oak bark. I placed some of the bark on my cut. It wasn't necessary when healing myself, but it helped me complete the spell quickly and harbor what little spell strength I had. I directed a sliver of vibrant energy from the whorl, through the bark and my wound, causing the bleeding to stop and the cut to heal closed.

The clan chief's son pointed and laughed. "That is it?"

"That is all that is necessary," I said, "to have standing. Am I correct?"

The clan chief nodded, but looked unimpressed.

Enchantress Thulease said to the clan chief, "I desire proof that your son is a practitioner of the arcane. That he has standing."

Jeers and laughter arose in the hall. It was hard to tell if it was directed at Enchantress Thulease, or the clan chief's son. Possibly both.

The clan chief's son reached into his pocket and tossed three gold coins in the air. He spoke a sharp enchantment as they arced toward us, but certain to fall short. As they started to fall, the coins lost their shape, transforming into globs of molten metal that splattered when they struck the marble floor.

She shrugged. "That is all that is necessary. In my eyes, he has standing."

"Then," said the clan chief, rising from his throne. "Let us proceed to the pit."

A roar of excitement followed.

CHAPTER 36

Sergeant Drux helped Barkey pull up the rope ladder. As we'd walked the short distance to the pit, the thrall had squeezed between me and Enchantress Thulease. "Get rid of that gun on your hip," he warned me in a whisper.

I was already going to do that.

"He's got some deadly spells," the thrall had added. "Quick an' deadly, but he's got no endurance with them. He'll disarm you and probably try to cook your innards—get the juices in your stomach boiling if he can. Makes it tough to fight when that's going on. Metal'll block him some, but you saw what he can do with that. So it's a whole 'nother problem.

"Just giving you warning," he'd finished before scurrying ahead.

The round pit was about fifty feet across with layered slate walls, ten feet high and steeply angled. There was no way I'd be able to jump up and reach the granite lined rim, not in armor. The floor was polished black marble. Blood would make it slick.

Across from me, two Svartálfar soldiers pulled up the clan chief's son's ladder.

He was armed with his rapier, a long dagger with a guard designed to trap blades, and two throwing daggers strapped to his thighs. I guessed spells would be his first choice.

I knew my spear could pierce his light chainmail shirt he'd thrown over his leather jerkin. He kept on his wolf-skin vest and had high leather boots, black like his jerkin.

Just as I was appraising him, he was looking me over. From my steel helmet and breastplate, down to my boots. I had my boar spear, broad-bladed short sword and dirk. Plus pouches with things like salt, iron beads and white oak bark.

He looked up behind him and said something in the Svartálfar tongue to one of the two soldiers pulling up the rope ladder. They both laughed. Next to the soldier stood the clan chief. He didn't look ready to laugh. Maybe Jadd's words were getting to him?

Two rows of Svartálfar lined the pit's edge. The front row knelt on one knee while the second row packed in close behind, with a third trying to shift back and forth to get a half-good view. No thralls were among them.

Above me, Lilly knelt next to Enchantress Thulease, on her right. Barkey knelt on the enchantress's left. The supreme enchantress stood tall, near the edge like the clan chief opposite her. Although I couldn't see from my angle, I knew that Enchantress Thereese lay unconscious in front of her, just beyond the granite-lined rim. Jadd stood behind Lilly and Drux behind the thrall, casually observing the pit but mostly watching for potential danger. There wouldn't be any, with all attention focused on the violence near to beginning.

The clan chief raised both hands, with chest puffed out it appeared something he was proud to be able to do once again. When there was silence, he stared down at me in the pit. "Mercenary," he said in Sea Spittle, "the battle goes until one yields, is unconscious, or dead."

"How will I know when he's done?" I asked. "Throws down his weapons?"

"No," the clan chief said. "When you've been beaten, Mercenary, you say, *Jeg gir opp.*" He grinned wider than even his son could manage. "That way there is never confusion. Discarding a weapon for another, preparing a spell or whatever else might occur."

He crossed his arms. "So don't forget. *Jeg gir opp.* Maybe you'd like a moment to practice those words?"

"I will wait while you practice," the clan chief's son said, almost shouting, so he could be heard above the Svartálfar laughter and jeers. "*Jeg gir opp.*"

I shrugged, saying, "Smoothly as that phrase rolls of your tongue, tells me those words are second nature to you."

At that, Drux laughed loudly. Quickly followed by Jadd and Lilly.

The clan chief raised his hands again and the hall fell silent. "Once begun, none may interfere. No physical support, no spells, no components, no weapons, shields or armor into the pit, under punishment of death."

With that, the noise rose so that it was near impossible to hear anything. The clan chief held a black rag, ready to toss it into the pit. When it landed on the floor, the fight began. Battlefield noise was worse, the cries of dying men. I shoved aside what was raining down from above and gripped my spear, prepared to charge.

As the clan chief cocked his arm back to throw the rag, I felt something on the air. Vibration, a music that I'd not heard since fighting alongside Crusader Roos. One of the Crusader battle hymns. It wasn't as pervasive or strong, but it was there—there in Lilly's voice, penetrating the Svartálfar ruckus. It pierced the cheering and encouraging of their kin.

"*Stoppe henne! Ta henne ned!*" the clan chief shouted, pointing at Lilly. "Seize her!"

The Svartálfar must've felt Lilly's song too, as they rose as one, prepared to leap and overwhelm her, the enchantress, Jadd and Drux. They already had their weapons drawn, except for Enchantress Thulease, who raised her hand to full height, revealing a locket. "*Stanse eller jeg vil frigi sollys til dette stedet!*" she shouted, her voice, louder than it should've been, reverberating like thunder. That, and whatever she said, caused the dark elves to hesitate.

I turned to see the clan chief's response, but kept an eye on the clan chief's son, should he try to intervene on what was happening beyond the pit.

The clan chief pointed at Lilly. "She intervenes with Crusader null magic."

The Svartálfar mob stood poised to overwhelm my companions.

"That is an untruth, Clan Chief." Because many Svartálfar cautiously stared upward, I guessed Enchantress Thulease still held the locket aloft, thumb ready to release its burst of sunlight.

The clan chief said, "Put the device containing shards of sunlight away, Supreme Enchantress."

"Recall your order. Your men."

The clan chief pointed again. "Her life is forfeit."

"First, Clan Chief, you still hold the black rag. The contest had not commenced. Second, my scout lacks both knowledge and ability to cast spells. Look closer, Clan Chief. See her aura. Among the Crusaders of the Reunited Kingdom, she is a cursed one." After a breath, she asked, "Explain then, how she wields their magic of which you have accused her?"

The clan chief's arm drooped, unsure. He probably felt what I'd felt in Lilly's words, but even more strongly. Many, if not all of the Svartálfar, probably had as well.

"You question my ability to sense such magic in my own hall?"

"Scout," Enchantress Thulease said. "Demonstrate his folly."

"As you wish, Enchantress," Lilly said, an eager boldness in her words.

I'd seen Lilly transform into a werebeast—a giant muskrat. It took only a short, painful span of time to complete. From the gazes of the on looking Svartálfar, she was undressing. Soon the sound of bones and tendons reforming, like twisting, snapping celery, confirmed her shifting. As did the mixture of looks on the Svartálfar faces. Some confused or disgusted. Others amused. Several filled with lust.

Enchantress Thulease said, "As you can assess with your own sight, Clan Chief, she is *not* a Crusader of the Reunited Kingdom. She cannot be both a lycanthrope *and* spread, as you name it, Crusader null magic."

The clan chief's son apparently saw Lilly as a werebeast as his hopeful face transformed, leaving him huffing and scowling, more ready to kill than before.

"If you insist on slitting the throat of my scout," Enchantress Thulease said, "I insist you do the same with each and every dark elf uttering any sound in support of or to encourage your son."

The clan chief ground his jaw in thought. Taking a deep breath he said, "I may have been…in error."

The admission drew a chorus of grumbles and a few gasps.

"However," he continued. "The contest in the pit shall be observed in silence. Or near silence. Nothing above a whisper." He stared across the pit, probably at Lilly. "And no lyrics of any sort."

I wanted to speak up and say that her beast couldn't sing, but thought better of it. I had to refocus, and ready myself for the struggle.

Enchantress Thulease said down to me, "Flank Hawk, as before, I anticipate your victory. My daughter, your fiancé awaits." Then she said to the clan chief, "Agreed."

I wasn't nearly as confident as Enchantress Thulease sounded. I'd survived life and death battles against beasts and opponents far more fearsome than the clan chief's son. But those had no bearing on what I faced at the moment. The dark elf wielded spells unfamiliar to me, and was said to have that backed up by skill wielding steel.

I rechecked my helmet, pouches, armor, sword, dirk, and javelin strapped across my back, before gripping my boar spear with both gauntleted hands. Boar spear versus rapier. His blade lacked the stoutness to effectively turn my weapon. Closing the forty-five feet between us…if I couldn't do that, both me and Thereese were doomed.

The clan chief turned his gaze from left to right, a hard warning stare to his people before he tossed the black rag up. I kept my eye on the dark elf across from me as it fluttered down to the floor between us. Before it was half way down I reached back and pulled my javelin free, and hefted it to throw.

As soon as the rag touched the polished floor I hurled my javelin while trotting forward rather than with reckless abandon. The javelin forced my foe to sidestep, but it didn't disrupt whatever spell he'd prepared. Before I was halfway across the pit, my spear's shaft warped, quickly curling the tip down. Without waiting I flung my ruined spear at the dark elf across from me, ready with his rapier and dagger drawn, but uttering another spell.

Before I reached him, a searing heat took hold of my scalp. Scalding heat radiated down from my helmet, including the drooping brim. I abandoned drawing my sword and yanked my helmet off. Rather than ponder, I hurled it at the dark elf before it burned my hand through my leather gauntlets.

He ducked and shuffled to his left and my bespelled helmet struck the slate wall with a *thud* rather than a *clang*. It collapsed like wet canvas when it struck the floor. The clan chief's son continued to shuffle left—to my right—with a look of disbelief on his face. But his lips were still moving.

He stopped and again released a spell at me.

I decided to take a chance and reached into my biggest pouch. Striding toward him I hurled a handful of iron beads and a scattering of salt. He flinched and ducked as the fine salt crystals spread across the floor. The heavier beads that struck plinked off his chain armor and jerkin. The rest rebounded off the wall behind him.

"Fool!" He laughed as I drew my resin-covered sword. "My magic's not fey."

Even as he said it, I felt heat rising from my breastplate like it was a cast-iron pan—red hot!

It was now or never. I charged, releasing a fierce war cry that mimicked a black dragon's screeching roar. My foe tried to shuffle right but nearly lost his footing with the iron beads underfoot. That left him off balance with his rapier held wide, out of position. I slammed into him, gripping his sword arm's wrist and pressing my scorching breastplate against his face.

He bellowed as searing metal burned his cheek and jaw. Blocking his dagger thrust with my sword, he slammed against the wall and rebounded off. Both of us lost our footing upon the scattered beads and went down.

Piercing pain shot through my right thigh. He'd stabbed me with his dagger while getting on top of me. He was far stronger than he looked. He was uttering another spell, seared skin torn from his face, stuck to my breastplate. I head-butted him in the nose. Somehow he kept chanting.

He stabbed my leg a second time. I had to stop his spellcasting. With my leg wounded, if he got away I'd never catch him. He dropped his rapier the same instant I abandoned my sword and reached deep into my pouch.

A ball of darkness engulfed his right hand. I strained to keep hold of his wrist and the blackness away from me. Reaching into my pouch gave him leverage. He must've dropped his dagger, freeing his hand and giving him leverage to flip over and on top of me.

That was okay. It gave me the time needed to get a hold of my uncle's 'troll stopper.' I slammed the spore pod across his lower jaw as he pulled away, trying to get leverage to free his hand hidden in a cloud of blackness.

I held my breath while following through with my blow, knocking him off. I let go of his wrist and rolled away, trying to put distance between myself and the spores.

Pain lanced through my leg. My foe had left his dagger plunged into it. My movement dislodged it, causing me to bleed faster.

I looked up as the clan chief's son climbed to his feet still chanting, dark glowing hand held back, ready to slam it down on me. What the inky black magic would do, I didn't know.

My sword was out of reach so climbed I unsteadily to my feet after drawing my dirk from its booth sheath. We faced each other, about five feet apart. My armor was cooling, so I couldn't use that as a weapon. His burned and torn face twisted while still uttering a spell, black eyes gleaming in confident victory. Mine, I'm sure, were locked in grim determination.

Then his jaw drew open, like a wide yawn wrenching to his left—the side I'd struck him with the spore pod. His black spell faded and his eyes shot wide. His head turned to the right and his right shoulder flexed upward.

He staggered back, his left hand trying to reach across and turn his head back straight.

"Do you yield?" I asked, carefully pulling off my right-hand gauntlet, just to be safe. He staggered back stiff-legged. I followed slowly, my wounded leg not able to bear much weight.

I hurled my dirk, driving it into his right thigh, just above the knee. He fell backwards, rebounding off the wall and to the ground. His jaw looked like it had dislocated itself, and his head was turned so far to the left I thought he might snap his neck any second.

I picked up my sword and hacked down on his left knee, splintering bone and shattering it. I did the same with the right.

"*Stanse*!" Someone shouted. It was the clan chief. "Stop!"

"What?" I asked, looking up. "Might that be what she'd have cried out?" I pointed to where Thereese lay. "The young enchantress, might she shout that while he raped her? Would he, your son, *stanse*?"

Without listening to his answer, I hacked my sword down against his left elbow, shattering it as well. It caused him to grunt once and writhe on the floor. The fireweed resin in the wound probably wasn't even noticed. Wounding a downed and helpless foe, causing torturous pain, it tore at me. Deep inside I knew it was wrong, but kindness and mercy wouldn't be repaid in kind. The Svartálfar were a violent, cruel people. Threats and pain was the coin they traded and negotiated in. Enchantress Thereese's life and wellbeing was at stake. It was my duty to protect her and see her returned to health. I'd suffer through guilt and remorse, but not until later.

The clan chief's son, shattered legs and arm, jaw, neck and shoulder distorted in paralysis? He wasn't going to be an immediate threat, so I reached into my pouch for a fistful of white oak bark and held it against my wounded leg. It took a lot of spell energy to close up my leg wounds. Waiting much longer would've weakened me, maybe to the point of losing consciousness.

With my leg no longer bleeding and some of the skin and a small amount of muscle healed, I limped back over to my foe, still locked in agony. The pain lingering in my wound was nothing compared to my foe's. "Clan Chief," I said, looking up at him while pulling my dirk from his son's leg. "Will you swear not to take the young enchantress, who is to be my wife?" I tried to think how Grand Wizard Seelain would speak as I continued. "Refrain from abusing her mentally, physically and sexually, or in any other manner, and forbid all others to do so as well? And forbid anyone, or their agents, from taking revenge for what has occurred, and might yet occur in this, your meeting hall today?"

"If you kill him, none of you will leave this hall," the clan chief said, his arms crossed. "Bringing sunlight down upon us will not avail you. My people are too numerous for you to escape. You must know this, Mercenary."

"I will not kill him," I said, glancing at my melted helmet. "His spells were meant to maim and disfigure me. Shall I do the same to him?"

The clan chief laughed.

I asked, "You believe the sunlight to moonlight cycle will revive your son?"

He laughed louder. The rest of the Svartálfar joined in.

I pulled on the silver chain around my neck, drawing the pendant Belinda the Cursed had gifted to me. I held it up for the clan chief to see. "Road Toad—Major, told you I'd faced an angel that had once served the Crusader's God? This contains his blood. Do you know what it does?"

"I can guess, Mercenary. It's why you survived my son's spells."

"Using this, I can maim your son such that any number of stone piles revived by moonlight won't repair the damage inflicted."

He stood tall with gritted teeth. "You wouldn't dare."

I leaned close and asked his son, "Do you yield?" I'd ignored his hoarse groaning. "No reply, Clan Chief." Resting the blood-filled crystal over the clan chief's son's eye as he twitched and gurgled, I moved the point of my dirk closer. "For vexing me further, I ask for Barkey's service, his thrallspans granted to me."

The clan chief shook his head and warned, "You and all your people will pay."

Enchantress Thulease held the sun-filled locket in clear view for all. "It's my daughter that your son threatened to disgrace and make to suffer. See the result? The man sworn to defend her now stands over him.

"Now you, Clan Chief, will not promise to refrain from the same. She is my daughter. My daughter is Flank Hawk's wife to be. If you know anything of Keeseeans, Chief of the Svartálfar in this Mountainhold, you must know what this means to us."

There was something else that went between Enchantress Thulease and the clan chief. Unspoken, but a look of understanding crossed his face.

She cast her gaze across the hall, to all of the Svartálfar and thralls in attendance. "Also know this, Clan Chief of this Mountainhold. Break your oath, rending your words so that they mean nothing, and your fall from power will be swift. How could they follow? Why should they follow, even die for you if they cannot trust in and believe your clear and unquestionable promise?"

After looking around his hall the Clan Chief of the Iron Hoard Mountainhold stated the oath I'd proposed, reviewed and clarified in detail by Enchantress Thulease. He swore upon his blood and magic to keep it.

CHAPTER 37

Lilly was rubbing a salve on my neck and chin, trying to soothe my skin burned by my bespelled breastplate. Major Jadd gave it to her, saying it was good for blisters and chafing. It was helping some.

"Looks like it might be the worst sunburn ever, Flank Hawk. Like you were back out in that horrible desert."

The lantern's light probably didn't show how bad it really was. "Feels like it, Scout." I wanted to say her real name but knew better, even though we were sitting in a small room off the immense underground workshop that housed the Soul Forge. We were watching over Enchantress Thereese while Enchantress Thulease made preparations with the forge master. Sergeant Drux was with her. Major Jadd and Barkey were going to the surface to retrieve some of the necessary components from Grand Wizard Seelain.

"How's your leg?"

It was stretched out on the wooden bench where I sat. "Hurts, but it's not going to bleed and I can walk on it."

The room was filled with barrels of iron ingots. The walls held hammers, pliers, files, gripping tongs, and a host of other tools of which I didn't know their name or purpose. All hung from wooden pegs and steel hooks drilled into the stone wall.

"Limp, you mean."

"How's she doing," I asked, looking down at Enchantress Thereese.

"About the same." Lilly gripped the enchantress's frail hand. "I think she knows what's going on. Somehow listening in." Then Lilly's voice changed, giving off hints of anger. "Hope she knows what you risked, Flank Hawk. You just about died." Lilly adjusted the folded blanket under the enchantress's head. "If she doesn't, Flank Hawk, you can be sure I'll tell her."

I wanted to say, 'If she survives,' but didn't.

"What about…you know, who you rode next to halfway across that desert?" She'd almost said Nura's name, but didn't. Lilly put her hands on her hips. "What about you and her?"

I wasn't thinking about Nura when I stepped forward and claimed the enchantress as my fiancé. "I couldn't let her die," I said. I started to rub my hands on my thighs, but flinched when I caused the pain in my wounded leg to flare up.

"Your duty, right? Do you love her?"

I shrugged. "I like her. We get along pretty well. You know that."

"Not as good as…you know who. I've seen you together. Whatcha gonna tell her?"

"I haven't thought that far." It was true. I hadn't. I did the right thing—what had to be done to save Thereese. But that didn't mean part of me wouldn't regret it.

"Well, you better be thinking on that, Flank Hawk."

I didn't need that, not then. "Listen," I said. "I won't be anybody's husband for long. That spore pod that seized up that dark elf's muscles? That was how I planned to defeat Flayzin. So it doesn't really matter now, does it?"

That shook Lilly out of her anger. She bit her lip and clasped her hands together. Sadness filled her eyes.

"I'm sorry," I told her.

She leaned close and hugged me. Firm, but trembling. Just a little. "I don't want you to die, Flank Hawk. Nobody does."

I hugged her back, the pain in my leg and neck forgotten. "I won't," I said, forcing conviction into my words. I didn't believe them. I hugged Lilly harder, afraid she saw through my words as well.

The Soul Forge was immense. Red bricks, each etched with runes that seemed impossible to see clearly, formed the housing where rare metals, more rare than gold Barkey had said, were being melted. Teams of four Svartálfar thralls took turns working the two huge bellows that intensified the heat needed for the forge master's work. We sat on stools twenty yards away and watched him give orders to his apprentices in the underground smithy.

Although it might've been the most prized forge in the smithy, which rivaled the size of the Clan Chief's Meeting Hall, it was set off in a distant corner, far from the other forges, anvils, mounds of coal and other equipment. The place smelled of coal smoke and sweat, and the other dozen forges continued melting iron and steel which was being hammered and bent and twisted or flattened, or fashioned a half dozen other ways into works from swords and helmets to nails and chain links. It was sweltering and noisy, with hammering and clanging and the constant roar like the furnaces of hell, yet orderly and precise as if each smith, apprentice smith, and laborer shoveling coal or hauling buckets of iron ore to be smelted down was part of the finest orchestra ever to be seen or heard. There were other smithies and workshops in the mountainhold where the focus was on silver or copper or other metals, but the smithy with the Soul Forge was the largest.

Enchantress Thulease said the dark elves might be the most skilled blacksmiths in the entire world. Watching their focus, speed and precision they made the royal blacksmiths in the King's City appear slow, unsteady and unsure. And King Tobais's royal smiths were said to be some of the best on the Mainland Continent.

Enchantress Thereese now rested on a long cart. Her shallow breaths, the faint rising and falling of her chest, were the only signs she yet lived.

Enchantress Thulease sat next to Thereese, holding her daughter's hand and humming a tune that reminded me of a child's lullaby. Lilly stood a few paces off. Drux stood at attention, between Thereese and Enchantress Thulease, and myself, and the Soul Forge. His hawk-like gaze taking everything in.

How much longer, I thought. We'd eaten dark bread and venison, washed down with frothy ale. The forge master said not to feed Thereese. Better she undergo the ordeal with an empty stomach. Water, however, she'd been given to replace what was certain to be lost through sweat brought out by the smithy's heat. I tried to imagine her as an apprentice, moving among and working with the far shorter Svartálfar and their thralls. I just couldn't see her bent over, hammering iron and steel, sparks flying with each blow.

The forge master was the greatest of the mountainhold's smiths, so maybe he would train her as a silver smith, where more delicate work might be focused on. I just didn't know and my mind went round and round, trying to imagine Thereese, in the smithy or walking crouched or bent low through the mountainhold's dark passages. In truth, I was avoiding thinking of the future, a future life with Enchantress Thereese as my wife, and what that would entail. It didn't seem worth the worry or concern, not with Guard Captain Flayzin awaiting my return. The challenge would be settled, one way or another, probably by noon after the first sunrise of our return.

Running away wasn't an option. Cowardice wasn't in me, and it would give Flayzin the satisfaction of believing his accusation was right. It would dishonor my family and friends and all that I had ever done. Most of all it would dishonor Prince Reveron's death. His sacrifice to save Keesee, the kingdom his family ruled and the people they'd sworn to protect.

Before I realized it, the forge master was standing before Enchantress Thulease, addressing her. "Supreme Enchantress, the Soul Forge has completed its objective. Its molten steel alloy is ready."

Moments after Major Jadd's return, he and Enchantress Thulease approached the forge master. The dark elven smith met them half way, leaving them within spitting distance of the massive, rune-adorned forge and its intense heat.

The stocky Svartálfar examined the contents of the steel chest Enchantress Thulease presented to him. Actually, Major Jadd handed it to one of his assistants before unlocking it with an iron key worn on a chain about his neck.

The first item the forge master examined was the core of a unicorn horn. Since my uncle sold it to the enchantress at my suggestion, I'd seen the foot long magical component up close before it'd been encased and wrapped for travel. It reminded me of a pure white icicle, hard as a diamond.

Next examined was the dragon egg held inside a steel-reinforced wooden box—a valuable commodity, especially with Keesee's shortage of serpent steeds. Oblong, like a goose egg but leathery and five times the size, the forge master asked Major Jadd a question and nodded while listening to the reply.

Third was a thumb-sized crystal vial holding a red liquid. The blood of a fairy, an immortal being. Enchantress Thulease said something that I couldn't hear over the noise in the hall and the forge master nodded once again.

Next, Enchantress Thulease lifted from the box a red cloth holding a brownish-black stone with a metallic luster. The forge master pulled a small nail from one of his pockets. It stuck to the lodestone as if held by magic.

The fifth item, the enchantress carefully removed from a padded box. Fragile looking glass, shaped like a large onion, it appeared empty.

Sergeant Drux spoke up, telling me and Lilly, "Breath of a fish. While you were trapping fairies, Flank Hawk, the major and I travelled to the northeastern portion of the Southern Continent, and sought out a lung fish."

"Lung fish," Lilly asked.

Drux nodded once. "Weird looking fish that can survive out of water, for a time. Mostly in mud I think. We hired a river fisherman near a fish market to get three of them for us."

"Those lungfish?" Lilly asked with a scrunched up nose. "They're still alive?"

Drux shrugged. "The alchemist had them in a wooden trough filled with muddy water, last I saw them."

The last item lifted from the chest was a small jar sealed with wax. It held a liquid that appeared opaque, whitish. I thought a giant's tears would be clear, like any person's. Upon inspection the forge master nodded in approval, and then directed his assistant to set the items on a work bench near the Soul Forge.

After the forge master's assistant took the chest filled with items and placed it as directed, Enchantress Thulease and the forge master spoke for a few minutes.

"Can't tell what they're talking about," Lilly said. "Only a word here and there." She shook her head. "Too much noise in here."

I split my attention between Lilly and Enchantress Thereese lying at my feet, hands resting on her stomach.

I knelt down next to the dying enchantress and placed my hand upon hers. "Hold on, Enchantress Thereese. Your mother has faced dangers and unspeakable horrors, pried concessions from King Tobias and successfully bartered with the Dark Elves of the North. She's done what sages and learned wise men said was impossible. All done to save you, the daughter that she so loves. Hold on, Enchantress Thereese. Hold on a just a little longer."

Lilly and Drux both heard me speaking to the failing enchantress, but stood, facing away, watching events and for danger.

"She and your father will see you healthy again. We all will." I took a breath, and finished, trailing off, "I will, at least for a time."

After Enchantress Thulease and the forge master finished their discussion, he signaled a female Svartálfar over to him. She was a half head taller than the smith, wearing dark garments, heavy boots and leather gloves and an apron, all covered in ash. Her long black hair was tied back in a trio of braids with a black leather band tied across her forehead.

The forge master's female assistant trotted over to us and said to me in halting trade tongue, "We must prepare her."

I asked, "How is she to be prepared?"

The female Svartálfar removed her leather gloves and pointed down at Thereese. "She must be unclothed and washed down. Thralls with boiling spring water are coming."

"The scout will assist you," I said.

Lilly stepped up next to me. "Me and you will do it, Flank Hawk. She can tell us anything special that needs done." She pointed a thumb over her shoulder to Drux. "The sergeant'll watch to make sure nothing happens."

I relayed what Lilly said to the forge master's assistant. She nodded and signaled for a thrall to bring her a large sack and handed it to me. "Make sure the weak enchantress is clean. Braid her hair and tuck it under her back so that it doesn't fall in the forge table's gutter."

The female Svartálfar's command of the Trade Tongue became smoother, as if she'd pulled it from an old shelf and dusted it off. "There are silver cords. Tie off the end of her braid. Use the longer ones to secure her arms along her sides and her ankles together so that they remain in place during the forge spell."

She signaled to another thrall who hurried next to her and offered me something shaped like a folded blanket wrapped in a white cloth.

"Use this leather wrap, scribed with powerful runes to cover her." The Svartálfar assistant ran her gaze along Enchantress Thereese, and nodded to herself. "As the forge master warned, it's too short to cover all of her legs, but he said that won't matter to the spell's result. That it covers her head, heart, lungs and woman parts is what is necessary."

Four thralls arrived bearing four polished steel pails, half of them filled with clear water, and four cast-iron kettles with steam rising from them. The hint of exotic ingredients, like when I'd visited herbalist shops, rose with the steam. The medicinal smell was strong enough to cut through the forge hall's coal smoke and molten iron, even as it tingled in my nostrils.

Lilly wrinkled her nose, but took the buckets and sat them next to Enchantress Thereese. Drux took the hot kettles and did the same, but without a hint that he noticed any unusual odor.

The female Svartálfar said to me, "Do a good job cleansing the ailing girl, but it doesn't have to be perfect." She stepped left to speak around me to Lilly. Wash your hands and arms first from one bucket. Then unclothe the girl, and wash her from head to toe."

"Enchantress," Drux said to the female Svartálfar. "Not girl. En—chan—tress."

The forge master's assistant ignored Sergeant Drux and looked back to me after signaling one of the bucket-bearing thralls to hand me a satchel. "Clean rags for cleansing," she said.

The Svartálfar were a type of elves, and thus long-lived, if not immortal. They probably thought all humans as somehow inferior. Still, that didn't excuse her insult and I should've caught it, as Drux did. If Lilly spoke the Trade Tongue, she would have. I was letting the situation distract me.

"For cleansing who?" I asked.

The female assistant pointed her dark-nailed finger. "Her."

"Her, the enchantress," I insisted.

"Her, the enchantress," she replied.

Lilly asked, "Do her hair too?"

I relayed Lilly's question and the assistant shook her head. "No. Not necessary."

Lilly guessed the assistant's answer and said to me, "We will anyway."

"Be quick," the assistant said, looking over her shoulder. It sounded like an urging so that we didn't keep the forge master waiting. The faster we got to it, the better it would be for Enchantress Thereese anyway.

I remembered, as a child, helping my mother bathe my grandfather, as he slowly died, weakened by illness. As Lilly and I washed our hands and arms, I said to her, "I'll help you undress her. You bathe her and I'll assist, pouring water, wringing out rags, lifting arms and legs and holding her as you need."

Just before we began, I looked up at Sergeant Drux.

He put his hand on the hilt of his sword. "Move along," he said to the thralls standing nearby. Years serving as a guard in the worst parts of the King's City echoed in his command. The four thralls didn't look for permission from the female assistant before shuffling off, grumbling to onc another.

After we'd undressed the enchantress, two young female dark elves approached with a steel litter. The forge master's assistant said, "Place the enchantress upon this once she is cleansed and bound with the silver cords. Tuck her hair under and place the rune scribed leather over her body."

The litter was hard and flat. Even the quarter moon-shaped grips were metal. Nothing about it appeared comfortable. Holding the enchantress's head up while Lilly adjusted and rinsed her long dark hair, I knew Thereese wouldn't notice. Her skin was white and lifeless as marble, and her muscle tone showed that she'd been unmoving for months. She should've looked weaker, but didn't, possibly owing to magic and her father's alchemical brews. Even in her fragile state, Enchantress Thereese retained her beauty.

Lilly completed the task in under ten minutes. She might've even impressed the female Svartálfar. After washing her hands, the dark elf helped me and Lilly lift and move the enchantress to the metal litter.

The leather wrap was white, retaining the fur of what possibly was a giant mountain goat, trimmed short and branded with a host of unreadable runes—at least unreadable by me. Lilly and I finished to the assistant's satisfaction, leaving part of the wrap turned down so that it didn't yet cover the enchantress's face.

"I shall return," she said and turned on her heels and strode toward the forge master who was instructing several assistants gathered near him.

Drux inspected our work while Lilly stuffed the enchantress's boots and clothing into the sack that had held the rune-scribed wrap. He said, "Those thralls have been rotating at the bellows, building up quite a sweat. A smith used long-handled tongs and, I guess you'd call them extended spoons or scoops, to add the rare the things gathered by the enchantress into the molten metal alloy inside the forge. All except the unicorn horn. I didn't see them add that."

Enchantress Thulease stopped observing activities around the magical forge and came to kneel next to Thereese. She placed a hand on her daughter's head, bent low, and whispered into her ear.

Major Jadd had remained near the forge. He caught my attention and signaled me over to him. A tip of his head directed me to stand several paces off to his left while he finished a discussion with the female assistant.

A tingling ran across my skin, especially on my right side, which faced the Soul Forge. It was magic, not quite like any I'd experienced before. It felt pulsing and persistent, and hot, like prickling spices rolling across my skin, penetrating to my muscles. Somehow I sensed a blunt, hammering force contained, restrained within it.

Jadd then moved to stand next to me, put an arm on my shoulder and spoke into my ear. "The enchantress and I have been warned that the forge casting process is both loud and ritualistic, and difficult to witness." He paused. "I interpret that to mean the enchantress will experience pain. Weak as she is, there is even more reason to believe she may not survive the spell."

We all recognized this possibility and I wondered why he was reminding me. I turned my head and spoke into his ear. "Understood, Road Toad."

"We've been warned," he continued. "No matter what happens, not to interfere. If we do, the forge magic's backlash will assuredly slay the enchantress, and could do the same to those nearby. The forge master, his assistants, us…any and everyone in this hall."

"Understood, Road Toad."

"Normally observers are banished from the Forge Hall during the spell, because of this. However, the enchantress convinced the forge master that our presence will increase her daughter's chance of survival. How, I don't know, but she convinced the forge master."

"Okay," I said.

He then looked me eye to eye, an arm on each shoulder. "I will stand prepared to restrain the enchantress."

"Do you think that will be necessary?"

"No, but better to be prepared. I am assigning you to explain this to our scout. I believe she'd listen to me, but you're the man for the task. Further, I expect both you and the sergeant to stand prepared to restrain her. Make sure she doesn't interfere."

I nodded.

"Now for the tough assignment," he said.

That got my attention.

"The enchantress desires that you do interfere, if you observe or feel something is amiss."

That caught me off guard. "What do you mean, Road Toad?"

The enchantress believes she is too emotionally involved in the situation to evaluate objectively as it unfolds. You have experience, confronting and dealing with unknown magics and situations." His stance shifted. "So she is relying on you. On your experience and instinct."

He placed a hand on my shoulder. "More experience than me. Like her, I'm confident you'll intervene as necessary, if it becomes necessary."

I took a deep breath and nodded once. They had more confidence in me than I did.

Suddenly my hands felt empty and useless without my spear.

CHAPTER 38

Lilly and Drux stepped back after placing Enchantress Thereese's steel litter onto the slats set into the iron table's frame. She lay with her head nearest the Soul Forge, her head elevated slightly higher than her feet. A shallow gutter ran along the edges of the table, inches from her head, arms, legs and feet.

I didn't know much about forges and smiths and their tools, having spent time around them only when I needed horse shoes or my armor worked on. Even then, I rarely watched. From what I could tell, metal from the Soul Forge would travel along a clay spout into the gutter. What would happen from there, I would soon find out.

The forge master stood next to the spout, near Enchantress Thereese's head. Sweat glistened on his dark face and muscled arms. He gripped a heavy hammer in one hand and a pair of tongs in the other. Both might've had runes carved into them. Age, and soot, and the shadowy light made it difficult to be sure.

Along both the young enchantress's left and right stood two additional Svartálfar smiths, hammers held in leather-gloved hands. At the enchantress's feet stood the female assistant, also a Svartálfar smith, with heavy hammer held poised and ready.

Across from us, a pace back from the smiths stood Enchantress Thulease, with Major Jadd to her right. Her face and stance appeared weary, yet her eyes were alert and expectant. Lilly stood between me and Sergeant Drux.

The smell of sweat swirled with the coal dust in the hot air, moving past us, drawn in by the Soul Forge's heat. The Forge Hall felt even more foreign to me, now silent with all other work halting and only a few assistant smiths standing ready in the distance. The straining of the four thralls pumping the giant bellows, sending gusts of air was drowned out by the Soul Forge's burning roar.

Even so, I heard Lilly whisper into my ear, "Its magic's crawling into my skin."

I felt it too, more intense than before. I nodded once and gripped her hand, briefly. After that, she fell silent.

The forge master made eye contact with Enchantress Thulease before reaching with the tongs and pulling the white leather wrap over her daughters face. It had been tucked under the rest of her body down to her ankles. A second, smaller leather wrap, white with a single rune mark, covered her feet. Placed there by the female assistant.

Sergeant Drux stepped away, to watch from a distance, and make sure no one interfered. Barkey had assured Enchantress Thulease that he would watch and warn, but she felt he might not be enough, and maybe not trustworthy enough. He was half Svartálfar.

I glanced at the female Svartálfar. For some reason, I wondered at her name—her common name, not the secret one. Barkey, who I spotted standing next to one of the distant smiths, probably knew.

Lifting his hammer, the forge master initiated a guttural song. It was deeper in tone than I expected a Svartálfar could produce, repetitive and indecipherable to me. It took a moment for me to realize that they were singing it as a round. The same song started by the forge master, then the next two smiths facing each other picked up part way through, followed by the next pair and ending with the female Svartálfar. Same magical song, or chant, in four parts.

This went on for several minutes. Next to me, Lilly shifted from one foot to the next. Nervous or in anticipation, I wasn't sure. Maybe she felt something of the Svartálfar magic, maybe amplified by the roaring Soul Forge.

Enchantress Thulease and Major Jadd across from us stood absolutely still. His face held no emotion. The enchantress's eyes shifted their focus, from her daughter, to the forge master, and then to something in between. Maybe the magic being woven by their song.

Then the forge master slammed his hammer down on the outside rim of the table's gutter. The others did as well, timed with the rotation of their spell song. It was loud, and each hammer seemed to strike a different note. I wasn't sure if it was the individual hammer, the place each struck along the gutter, or both.

After another several minutes of this, causing me to grit my teeth and figuring it would leave my ears ringing almost as bad as having a Crusader's muzzle-loading rifle discharge beside my ear, the forge master lifted the set of iron tongs. At that signal a Svartálfar smith behind the forge began shouting directions to a half dozen thralls—or I guessed by his actions and spittle spraying that he was.

A few seconds later, glowing hot metal began to pour from the Soul Forge's mouth, down the clay spout and into the gutter. The instant it did, the forge master used the tongs to drop the core of the unicorn horn into the molten metal's path.

I expected the magical horn to be consumed by the liquid metal, or at least get caught up in its flow. Neither happened. It remained in place, as if anchored. But the metal that flowed past, touching the unicorn horn, changed from orange-yellow to a yellow-silver color, with thin streaks of red, or maybe purple. From my distance and the hammer-swinging smiths spaced between me and the gutter, and the wavy distortion the rising heat caused, I couldn't be sure of the colors.

The moment the flow along the two gutter channels met in front of the female smith, the forge master brought his hammer down on the unicorn horn, crushing it and immediately solidifying the molten metal mixture.

Without missing a beat the Svartálfar smiths shifted from hammering the gutter to hammering the silvery yellow metal. Sparks rose a foot or more in the air, and arced in toward Enchantress Thereese.

Then the spell song shifted, as did the hammering pattern. The forge master shifted to his right, to stand alongside Enchantress Thereese near her shoulder. The other two smiths on his side moved to accommodate, remaining equal distant, spread down to the enchantress's knees. The same happened with the female smith shifting around to stand along the enchantress's left knee and the other two smiths moving to stand across from a hammering partner.

Now the left hammered and the right followed, back and forth, sparks rising and falling all inward, all toward the rune marks upon the white leather wrap. They touched but didn't burn the wrap.

A mist began rising through the white leather—at least that's what I thought it was, at first.

Besides the wraith, I'd seen a ghost before. I'd summoned it. The mercenary Short Two Blades through his talisman, to fight on my behalf against a lamenting soul trying to possess me.

Where the ghost of Short Two Blades and been smoky and gray, this one appeared more misty and white—it was Enchantress Thereese! Her sprit. Her soul. She was dead, if not dying.

Lilly recognized what was happening too. I placed a restraining arm on her shoulder. Out of the corner of my eye I saw her look up at me, shouting something I couldn't hear over the roar of the Soul Forge, still burning, the hammering, and smiths' song spell.

They were still chanting, still hammering out their arcane magic. If it didn't work, the enchantress was dead anyway. Her only hope was for them to continue, uninterrupted.

Across from me, Jadd followed my lead and placed a hand on Thulease's shoulder, reassuring her.

Then, after the smith across from the forge master hammered down, sending sparks arcing through the rising spirit, the forge master reached forward and swung his hammer down, passing through Thereese's spirit, striking a rune mark on the leather above her sternum.

I gripped Lilly harder, hearing her shout, "Flank Hawk!" It sounded like a muffled cry from miles away.

The hammer's force jolted the young enchantress's body, but didn't cave in her chest as it should have.

The song continued. Those opposite the forge master's side hammered the silvery metal, creating sparks, now pink sparks and purple, followed by the forge master's side hammering those colored sparks into the rune marks. At some unknown signal, the sides switched off.

Slowly the misty image of the young enchantress settled, flowing back beneath the leather wrap, back into her body.

Although the song remained strong, the sparks returned to whitish silver, lessening in intensity, and the sides switched back and forth, their task of hammering metal or pounding sparks into the runes. As they did, the metal in the gutter lost its silvery luster, and its reddish-purple streaks, if it ever truly had them. It all seemed so distant, so unreal, like a half-remembered dream.

As I was trying to clear my thoughts, the chanting stopped. The Svartálfar smiths brought their hammers down in unison, and Enchantress Thereese bolted upright, to a sitting position.

CHAPTER 39

Within ten breaths of Enchantress Thereese's recovery, a company of Svartálfar soldiers marched into the Forge Hall. The few smiths, apprentice smiths, and thralls observing from a distance made their way to cover along the walls and behind forges, equipment and piles of iron ingots and coal.

Barkey rushed toward the captain, shouting in the dark elf tongue and waving his arms, but was knocked aside.

"Musketoons and blunderbusses," Jadd said, stepping in front of Enchantress Thulease, hand on his sword's hilt, but not drawing it. His voice was grim as was his hard gaze. Drux strode to join him, and angry sneer etched across his face.

I knew enough about guns to know we'd face a hail of steel and lead. If we survived that, we'd have to contend with the steel of their rapiers and curved daggers. Their armor of layered scales and rings said it wouldn't be easy. And the noise of another company mustering just beyond the Forge Hall's doors signaled that it if came to a fight, they'd come at us in waves.

And we were deep within the mountain, over an hour from the surface at a dead run.

I moved to stand between Thereese and the oncoming soldiers. She was still seated on the table. Lilly leapt to help her remove the silver cords still binding her wrists and ankles.

Enchantress Thulease stood with her saber held in one hand at her side, and a locket, probably holding a flash of sunlight, in the other. If it came to a fight, we'd win the first round and have guns in hand for the second. But there were too few of us, and certainly a limited supply of sunlight.

The forge master and his assistants formed a line between us and the soldiers. His twisted face made Drux's sneer look like the aft-guard was enjoying a favorite dessert. In his right hand the master smith held a war hammer, a faint glow of blackness surrounded its head…or maybe the head devoured any light that came near it.

A Svartálfar sergeant formed the soldiers into a line, a long one arcing to encompass us while the captain announced, using the Trade Tongue, "By order of the Clan Chief of the Iron Hoard Mountainhold, the enchantress and her company are ordered to depart, leaving the revived young enchantress behind for the agreed upon single thrallspan."

Barefoot and draped in the rune-scribed cover, Enchantress Thereese came to stand next to me. Surprised, I looked up out of the corner of my eye. She could stand?

"Remain behind me," I said, once again stepping between her and the Svartálfar soldiers. I'd forgotten how tall she was. I wanted to tell her to sit back down, or at least hunch down, but knew she wouldn't.

"Listen to Flank Hawk," Lilly hissed and moved up to my left.

As the forge master raised his hammer above his head, I whispered to Lilly, "Watch our rear."

Enchantress Thereese leaned close and responded, "Allow me to do that, at least."

I nodded once, splitting the rest of my attention between the master smith and the captain in front of me, and Enchantress Thulease standing poised for action behind Jadd and Drux, two paces to my right.

The forge master's voiced boomed, "This is *my* hall. I determine who comes and who goes, and when my spellcraft is complete."

A sinister grin crossed the captain's face. "Are you referring to the young enchantress standing behind you?"

"I am referring to you and your men soon to be lying dead in front of me." At the forge master's words, the smiths and thralls I thought were seeking cover emerged, holding loaded crossbows. At the same time the hall's great iron doors slammed shut, the sound reverberating off the walls and arched ceiling. "If you continue to interfere with *my* spellcraft," he finished.

Without a verbal command, six of the soldiers on each end of their line turned, with firearms ready to face the new menace.

The captain scoffed. "You claim your spell is not yet complete?"

Still holding his dark hammer above his head, a stance that appeared effortless, the forge master replied, "To the untrained, a sword may appear complete after quenching. No, it is brittle and must be tempered before it can be finished."

"You are saying the young enchantress has yet to be tempered?"

"Leave now, so that I may finish my work." The great iron doors swung open. "Await outside if you desire, to escort the enchantress and her companions from this mountainhold."

"Except for the young enchantress," the captain clarified.

The forge master lowered his hammer and cocked it back, shifting to a battle stance. "Must your thick skull be cracked for my command to enter?"

The captain's sinister smile returned. "Complete your casting. I and my men will await outside this chamber to do as our clan chief commands."

With that the company turned, reformed and marched out of the Forge Hall.

Lilly asked me, "You think it's really not finished?"

From behind, Enchantress Thereese said, "No, Scout. I can feel that it is not."

Jadd ordered Drux to post near the doors with Barkey while Enchantress Thulease tucked away her locket and sheathed her saber.

Lilly looked up at Thereese. "You know to call me Scout?"

With a mischievous grin, Thereese said, "I know a great many things. I heard everything, but as if in an unending dream. Thank you, Flank Hawk. For stepping forward." She took my hands in hers. "For fighting for me, my husband to be. I have dreamt of it since the day we met."

It took me a breath to reply, "I did what—"

Lilly stepped on my foot, interrupting me. I think Enchantress Thereese saw her do it.

"You're welcome," I said. "It'll be an—my honor."

I wasn't sure she believed my words, but her mother came up to her and they embraced. Lilly caught and held the white wrap over the enchantress's back while I turned away and met Jadd's gaze. With a tip of his head he signaled for me to follow him, out of earshot of the enchantresses and the smiths and thralls working to rebuild the Soul Forge's heat and magic.

When Jadd and I stopped, I realized I needed to act on my choice. "Road Toad, if it's possible I think it would benefit the enchantress if we were wed before we're separated."

A smirky grin crossed his pockmarked face. "I was prepared to suggest just that." Then his face straightened. "You don't look so convinced."

"It'll safeguard her here, but how do I tell her…"

He finished my thought. "About your crossing of swords with the guard captain?"

"Yeah," I said, "that'll be hard news. Especially with things being rushed—can it even be done? Properly done in the eyes of the king and of Keesee?"

"I believe her mother is explaining some of…your concern as we speak. She and I discussed it briefly while you and Lilly were preparing her daughter for the Forge."

"I hadn't really expected this," I said.

He put a hand on my shoulder. "I know. You did what was right. Perhaps what was destined to happen."

"You believe in fate like that?"

He laughed. "You've been in the Imperial Seer's chamber, haven't you?"

"Nothing is for certain. I learned that."

"I think the guard captain will learn that too."

"Maybe," I said, looking back towards Thereese and her mother huddled close, and Lilly standing nearby, watching for danger. Imperial Seer Lochelle predicted my death if I faced Flayzin in combat. It'd take interference from someone powerful, an immortal being or a god to foil her visions. I had none of those backing me.

"All we have here now, Flank Hawk, is the moment. As an officer of rank, leading a mission, I carry the authority to perform a marriage in the name of the king."

"I have to ask her formally," I said.

"I think she'll accept, my friend."

"What about a ring?"

He whispered into my ear, "Actually, our sergeant is carrying a ring."

"He is?"

"Promise of silence," Jadd warned. He gazed over at the forge master, shouting new orders as the thralls worked the bellows and the Soul Forge's fiery heart roared back to life. "Although she may piece things together. She is pretty wily when it comes to such things."

"What?" I asked.

He leaned closer and continued whispering into my ear. "Our sergeant has been trying to build up the courage. Find the right time to ask our scout."

I stumbled back a step. "Really?" I meant it as a whisper but it came out louder.

He nodded once in assurance.

Drux was Jadd's aft-guard, and fellow Sun Fox brother. Of course he'd know.

"Knowing our sergeant, it'll be a year before he finally settles and asks her," he whispered. "He just carries it in case he suddenly decides to ask. You know our scout. He's afraid she'll be ready the moment he asks, and he'll need the ring on hand."

In my mind's eye I could see it. Lilly dragging him off to a magistrate or Algaan priest—whichever was closest.

Jadd continued whispering, "I'll secure the ring from him. It'll help keep her in the dark. And I'll get Barkey to secure a ring for you." He looked over at the smiths and thralls. "One of these smiths must have at least an iron or copper one between them."

I leaned in even closer. "You know, I'd've never guessed…our scout and sergeant."

"Stranger things have happened."

"You don't have to convince me," I said. We both laughed as he patted me on the back.

"Thanks, Road Toad."

"You're most welcome, my friend."

CHAPTER 40

We emerged into the sunlight, on a mountainside ledge littered with frosty rocks and scrub pines.

The tempering of Enchantress Thereese consisted of burning the rune-scribed leather wrap and her breathing in the smoke released, carrying the Soul Forge's finishing magic into her body, binding her revived soul to every organ, muscle, bone, and her blood.

The forge master allowed us passage up the long narrow stairway that reached the mountainside. The secret passage was necessary. It provided access to the outside, allowing the smiths and their thralls the ability to reach and maintain ventilation shafts necessary for their forges and craft. It also offered an opportunity for Enchantress Thereese and me to wed, exchanging vows using our names out of earshot of any Svartálfar, including spies of the clan chief and especially his son.

The forge master agreed that our marriage binding would offer Thereese additional protection, especially if word of my demise reached the clan chief or his son. As a widow, a period of mourning, equal to two thrallspans was part of their culture and tradition.

The female Svartálfar smith had climbed the steps ahead of us, silencing protective wards as we went. She remained within the mountain's shadows, behind the granite door, beyond the sun's reach.

And there I stood, upon a flat rock to elevate me closer to my bride's height.

Thereese was beautiful, despite being garbed only in her travel robes, cleaned and turned white by her mother's magic. Drux stood to my left, as my best man and Lilly preceded the young enchantress, as her maid of honor, carrying a half dozen budding flowers. Tiny, the size of corn kernels, but they were flowers. Major Jadd stood to my right, awaiting the two enchantresses as they approached, Thulease giving her daughter away, with the thrall Barkey, Braden Coaliron, following behind, both a ring bearer and witness for the Svartálfar.

Besides learning Barkey's given name, shared because the ceremony required Thereese and I to speak ours, I don't really remember much of the ceremony, other than staring into Thereese's eyes, noticing purple flecks scattered within their green. It was then than I promised to love, care, and cherish her, until death might separate us, and slid Drux's gold ring, etched with a vine of flowers, onto Thereese's long, slender finger.

Our embrace and kiss…it dashed many doubts that I'd made a bad choice, until our few moments together, left alone to speak before returning to the mountain below, and our separation.

We stood along the mountainside, in a small alcove to avoid the chilling windgusts.

Thereese began, saying, "You don't really know me, Krish. My husband. And after the Soul Forge's spell, I cannot say with certainty that I have full measure of who I am."

"That is true, Thereese. My wife. But do you really know me?" She started to say something, but I reached up and pressed a finger over her lips. "Seven years stand between us."

I took a breath, setting aside what I faced upon returning to Keesee, to the King's City. "Seven years where we will grow and change, so it matters not how well we know ourselves, or each other at this moment."

She kissed my finger before pulling it away. "I know you are a loyal man. A man of duty. That is something you will always be."

She tilted her head, flicked back the hair a wind gust had blown across her face, and smiled. "You married me because of loyalty. Because of duty. You saved my life and I will never, ever forget that."

I took her hands. "Thereese, it is enough to know that the seed of our love has been planted here, on this mountainside. It'll lie alive but dormant, until our reuniting, awaiting its chance to grow. To flourish. That is something I hope you look forward to."

"I hope it is the same for you, Krish."

"Until my vows made to you, I was unsure, Thereese. Now, I am not."

She grinned from ear to ear. "That's the loyalty in your heart. I will carry it forth, this day in my heart, to get me through the grim years under this mountain."

Then her face lost its bright smile and her eyes glistened, with forming tears. "Promise me, Krish. Promise me, Mercenary Flank Hawk, that you will prevail over Captain Flayzin. Be alive for my return."

I took a deep breath, preparing a steady voice. "I have faced far worse than Guard Captain Flayzin, Enchantress."

When I said no more, tears began to flow. "That isn't a promise," she said.

"Because, it's one I cannot give."

She stood tall, gripped my hands firmly, almost so it hurt. "I will promise you this, my husband. If Guard Captain Flayzin slays you, he will not survive the day of my return."

"You know, Thereese, that is not how it works."

"I am well aware," she said. "A challenge ends with the two combatants, whatever the result. Otherwise endless reprisals and death would follow." She took a half step back. "I am neither mercenary, nor soldier and refuse to be bound by that code."

"You would dishonor me, my name?" I asked, and broke our grip upon realizing I was squeezing her hands in return.

"It shall not matter," she said. "You shall not have a say. If you are dead." She turned away. "Maybe knowing that that will encourage you to fight all the more fiercely."

I turned away too. "You don't know me," I said. "Live or die, it may be that you never will."

That wasn't how I expected my wedding day to end. I'd have wagered all the coins in the King of Keesee's treasury that it wasn't how Enchantress Thereese expected hers to end, either.

My stomach turned that, after the last moments of conversation, I no longer thought of it as *our* wedding day.

Guard Captain Flayzin's challenge? No matter Imperial Seer Lochelle's vision. It'll be a grim day for him, I promised, however it ends.

CHAPTER 41

Grand Wizard Seelain approached me near the end of my midnight watch. Our camp was well within the northern reaches of Keesee and we'd reach the King's City not long after tomorrow's nightfall, if we pressed our mounts. Something I didn't care to do.

"Flank Hawk," she said. "You have remained even more isolated and melancholy than usual. I know you are a man prone to keeping a distance from those you serve, to more effectively perform your duty."

I turned to acknowledge the grand wizard and returned my gaze to the distant hillsides. "How would you have me perform my duty, Grand Wizard?"

"In a way that doesn't cast a gloom over Lilly." The grand wizard stood next to me, her white hair flowing over her shoulders catching and reflecting some of the orange firelight. "She is both seething and miserable."

I shrugged. "Lilly's moods, just like her views, they are hers and steered by none other. Most of the time they're hidden, so that she might fit in, or serve. You know that as well as I do, Wizard Seelain."

"It is not difficult to determine what is affecting our scout's mood. Thulease believes, now that you have wed her daughter, Flayzin will relent in his challenge. Her husband's words added to hers."

I turned to her with a skeptical eyebrow raised. Certainly the firelight caught my expression.

"I am of the same mind as you, Flank Hawk. I know my cousin. Rare, exceedingly rare, are the words or deeds that might alter his trajectory once it is set. I believe nothing will dissuade him, even the point of your spear at his throat."

I shrugged once again, staring off into the night. "I have lost my spear."

"You will have one," she said.

After several moments of silence, where the air wizard joined me watching for danger in the night, she asked, "Have Jadd or Drux any advice? They are wise in the ways of combat."

"With them, I've practiced attacks and maneuvers aimed at foiling Flayzin's blade." She'd witnessed that. "You know your cousin is the better swordsman. I'll have no tactics, no tricks that he'll be unable to counter."

"Then you've given up?"

"No." I turned to face her. "When Prince Reveron tasked me to carry on for him," I said, ignoring her flinch at the mention of her dead fiancé.

"To bear the Blood Sword over land and ocean to the Colonel of the West, it seemed hopeless. Yet I persevered, and succeeded." I didn't add that others, Lilly and Roos aided in the task I bore. Against Flayzin, I'd stand alone.

"Good," she said. "If, after this ordeal, you desire respite from the King's City, I offer my estate. Not as a guard, but as a resident—a neighbor, for the time you might desire."

"I imagine my mother-in-law would have other ideas," I said, cracking a small smile.

"Indeed, she does not know you as well as I do, Flank Hawk. She envisions you serving in Flayzin's place. You, tethered as a guard captain for seven years, awaiting her daughter's return?" Then she laughed quietly. "In truth, that is her desire, not her expectation."

"In truth," I replied, "I can say that I know neither you, Grand Wizard, nor the supreme enchantress."

"Then you must take me up on my offer, part of a season at least. Lure Lilly to accompany you. Do not dispute with me that Chief Gardener Orich manages to get under Lilly's skin. I believe Lilly befriending Abigail, my apprentice, would benefit both."

I thought about her offer a moment. "I will visit your estate," I said, "if you promise to accompany me, and some other friends, to the One-Eyed Pelican."

"Me? Dine at that, from what I have been informed, unsavory establishment."

It was true, she wouldn't fit in with the usual patrons, but woe to any that directed rudeness, or worse, toward her.

"It would be a shared experience, Grand Wizard. A minor adventure. And our scout, Lilly, will be thrilled. I only ask to be nearby when you announce to her that I have invited you, and of your intention to accept."

"I will, Flank Hawk, for two reasons. Witnessing Lilly's smile is something to cherish. And naming me a friend, as you just did." She wrapped an arm around my waist. "I deeply regret how I abandoned you after the loss of Reveron. I fled you, King Tobias, his queen, the palace, the King's City. Everyone and everything. Believing it was me that had failed him."

I placed a hand around her shoulder and pulled her close. "Thank you, Grand Wizard—"

"Seelain, if you prefer."

"Grand Wizard, for now," I said. "Part of me says I failed him, not slaying that ogre. I believed part of you blamed me as well." I gripped her shoulder. "You must not blame yourself for what happened that day, what we were unable to do. It was war. People die in war, no matter what we do. Even loved ones are taken from us, sometimes while standing as close as the two of us are now."

I stepped back, meeting her gaze, despite the darkness. "Fendra Jolain, the Cult of the Long Tooth Tiger. *They* are to blame."

"At least the goddess paid," Grand Wizard Seelain said. "We have you to thank for that. She glanced over her shoulder, to Sergeant Drux, snoring in his tent. "And him. You made good on what my prince had started, bearing the Blood Sword on his behalf. That is why he called for you to fight alongside him, in the company of one of his Sun Fox brothers. And you carried on a second time, when he could not. As I believe he knew you would."

I took a deep breath. "Thank you for lifting that burden from my heart, Grand Wizard. Seelain. I've looked away from it. Ignored it, not recognizing its weight."

We stood silent next to each other for several minutes.

Finally, I inhaled a deep, refreshing breath. "In truth, I now feel better prepared for what is to come."

CHAPTER 42

Guard Captain Flayzin knew of my return the moment Enchantress Thulease walked onto the grounds of her tower. I wasn't going to alter my actions to avoid him.

The first place I went was to my parent's apartment. It was close to midnight by the time I arrived.

Everyone woke to greet me, my father and mother, my younger sister Katchia, and Rin, my adopted brother. My mother wanted to know if I was okay, my brother and sister wanted to hear the tale of what had happened. My father, looking into my eyes, wanted to know what other news I bore.

I told them of my marriage first, and worked back from there. I asked them not to share the news, at least not yet, until an appropriate announcement could be made. It's what Supreme Enchantress Thulease, my mother-in-law desired.

My mother was excited for me, yet saddened that she and the family were not part of the occasion. Katchia thought it was neat that Lilly served as the flower girl and maid of honor both, although she said she'd've done it for me, if I'd've asked. Rin was more interested in the dark elves. My father, he just seemed relieved that I'd once again returned home.

After a quick meal of leftover stew and day-old bread, everyone went to bed but my father and me.

Sitting near the fireplace, watching the dying flames, he asked, "Son, what do you intend to do now?"

He knew of my impending confrontation with Flayzin. Rin did as well, and so did my mother. He, better than they, knew the likely result.

"I'm going to get myself a new boar spear," I said. "Tomorrow morning, Dad. I'd like you to come with me."

He nodded once. "Then you can sleep here tonight. We shall depart at first light, if you like."

I shook my head. "No, let mother cook breakfast for us all. If the stablemaster won't give you trouble at the Royal Stables.

He laughed, reached over, and patted me on the shoulder. "Someone got wind that I might be thinking of returning to our farm up in the Doran Confederacy, so they made me the Royal Stable's Foreman to the Stablemaster."

I couldn't help but grin. "Well deserved, Father."

He shook his head. "I don't know about that, Son, but the stablemaster will understand if I don't show up on time this once. And with your wyvern mount returned to the roost, they'll know why Rin is late."

Rin had weapons sparred with me in the practice yard earlier in the afternoon. He'd grown so much, not only in stature but in confidence since I'd departed for the Southern Continent with Enchantress Thulease, that I invited him to join us at the One-Eyed Pelican. He was both surprised and nervous, but he needed something to occupy his mind. He kept looking over his shoulder, expecting Flayzin at any moment to show up and formally announce his challenge.

I guessed Enchantress Thulease refused to release him from his assigned duties, at least until late afternoon. Although I didn't try to avoid him, we didn't cross paths, even as Rin, Lilly, Nura, Grand Wizard Seelain and I made our way from my boarding room to the run down tavern near the docks.

Working as an apprentice for Alchemist Butlir, Enchantress Thulease's husband, Nura had learned of my marriage to Thereese. She was all smiles, but twice our eyes met from across the table, and hers held that look of *what might have been.* The same that mine must've held.

But what was done was done. I'd concern myself with sorting out the tangles my life had gathered should I survive the next few days. There was Nura, a differing relationship with Grand Wizard Seelain, figuring how Drux and Lilly might end up as a pair, the chasm that still remained between my older sister Raina and myself, and how my life would change, being son-in-law to Supreme Enchantress Thulease, one of the most powerful spellcasters on the Mainland Continent. And who I'd be and who, even what, Enchantress Thereese would be upon her return.

It was a logjam that could wait to be sorted out.

My fish soup, greasy red broth and stale bread sat in front of me, with a mug of bitter ale. To my right Wizard Seelain sat, in her leather traveling outfit, her hair tucked up and hidden under a brown wool hat. Next to her sat Major Jadd and the woman he promised to bring, Colonel Isar, of Keesee's m'unicorn cavalry. The deep scar above the left eye of her tight, leathery face had healed over. She wore a black wrap over the stump where her left hand had once been, lost in battle. Bitten off by a griffon, just before she slew it.

I'd only seen and heard her talk in councils of war, often within Imperial Seer Lochelle's dark chamber. Around the table, she had a wry smile and sharp memory for poems, most being humorous and tending toward the lewd. She left Rin, sitting to my left, blushing more than once.

Drux, next to Rin, laughed at my brother's youthful embarrassment, yet encouraged Rin to join in the conversation—and drink only hard cider. Lilly sat between Drux and Nura.Both women laughed and grinned while catching up. They focused on what Nura thought of the King's City, Lilly being able to understand, having only come to the city after befriending me and accompanying me to deliver the Blood Sword to the Colonel of the West. To Nura's surprise, Colonel Isar, sitting next to her, spoke the dialect of the Southern Continent that was Nura's native tongue. The only person not surprised was Major Jadd.

I found it hard to see both Jadd and Isar, battle-hardened veterans, as potential lovers. I wasn't sure that they were. They were definitely companions that could understand each other, but their eyes met in a different way than mine and Lilly's did. Of course, I once found it difficult to imagine Enchantress Thulease as a loving mother.

It was a jovial round table, with bits of stories, both heroic and humorous, remembering friends and comrades lost, and learning the whereabouts of those still alive. Drux, pointing out the rats in the rafters, made Rin laugh the most. My young brother even pitched a spoon at one, nearly knocking it down upon our table.

Jadd was telling of a time scouting along the borders of the lesser kingdoms and he came upon a goblin camp. He swooped down over them, and his dragon unloaded its bowels on the horse they were cooking. And upon his return trip an hour later, he discovered them feasting upon that same horse. That was when Lilly's laughter fell silent.

Her eyes shifted toward the entrance and a scowl fell across her face.

Guard Captain Flayzin, haughty, with chest puffed out, made his way to our table.

Normally men and women coming and going were ignored by the Pelican's patrons. It was a place of privacy, where you and your business were ignored, and you were expected to do the same. Tonight almost half halted their drinking and raucous discussions. That led to the rest turning to see what was happening.

It was just what Flayzin desired.

He was dressed in his chainmail, polished, with sword on his hip. He lacked the arm band, brown and green, indicating service to Supreme Enchantress Thulease and her husband.

Two men followed him in. Pault, still wearing the enchantress's colors and the stocky, battle-scarred mercenary named Bent Iron. He was a quiet man prone to quick violence with his battle axe.

I caught a glimpse of momentary confusion in Flayzin—he didn't expect to see Seelain seated next to me.

As the former guard captain prepared to speak, Grand Wizard Seelain, to my right, said, "Cousin, have you and your associates ventured to this establishment to join us?"

A sneer crossed Flayzin's face. "That is hardly the case, Cousin Seelain. I find your choice of companions odd, considering."

"Considering?" she asked. "I consider those seated with me proper company. I am unfamiliar with your associates. However, I am familiar with you, and your current line of errant belief."

"Let me be about my business here, then, so that you may return to your…celebration?"

Flayzin then turned to me. I didn't bother to stand. Doing so would have offered a small courtesy, which I didn't feel he deserved.

"Mercenary Flank Hawk," he said, "weaseling your way into the enchantress's family will not avail you. I again name you a coward and the primary cause of Prince Reveron's death. What say you?"

I pushed my bowl of fish soup away from me. "As before, I dispute your ignorant claim, Former Guard Captain. We can meet tomorrow at the practice yard at the time of your choosing to settle this dispute by crossing steel."

He nodded once and smiled. "As you appear to be enjoying yourself, I expect that you might have a late night. Say, an hour after noon tomorrow?"

"I'll be there," I said.

His task accomplished, Flayzin turned and left with his companions.

Drux looked at me with a raised eyebrow. I gazed at some of the patrons, several of which I recognized as sailors and dockworkers who'd come to my and Jadd's support almost two years ago when Colonel Brizich had surrounded us with a company of men, intending to kill us.

Meeting Drux's stare, I shook my head. He, in turn looked to his friends, if the thugs and ruffians could be called that, and shook his head once.

Flayzin would make it home alive and uninjured, to face me tomorrow.

Needless to say, the mirth surrounding our dinner never returned.

It was a long walk home, members of the group peeling off to go separate ways.

Rin was the last to be with me. Before leaving him at my parent's apartment and heading to Snyder's Boarding House not far away, I said to him, "Whatever happens tomorrow, those you met tonight…they are the best of what mankind has to offer. Each is different, Rin. Born of different places, and stations, and experiences. Yet each remains loyal to those they name friend. You're now among them. If I'm not around, and you find yourself in need—"

Rin cut me off. "You're going ta win tomorrow!"

I gripped his shoulders. "I intend to, Rin."

He looked away. "Ya shoulda killed him the first time. He's…he's…"

"He's better with a sword than me, Rin. That doesn't mean I'll be defeated."

"Who would you bet on, Flank Hawk?" He looked up and the nearby street lamp revealed expectant sadness in his eyes. "You or him?"

"If I fall tomorrow, Rin, that doesn't mean Flayzin will walk away."

Rin knew what I meant. I'd told him in the past, 'Even if you lose that doesn't mean the other guy has to win.'

"You've faced worse than him—and you're still here," he said, and hugged me tight.

I hugged him back. "You're right, Rin. You're right."

Chapter 43

My first man, Major Jadd, walked with me toward the center of the Arms Practice Yard, where Flayzin, along with his first man, Bent Iron, awaited. Preston, the yard's regular guard, stood there as well. His responsibility was to oversee the challenge's start. After that, whatever happened, happened.

Along the six-foot stone wall, to the left of the entrance gate stood my supporters: my father, Rin, my sister Raina, Enchantress Thulease, Lilly, Drux, Wizard Seelain, Captain Bray, and Snyder, owner of the boarding house. The last surprised me.

To the right of the gate stood three men who I didn't recognize, armed and armored, along with Coachman Pault and Alchemist Butlir. That the enchantress and her husband stood as supporting opposites on the challenge said something, but it was something else to ponder later, if I survived.

Flayzin wore his chain armor over a sturdy leather shirt and leggings, including metal shin and shoulder guards and gauntlets. He had a round shield, painted white, and his steel helmet was open-faced, but extended down to protect his ears and the back of his neck. His long sword hung on his left hip, a long dagger on his right and a bandoleer of three throwing knives hung across his chest.

I'd have better luck piercing than slashing with my boar spear, broad-bladed short sword, or dirk, if it came to that. I had my breast and backplate that Lilly had polished that morning before Jadd helped me dress, over my leather armor. Lilly's work made my armor's combat scars stand out. I wore leather gauntlets with metal plates sewn into them, a gift from Wizard Seelain several years back. I carried a round shield slung over by back, new and provided by Enchantress Thulease, and painted emerald green. And my old helmet with nose guard, a feature I'd never fully gotten used to, even after wearing it through countless battles.

The throwing knives were something I hadn't expected. But Drux had provided me with something Flayzin might not expect. Instead of salt in my pouch, which out of habit I carried after my experiences with zombies and other undead, it held bits of broken and ground up glass. It wouldn't prove deadly but, if properly employed, irritating, painful and even crippling.

I stopped two paces from Flayzin, and we locked gazes.

"A challenge has been issued," Preston announced, loud enough for all in the yard to hear while gesturing with a hand to Flayzin." The guard then gestured to me. "And has been answered."

Flayzin said to me, "Admit to your cowardice and live."

"I've stood to far worse than you," I replied.

He grinned. "That's the last time you shall utter that boast, Mercenary."

"I've stood to far worse than you, Former Guard Captain."

Major Jadd snorted while trying to stifle a burst of laughter.

Bent Iron grunted while Flayzin addressed my first man. "Honorable attempt," he said, "attempting to turn my righteous determination to ire upon you, Major." His words weren't able to conceal his irritation, not quite anger. "Let this be settled."

Guardsman Preston stepped back. "Once begun, none other shall interfere."

"Make it quick," Bent Iron urged, stepping back.

"Do what's necessary to finish this," Jadd said, before moving along with Preston and Bent Iron to the customary fifteen stride distance. Before me, Imperial Seer Lochelle's prediction echoed, what she said would result if this moment came. I'd die.

Gripping my spear and standing ready, I prepared to prove her wrong.

Flayzin drew his sword and readied his shield. "If only you'd shown such fortitude when fighting alongside Prince Reveron."

I pointed my spear toward his face. "My fortitude will prove to be your bane."

"Hah," he said and charged.

"Halt!" boomed across the Arms Practice Yard.

I recognized the voice, backed and sidestepped, even as Flayzin slowed his charge and lowered his sword, recognizing the crown prince by sight even as I did by voice.

All in the yard had bowed upon recognition, supplemented by the sergeant of his guard's proclamation: "Halgadin, Prince of Keesee, walks before you."

Both Flayzin and I laid down our weapons, knelt and bowed our heads as well.

The prince stopped two paces from us and said, "Rise, combatants, and face me."

We did.

Prince Halgadin was little changed from the time I'd last seen him armed for battle, confident and strong. His hair and dark beard were better trimmed and his breast plate and chainmail were clean and polished bright. To the prince's right stood his personal guard, a burly dark-skinned soldier that almost made Drux look like an easygoing fop.

The prince said, "I have recently learned of this challenge, fought over the cause of my brother, Reveron's, death." His voice was both deep and filled with confidence.

I'd never been one of the prince's favorites, owing to my friendship with Major Jadd, once exiled by Prince Halgadin under threat of crossing swords unto his death should Jadd ever return to set foot within Keesee. Jadd had told me more than once that if he ever crossed swords with the prince, the outcome was both assured and grim. I'd witnessed Prince Halgadin in battle. His speed and skill—he was the best I'd ever seen. Had he been a spellcaster and able to wield the Blood Sword, the goddess Fendra Jolain would've swiftly fallen to his blade, far more swiftly than Prince Reveron, who was an accomplished swordsman, could achieve.

"It is my understanding," the prince continued, assessing us, "that the mercenary, Flank Hawk, is accused of my brother's downfall, owing to the mercenary's…cowardice." His hard gaze remained upon me. "This mercenary, the chosen of my brother to accompany him in the final battle with the now fallen goddess. This mercenary, who took up my fallen brother's sword, and completed what my brother and I had begun, a task set upon under the direct order of my father, King Tobias of Keesee."

His gaze then fell upon Flayzin, who stood proud and unflinching. "I was there," the prince said. "A witness to this, even as I and others fought to keep the minions of the goddess, now defeated, from falling upon my brother and his chosen, Sergeant Drux and Mercenary Flank Hawk."

The prince's hands moved to rest upon his hips. "Flayzin, son of Raszlin, your accusation names my brother unwise. Names him a fool."

The prince's left hand slid down to rest on the jeweled pommel of his sword. "My brother recommended this mercenary to accompany us on our mission to slay the goddess who brought war to this land, after we repelled and defeated the forces of the Necromancer King. Owing much, I will add, to the actions of the mercenary in question, *also* called upon then to step forward and do his part by my now fallen brother. More to the point, you name Reveron unwise and a fool for calling this mercenary to his side. My brother, having done so prior to his final battle."

The prince stepped closer to Flayzin. "I know this, Flayzin, son of Raszlin, because I was there, whereas you were not. My recollection declares your name was neither mentioned nor considered when forming the assault force to bring the goddess down.

"Speak, Flayzin, son of Raszlin. What do you have to say?"

Without hesitation or faltering, Flayzin said, "I stand by my belief, Crown Prince Halgadin, that the cowardice of Mercenary Flank Hawk, causing slowness of action on his part, caused the downfall of your brother, the beloved Prince Reveron."

"What leads you to this conviction, such that it has come to crossing of steel?"

"Heart and mind, and loyalty to Keesee and its rulers, my prince."

Prince Halgadin's eyes became narrow. He turned and faced away from Flayzin and myself. His personal guard did not.

That the prince knew who Flayzin was, meant that he'd showed up knowledgeable of the situation. Why I'd thought otherwise, even for a moment, surprised me. Out of the corner of my eye, I observed Flayzin, standing straight with a stern look on his face. He was probably coming to the same conclusion I had. And the prince turning is back on us? He knew what he was about. The time offered was for me, and for Flayzin to think and consider—or so I figured.

I couldn't see the prince declaring an end to the challenge. But, as Crown Prince, he could, and maybe he would. If that was his decree, the notion that cowardice lay nestled within my actions would linger—actions some might come to believe resulted in Prince Reveron's death.

Prince Halgadin turned on his heel, stopping to face Flayzin. His voice boomed as he said, "This man, Flayzin, son of Raszlin, has questioned the wisdom of my brother, Reveron. Named him a fool for setting a coward at his side in a crucial battle for the safety of Keesee, a confrontation that cost my brother his life. As my brother is not here to defend his judgment, defend his name, I shall stand in his place, as is my right, both as his brother and as the Crown Prince of Keesee."

He motioned for Jadd to approach and then turned to face those watching along the wall. "I am honored that the Mercenary Flank Hawk stepped forward to defend his honor and, in doing so, defending that of my brother. My claim to defend the honor of my brother supersedes the claim of the mercenary which my brother, Reveron, called to his side for his final battle."

Prince Halgadin then turned to face Flayzin. "Do you persist in your claim, Flayzin, son of Raszlin?"

Flayzin's voice was strong and steady. "I do, Crown Prince. I cannot do otherwise."

"So be it. The claim will be settled with steel between us." The prince turned to me. "Mercenary Flank Hawk, will you do me the honor of standing as my first man?"

That caught me by surprise, but there was only one answer. I nodded once and said, "I would be honored to do so, Prince Halgadin."

The prince turned to his guard. "Stoadin, stand aside." The guard nodded once before pulling a flanged mace from his belt and handing it to the prince. Hefting the mace in his left hand, the prince turned to Major Jadd. "Your support of my brother's man does me honor, Jadd."

Major Jadd observed the tone of dismissal and nodded once. Following the imposing Stoadin, he marched toward a spot along the yard's wall. Beyond it, men waited atop their mounts, observing. All were armored soldiers except one. His fiery red hair and ruddy skin marked him as a fire wizard.

The prince backed away from Flayzin several steps and nodded to me. I moved to stand next to Bent Iron.

Loud enough for all to hear, Prince Halgadin asked, "What is the substance that stains your blade, Flayzin, son of Raszlin?" Without waiting for an answer, the prince said, "Poison, without a doubt. Truly a sign of honor."

I'd reached the fifteen paces and turned to stand next to Bent Iron just in time to see the prince raise his hand before Flayzin could utter a reply. "Take up your tainted blade, opponent. It may be your only hope of victory, if the vile substance is from a highly virulent brew.

Flayzin did, and stood for combat, sword and shield held ready.

The prince drew his long sword. Its metal gleamed silver, reflecting the sun's rays. In contrast, the steel of his mace was dull gray, reminding me of lead.

I muttered to myself, "Flayzin's conviction is unveering."

Bent Iron must've heard me and responded, "He's a fool."

At an unseen signal the prince and Flayzin clashed.

It wasn't going be a drawn out fight, with each man a fury of dodging, striking, and parrying. While Flayzin had more finesse, thrusting and slashing with his sword, he finally began giving ground to the prince's hammering dual-weapon onslaught.

Both men wore masks of grim concentration, but Flayzin's showed cracks of frustration.

Prince Halgadin sidestepped a thrust, further knocking it wide with a flick of his mace, and quickly advanced. Flayzin slammed the prince with his shield, driving the man of royalty staggering back. But, when Flayzin moved to press his advantage, his left leg buckled.

A thin line of blood covered one edge of Prince Halgadin's blade.

Closing on the crippled former guard captain, the prince hammered down with his mace. Flayzin deflected it with his shield but left himself open, earning a kick to his shoulder that knocked him onto his back.

The prince was on Flayzin, parrying a determined thrust. His sword's tip ended less than an inch from Flayzin's throat.

"Yield, and renounce your claim against my brother!"

Flayzin shook his head ever so slightly and replied, "I cannot. Mercenary Flank Hawk is—"

A swift thrust of the prince's sword cut short Flayzin's last words.

"Died brave," Bent Iron said. "A brave fool."

Before I could consider the battle-scarred mercenary's statement, something slammed into my right thigh, causing it to collapse. Using my spear for support, I didn't go to the ground.

Bent Iron reacted quickly, his eyes searching the direction from which the crossbow bolt had come.

"Ambush!" Jadd shouted, sprinting toward the prince. Everyone was coming to the prince's defense, except for my father, Lilly and Rin. They raced toward me. I saw a whirlwind raised by Grand Wizard Seelain, and Enchanters Thulease releasing some sort of spell.

"Let's move from here," Bent Iron said, lifting my arm over his shoulder.

My leg went numb. My boar spear fell from my hand. I tried to say, "To the wall," but all I could muster was a spittle-filled whisper, my breath and strength fleeing me. Slumping and supported by Bent Iron, I struggled to draw another breath—and couldn't.

EPILOGUE

Every muscle hurt. Even when I took a shallow breath, it felt like flames stretched across my stomach. It was nearly worse than the night of a full moon spent in the company of Belinda the Cursed, fighting off lycanthropy, vanquishing the beast trying to wrest hold of my body. Wrest hold of my soul.

Heidi Lynn, I was pretty sure it was her speaking to me. She lifted my head and gave me a sip of water.

It hurt to groan. It hurt to move, but less than it did to resist. Despite the dim candlelight and fuzzy vision there was someone else. Wearing green, tall, standing close behind Heidi Lynn.

Then I lost focus and slept, escaping the pain

The next time I awoke my body ached like a dozen mules had stampeded over me. A vast improvement.

Lilly was at my side, holding a flickering lamp. A grin broke across her face. "Betcha feel bad," she said. She kept her voice low but it was filled with excitement. "Don't move. You thirsty?"

Looking around without moving my head much I saw that I was in my boarding room. "I am," I said. Other than my parched throat, it didn't hurt to talk.

"Just a minute," Lilly said, setting the lamp on a table next to my bed. She returned with a wooden bowl and spoon. "Your mom just left. Rin too. She left some broth for you. It'll help you get your strength back."

She placed the bowl and spoon on the table before propping me up with another pillow. Being moved hurt, but groaning didn't.

After a couple spoonfuls of warm chicken broth, I asked, "How long?"

"Since you've been here?" Lilly responded. "Let me tell you all what happened so you don't have to ask a lot of questions." She held up the bowl. "Just let me know when you don't want any more."

I nodded once.

"The prince has a guard standing down the hall, guarding you, until you're back on your feet." She glanced at the door and then back to me. "Your mom and the enchantress argued about where you'd be taken. That was after the prince's healer got something from a vial into your blood.

"I think when the prince said Flayzin had poison on his sword—you know the prince killed him, right?"

I swallowed a spoonful of broth and nodded once, noticing a quilt from my younger sister's bed covering me.

"Well, the prince must've said it to signal his enchanter sitting behind the wall. A message got to the palace and a healer was sent straight away to the Arms Yard. Anyway, you stopped breathing. That big guard Stoadin, he cut your arm and put the vial to a vein. Enchantress Thulease spelled the yellow sludge in it to go in your vein. Then the guard pushed up and down on your chest. He had me breathe in your mouth every now and then till the palace healer got there. Your sister, the healer one, she healed up your arm but couldn't stop the poison in you. It made her cry, Flank Hawk.

"Anyway, Road Toad rubbed your healed-up arm to get the yellow stuff moving up it and into the rest of your body."

She pulled the bowl back. "Are you full?"

"Yes," I said, nodding once. My throat felt better.

"We did this until the healer showed up," Lilly said. "Once they figured you were going live, your mom wanted to take you to her place. Enchantress Thulease argued that her estate was just as close and better staffed and equipped. That got your mom mad, so I said you'd want to be in your own room. Major Jadd agreed, and told them that they could visit and that's when the prince said he'd order a guard to help watch."

"We've all been here. Jadd, Drux, Bray, your mom, dad, both sisters, Rin, me, the enchantress and Wizard Seelain, and Nura too. Then that Heidi girl helps out when she isn't cleaning and Snyder keeps people out and feeds everyone that stays with you. I think the enchantress paid him. She beat your dad to it because he didn't have the coin on him."

It didn't sound like my family and Enchantress Thulease were getting along. I shouldn't have been surprised.

"The enchantress told me she and the prince talked to—they said, 'consulted'—that Imperial Seer Lochelle. She's kind of scary, Flank Hawk, don'tcha think?"

"She can be," I said.

Lilly looked at me skeptically. "Well, Enchantress Thulease said that the woman that shot you—yeah they don't know a lot but think it's a woman. Anyway, she wasn't hired by Flayzin, which I agree with. He was a lot of rotten things, the way he thought about you. But he wasn't someone who'd hire an assassin."

I agreed. Flayzin expected to win. Even if he didn't win, he had too much honor to want things to end that way.

"Anyway," Lilly continued, "she had some magic, that lady that shot you. It had to be a big crossbow too, because that mercenary, Bent Iron, thought he saw someone on the shoemaker's roof. He said he looked kind of shadowy—but it turned out to be a she, not a he."

I adjusted my position in the bed. Doing so hurt, but felt better afterward. "Do you...do they know any more?" I asked, thinking about the guard in the hallway. Why would someone want to kill me, then and there? Who would?

"The king's seer thinks the person that tried to kill you is part of the Long Tooth Cult. She can't be sure but Enchantress Thulease believes her. Says it fits, and how she escaped the soldiers Prince Halgadin sent right away to catch whoever shot you."

Lilly scooted her chair closer. "Road Toad told me more than I ever wanted to know about the Long Tooths. They're the enemy of him and his Sun Fox Brotherhood."

I nodded. "I know a little about them."

Lilly leaned close and gently hugged me. "I'm glad you're alive, Flank Hawk." I embraced her. It was weak, the best I could manage.

My friend sat back on her stool and crossed her arms. "Soon as you're better, Flank Hawk, we're going after her. That woman that tried to kill you. Me and you."

Lilly's gaze drifted away from me, toward the shuttered window. Her face hardened. "Whoever she is. Wherever she's hiding."

The End

ABOUT THE AUTHOR

Terry W. Ervin II is an English teacher who enjoys writing fantasy and science fiction. His *First Civilization's Legacy Series* includes ***Flank Hawk***, ***Blood Sword*** and ***Soul Forge***. His short story collection, ***Genre Shotgun***, contains all of his stories previously published in magazines, ezines and anthologies. ***Relic Tech*** was Terry's first foray into novel-length science fiction. He is focused on completing ***Relic Rescue*** (working title), the second novel in the *Crax War Chronicles*.

When Terry isn't writing or enjoying time with his wife and daughters, he can be found in his basement raising turtles.

To contact Terry, or to learn more about his writing endeavors, visit his website at www.ervin-author.com and his blog, *Up Around the Corner,* at uparoundthecorner.blogspot.com.